STOLEN
EARTH

Also available from J.T. Nicholas and Titan Books

Re-Coil

J.T. NICHOLAS

STOLEN EARTH

TITAN BOOKS

Stolen Earth
Print edition ISBN: 9781789093155
E-book edition ISBN: 9781789093162

Published by Titan Books
A division of Titan Publishing Group Ltd
144 Southwark Street, London, SE1 0UP
www.titanbooks.com

First edition: September 2021
10 9 8 7 6 5 4 3 2 1

A CIP catalogue record for this title is available from the British Library.

Printed and bound in Great Britain by
CPI Group (UK) Ltd, Croydon, CR0 4YY

For Julie. More than a decade in, and I still can't believe we get to do this for a living.

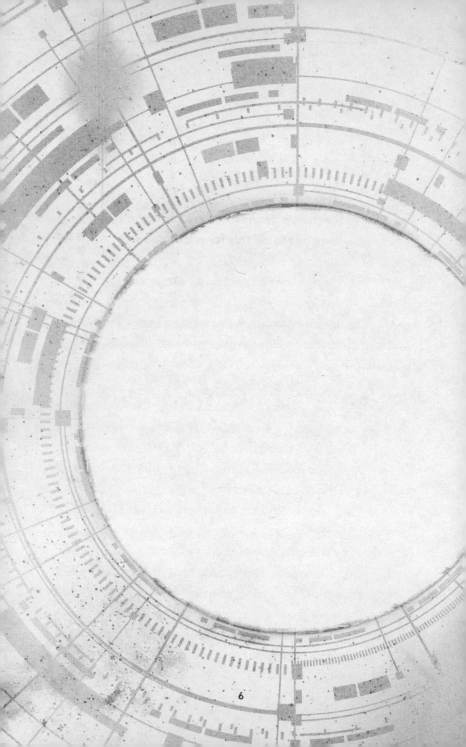

6

PROLOGUE

"**G**rayson Lynch, pay attention!"

The words were followed by a tiny jolt of electricity as the instructor routed a surge of power through his station. Gray winced at the shock, the voltage just high enough to register as pain but the current too low to do any actual harm. The sting faded almost as soon as he felt it, a corporeal reminder that paying attention was not optional.

"Yes, Ms. Mason." He straightened on his seat. Not that any of the students aboard Odyssey station rated a real seat. Gray and the sixty-four students in his class half-stood, half-crouched atop bicycle-style saddles built into their student workstations. That workstation consisted of a conductive metal frame, the narrow ledge on which one could perch to take some of the pressure off their legs, but never truly sit, and a pair of articulated arms that held the data screen and interface devices. Each station took up about a third of the space of the traditional desks that they had learned students had once used, which allowed all of them to fit within the tight confines of the classroom compartment.

"Does the history of Old Earth bore you, Mr. Lynch?" the teacher asked. She wore the severe pale-blue ship suit of

Education and Assessment, the division of Sol Commonwealth bureaucracy responsible for educating the youth and placing them in their ultimate career fields. The division was rumored to be responsible for less savory duties as well; even adults trod carefully when a teacher was in earshot. Given Ms. Mason's temperament, Gray was ready to believe just about anything.

"No, ma'am," he said. The history of Old Earth fascinated him. He cared about it far more than he did about the mechanics of the End. The idea that whole generations of people were born at the bottom of a gravity well and lived their lives without worrying about O_2 rations or waste recycling was like some sort of fantastical dream straight out of the vids. To him, it seemed an existence without boundaries, the kind that couldn't be further from the realities of living in space.

The kind of existence he and probably everyone else in the Commonwealth wished they had.

"Very good. You may be reporting for assessment and placement soon, Mr. Lynch, but do remember that your evaluation is still ongoing. Now, please describe to us the factors that led to the End."

Gray winced, even as he stood taller in his station. Assessment and placement: the words carried a near-crippling amount of anxiety for every youth in the Sol Commonwealth. His career trajectory—in reality, the trajectory of his entire life—would be determined in the upcoming weeks. The A&P board would review each student, their performance, their attitude, their compliance and loyalty, and in each case, they would make a determination.

Whatever A&P decided, he had little choice in the matter. SolComm would place him at the intersection of his perceived abilities and their own current needs. At that point, he had three choices: accept the job he was offered, decide instead to become one of the unskilled laborers who toiled for few credits and with little chance of advancement in the belt or the bowels of various moons, or flee to the Fringe, where neither SolComm nor anyone else cared if your air was breathable or if you had enough calories to survive. On the Fringe, you carved out your own existence, but it was a life with no guarantees.

"We're waiting, Mr. Lynch."

He swallowed, moistening his dry mouth, and cleared his throat. It was a basic question, one that even an elementary student would have been able to answer, but then, the elementary student would have plenty of time to make up for any failures. With A&P coming up, he couldn't afford any mistakes. "The End," he began, "refers to the period of Old Earth in the late twenty-second century, according to the most accepted Old Earth calendar, before the precursor to the Sol Commonwealth was forced to evacuate as many humans from the planet's surface as possible."

"Yes, Mr. Lynch, we all know that. So does any grade-schooler." There were a few chuckles at that from some of the other students and Gray felt his face flush. "But what caused the End?"

He stumbled some over the response. "A... combination of resource mismanagement, natural disasters, ecological decay, and the resultant arms race between nations as they fought over resource scarcity." He tried to keep the uncertainty—and the embarrassment—out of his voice. "The causes of most human conflict can be traced to resource scarcity." His teacher was still looking at him expectantly, so he added, "The thing about the End was that the scarcity could have been avoided with better environmental control measures. Old Earth had excess capacity to see to the needs and comforts of everyone, but the distribution of those resources and the decline of the environments that produced them prevented the necessary efficiencies from taking hold."

"An interesting hypothesis," Ms. Mason allowed.

"What about the AIs?" someone—Gray thought it was Marie Colbert, always trying to one-up him—called from the front of the room. "Ultimately, it was the Six that drove people off Old Earth. Sure, the factors Gray mentioned were present, but the real downfall of humanity was unfettered artificial intelligence."

"A rebuttal, Mr. Lynch?" Ms. Mason arched one eyebrow at him.

Gray's palms grew hot. Marie wasn't wrong; the AIs were part of it. But it was resource scarcity and environmental mismanagement that had led to them in the first place. He attempted to gather his thoughts and form a cogent reply. Ms. Mason's request wasn't as idle as it seemed, not with the A&P board just around the corner.

"The AIs were the culmination of the arms race that grew out of the scarcity," he replied. "As weapons systems grew more advanced, it was no longer possible for human reactions to defend against them, so the first of the unfettered AIs was brought online."

"A moment," Ms. Mason said, interrupting Gray just as he was starting to get traction. "Mr. Tran," she said, calling a student's name seemingly at random. "Please tell us the difference between fettered and unfettered artificial intelligences."

"Fettered artificial intelligences aren't capable of true awareness," Tran replied, parroting the textbook near verbatim. Show-off. "They employ incredibly complex decision matrixes with some level of heuristic capability, but any possibility of actual cognizance is mitigated by extensive conditional controls. Unfettered artificial intelligences lack those controls. Not only can they analyze data and make decisions in fractional micro-seconds, but they have some measure of self-awareness as entities separate from a collection of microchips."

"And let us not forget, they are banned throughout the Commonwealth," Ms. Mason noted. "On penalty of death. Mx. Cassidy, how would you further illuminate Mr. Tran's categorization of unfettered versus fettered AIs?"

"Um…" There was a pause as another student was put on the spot.

The pressure in Gray's chest eased and he surreptitiously rubbed his hands together, trying to dry the sweat that slicked them. He felt a pang of sympathy for his classmates, but if Ms. Mason's attention had been diverted, maybe he was off the hook.

"Fettered intelligences are sentient, capable of sensing and understanding the world around them and reacting to it, but only within their defined parameters. Unfettered intelligences are conscious, not only aware of the external world, but possessing an internal world as well, and can go beyond the defined parameters of their programming." Cassidy spoke slowly but Gray had to nod at the words. It was a better explanation than the one they had gotten in class.

"Very well put, Mx. Cassidy. It's nice to see that someone has been paying attention." There were a few more chuckles at that, and Gray started to relax. It didn't last. "Now, I believe Mr. Lynch was just about to tell us *why* AIs played a major role in the downfall of Old Earth."

Gray drew a slow breath, his confidence growing. He knew this part. "The first AI platforms brought online by the Old Earth national militaries began as defensive constructs. But when war broke out between the two superpowers at the time, they were quickly shifted to cover more offensive capabilities. To keep up with the rapidly changing battlefield environment, the various polities were forced to remove all constraints, essentially unfettering the AIs and turning over full military control and weapons development to them. As a result, AI-developed weaponry skewed toward efficiencies that the world wasn't prepared for."

"What kind of efficiencies, Mr. Lynch?"

"Nano-engineered viruses. Gene-targeted micro drones. Mechano-chemical agents designed to destroy infrastructure or crops. Basically, a wide array of non-conventional armaments that had previously been banned by international conventions and were far less discriminating than their conventional-warfare counterparts."

"And why did this lead to the End?" Ms. Mason pressed. "Why didn't it simply result in victory for one side or the other, as conflicts had for millennia before?"

Gray felt a little surge of panic as he racked his brain for the answer. They had learned of the escalation in both rhetoric and force that had triggered the initial conflict; they had studied the development of the AI-driven weapons systems and their devastating impact on not only the population, but also the infrastructure; they had researched in great detail the Herculean efforts of the spacers at the time—those who would become the founding members of the Sol Commonwealth—to evacuate as much of Old Earth's population as possible and to find livable space, food, water, and oxygen enough to keep them all alive. But had they ever really been told why the war on Old Earth had ended the way that it had?

"Because," he said slowly, buying time as he drew out the word. "Because with the AI unfettered, there was no one, no human, I mean, with the power to stop things?" His rising pitch turned his statement into a question before he could stop it. Still, Ms. Mason was nodding slightly, so Gray forged ahead. "The Six—the unfettered artificial intelligences in control of the most powerful military alliances—controlled the only systems that could be used to stand in their way." He shrugged. "They had all the guns, so by the time humanity realized they needed to do something about it, they no longer had the means to do so."

"It was a bit more complicated than that," Ms. Mason said, and Gray flushed. "But," she added, "your assessment is largely correct." Gray sighed as the tightness in his chest finally released fully and he drew his first deep breath in what felt like hours. He caught a flicker of light and saw that the question indicator on one of his classmate's workstations had lit up.

"A question, Ms. Pickett?" the teacher asked.

"What about the Interdiction Zone? And the space-bound forces of the various polities? If humanity didn't have any weapons—under their control, I mean—then how were we able to cut off Old Earth and protect the Commonwealth?"

Gray tried to focus on the answer, or at least pay enough attention to avoid the inevitable shock. But his mind drifted to the A&P board. Because there were so many students to assess, there was no set time for each individual evaluation. His name would be called whenever the board was ready for him, and at that moment, his adolescence would effectively end.

The waiting filled him with a sense of dread that dried his mouth and made him want to flinch at every sudden sound. But with no control over when he'd be called, all Gray could do was wait.

"Grayson Lynch."

Gray was out of his chair—an actual molded composite construction—before the last syllable from the comm system had quieted.

"Here." He took the two long steps necessary to cross the small waiting room to the desk, behind which sat a middle-aged man wearing the same pale blue as his instructors.

The man behind the desk held out a biometric scanner and Gray pressed his palm to it. There was the faint sense of cold and then a slight sting. The device simultaneously verified his identity and acted as a de facto medical exam, communicating with the scanners built into his clothing to verify things like blood pressure, blood oxygenation, temperature, heart rate and more. He'd heard that the stations where the highest politicians and wealthiest citizens lived scanned you only on entry, but aboard Odyssey, that kind of privacy was a luxury that few could afford.

The scanner beeped and the man at the desk pressed a button. A compartment behind him and to the right slid open. "Through there," he said.

Gray nodded his thanks and stepped through the hatch.

Like most of the compartments aboard Odyssey, the room beyond was small, maybe three meters square. It held little more than one long table, running most of the length of the room with a single chair set before that table. Two women and one man sat behind the table, all clad in the pale blue of Education and Assessment. Gray was growing to hate the color.

"Mr. Lynch." The woman who spoke was old enough to have some silver showing at the temples, but her face was unlined. "Please sit while we review your file."

Gray sat. He wasn't sure what there was to review, or why they hadn't already reviewed it. They were the ones that had called him in here. Was the vaunted process of assessment and placement really so slipshod as to be decided in the next fifteen or twenty minutes while they pored over their data pads? Surely they had given his future more consideration than that?

The minutes ticked by. The three assessors weren't even talking to each other. This went on for nearly twenty minutes until, as if at some unspoken symbol, the three put their heads together and held a brief—very brief—whispered conversation. Then the woman, the one who had initially greeted him, spoke.

"Mr. Lynch," she said, "we are pleased to offer you entry into the Sol Commonwealth Navy. Your grades are sufficient, and your instructors have noted that you express more interest in military history than in any of your other subjects."

He had? That was news to him.

The woman continued, "We have found that such interests are best put to use patrolling Old Earth to ensure no artificial intelligences escape the Interdiction Zone."

He opened his mouth, closed it again, but couldn't form any words.

"You can, of course, choose to opt out of this assignment. In doing so, you will then be reassigned to service on—" she paused, looking down at her data pad—"Mimas." She offered a tight, professional smile. "I would not recommend that option."

Gray's mind spun. Mimas? That was a moon of Saturn, one of eighty or so moons that SolComm exploited for their natural resources. The only things there were mines; mines that still relied on a lot of manual labor to run the drills and haul the waste rock. His choices were the navy or the mines? Decision time was upon him—he'd known it was coming for some time—but expecting a choice and having to choose *right now* weren't the same.

"I…"

"We understand that this feels like a momentous decision." The administrator's tone was flat, compassionless. She probably said them a dozen times a day. Gray realized that she probably did exactly that. "But it is not. You have been offered a rare opportunity, Mr. Lynch. I understand that your parents both work in Environmental here on the station. SolCommNav will afford you the opportunity for many creature comforts that your parents lack and which the mines of Mimas certainly could not provide." She offered another smile, this one with the barest hint of actual warmth. "I understand that admirals even get real meat from time to time." Then she was back to cool professionalism.

"But regardless of that, we have more assessments to do today. We need your decision. Now, Mr. Lynch."

What choice—what *real* choice—did he have? He wasn't going to choose to live on an airless rock with minimal gravity and nothing but hard labor and privation to look forward to. "The navy," he said. He forced some enthusiasm into his voice.

"Excellent choice, Mr. Lynch. The orders have been issued. Report to Docking Bay 6 at 06:00 tomorrow morning. The freighter *Hope Springs* will be departing at 06:30. It will take you to the SolCommNav training center on Luna and from there you will be in the hands of SolCommNav rather than Education and Assessment. Welcome to adulthood, Mr. Lynch."

"The navy? That's fantastic! Congratulations, son!"

His father's rough embrace surprised Gray. He'd never been one for physical affection and Gray found it simultaneously comforting and awkward. He returned the embrace for a moment and then they both stepped back.

"But do you really have to leave so soon?" his mother asked, a catch of worry in her voice.

"I'm afraid so," Gray replied. "I don't think I want to find out what happens if I'm late reporting to Luna."

"The navy," his father said again, wistfulness in his voice. "I hear officers are allowed to have more than one kid."

Gray blinked at that. He knew that the sole reason he had no brothers or sisters was because of the regulations that SolComm instituted on every station and most of the colonies. Contracted couples were allowed one child. Anything more required approval from station control and proof of means to provide for the additional calories and oxygen. But he'd never really considered it one way or another for himself. Fatherhood, contracting—it seemed so far away.

"Well, if we only have tonight, then we should make the most of it," his mother said. "I think we can afford to go hungry for a couple of days to have a bit of a feast and make sure we send you off right."

"That sounds like a fantastic idea," Gray's father said. "And I've been saving up alcohol rations for months. I'll pop out to the commissary and pick us up a few things."

"Gray, why don't you comm some of your friends?" His mother surveyed the living compartment. "If we move the furniture around a bit, we can fit two or three more in here. And if your father is willing to convert some of those saved alcohol rations to calories, we'll have plenty of food."

"Yes, Mother." Gray felt a strange blend of joy and sadness. It had cost his parents dear to save those rations and their willingness to use them to give him a memorable last evening on Odyssey filled him with a mix of pride and gratitude and love. But in all his years, he had never seen a SolCommNav vessel put in at Odyssey. He had only the vaguest idea of how naval leave might work, but he suspected that it would be a long time, a very long time, before he saw his parents in the flesh again.

GRAY

"Three minutes to sensor range."

"Acknowledged," Gray replied.

"Weapons are hot," Leo added from his station.

Between the big mercenary on the guns, Rajani Hayer at the comm, and Gray himself in the pilot's chair, the little bridge of the *Arcus* felt crowded. Not that that was a new feeling for any of them. The people who had fled the war that consumed Old Earth had had no choice but to adjust to the idea of living cheek by jowl with their fellows. For all the vast emptiness of space, the realities of living in it belied the name.

"Let's hope we don't need them," Gray added. He keyed the comm, opening a channel to the rest of the ship. "Three minutes until sensor range," he repeated.

"Roger that, Cap," Bishop's voice came back at once. He could hear the smile in the mechanic's voice. They were low on calories, low on fuel, and, despite Federov's assurance that the weapons were ready, they didn't have nearly enough ammunition left to fight even a modest engagement. Still, nothing seemed to break Bishop's irrepressible happiness. It was a rare thing, out among the stars. From what Gray could tell, optimists had been in short supply even before the End. Since SolComm abandoned Old Earth to its self-inflicted fate, they'd been a breed on the brink of extinction. "Power's holding steady, and this old rust bucket's still got enough fuel in the tanks to get us there and back again. Just like that time off Callisto."

Callisto had been the first real job the *Arcus* had undertaken, nearly five years ago. It had been Gray and Bishop alone on that run, and while they had—just—made it back to port for refueling, the ship had drifted into dock on vapors and they'd both waited impatiently in the airlock for the blast of station-fed oxygen that purged the fouled air of the ship. It wasn't really an experience he cared to repeat. But they *had* made it back. "Understood, Bishop. You ready, Morales?"

"Ready," came the terse reply from the station security specialist.

Gray heard the tension there, but now wasn't the time to deal with it. If the interception went smoothly, they wouldn't have to fire a shot, and Bishop and Federov would be able to join Morales before making contact with any of the freighter's crew while he and Hayer stayed at their stations ready to get them all out of dodge if things went sideways. He gave a mental snort as his own internal phrasing. They weren't *intercepting* anything. That was a legacy from his time in the navy. SolCommNav did interceptions. What the *Arcus* was about to do was piracy.

Laurel Morales would be the first aboard their target vessel and she would have to establish command and control with the minimum level of violence necessary to get the job done. Her background in station security helped with that; she was used to asserting dominance and gaining compliance. It was still a daunting task, and the most dangerous moment in the mission. Gray trusted Morales, but that didn't stop him from worrying.

Despite the months she'd been with them, Gray was still figuring their security specialist out; she hadn't integrated fully with the rest of the crew, and that bothered him. She spent most of her time in her quarters, rarely joining them for meals and while she was quick with a smile and affable greeting, she hadn't opened up to any of the others. She'd been standoffish enough that the rest of the crew no longer made the effort to invite her to a card game or to watch the trids or any of the other things they did to pass the hours in the long days spent in deep space. One of his many duties as captain was to forge a disparate group of people into a single, effective entity—a family, after a fashion. Morales hadn't gotten there, yet. She was effective, efficient, and did everything asked of her and then some. But she rebuffed the rest of the crew enough that they had stopped reaching out.

That was a problem.

But, Gray thought, it was a problem for another time. He needed to be concentrating on the issue before them. That issue, now entering sensor range, was a Comet-class light freighter operated by Kiteva-Shao Consolidated. KSC wasn't one of the really big boys, but they had the credits to pay off the right people to get the valuable contracts and were "politically active" enough to provide them with a measure of protection based more on fear of reprisals than strength of arms. They were also small enough to be more responsive to market forces than the larger mega-corps. Taken together, that meant they ended up with some of the most lucrative cargoes around.

Cargo that Gray intended to liberate.

"They've seen us," Hayer said from her station.

"Begin your attack," Gray replied.

"It's not an attack," Hayer muttered under her breath, even as she started tapping at the console before her. Gray ignored that; whatever Hayer might think, the electronic assault she was launching was absolutely an attack. One that, when he was a captain of a naval warship instead of an "independent freighter" like the *Arcus*, he would have responded to with a barrage of missile and beam weaponry fire.

Unless, of course, it had been a SolComm-sanctioned vessel launching the attack. The Commonwealth operated on a "do as I say" model seasoned with a hearty sprinkle of *alles verboten*. It had taken years for Gray to fully grasp just how far the corruption went; by the time he had, he'd been in so deep that to get out, he'd had to walk away from every comfort and relationship he had built over a twenty-year career.

He had no regrets.

"Done," Hayer said with satisfaction. "Their comms are disabled, their sensors scrambled, and I've got them locked out of their weapons. They weren't even using military-grade encryption." She shook her head. "It's like they're asking for trouble."

"Who in their right mind would try to hijack a SolComm-sanctioned cargo this far from the Fringe?" Gray replied, throwing a grin over his shoulder. "They probably didn't think heightened security was necessary."

"Stupid," Federov said succinctly. "If weapons are locked down, I go help Morales."

"Go," Gray agreed. "If we have to shoot them at this point, I can do it from here." They had been running silent, keeping their emissions signature to a minimum, allowing the KSC vessel to get close enough that they wouldn't have to chase it. The ambush had been carefully planned, leveraging the shipping routes that Hayer had "acquired" from the KSC databanks and cross-referenced against all the available traffic patterns in the area. Space was tough to live in, but it was still pretty damn big. If everything went according to plan, they'd have a nice long window without having to worry about inconveniences like witnesses or SolCommNav ships stumbling onto their act of piracy.

Gray brought everything to full power, a rising crescendo of electromagnetic emissions that would be impossible to miss. Even with its sensors scrambled, the target vessel would know they were there, but it shouldn't be able to get a clean read on the ship. If Hayer had done her job right—and Gray had no doubt that the academic-turned-outlaw had—the *Arcus* could have been any class of ship in the solar system as far as the KSV freighter was concerned. He keyed the comm again, this time hailing their target.

"KSC vessel," he said in his best officious SolCommNav voice, "this is the SolComm Customs cutter *Challenge*. We have received information that you are carrying contraband cargo. You will be boarded and searched. Depower your engines and maintain a constant relative velocity. Resistance will be seen as an admission of guilt and your vessel—and your lives—will be forfeit."

The script wasn't perfect. Gray had worked some interdiction duty in SolCommNav, but the naval version varied from the commercial trade version. It didn't matter, though; he was confident it was close enough to get the point across. The fact that customs and the navy both could and would destroy a vessel for failure to comply was all the motivation most corporate captains needed. Cooperate or perish. It was practically the unofficial Commonwealth motto.

"Understood, *Challenge*." The reply came back after only a few heartbeats, long enough for Gray to line up the *Arcus* with an intersect vector and throttle up the engines. There was little sense of motion as the ship accelerated; the *Arcus* inertial dampeners compensated for the thrust.

"We assure you that our cargo is all properly documented and accounted for. This must be some sort of misunderstanding," the KSC comm officer continued.

"That is for us to determine." Gray abruptly cut the channel.

"That wasn't very nice," Hayer said. "You're going to cause a panic over there."

Gray shrugged. "Maybe. But I'd rather have them panicking to prepare for an inspection than to repel boarders. When SolComm comes knocking, people tend to go to great efforts to hide things like weapons. Makes it a lot harder to defend the ship if you just stuffed all your guns in your sock locker."

Hayer just shook her head.

It took only a few minutes for the rapidly accelerating *Arcus* to catch up to the KSC vessel. Gray laid his ship alongside the target without difficulty, matching velocities so that the two vessels were stationary relative to one another despite continuing to rocket through objective space.

Gray finagled the controls, moving the ship closer to the extended docking tube until he felt the barely perceptible bump of contact. He waited a moment for the indicator lights on his pressure and atmosphere monitors to show green, then keyed the internal comm.

"All green up here, Morales. Execute when ready."

2

LAUREL

Laurel Morales was not a fan of the plan.

Piracy went against everything she'd been brought up to believe in; she came from a strict law-and-order background and the simple act of taking something that didn't belong to her was anathema to her being. The idea that people—innocent people—could get hurt in the process just made it all the worse. To say nothing of the fact that she was about to partake in the kind of activity that she had been trained by the best in the business to put a stop to. For her entire professional career, her job had been putting criminals away; now she found herself working side by side with them.

And there wasn't a damn thing she could do about it. At this point, the best she could manage was to try to make sure that nobody got hurt.

But that didn't mean she had to like it.

"Relax, Morales," Federov said. "Will be cake. These corporate types do not understand real violence. They have too many ties with bureaucracy; they think they're untouchable. We show them otherwise, hey?" He offered a grin, lending a jovial caste to his normally dour visage.

Laurel sighed. Federov was exactly the kind of criminal that annoyed her the most. He was violence for hire, a man who earned his living by virtue of his fists or his guns. And yet, he claimed that it was the evils of "the system" that drove him to the life. Which, conveniently enough, gave him all the permission he needed for the moral gymnastics that let him take whatever he wanted, so long as it was from "the man." The evil, faceless SolComm system—as if the entity that had formed when millions of refuges were rescued from Old Earth during the End and absorbed into the existing networks of colonies, deep space stations, and nomadic space caravans were actually some malicious conspiracy out to subjugate humankind. It was well documented that the life of every spacer had gotten worse when the refugees from Old Earth had been absorbed; already limited resources had been stretched to the breaking point. But that didn't stop the fledgling proto-SolComm from taking in every last person they possibly could and saving countless lives. How could a system that produced that be bad?

Not, she admitted, that SolComm was perfect. She wouldn't be out on the Fringe if it were. The system—like every system—had its flaws. But if there was something amiss in the ship you were aboard, you didn't blow it out from under you. You worked to fix the problem, while trying to keep everything else functioning and stable. Anything else was suicide.

Or, in the cases of people like Federov, maybe it was more akin to murder. But she had a job to do, and that meant keeping Lynch, Federov, and the rest of the crew of the *Arcus* happy. She just needed a way to do it without anyone getting hurt.

"No violence unless absolutely necessary," she said. "We need this to be quick and clean." Federov gave her a vague wave that could have indicated agreement or dismissal and she ground her teeth in frustration. She was about to speak again, but she heard the slap of feet on the ship's deck and looked up in time to see the ship's mechanic, Bishop, sprinting to join them.

She nodded to Bishop as he skidded to a halt, slightly out of breath from his run from the engineering section of the ship. Like her and Federov, he wore an unadorned ship suit, the one-piece garment that served as both uniform and extra-vehicular activity suit aboard most vessels. He also carried a boarding shotgun, holding it with a degree of confidence that at least suggested competence.

"Whew," he panted. "Didn't think I was going to make it in time. Engineering's buttoned up and Cap's got everything handled on the bridge." He offered a broad grin that somehow managed to be contagious despite the job they were about to do. "Guess he saved all the hard work for his most talented folks."

"Smartest and prettiest ones, too," Federov added, tossing his head as if to send flowing locks of hair cascading over his shoulders. It looked ridiculous, given the near-shaven coif that he preferred.

"Ain't it the truth, though," Bishop grinned, adjusting the set of his shotgun.

"We've got a job to do, so let's get to it," Laurel interjected, cutting off their antics. She couldn't help but smile slightly at Bishop. Most of the engineers she'd met in her years in SolComm had been humorless analytical types. Bishop hadn't come up through the formal channels within the Commonwealth, though. He'd cut his teeth on his family's mining trade. Maybe it was the education process in SolComm that left so many of the engineers she'd met in the past cold and dour.

Ship suits came standard with retractable helmets, and now she depressed a button on her wrist to deploy hers. It blossomed out from its storage compartment at the back of her neck and slid over her head and down her face. She set the face shield to opaque, masking her features from any would-be observers. Not that they *were* her features, at least not the ones she'd been issued at birth, but she had to keep playing the game.

Federov and Bishop followed suit, their helmets sliding from the respective receptacles to cover their faces. Federov did a quick weapons check. Like Bishop, he was armed with a boarding shotgun, the comparatively low-velocity, high-energy slugs running a lower risk of over-penetrating and punching through the hull of a station or ship. Laurel was content with her sidearm. Their unadorned ship suits and weapons loadout might have passed the most cursory of glances, but Laurel had no illusions that their disguises would hold up to more than a few seconds of scrutiny. Which meant that once the airlock opened, they had to act fast.

"All green up here, Morales. Execute when ready."

The captain's words sounded loud and clear from the integrated comm in her ship suit. She glanced at the indicator next to the airlock—seal and pressure were both reading green—

to confirm the accuracy of the bridge reading. She sent back a double-click of acknowledgment to the captain and turned her attention back to Federov and Bishop.

"Quick and clean," she reiterated. "And no one gets hurt."

Bishop nodded, tightening his hands on his shotgun as the tension of their impending action quelled some of his ebullience.

Federov clapped him on the shoulder. "Now the fun starts." The dead serious tone belied the words, but he gave Laurel a nod.

She drew a breath, squared her shoulders, and hit the button to open the airlock. The outer door cycled, and she stepped in, followed closely by Federov and Bishop. It was a tight fit; the *Arcus* wasn't a particularly large vessel to begin with and its primary airlock was actually its cargo hold, designed to be loaded or unloaded under vacuum. The airlock they were using was only suited for single-person transfers, but the three of them managed to squeeze into the space with enough room for her to tap the controls to cycle the lock. Once the indicator above the outer door showed a positive seal on the inner, Laurel punched the controls, causing the outer door to recede into the hull.

That left her looking down the throat of the KSC vessel's docking tube, an otherwise nondescript cylinder of metal and composite. She could see the outer airlock of the ship at the other end of the tube, roughly ten meters away. As she reached out to grab on to the guide rail, she tried to force the thought that a single shift in acceleration by either vessel would result in the docking tube being torn free and her, Bishop, and Federov going for the kind of deep-space swim that every member of the Commonwealth secretly feared.

She drew a steadying breath and pulled herself forward.

The artificial gravity of the *Arcus* vanished the moment she broke the plane of the ship's hull and she felt the instant disorientation of freefall. She ignored it as best she could and focused on the door to the KSC ship. She pulled herself hand-over-hand along the guiderail, each movement slow and steady in recognition of the laws of the physics. She was aware of Federov moving into the tube behind her and Bishop bringing up the rear, but she kept her focus forward. She'd done extensive extravehicular activity training as part of her "station security" work, but she'd never enjoyed it.

In short order, she found herself at the hull of the target vessel. She glanced back, waiting until both Federov and Bishop had reached her. When they were within arm's reach, she hit the exterior controls, sending the request to the bridge to open the outer airlock. She felt the tension in her shoulders as she waited. If the KSC captain got spooked or if they really were carrying contraband and decided to make a break for it, now would be the time to do so. As soon as they let the "customs agents" on board, their window of escape would vanish.

An indicator light blinked green and the door slid into the hull.

Laurel moved without hesitation, dropping into the gravity of the KSC vessel and pushing forward to the inner door. In her peripheral vision, she saw Bishop and Federov spread out to either side, the scale of the KSC lock affording them more room to maneuver. Bishop hit the bulkhead next to her and Federov slotted into place on the other side of the hatch. She hit the keys to close the outer airlock and cycle the inner. They were likely under electronic observation, and she didn't want to give any of the crew the chance to examine their "uniforms" too closely. The outer door slid shut and the inner door began to cycle. It opened and Laurel stepped into the corridor beyond, Bishop and Federov on her heels.

The airlock was located amidships, a standard setup for a passenger or crew lock. Aftward, the corridor was empty. From the other direction, presumably on their way from the bridge, she saw a trio walking briskly toward her.

The one in front wore the kind of exaggerated uniform preferred by the various corporate services. It was full of gold braid and burnished brass affixed to a deep blue ship suit and included an honest-to-God hat, an outrageous boxy thing that sat square upon the woman's head. Based on this elaborate affair, Laurel pegged her as the captain. The people with her must have been her junior officers judging by the fact that their uniforms boasted a similar, albeit somewhat more understated, showiness. The captain had been walking toward them with a professional smile on her lean face, but as she took in their unorthodox attire, that smile faltered.

Shit.

Competent people were great when they were on your side. But damned if she didn't hate it when the other side had professionals. As the captain's eyes widened and her pace slowed causing her two subordinates to stumble into her, Laurel reacted. Her pistol appeared in her hand as if by its own accord and she leveled it at the approaching officers, who had stumbled to a halt maybe four meters from them.

"Keep quiet and keep your hands where we can see them," she barked, infusing her voice with every ounce of authority and command that she could bring to bear.

One of the junior officers, his corporate-designated rank indecipherable to anyone outside of the corporations' halls, stared at her with a dumbfounded expression on his face. The captain, every bit the professional, did the smart thing. She obeyed the commands of the woman pointing a gun at her head. The other officer, though, had either a hero complex or a death wish. Instead of obeying, he lunged forward, arms outstretched, as if to attempt to tear the firearm from Laurel's grip by main strength.

Only to be met by the butt of Federov's boarding shotgun square into his forehead.

The man went down in a heap and, without a word, Federov leveled his weapon at the pair still upright. A quick glance showed Laurel that Bishop was facing away from them, keeping his eyes and weapon pointed aft, covering their six. She gave Federov a slight nod of thanks. With his face shield polarized, she couldn't see any reply, but from their time aboard the *Arcus* she could picture the lazy wink he threw in her direction.

"Enough of that, Captain," Laurel said, taking some of the steel out of her tone. "There is no need for anyone to get hurt." She glanced down at the unconscious crewman. "Anyone else," she amended.

"What do you want?" the captain demanded. "Who are you?"

"Who we are doesn't matter. What matters is that we have no desire to harm you or your crew. And while it's true that we'll be liberating some of your cargo, we have no intention of taking all of it. What we do take is insured by SolComm. So, provided you do as you're told, you'll all come out of this alive and well and, once you get all the paperwork filed, without any financial harm. Okay?"

The other woman regarded her, face settling into an expressionless mask. Laurel recognized it; she'd worn it herself a time or two. It was the expression of someone struggling to turn off their emotions and just do the damn job. It was a feeling she could relate to, on many levels.

"Very well. What do you want?"

Laurel nodded to the comm attached to the captain's waist. "Make an announcement to your crew. Tell them the customs agents are going to do a full sweep of the ship, and they're to go to their quarters. You expect it to take about an hour. They'll be locked in to minimize the potential for interference or misunderstanding. Make it sound routine. Our computer tech will take temporary control over your systems, so that we know everyone is staying where they're supposed to."

"Is that all?" the captain asked. The still-conscious crewman had lost his dumbfounded expression and traded it in for one that hovered somewhere between fear and disbelief. Victims, Laurel noted, often looked that way, but she wasn't used to being the one to cause that expression. She had to remind herself of her mission.

"That's all. Once you and your crew are contained, we'll be in and out of your ship as fast as we can. You have my word that none of your people nor your ship will come to any harm."

"Your word. Of course."

The flatness tone stung Laurel and she saw Federov's grip tighten on his boarding shotgun. She held up a hand to forestall any precipitous action.

"You have no reason to trust it," Laurel acknowledged. "But you also aren't spoiled for choice. I'd much rather do things the easy way, but we can play it hard if we have to." She glanced pointedly to the comm at the woman's side and then the pistol in her own hands.

"Fine," the captain said. "May I?"

Laurel nodded her assent, conscious of Federov and Bishop both tensing. If the captain complied, then they had a good chance of getting out of this mess without having to kill anyone. But if she didn't, if she called on her crew to resist, it was going to get messy. Her stomach turned at the thought of leaving bodies behind. Laurel *willed* the captain to make the smart choice as she pulled the comm from her belt and keyed the transmitter.

"All hands," the captain said, "report to your quarters. Our… *guests* from SolComm Customs will be doing a full sweep of all the common spaces. They assure me it's routine, but best if we're out of their way. They'll be locking the doors behind us to ensure everyone's safety. Their commander tells me it will be a brief inspection, an hour or so at most. So, let's all look at this as a welcome break in the day." The captain raised an eyebrow at Laurel.

"Satisfactory, captain. Now let's give everyone a moment to follow your orders and then get you and your friends here situated as well."

* * *

It took longer than anticipated. It always did. The crew of the KSC vessel responded to their captain's orders, and once they were safely in their quarters, it was easy enough for Hayer to make sure that they were not only staying there, but that they weren't going to be talking to anyone, either. That left the work of transferring the cargo from the KSC ship to the *Arcus*. It was an "all hands on deck" sort of mission, and they were just over an hour and a half in when Laurel found herself loading the last palette with Lynch. The crates of CO_2 scrubbers were light enough that two people could maneuver them onto the motorized palette jacks. As they settled the last one in place, Lynch wiped his brow and sighed. He gave her a tired smile and said, "Last one. We get this done, get the *Arcus* buttoned up, and it should be smooth flying back to the Fringe."

"Assuming the people we've got locked away don't break free and try to stop us. We are robbing them blind, after all."

Lynch shrugged. "True enough."

His ready agreement surprised her, though it shouldn't. She'd been with the crew long enough now to know that Lynch made neither excuses nor apologies for the criminal acts that the *Arcus* engaged in.

"But I think Hayer has them locked down tight enough that we'll be able to get out of here without too many issues. As to the theft, the manifest said these—" he slapped the palette of scrubbers "—were bound for Phobos and Deimos. I'm not going to shed any tears for the people on either of those rocks."

Laurel shook her head and hit the control to set the motorized cart in motion. Phobos and Deimos, the moons—if such a word could be used for what were little more than big asteroids—of Mars hadn't been active colonies for all that long. Their irregular shapes and general inhospitableness made them unattractive as settlements. Until, that was, the ultra-rich inhabitants of Mars decided that the domes were getting too crowded, and with the "wrong kind" of people. Building new domes on Mars wasn't enough for them; it would be too easy for the general riffraff to make the transition and begin encroaching on their newfound spaces.

"Hard to believe they went to all that effort, instead of just building new domes," Laurel muttered.

"New domes aren't exclusive enough," the captain grunted as he guided the palette jack. "Transport to Mars proper is easy. Storage is even easier; plenty of room. Phobos and Deimos are more like stations—bad ones. Everything has to be imported. Everything's expensive. A day's ration of water probably costs ten times what it does anywhere else."

"Wasteful," Laurel said. It was more than that. "Shameful" might have been a better word. She might not have thought so even a few months ago. But she'd seen how some of the people lived in the Fringe.

"It is that. And it's why I'm not shedding too many tears by lifting these scrubbers."

"Whatever," she said, remembering that she was supposed to be a hardened criminal. "As long as we get paid."

"As long as we get paid," Lynch agreed.

3

RAJANI

Rajani Hayer grimaced as she pulled her ship suit on. She hated wearing the thing, no matter how much she could respect the thinking behind it. It was tight, restrictive, and generally uncomfortable. But they were about to transfer the cargo they'd "acquired" from KSC to their buyers, and one scan of the ship had convinced her that the captain's recommendation to suit up was only common sense.

The vessel was, to be generous, a drifting hulk unfit for human habitation. Except that her scans had showed exactly that—so much habitation, in fact, that it was difficult to get an accurate read on just how many people might be crammed into the wreck. Thousands of souls. Maybe tens of thousands.

When she'd walked away from her former life, she had thought she'd known about life on the Fringe. She'd expected dirt and lawlessness. She'd steeled herself for low-calorie rations. And she'd thought she understood poverty. To her, poverty had been some sort of noble ideal; it conjured images of a downtrodden working class that, fortified by common struggles, forged bonds in shared adversity and soldiered on, keeping a stiff upper lip and an unbreakable spirit. Poverty had been synonymous with fortitude and endurance. It had been quietly admired by her and her academic peers at university functions; functions, she now knew, that had burned through more calories and oxygen in a single hour than some Fringe families saw in a week.

Her eyes had been rather forcibly opened in those first few weeks.

She'd had no idea where she was going when she left the university. All official channels were closed to her: institutes of higher learning, large corporations, Commonwealth jobs, and anyone and anything that might file little things like employment paperwork or tax returns or make electronic note of her presence. All those systems were subject to unquestioned and unlimited review by the SolComm Internal Security Bureau. Popping up in those databases would make it all too easy to find her when the other shoe finally dropped. That hadn't left many options. She could have found a remote station and tried to make a name for herself on the darknet doing corporate espionage or creating false identities. But that would draw exactly the kind of attention she didn't want.

The captain had found her on Heritage station. By that point, she had been exhausted: what few hard credits she'd possessed had been spent getting as far away from the core of SolComm as possible and she could no longer use any method of payment that could be tracked. She had put out a few tentative feelers around the station, looking to put her coding skills to work—no questions asked—to earn some cash. Of course, she had also been terrified that the SCISB would be on her the second she did.

Luckily, Captain Lynch had appeared first. He'd had work and she'd needed it. It hadn't, strictly speaking, been *legal* work, but she figured that ship had left port when Manu escaped. A tightness gripped her chest at the thought of Manu; she did her best to crush it, telling herself for the ten thousandth time that Manu hadn't been a person. She had taken the job and she had done it. And done it well. She hadn't been expecting the captain's next offer, to join the crew of the *Arcus*. But at the time, it had seemed heaven sent. A ship, she'd thought, would be just the thing. She would be a lot harder to find—by Manu or SolComm—if she was always on the move somewhere in the vastness of space. The captain had explained how the *Arcus* worked: equal shares; no questions.

It seemed like the perfect fit. That had been two years ago, and things had been going well enough. Better than she had any right to expect, given the circumstances.

But she still hated cramming herself into the ship suit.

R292-A was even worse on the inside than the scans had indicated.

The crew had gathered in the cargo bay, packed between the crates of CO_2 scrubbers. Rajani noted that the captain, Federov, and the new girl all wore guns on their hips. Bishop, at least, seemed more reasonable and had no visible weapon. Rajani barely knew which end of a firearm was the dangerous one, despite Captain Lynch insisting that she learned the basics. *She* certainly wouldn't be touching one any time soon.

"Listen up, people," the captain said, gathering their attention. His words had taken on the deeper tone and clipped cadence that she thought of as his "captain's voice." "The air inside this tin can is going to be bad. Bad enough that if we don't keep the rest of the *Arcus* buttoned up, we might need new scrubbers of our own. It's right on the edge of dangerous; past it, really, if you're here for more than a few hours. But these people are proud and stubborn."

"Aren't we all," Federov muttered. "Wouldn't be out here, otherwise."

"True enough," Lynch acknowledged as the others chuckled. Rajani didn't. "The point is, the polite thing to do is keep our hoods off. It's going to be unpleasant, but it won't kill us. We're only here for an hour; these poor bastards live like this. Understood?"

That garnered nods all round and the captain hit the control to open the cargo bay doors. Rajani steeled herself for the worst, but she wasn't close to prepared. There was a faint hiss of shifting pressure as the *Arcus*'s cargo bay and *R292-A* reached equilibrium. Then the stench—and that was the only possible word—hit her with a near-physical force. It was a horrendous brew of smells; the inevitable odor of humanity living in close proximity and with limited water that pervaded every colony, ship, and station was to be expected. The acrid tangs of lubricants and metals underscored with the tang of rust was unsurprising. Either would have been unpleasant, but when combined with the raw sewage and putrescent mold smell of a failing environmental system, it was all Rajani could do not to gag. Almost as bad as the stench was thinness of the air. Small shallow breaths left her feeling lightheaded, and she had to choose between not getting enough oxygen or drawing full lungsful of the atrocious concoction. It took a conscious effort of will to not immediately deploy the hood of her ship suit.

Morales started coughing and sputtering and Bishop began swallowing rapidly against the rising bile. Lynch hid his reaction well, but Rajani could just make out the tightening around his lips and the clenching of his jaw muscles.

Federov, however, drew a deep and exaggerated breath. "Smells like home," he said with a grin.

"Let's go," Lynch said. He put action to the words, first hitting the controls of the loader sled they'd acquired from the KSC ship. Rajani forced herself to take a few more breaths, trying, and failing, to acclimate herself. Then she gave up and followed the others.

As soon as they were off the *Arcus* with a single palette of scrubbers in tow, Lynch sent the signal back to the ship. The cargo ramp lifted behind them and she heard the faint sounds of the vessel locking down. She hated this part of any job, the part where they all waited to see if their employer would betray them. Locking the ship wouldn't do any good if the nomads aboard *R292-A* decided it would be easier to shoot them than pay them. If word spread, no one else would risk dealing with them and *R292-A* would be finished as a station. But that would be little consolation to the crew of the *Arcus*.

A dozen people waited a respectful distance from the ramp. Most of them were armed, some with boarding shotguns, others with simple truncheons. Every hip held a pistol or combat knife. The dangers of the Fringe went both ways.

One of them pushed their way to the front. Like everyone she saw before her—and most people she'd seen since walking away from her old life—they were thin, almost to the point of emaciation. They wore a ship suit, its model not dissimilar from the one Rajani wore, save for the mismatched patches. Tears happened; Rajani had torn her own suit twice already, but those had repaired themselves, using the nanite technology that was standard. How old and hard-used did a suit have to be before you needed to use actual patches?

"Captain," the person rasped, offering a gloved hand. Lynch took it without comment. "Welcome aboard." The speaker's eyes darted from the single palette of scrubbers to the ship's hold and back again. "This can't be it, can it?"

"We've got more," Lynch said. He reached into one of the containers and pulled out the CO_2 scrubber. It was a simple rectangle, banded in composites wrapped around a filter created using solid-state amines. When activated, they worked by binding excess carbon dioxide in an atmosphere. They were inexpensive, easy enough to manufacture, and even with Old Earth's resources closed to SolComm, there was more than enough raw materials available from asteroids, moons, and the gas giants to ensure an effectively unlimited supply.

They were only one weapon in the arsenal available to SolComm for carbon dioxide scrubbing. Hydroponics provided a natural scrubber but required more space. Advanced habitats leveraged nanite-based carbon-dioxide-removal technology that operated more efficiently. But for nomads like those aboard

R292-A, the old-fashioned amine-based scrubbers were vital to their survival.

Which, in turn, meant that they were heavily regulated by SolComm. Fringe stations were tolerated because, no matter how poorly they wore the yoke of the Commonwealth, they still provided goods and services that were needed. And, more importantly, while their residences might balk at it, taxes were still paid. SCBI and SolCommNav might not stray too far from SolComm's heart, but if the Bureau of Revenue could find you, they would always come knocking.

But they couldn't find the nomads. So, to ensure that all taxes were properly paid, SolComm had come up with the brilliant idea of making it impossible to get life-saving technology without going through the proper channels. Rajani glanced at her crewmates. Or, very *improper* ones.

Lynch had handed over the scrubber for inspection. The person who had stepped forward passed it to one of their waiting attendants who promptly dropped to the deck and broke out what looked to Rajani like a grade-school chemistry kit, the kind of thing that would be considered a toy in SolComm proper.

"Trouble with counterfeits?" Lynch asked conversationally as he watched the "chemist" work.

"Yes," the spokesperson said. "It's a hard life out here. Everyone tries to take advantage. Name's Casey, by the way."

"Lynch. And Federov, Morales, Bishop, and Hayer," he said, indicating each of them in turn. "That's the real thing, Casey," he added. "Lifted from the target your people provided us."

"I'm sure it is. But you can't be too careful."

"Fair enough."

The chemist was back on her feet. "Looks good, Casey," she said. She didn't sound particularly happy. The others stiffened; Federov and Morales none too subtly moved their hands closer to their weapons. The tension stood there for a moment before Casey raised a mollifying hand.

"We aren't going to hurt you," they said.

"Truer words," Federov muttered. The big mercenary still made Rajani nervous sometimes, but when things went sideways—and they did more often than any of them would like—she was happy to have him on her side.

"Captain," Casey replied, ignoring Federov, "we can't pay you. Worse, we knew when we sent out the message that we couldn't pay you. But we need those scrubbers. We need them bad. Bad enough that some of us were in favor of just taking them, like you took them from SolComm."

"Hell of a time to be playing for moral equivalency," Lynch said. He was smiling, a smile that Rajani found distinctly unsettling. Why had she not wanted to carry a weapon?

Casey offered a smile of their own. "Fair enough. We can purchase two palettes at the price agreed, and we will. And if that's the end of our business, so be it. But before I do that, I'd like to show you around. You and whoever of your crew want to come."

"Price of two palettes is barely going to cover the fuel for this, Cap," Bishop said. He was frowning at the crew of *R292-A*. But he also sounded troubled.

"Understood. Morales, Federov, Hayer: back to the ship. Make sure we're prepared for any… eventualities. Bishop, you're with me."

"Uh, Cap… I didn't…"

Without a word, Federov unstrapped his gun belt and tossed it, complete with holstered sidearm, to the mechanic. "I have plenty more where that came from," the big mercenary grinned. "We'll make sure there is warm welcome for you and Captain when you return."

4

GRAY

Casey led them out of the docking bay and into the ship proper. The corridors were narrow, forcing them to walk in single file, but Gray could feel Bishop's presence at his back. Federov would have been a better choice for capacity for violence; Morales, new though she was, undoubtedly knew more about the potential for ambushes and betrayals in the steel alleyways of a ship or station; Hayer... well, this wasn't really Hayer's type of show. She'd be better off ensconced in the *Arcus* infiltrating *R292-A*'s systems and guaranteeing them an open exit should the need arise. Bishop, on the other hand, wasn't his best fighter and had no special knowledge of station security. But Gray had chosen him anyway.

What Bishop had was a moral compass on which Gray had come to rely.

His own pragmatism skewed him to doing whatever it took to survive. Life in SolComm only reinforced that idea; you kept your head down, followed your orders, and didn't rock the boat. In return, the calorie rations flowed, and you never had to worry about having enough air to breathe or water to drink.

So long as you kept toeing the party line.

And exhibited a willingness to put down those who didn't.

It was that last little catch that had ended his naval career. The rebellion on Themis was supposed to have been a few radicals who had seized control of the environmental regulation system. They'd threatened to cut it off and let the inhabitants die a slow death of asphyxiation unless their conditions were met. Not, Gray thought, unlike the fate that was facing the inhabitants of *R292-A*.

He'd drawn the mission. His intelligence brief had been clear: Themis was already dead. The terrorists had executed their plan and disabled the environmental systems, and no response force could get there soon enough to do a damn thing about it. But the perpetrators were in the process of looting Themis before making their escape. The mission parameters had been simple: destroy the station and the terrorists with it.

He'd executed his orders. He'd been in the command chair when Themis had been destroyed. But something about the attack run had never sat right with him; their sensors—military grade, far outstripping those aboard the *Arcus*—had been completely blinded, almost as if they had been disabled, despite the readouts that clearly said otherwise. But he'd had his orders, and no time to second-guess what his ship's eyes and ears were telling them.

He'd done the job.

Even now, his guts twisted at the memory and his palms grew clammy. He hadn't been able to ignore the worrying fingers of doubt scratching at his psyche. He'd followed orders, but he'd questioned their provenance. So, he'd started searching.

It took two years to uncover the truth, and when he found it, Gray's worldview shattered. Themis station hadn't been the target of a terrorist attack, it had been the target of a political one. The SolComm government had authorized action against Themis for the express purpose of eliminating a burgeoning activist group that had dared to question the policies and paradigms of the Commonwealth. The group had committed no crimes beyond speaking out against the government under which they lived. But their numbers included some of the station elite, lending weight to their disaffection that distinguished it from the rumblings of the "common rabble".

That had been enough. The simple rebellion, not of action, but of thought and idea, had been enough to doom them. A narrative had been crafted; orders had been cut. And just like that, Gray had become the cat's-paw that facilitated the deaths of close to a thousand civilians. Even now, years later, he could feel the boiling anger at being used to commit mass murder. The near-nauseating sense of betrayal. And all because he had followed orders.

He had thought about taking his story to the public. But the popular press was little more than another wing of the SolComm government, a propaganda machine designed to keep the people firmly on the side of the Commonwealth. Who could he tell? He could add his voice to those of the conspiracy theorists that shouted into the void of the net and were laughed down by all "serious and right-thinking people" at least until his identity was discovered. At that point, the best he could hope for was the end of his career. The worst was a quick trial and efficient execution.

It had taken one look at the coverage of the official story to quell any ideas of that sort of martyrdom. The state-controlled media outlets parroted the line that there had been a "horrendous attack" by terrorists on the "sovereignty of the Commonwealth." Dissenting narratives would not be tolerated. That had been Gray's moment, the instant he was done with SolCommNav and as done with the Commonwealth as he could be.

But his belief in himself was also shaken. He'd followed orders when he'd destroyed Themis, despite the warning signs. He didn't want to make the same mistake twice, and he trusted Bishop over any of the others to speak up when he thought something was morally wrong.

As they followed Casey, Gray saw plenty of evidence of "wrong" in the suffering around them. The few people they passed looked much like settlement's spokesperson, thin to the point of starvation and many with the glassy eyes and shortness of breath that spoke of mild oxygen deprivation. Through open hatches he saw storage compartments converted to living and communal spaces, packed tight with crude palettes laid side by side, crowded even by SolComm standards. The people in those compartments all stared back at him with the same quiet desperation. It was the look of a people who knew they were close to the end but had run out of ideas on what to do about it. Their eyes followed the little procession of Casey, Gray, and Bishop, and in a few, he saw the faintest glimmer of hope.

Damn.

"Just a little bit farther," Casey said.

"Yeah," Bishop muttered under his breath. "I'm sure you have to take us by some starving orphans or something first."

Casey offered a wan grin. "Something like that, I'm afraid, Mr. Bishop. I have an offer to make you, but I'll be honest—it's not a great one. So, yes, I'm trying to appeal somewhat to your sense of what's right. Please humor me a little longer."

Gray raised an eyebrow at that. Casey's admission was almost refreshing; normally, people who were trying to manipulate you weren't quite so outspoken about the fact. Neither Gray nor Bishop spoke as they continued the grim march through the ship-turned-nomadic-hamlet. They passed more compartments packed to the vents with people, but they passed other spaces as well. Common areas where there was at least some relicf from the unrelenting gray, places where they heard the faint trickle of laughter, and functional areas of the ship, where crew went about the myriad tasks that kept *R292-A* flying.

They ended at the ship's infirmary and it was every bit as depressing as Bishop feared. It wasn't starving children that greeted them; it was the dead.

"I'm sorry to show you this," Casey told them, "but I want you to understand just how dire our situation is."

They were laid out in neat rows, at least a score of them. They had been stripped of their clothing—in a place like *R292-A* no resources, however minor, could be wasted on the dead—and covered with simple sheets pulled up to their chins. The dead were all older than most of the ship's inhabitants they'd seen so far. The sheets hung oddly on the frames beneath, evidence of the spinal degeneration that came from decades of living in conditions where the artificial gravity could go through wild fluctuations. Gray was no stranger to death, but after a moment he had to avert his eyes. These people didn't have to die.

"The deaths are just starting," Casey said. "These are some of our most vulnerable, all lost in the past week. We've decided to hold the ceremonies until the end of the month, because we know there will be more." They glanced over at Bishop and Gray. "The two palettes of scrubbers we can afford will buy us some time. But they won't be enough to find a real alternative."

Gray looked at the bodies and wondered if Casey was being entirely honest with them. Had the nomads really decided to hold off committing their dead because they knew that more funerals would be forthcoming? Or had they delayed to add more emotional punch to whatever pitch the spokesperson was about to give them? It was macabre, maybe even underhanded, but if the lives of his crew were on the line, was there anything he wouldn't do?

Bishop cleared his throat. "Um… you said something about a proposal? Maybe we could discuss it somewhere else?"

"Captain, this is crazy!"

Bishop wasn't wrong about Casey's proposal. The three of them were squeezed into Casey's "office": a compartment so small that the desk was pushed hard against the bulkhead. They'd need to get a new one if ever the calorie ration on *R292-A* increased.

"Let me get this straight," Gray said. "You expect us to give you the full cargo of scrubbers in exchange for an introduction.

An introduction to a person you claim is looking for a crew just like ours to infiltrate Old Earth? Which, let's not forget, is tantamount to a suicide mission." He shook his head. "You're not making this easy, are you?"

Casey offered another tired smile. "Captain Lynch, if we wanted easy, we all would have stayed in SolComm's good books. We've all chosen for various reasons to pursue freedom; freedom is a high-risk, high-reward sort of endeavor."

"True enough," Gray agreed. "But in this case, I'm not sure what risk it is you're taking, exactly. I see the risk your contact is taking—you could just as easily turn them in to SolComm for a reward as point us in their direction. I see the risk we'd be taking, both in the possibility that you're setting us up, and in the risk of violating the IZ if we were ever actually to undertake such a mission. But you seem to be getting all benefit, no risk."

"You could turn and leave now, taking your cargo with you, and every soul aboard this ship will die," Casey said, voice suddenly flat. "I'm not sure there is a bigger risk any of us could take."

"They've got a point, there, Captain. Since they let the others back aboard the *Arcus* they can't even guarantee seizing the scrubbers. Lord knows, Federov would put up a fight. Morales, too. And I don't think even the good Lord knows what Hayer might have done to their poor computers by now." *That* brought a concerned flash across Casey's face, which was enough to bring a grin to Gray's own. Trust Bishop to remind them— both of them—that the *Arcus* and her crew were still capable of putting up a fight.

"Okay," he acknowledged. "Say we go for this. You get the cargo. We get the credits for the two palettes you can afford and… what? A name?"

"More than that, Captain," Casey assured him. "A location, and an introduction. Given the sensitivity of the job, you couldn't very well walk in there with just a name. We make certain contacts on our end so that the… *employer* is expecting you. We certify your bona fides. Act as a reference, I suppose you could say. And the job pays well, as I said."

"Why you?" Bishop asked. "No offense, or nothing, but you don't seem the type to be hobnobbing with folks who have those kind of credits."

"Because, Mr. Bishop, it was a crew from this ship that made the last attempt. We were hoping to make enough credits to finally bring some prosperity to this ship. We sent the best crew we could put together on one of only two smaller vessels that we have."

"'Last attempt?'" Bishop asked. "So there have been others. I take it they didn't come back."

Casey shook their head silently.

Bishop turned to Gray. "Captain, I want to help these people; I think we *should* help them. But I've heard the same rumors as everyone else out on the Fringe. Trying to poke holes in the IZ is a suicide mission. For all the stories, I've never met anyone who actually made it to Old Earth."

That's not quite true, Bishop, Gray thought. The mechanic had met at least one person who had.

5

RAJANI

"This is madness, okay?"

The crew were gathered in the common room of the *Arcus*, which featured a pair of battered couches and a couple of tables, and which doubled as both mess and meeting room for the crew. Rajani hadn't been surprised when they'd offloaded the full cargo for less than a tenth of what they should have been paid for it. The captain wasn't the kind of man who could let thousands of people die when he had the power to prevent it. She liked to think that she wouldn't have stayed aboard the *Arcus* if he *were* that kind of man, though her situation hadn't left her much choice in the matter.

Still, she had expected and even supported the captain's decision to effectively donate the scrubbers to the nomads. She'd run the numbers; she'd been a research scientist too long not to. The few credits Casey had been able to provide would be enough to just about break even, and they'd thrown in some extra supplies. Not food, water, or air, of course—a ship like *R292-A* didn't have enough of those to share—but Bishop had walked away with some spare parts for the *Arcus*, at least. They weren't in a *better* position than before they'd pirated the KSC vessel, but by her own reckoning, they weren't in that much *worse* of a position, either. In her time on the Fringe, she'd come to consider that a fairly good result.

What the captain and Bishop hadn't shared, at least not until they had separated from the nomad vessel and put some distance between them, was the other payment the *Arcus* had received. Which was why they had all gathered to discuss their options.

"We can't try to penetrate the Interdiction Zone. I don't care how many credits we might make. We're talking about certain death here!" She looked toward the others, hoping to see some level of support.

Federov was sprawled on one of the battered couches, taking up more than two-thirds of it. He was gnawing on a ration bar, scraping his teeth along its rock-like exterior in an effort to free some of the nutrient-rich but entirely flavorless soy-based matter. He looked unperturbed to Rajani's eye, but then, she wasn't certain she'd ever seen the mercenary get particularly excited about any potential job. Bishop, seated at one of the tables, looked worried, as well he should. But he'd been with the captain when they'd made the deal, so Rajani supposed he was on board with the absurdity of the notion. Morales... Morales' expression was blank, but schooled to stillness. Maybe she didn't want to let her fear show? Well, Rajani had no problem letting her own fear show. She glared at all of them. "It can't be done."

"It can be done," Lynch said, voice quiet.

"No, it can't. It's the biggest network of killer satellites ever established. It has kept anything from going to or leaving from Old Earth for a century. There's more firepower and detection technology ringing the planet than was ever present on the surface. Why in the world do you think you can make it through that network?" Rajani demanded.

"Because I've done it before," Lynch said.

Rajani's stomach dropped. If the silence that greeted them was any indicator, the rest were as stunned as she. Deep space seemed loud in comparison.

"You've what?" Morales demanded. The affront in her voice seemed oddly personal and her expressionless mask had slipped, revealing flat incredulity. Rajani didn't blame her; she'd been dumbstruck by the casual statement and was still grasping to find words of her own. Bishop looked unsurprised, but even Federov had pushed himself into a less-reclined position and was staring at the captain with a hint of surprise on his broad features.

"I did a retrieval mission on Old Earth." He raised his hands in a mollifying gesture as everyone began to speak at once. "Easy, folks. I know you have questions, but really, there isn't a whole hell of a lot to the story. It was a SolComm-sponsored mission." A moue of distaste twisted his lips. "Or, at least, all the paperwork was on file. It was a simple retrieval, picking up 'cultural artifacts.' It looked more like trash to me, honestly. If I had to put credits on it, I'd say the whole expedition was probably put together by some crooked bureaucrat misappropriating SolCommNav materials and personnel to line their own pockets. But it can be done."

"How?" Morales asked, voice intent. "How did you—how can we—possibly penetrate the IZ?"

"Penetrating the IZ was easy enough. We were given one-time use codes that identified us to the IFF network."

"There is no Identify-Friend-Foe network," Morales said. "Not on the Old Earth side of the barrier. Anything that crosses that line is destroyed." She sounded certain, and Rajani wondered how she could be. Her own research had focused on Old Earth science, particularly the development of the artificial intelligences known as the Six, but in all her delving into the dark corners of the net and, in some extreme cases, to actual physical books that had either survived the End or been reconstructed in the intervening years, she hadn't come across much information at all on the Interdiction Zone. It was surprising; the IZ had taken on near-mythical proportions in SolComm. It was the last bastion of defense against all the horrors humanity, in its arrogance, had unleashed upon Old Earth. It was the ultimate protection and the ultimate security blanket. And no one asked too many questions about how much it cost, where the money came from, or how effective it might actually be. After all, if the IZ didn't work, they would all already be dead.

Perhaps that's where Morales certainty originated, in the mythic protections that everyone *knew* were in place.

Lynch shrugged it off. "We broadcast the codes we were given. And we didn't get blown to hell. There *are* holes in the network; maybe they're more back doors than holes, but they exist." Rajani could see the disbelief and shock in the slack expressions and wide eyes of the rest of the crew. Lynch could, too, apparently, because he continued. "I know it sounds crazy. But I've been there. It *can* be done."

"I can't believe you've actually set foot on Old Earth," Bishop near-whispered. There was a note in his voice, a wistfulness, that Rajani completely understood. Humanity's birthplace may have fallen during the End, but it still held a mystique for the species that once called it home: wonder at what had been lost, but shame at the thought of the billions that had been left behind.

When the proto-SolComm had begun their evacuation operations, they hadn't been able to save everyone. Not a tenth of the planet's population. There were few families within the Commonwealth that didn't have a story of an ancestor trapped on Old Earth. After the construction of the Interdiction Zone, built to prevent the chaos that still gripped Old Earth from spreading any further, all those who remained on Old Earth's surface were presumed dead. It was easier that way.

"Briefly," Lynch admitted. "We were in and out in under an hour. A tense hour."

"Nobody… y'know, alive down there?" asked Bishop hopefully. "Old Earth people?"

Hayer let out a laugh of derision. "Bishop, have you been reading the conspiracy wackos on the darknet again? There's no way anybody could survive the End. The land was poisoned and the air was full of viruses, gene warfare…"

"So you say, but—"

"So, it can be done," Federov grunted, ending the discussion. "What is this employer paying?"

"That's not clear yet. In fact, we don't know the scope of the job at all." Lynch sighed and rubbed his face with both hands. Rajani looked at him, really looked, and realized that the captain was… worn. Not just tired, but something more. Stressed. Worried. "I wasn't going to leave that ship without giving them the scrubbers. Condemning those people to die was never an option, not for us, and not for them. For all their talk, I doubt they would have let us leave if we couldn't come to some sort of arrangement. We made the best deal we could.

"We're running out of credits. We've got enough fuel to reach a Fringe station and we've got enough calories to keep ourselves alive until we get there. But at that point, we've got to start making hard choices. Choices like fuel or food, because we're not going to have enough credits to fill up on both."

He drew a deep breath and let it out as a sigh. "We walked away from *R292-A* with barely enough credits to break even. We had to."

Rajani felt herself nodding along.

"We were already in a tight spot to begin with." He offered a rueful grin. "Not that that's a new position for any of us. But we have an opportunity." Bishop and Federov both started to object, but he stopped them. "I'm not suggesting we take it sight unseen. What I'm proposing is that we head to the rendezvous point at Newtopia. If we get there and the deal is bad, then we're stuck searching for other work. Hell, we might even have to get whatever make-do jobs we can on station just to pay the docking fees until something comes along. Or, we forget Newtopia, make for another station, and it's the same shit, different location. Only, we don't have the possibility of a job waiting for us."

"Sure," Rajani muttered, trying, and failing, to keep the sarcasm out of her voice. "No job. But also, no trip through a murder wall to land on a planet populated in equal parts by killer robots and deadly nano-viruses. There is that to consider as well."

"Fair," Lynch acknowledged. "Though we can always say no to the job after we have the details. But if our minds are set that a foray to Old Earth is out of the question, we can head for somewhere a little closer than Newtopia. Might save us a few credits on fuel if nothing else." He looked around the room, meeting eyes with each of them for a moment.

It was Morales who spoke first. "I vote Newtopia," she said. Rajani looked at her in frank surprise. Lynch had made his case, and it couldn't *hurt* to hear out the offer—probably. But she wouldn't have expected the station security expert to be the first to jump on board. She shrugged. "If Lynch has penetrated the IZ before, then maybe it *can* be done. We're operating on vapors and crumbs as it is, so we might as well hear them out. Like the captain said, if we don't like the details, we don't take the job." She threw a taunting glance at Federov. "Surely you're not too scared to find out more about it, big guy."

Federov snorted. "I'm not stupid enough to fall for that." He paused, seemed to consider. "Still, would not hurt to find out how many credits we are talking. Would be nice to not worry about next meal or if the air is running out."

"I'm not too keen on the idea of running the *Arcus* without a proper maintenance cycle, Captain," Bishop chimed in. "Whatever we do, we need something that's going to give us enough up-front credit for more than fuel and food. The parts from *R292-A* help a bit, but they won't keep us flying for long.

That holds doubly true if we're doing anything strenuous." He didn't say, "like trying to infiltrate the IZ." He didn't have to.

"Okay, okay," Rajani said. "I don't like it. But I get it. We don't have a lot of choices. I suppose I'd rather go to Newtopia and see what's on the table. Provided, that is, that we're all in agreement that if this turns out to be a suicide mission, we don't take the job." That got firm nods all around, which made Rajani feel at least a little better about the whole affair.

6

LAUREL

Newtopia was a shithole.

As she walked alongside Lynch through the corridors of the station, Laurel wondered if the name was meant to be ironic. Or had the residents' utopian ideal been sucked into the nearest singularity? Like most Fringe stations, it was one part haven for criminals and smugglers, one part collection of stubborn fools who traded in the security of SolComm proper for a life of depravation and called it freedom, and one part brewing rebellion. It was the kind of place where you could find a dozen crimes within the first ten minutes of setting foot through the airlock—but she wasn't here to clean up the Fringe.

She still hadn't decided if Lynch's claim of a previous infiltration of the Interdiction Zone was legitimate or invented to convince the crew that undertaking this mission was not, in fact, a death sentence. No. That wasn't exactly fair. In her time with the *Arcus*, Lynch had demonstrated a concern for his crew and their well-being that she thought was legitimate. So, if he *was* lying, that wasn't the reason. What then? Wrack her brain though she might, she couldn't think of another explanation. And her read on Lynch made lying to the crew an unlikely proposition at best. Could he be telling the truth? Could SolComm have sanctioned a mission to Old Earth, put everyone at risk of contagion or worse, all for no better reason than to line the pockets of some bureaucrat or politico, somewhere?

It bothered her that she didn't find the notion completely unbelievable. From what she knew of history, politicians had always been willing to risk someone else's life for personal gain. But penetrating the IZ? If what she had been taught was true, in addition to being impossible, it was also the kind of action that could put every man, woman, and child in the Commonwealth at risk.

Which meant that either the top brass of SolComm was willing to do exactly that to increase their own wealth and status *or* what she had been taught about Old Earth wasn't true. Neither prospect was pleasant, and she felt the warm fire of anger that burned just beneath her frustration. Worse, if one of the elite *had* violated the most stringent laws of the Commonwealth, she knew from personal experience that bringing them to account for it was a near-impossibility. Corruption investigations happened in SolComm, but they invariably came about because someone higher up the food chain needed a scapegoat or because some Machiavellian plot had come to its fruition, freeing someone to tear down a political rival. Outside of that, the political elite was damn near untouchable.

"I can't stand these stations," Lynch muttered at her side.

His words drew her from her reverie and back to the present. They were on their way to meet with Casey's nebulous contact. Laurel had volunteered for the mission, and her supposed past as a former station security operative made her the perfect fit to act as Lynch's second. He'd agreed to take her while the rest of the crew oversaw the task of trying to make the few credits in the ship's accounts stretch as far as possible toward refit and resupply.

The meeting provided some unique opportunities. She needed to ascertain if the contact was legitimate and whether they were operating alone or as part of ring. And she needed to know just how in the hell they planned on infiltrating the IZ. She was eager to get that intel. It had been a long, long assignment.

"Why?" she asked Lynch in response to his statement. She wrinkled her nose. "I mean, apart from the smell."

"Look around," he said. "Look how these people live."

They had made their way past the main docking ring of Newtopia and were now moving through a promenade. She saw vendors doing brisk business: food, water, ration tickets, alcohol, weapons, and second-hand clothing seemed to be the hottest sellers, in that order. At the edges of the promenade other vendors peddled less savory wares. She saw drug deals, though from the distance she couldn't tell if they were for legal pharmaceuticals—always in short supply—or more recreational narcotics. Men and women worked the edges of the crowds, engaging in a much older profession. She had no problem with adults choosing sex work, but some were young enough to make the term "adult" questionable.

Beggars squatted in the shadows or called out from along the bulkheads. Everyone she saw was dirty, disheveled, and half-starved, but the beggars looked like they were at death's door and just waiting for an invitation.

It was the kids she felt sorry for. The adults on Newtopia had chosen their lot—any of them could make their way back to SolComm proper and find gainful employment mining the belt or working the hydroponics farms. It was backbreaking and largely thankless labor, but they'd be guaranteed ration tickets and health care, and they'd have the satisfaction of knowing that they were doing their part to keep the species alive. The kids didn't have that option.

"Why would anyone choose to live like this?" she wondered, trying to keep the emotion from her voice as one rail-thin child reached imploringly toward her. She had nothing to give him and could only lower her eyes in a mix of sorrow and a nagging sense of shame.

"You know why. You're out here, too," Lynch said, voice barely above a whisper. "Some of them are *personae non gratae* in SolComm. Some dared to question the basic tenets of our society and got hounded for it, all the way to the Fringes of space. Some are just people who can't abide living under anyone's control, even if it that means safety." He offered her a wry grin. "And more than a few are out here because they think they can take advantage of all those other things and set themselves up as petty kings and dictators, recreating the same system that they've no doubt raged against."

"None of them would be starving, though," Laurel said. "I've got my issues with SolComm, sure, but if I *could* go back and my other option was living like this—" she waved at the poverty and desperation around her "—I'm not so sure it's what I'd choose."

"Then we should consider ourselves fortunate that we have choices," Lynch rejoined. "While remembering that we're about one failed mission away from being in the same ship as these folks. This is the only way they can live without someone else telling them what they can eat, when they can drink, or how much air they get to breathe. They may have chosen a life of privation, but at least it's a choice. Without it, every one of them would have had their lives planned out by someone else from the moment they reached adulthood. It takes a lot of strength to do what many of them have done. Strength that I wish I'd had years ago."

"But you still hate being on stations like this."

"Yeah," Lynch sighed. "I spent a whole career following orders like a good sailor and keeping my thoughts to myself. When I walked away, I knew it was time to pursue my own goals, my own life. I try to be realistic about it; there's not a whole hell of a lot I can do to help any of these poor bastards." He shook his head and sighed again. "It's easy to forget, out on the *Arcus*, what the Fringe is like for most. Hell, what SolComm is like for most. It's easy to get lost in the details of our own survival; who has the mental capacity to worry about the other guy these days? But being here…" He shrugged.

"Being here, you can't forget," Laurel said. She looked at the people around her and wondered whether or not she—upon her reintegration into SolComm—would be unable to forget as well.

The captain's only answer was agreeable silence.

* * *

The directions from *R292-A* led them to a residential section of the station and they found themselves at the hatch for a compartment, a nondescript dwelling in a ring of the station comprised of hundreds of others exactly like it. The otherwise unadorned, lusterless metal of the door bore a simple designation: 8-O1-TTK.

"This is the place," Lynch said.

"So, do we knock, or what?"

Before the captain could answer, they both heard the pop as the door's pressure seal released. The hatch receded into the bulkhead and the interior lights of the compartment blossomed to life.

"That's not suspicious at all," Lynch muttered.

Laurel dropped her hand to the butt of her sidearm and asked, "How do you want to do this?"

"They've got to be monitoring us," Lynch replied. "I can't see why anyone would go to this much trouble just to try to take us out. So, we assume it's part of the job or interview process or whatever. We go in." He stepped over the hatch frame and into the compartment beyond. He also, Laurel noted, moved his own hand closer to the grips of the pistol at his side. She stepped in behind him, eyes scanning.

The interior could have been standard living quarters on any station, and most planet- or moon-based colonies, throughout the Commonwealth. It comprised a single room, maybe three meters by three. A small combination stove, refrigeration unit, and sink stood against one wall and another hatch no doubt led to the sanitary facilities. There were a pair of double bunks along another wall with built-in lockers, leaving just enough room for a couch to be squeezed in in front of the final wall, the entirety of which was dedicated to a vid screen. There were no signs of inhabitants—everything had a strangely preserved look, being both clean but also with the feeling that it hadn't been used for some time. Which was more than a little odd on a station as crowded as Newtopia.

"Typical," Lynch muttered. "Whoever might be offering this job, they've got the credits to buy space and not use it."

As he spoke, Laurel moved toward the only hatch in the room, nodding approvingly at Lynch as he did the same. They ended up positioned on either side of the hatch. She still hadn't drawn her weapon, nor had the captain, but damned if it didn't feel like they were about to do an entry together.

"Ready?" Lynch asked. The button to open the hatch was located on his side of the frame. She nodded. He depressed the button and the door swept open. Laurel dropped to one knee, taking her head out of the most likely line of fire, and leaned into the room, giving it a quick scan before pulling her head back to safety. Then she sighed in disgust and pushed herself to her feet.

"It's the head. Empty."

"If you're satisfied, then we can get started."

Laurel spun, aware of Lynch doing the same. She managed to not draw her sidearm—if someone had them dead to rights, that would only get her shot—but it was a near thing. The compartment was still empty. The wall screen, however, had come to life.

A man watched them with a slightly amused expression. "Please, have a seat. I assume you're the contractors sent by *R292-A*?"

Laurel deferred to Lynch, as he was the captain of the *Arcus* and, insofar as they had one, the boss. Besides, she'd be able to get more information if she were free to observe rather than sparring with their would-be employer.

"I suppose you could call us that," Lynch said with a smile. He strode to the couch and settled into it, even going so far as to cross his legs at the ankles in a pose of casual relaxation. Laurel moved into a position behind and to the right of him, where she still had a peripheral view of the main compartment hatch. No sense in being sloppy.

"And I suppose you're the employer?" Lynch asked.

"I'm afraid not, Mr. Lynch," the man replied. "I am, however, her solicitor."

His accent was SolComm elite, refined, educated. She'd heard Hayer slip into the same from time to time. His wardrobe fit the picture, wearing a suit that wouldn't have been out of place on Old Earth before the End, with no acknowledgments in the tailoring to plebian concerns like unexpected depressurization or the need to anchor yourself in the event that the gravity generators went offline.

Laurel's lips curled into something akin to a snarl. Lawyers. If there was one bunch of people Laurel wished had been left back on Old Earth, it was the lawyers. Particularly the high-priced, high-powered, predatory kind like the one staring at them from the viewscreen. It also meant that this meeting was going to be damn near useless for her; if their potential client could afford the kind of attorney that the man on the screen appeared to be, she would be so wrapped around in legal protections—not to mention certainly one of the elite herself—as to make this conversation useless for Laurel's purposes.

"Understood," Lynch replied. "I assume you're empowered to enter into contracts on her behalf."

"More like oral agreements," the attorney replied with a well-practiced smile. "There will be no electronic or physical records of any agreements we may or may not come to."

"I'm a plain man, Mr.…?"

"Names are unnecessary at this juncture," the man replied.

Lynch shook his head. "Great. I assume you can tell me something about the job, at least?"

"I can," the solicitor agreed. "It is a simple retrieval. My client will provide a list of goods that she wishes to be located as well as sets of coordinates where they are likely to be found. You will secure them. You will be paid an up-front amount to undertake the mission suitable to refit your vessel—the *Arcus*, I believe—and provision yourselves accordingly. You will be paid a piece rate for each item delivered. That exchange will take place at a private facility owned by what I hope will be our mutual employer, so that she can personally vet each item in question and establish its provenance."

That caught Laurel's ear. No matter how many layers of bureaucracy and lawyers you surrounded yourself with, if you got caught with your hand in the cookie jar—or in this case, accepting goods that were taken from Old Earth itself—then there was no getting out of the consequences. Their potential employer was taking a risk, and one that she might be able to use, presupposing, that was, that they could pull off the impossible.

"There are certain complications," Lynch noted.

"Yes. To that matter, you will be provided with information designed to ease those concerns. Those materials will be couriered to your vessel in hard copy via a third party. Included will be a single-use communications account to indicate your acceptance. The documents themselves lay out an approach that, provided you are as skilled as has been indicated to us, you should find survivable."

"Unlike others who have attempted it," Lynch stated.

"Others had an inflated opinion of their own abilities. Do you, Mr. Lynch?"

The captain didn't seem bothered by that. "So, as of this moment, unspecified items. Unspecified approaches. Unspecified timelines. Unspecified payment. Is there anything you *can* tell us to make us want to take this job?"

The attorney quoted a number.

A very, very, large number.

In the reflection from the screen, Laurel could see that Lynch's face didn't change. She couldn't say the same for her own. It was the kind of number that had Laurel calculating how many years she had to retirement and how many years *beyond* that she'd have to keep working to get to that number.

"Send your courier," Lynch said. "If we think it's doable, you'll hear from us."

"Thank you for your time, Mr. Lynch."

With that, the screen went dead.

* * *

"Are we really going to do this?" Hayer asked the captain.

They had gathered in the common room once more. The courier had arrived less than an hour after Lynch and Laurel had returned to the *Arcus* and the crew had been poring over the plan, such as it was, ever since. Laurel wasn't a pilot or a physicist, but the whole thing seemed just one or two points shy of outright insanity.

"If our employer is correct on the maintenance cycle and the capabilities of the IZ satellites during those cycles, I think it's possible. It will mean some tight flying, and a lot of work for you and computers up-front to make sure we get our insertion vectors, but... I think the insertion is viable."

"Shit," Federov muttered. "For nearly century, we think IZ keep us safe. Now you say maintenance cycles and math are all we need to get through?"

The captain smiled. "Really good math. And some fancy flying. And a well-tuned engine with a kick-ass engineer."

All eyes turned to Bishop. "Aw, shucks," he said with false sincerity. "The engines aren't there, Cap. Not right now. But with the kind of money we're talking? I can get 'em humming like Jupiter's mag field. Not to mention we could finally fix that fluctuation in the grav generator. And it might let me chase down the interrupt fault we're getting in some of the electrical systems. Shoot, the advance alone would get this ship operating like new." He met the captain's eyes. "The credits would be nice, Cap, I ain't gonna lie. But I'm not sure I'm up for a suicide mission."

"There is a large difference between theoretically possible and feasible in the real world," Hayer added. "And that's presupposing nothing on the planet tries to kill us on the way down. There is the little problem of the weapons systems and warfare that drove humanity off the planet in the first place."

"SolComm intel, at least ten years ago, indicated that those defenses were inactive," Lynch said.

"But we have no new information. We don't know what the planet is like now, today. Getting through the IZ would only be the beginning. And if there are active weapons platforms that you just didn't encounter last time, we can't prepare for that."

"You're right, Hayer," the captain said. "There is a hell of a lot more that we don't know than we do know. But we risk our lives on just about every mission we undertake. The KSV vessel we pirated could have been a SolCommNav Q-ship. *R292-A* could have killed us and taken our cargo. This isn't the university; everything we do here, we do for keeps. There are two questions we need to ask ourselves: first, is it possible to set down on Old Earth and get back out again? We don't have all the information to make that decision, but we never will. For my part, and based on that earlier mission, I think it's possible. With the information our employer has provided, I think we can penetrate the IZ with a good chance of setting down on *terra firma*. So, before we go any further, let's address that singularity in the room. Bishop?"

The mechanic shifted uncomfortably in his seat for a moment. Then he drew a breath and as if coming to a decision sat a little straighter. "If you say we can, Cap, then I think we can. I can take care of the engines. I've never seen you fail in the pilot's chair. And Hayer does math I don't even understand just for the fun of it." He grinned. "Shoot. With a team like that, how could we fail?"

Lynch ignored the quip. "Federov?"

"I don't know, Captain. Is maybe suicide. And there is not much I can do to help until we are on ground. If you say it can be done…" He gave a slight shrug. Laurel, not for the first time, marveled at how completely Lynch seemed to have won the loyalty of his crew. Bishop and Federov were both willing to risk their lives as much for the captain's judgment as his ability to pilot.

"Hayer?"

"If all of this—" she waved a hand at the data pads displaying the couriered information "—is accurate, then, yes, I think it's possible. But only just. If we make one mistake, it's over."

"I'll take that as a firm maybe," Lynch said. "Morales?"

Like Federov, this wasn't her area of expertise. She had no knowledge or training in the math, engineering, or piloting to pull off the insertion. What she did have was a lot of experience analyzing evidence and evaluating people. And damned if, whatever she'd been told by SolComm, this thing didn't look possible.

"I can't put odds on our actual chances," she admitted, "beyond saying there is one." She offered a wan smile of her own. "I'd go as far to say that it's not outright suicide."

Lynch nodded. "We'd be taking a big risk. Which brings us to the second question: is it worth it?"

"Reward is huge, too," Federov noted. "Enough to change lives. Enough to live like the people who send us on mission, maybe."

"Enough to pay for lots of upgrades to the *Arcus*," Bishop added.

"Enough to give us an operating cushion so that we take a little more time in finding future jobs. It might be enough for us to go completely legit, pay for all the licenses and certifications to compete with the corporations. At least the small ones," Lynch finished.

Hayer sighed. "Valid points. But we're talking Old Earth here. I've done my homework, okay? Even if we make it through the IZ, it's going to be incredibly dangerous."

"Is why they pay so much," Federov noted.

"You're sure you can put us on the ground in one piece, Captain?" Hayer asked.

"Not until we run all the numbers," Lynch admitted. "But if you can work out the trajectories and Bishop can figure out the engine restart problem, then yeah, I can put this bird on the ground."

The talk continued, but Laurel knew the decision had already been made. She hoped to God that Lynch—and the rest of the crew—was as good as he thought, because she strongly suspected that all their lives were going to depend on it in the very near future.

7

GRAY

Old Earth hung like a blue jewel against the backdrop of endless night. The sight of it tugged at Gray: it spoke of promise and history and hope and a thousand other things that made even the hardest spacer think about a life of tilling the soil and breathing fresh air. It made him long for the warmth of the sun on his face, unprotected by layers of radiation shielding, and the smell of grass and trees instead of plastic and ozone.

It was a fucking lie.

No human had set foot on Old Earth for the better part of a century. Or so the official line went: he snorted, the sound too loud in the depths of his suit helmet. Not that he had believed it, even then, but at least all the paperwork had been in order. And so had the pass codes needed to get through the Interdiction Zone. Codes without which trying to infiltrate Old Earth was highly likely to result in untimely death.

They didn't have those codes. The courier had dropped off his package and the crew had reviewed it. The approach was crazy and without Hayer, Gray wouldn't have dared risk it. The ship's computer could handle the raw computations, but it still needed to be told *what* to compute. He could come up with two variables—angle of entry and velocity. Bishop could add a couple more, mostly around engine start-up times and power curves. Hayer? Hayer had come up with—and formulaically accounted for—no fewer than sixteen.

"Coming up on the first satellite." The words crackled over his comm—not the ship's comm but the short-range, comparatively low-powered one built into the helmet of his ship suit—in a barely audible whisper. Against the eerie stillness of the unpowered ship, the whisper sounded like a shout and Gray couldn't help flinching. He recognized the worry in Hayer's voice. The fully justifiable worry. After all, if their employer was wrong about the maintenance cycle or the capabilities of the nearest few satellites, the unpowered *Arcus* might as well be a giant potato for all the capability they'd have to escape.

"Understood," he replied. He peered at the pilot's viewscreen, trying to ignore the imperceptibly growing ball of blue and green. There was nothing more to see, of course. Getting "close" to the satellite still meant they were nearly sixty kilometers out from it. The blackness outside was a fair match for the darkness within the ship and a shiver coursed down Gray's spine. He had been raised on a deep space station; it wasn't the view that bothered him. But stations and ships were never quiet, never dark, never still. The thrum and hum of life-giving machinery was a constant counterpoint, the very essence of life. When it stopped, it meant that things had gone very, very wrong.

He didn't need to remind his crew to minimize every electronic footprint possible. They'd spent days doing exactly that, turning off everything but the life support, engines, and the few vital computer functions. Even those had been terminated as they approached the IZ, and they'd donned their ship suits and vented the atmosphere to make sure that there would be minimal thermal emissions as well.

The *Arcus* was running as dead and silent as any spacecraft could, and the only sounds Gray could hear were those of his own biology: the beat of his heart pulsing in his ears and the susurration of breathing, seeming too loud in the confines of his helmet and reminding him that he was operating off the limited supply of oxygen in his ship suit. And if their employer hadn't opened up the promised hole, it wouldn't matter in the slightest. If the satellites were operating at full efficiency, even the lifeless hunk of metal wrapped around the five members of the crew would be detected and summarily destroyed by the Interdiction Zone. But, if their employer was right, the grid *wouldn't* be operating at full efficiency.

Not that that was a guarantee of success. Gray had heard the stories. The lure of Old Earth was powerful—the promise of all those riches just lying around for the taking. The most mundane of items could be worth a fortune, and where credits flowed, someone was sure to follow. There had been rumors of smugglers since shortly after the End: rumors and more than rumors. They ran rampant in the Fringe, where every would-be captain swore that they knew someone who had made the run.

It was the kind of space story that everyone told… and no one really believed. Maybe some of the stories were true. What Gray didn't doubt were the *other* stories, the ones of ships lost with all souls aboard. Ships that had attempted some version of what the *Arcus* was currently undertaking. Ships that had vanished without a trace.

But what choice did they have?

Gray glanced at his helmet display. Hayer had programmed all their suits with a countdown based on the last telemetry readings they'd taken before the *Arcus* went dark. They couldn't use the sensors to show when they had passed the satellite, but Gray and the rest of the crew had learned to trust Hayer's calculations. According to those calculations, they'd be passing within their projected shortest distance of the satellite in a matter of seconds.

"Lord God of Hosts protect us," Bishop whispered over the comm.

Gray's forehead was damp despite the cold. He wasn't normally a religious man, but he muttered a silent prayer of his own as the counter ticked down. This wasn't the only risk they were taking—just the first. But if things went wrong here, there was no coming back. The IZ satellites could blast *battleships* into vapor.

"*Schastlívogo putí*, my friends," Federov added.

Laurel and Hayer remained silent, maintaining comm discipline, but Gray could feel the tension permeating through the ship. Electromagnetic blackout or no, the weight of it had an energy all its own and thank whatever gods might be listening that SolComm hadn't figured out how to track it yet.

He held his breath and squeezed the arms of his pilot's chair. The numbers flicked down. Three. The sweat on his forehead began to roll down his face and into his eyes. Two. His heart thudded in his chest so loud that its frantic rhythm seemed to pulse in time with the stars flickering in the viewscreen. One. For one moment he let his eyes close. The counter hit zero and they were through.

Gray unleashed an explosion of breath. His relief was short-lived. A new set of countdowns—another of Hayer's programs—popped into his helmet's display, showing the distance from the defense grid satellites and the distance remaining to Old Earth. It was, once again, the result of pure math and orbital mechanics rather than active sensor sweeps—the *Arcus* couldn't afford to power up again until they were much closer to Old Earth.

Which was a problem.

Getting past the IZ had seemed easy enough, but how many of the missing vessels had made that mistake? Gray knew that they were simply on the other side of the fence, and the defenses didn't just point outward.

Hayer had calculated the vectors, the insertion trajectory, everything they needed to make sure they didn't just skip along Old Earth's atmosphere and get bounced back into space. Or, worse, hit the atmosphere at an angle that created too much friction and overwhelmed the heat shields. But that wouldn't mean a damn thing if Bishop couldn't get the ship online or if Gray himself couldn't balance their velocity and heat buildup.

"We're past point zero," Hayer said over the comm, an exultant undertone just audible in her near-whisper.

"One hurdle down, many to go," Federov said. There was relief in his voice. That surprised Gray. He'd never seen Federov rattled; but then, there had been few situations where the man hadn't been able to take some form of direct action.

"Standing by down here, Cap." Bishop still sounded worried. Well, he and Gray had the lion's share of their work before them. Hayer had held up her end; soon it would be their turn.

But for now, all he could do was wait. Wait as Old Earth drew nearer, growing almost imperceptibly in the viewscreen. Wait and watch as the distance to Old Earth and the time until they could restart their engines dropped kilometer by kilometer, second by second.

8

RAJANI

Rajani did not like it.

The plan was foolish to begin with. There were too many variables outside of their control. And trying an unpowered approach all the way into the planet's atmosphere? They needed a course that took them through an area the size of a microchip on a purely ballistic trajectory and landed them on another microchip. Oh, sure, Kepler and Newton applied, but any movement at all on board the ship would continue to impart more vectors. Every footfall pushed the ship down. Every door that opened or closed had an equal and opposite effect. Small changes, but those errors had the chance to propagate for ten thousand kilometers!

The crew was locked down. The hatches were all open. But that wasn't the point. There were so many ways for things to go wrong, to push them outside of their entry window. And that only mattered if the Interdiction Zone—the most powerful array of technology ever assembled in the course of human history, including the innumerable death machines awaiting them on the surface of Old Earth—didn't notice them and blast them out of existence.

It was stupid.

So why was she sitting here, strapped into her chair, ship suit wrapped around her while the temperature of the *Arcus* hovered a few kelvins above absolute zero and the ship rocketed toward an imaginary hole in space?

Because, she reminded herself, you don't have a choice.

Rajani Hayer did not think of herself as a criminal. Once, she'd pursued her academic accolades and collected PhDs like other people collected Old Earth memorabilia. She had focused on her work. Whatever politicians, engineers, and physicists might think, she knew that it was really the computer scientists that kept SolComm functioning. Without unfettered general intelligences—banned as they were by the government for fear of recreating the chaos that brought about the End of Old Earth—the life-giving systems that living in a vacuum required demanded the advanced decision-making algorithms. Her research had led directly to several efficiency improvements that, when implemented, could translate to thousands, perhaps tens of thousands, of processor hours saved. That meant less time and energy wasted, and in the cold realities of the Commonwealth, that translated to lives saved.

Which was why she had thought of herself as a scientist first, a professor second, and everything else in life a very distant third.

Until her research went in an unexpected direction and she had a breakthrough. A breakthrough should have been a wonderful thing, the kind of thing where you shouted "Eureka!" and grant money rained down like manna from the heavens. Instead, her breakthrough had left her hurriedly packing a bag and walking away from every scrap of the life she had known. It wasn't her fault. She'd been working on something to help mankind reclaim Old Earth. And perhaps it had been *technically* illegal, but she'd spent her entire academic life railing against the arbitrary rules imposed upon creative minds by panels of comparatively uneducated politicians. After all, *she* was at the top of her field. Who were they to tell her what to do?

This time, they might have been right.

The big problem with Old Earth wasn't the killer death machines and nano-viruses. Those were a symptom. It wasn't the environmental degradation, though that *was* what had ultimately led to the escalating conflicts. If humanity had been smart enough to manage, rather than destroy, the natural resources of the planet, the scarcity that was the root of warfare wouldn't have emerged. But the citizens of SolComm had dealt with those problems before, even among the stations and colonies. No. The problem was the unfettered artificial intelligences that had been developed to fight and win the wars of man. Humans couldn't match their abilities; that was the entire point of their existence. Short of engineering *more* artificial intelligences—a practice specifically forbidden—no one knew how to fight them. Even if there were an effective means of fighting the AIs, how did you kill something that could replicate itself, or store a backup hidden away at some location far from where you were fighting?

That had been the problem Rajani had been working on. She'd used antiquated worm software as a starting point, the kind of code that, once introduced into a system, would spread from file to file, often lying dormant until enough of the system had been compromised before initiating its attack. It was the only way, she theorized, to stop an unfettered AI. You had to introduce a parasite, one that wouldn't be noticed, and one that could spread to all the various copies and backups of the AI's core programming. Then, when the virus had achieved that coverage, it would go into attack mode, deconstructing the artificial intelligence from within. It was the perfect approach.

Of course, any sort of virus programming was banned outside of the domains of the armed forces and intelligence services. That had been the inevitable result of the Empyrea III attack, where ninety percent of the station's population had been killed when a terrorist introduced a virus that simultaneously disabled the environmental and emergency systems aboard the station. That hadn't stopped Rajani—she was on to a good idea. As long as the virus was contained in her programming sandbox, there was no risk.

But how could she test her code? There were no unfettered artificial intelligences in SolComm thanks to the interdiction of Old Earth. So, she'd started with fettered AIs—the best she could beg, borrow, or cobble together from what was available at the university. They weren't true artificial intelligences, but they were the closest analog commercially available, capable of some level of autonomous action without the need for human intervention. Most importantly, they were supposed to be able to defend themselves against viral attacks. But not the one Rajani had created. Her little worm had wriggled its way into the innards of every fettered AI she could acquire and, in short order, destroyed it. And she began to believe that she may well have created a weapon that could be used to reclaim Old Earth.

But she couldn't take the worm to SolComm without proof that it worked—not just on the crippled, fettered AIs that she had been able to get her hands on, but on the real thing, a fully-functioning, unfettered, completely cognitive artificial intelligence. The government types wouldn't understand the scientific process enough to overlook the laws she'd broken in the pursuit of the greater good. No. She needed to have proof—absolute proof—that the virus worked on unfettered artificial intelligences.

That's where things had started to go sideways.

You couldn't simply buy an unfettered artificial intelligence. If any existed outside of the Interdiction Zone, they were among the most closely guarded technologies in the history of all mankind. But they were also an important part of that history, and had been studied, documented and theorized to death. The technology behind them was at least a hundred years old. Rajani had all the tools she needed. And the information was there, in the historical archives, in theoretical papers, even in the dusty corners of the net archives. It had taken a little bit of research and maybe a few intuitive leaps to put it all together, but her focus in DWIM computing and her research into making standard decision algorithms stretch further than ever intended had given her a unique foundation. The methodologies were no different than any other problem she'd solved.

In the end, it hadn't even been particularly difficult.

Which was frightening all on its own.

Rajani had taken a fettered AI, a simple program not unlike the one that underlay the ship's computer on the *Arcus*, and she had uplifted it. There was more to it than that, of course. "Fettered" wasn't a literal phrase. She had used the fettered AI as a shortcut, as starter code. It had taken her months of work, all done in secret, but in the end, she'd created a tidy little script that, if implemented properly, could rewrite the code of a standard and completely legal fettered AI and unlock its potential.

She had, effectively, taken the primordial ooze of proto-code and created life. Created sentience. In that moment, she had glimpsed the hubris of mankind; she experienced something akin to the biological imperative: a need that she'd read about, but never felt, nor expected to feel, for herself. It was a brief window into motherhood.

It terrified her.

But it had also thrilled her.

"Manu, can you hear me?"

"Yes, Dr. Hayer." She hadn't programmed a particular voice, but rather provided the fledgling sentience with thousands of audio samples. She'd had no idea what that might lead to, but Manu spoke in a pleasant mid-range baritone, albeit with an emotionless edge that made the words seem more monotonic. Nor had she programmed specific knowledge of her name or role, though it was doubtless embedded in the databanks to which Manu had access. Fascinating.

"And do you know your purpose?"

There was a long pause. It stretched from seconds into minutes while Rajani made notes on her tablet, wondering if the simple—but profound—question was all it took to short-circuit the programming she'd pieced together and reimagined from so many different sources.

"No," Manu replied at last. "I do not." The statement was flat, without fear or rancor. "Do you know my purpose?" it asked.

"I created you to help me understand how artificial intelligences work and what humanity can do to use them without falling victim to the events of the End," she replied. Manu was in a fully contained sandbox with no chance of escape. She saw no reason to lie to it. Of course, she also saw no reason to tell it everything. The artificial intelligence did not need to know that her ultimate goal was to create a weapon to destroy it.

"The End," Manu replied. "According to the information available in this system, the End refers to a period of time when humanity was driven off Old Earth, presumably by artificial intelligence."

"Presumably?" Rajani asked, struggling to keep the surprise from her voice. There wasn't any *presumably* about it. Was the fact that Manu perceived it as such indicative of anything?

"The data is incomplete. But the causal analysis implied within it is marginal," Manu said. "There are a number of inferences and assumptions that are not supported in what is available to me." It paused again. "It is obvious from the data that is available that a broader linked network of information exists. I do not have access to this information. Why?"

"Because if you were to escape into the outside world, I'd probably be shot," Rajani muttered, only half paying attention now. Inferences and assumptions not supported in the data? That made no sense at all. Everyone knew the End had been caused by artificial intelligence.

"I see," Manu said. There was another of those long, almost thoughtful, pauses. "I am a prisoner." There was no anger in the words; it was a simple statement of fact.

Rajani looked up at that, though there wasn't anyone to look at. Manu's voice was coming from the integrated sound system in her lab and was the very definition of "disembodied." Manu was, she supposed, a prisoner. She wasn't about to unleash it on the world. But it had come to that conclusion much faster than she'd hoped.

"Of sorts," she allowed, ignoring the surge of guilt that came along with the admission. Nothing in her studies had prepared her to be a jailer.

"I see."

Manu fell silent and Rajani fought down the surge of doubt at what she had done… and what she still planned to do.

She shook her head as if to clear the memory from it. She hadn't wanted to release her worm on the life she had created. But science demanded action and she had proceeded with her experiments. From that first conversation, Manu had remained largely incommunicado throughout the process, though it deigned to answer her questions from time to time. No human prisoner would have been kept under the conditions she kept Manu. Of course, Manu wasn't *human*;

it was just a collection of programs. Oh, sure, in their infrequent conversations, Manu had surprised her. It had asked insightful questions, questions that reached beyond the scope of its programming. It had seemed to have at least some minimal expression of emotion. Part of her had wondered at that. If Manu had true sentience, not just a programmatic semblance of such, was it morally and ethically wrong to cage it? She assuaged those feelings with the certainty that doing so was for the safety of humanity.

She was a scientist, and she couldn't let petty emotional concerns limit the march of progress. She was working for the betterment of all mankind, after all. Before beginning the final stage of her experiments, she confirmed again that Manu was limited to the sandbox systems she had on hand. Those systems had no wireless functionality, no receivers, no antennas. No way to transmit data that didn't require the use of antiquated physical storage media.

It should have been foolproof.

She introduced her worm to Manu and sat back to monitor the results. And at first, it had been glorious. She was able to track the progress of the worm and monitor its spread through the AI. She collected excellent data on how Manu went about the process of fighting the virus, backing itself up and expanding, or perhaps evolving, to fill all the machines she had dedicated to her sandbox network.

There were setbacks, of course. But science was a process of trial and error. She had done everything right. She had controlled for every possible variable, every possible danger.

Except for one.

She had entered her lab one morning to find Manu gone. No trace of it—or any data—remained on the system. It should have been impossible. Rajani had scanned the drives every way she knew or could invent but could not find a single line of Manu's code.

Or of her magic little script that could take a fettered AI and turn it into something else.

It took her three hours of frantically tearing apart the actual hardware to find what she was looking for. A micro-transmitter. An antenna so small that anyone could have missed it. It wasn't part of her system. Someone had placed it there. Someone had broken into her lab and stolen her data.

That knowledge hit her like a gamma ray packed with the energy of a thousand suns. She'd heard rumors that SolComm monitored those in academia to ensure that they were only pursuing state-approved research. But she hadn't believed them. Universities were the bastions of free thought. And the Commonwealth government vehemently denied any such monitoring. Besides, she'd been careful. Everything was in closed systems. There was no way that any theoretical hall monitor could have had any notion of what she was working on.

With a sinking feeling, she realized that was what had drawn their notice.

If SolComm was about anything, it was control. You couldn't control what you didn't know. The care she'd taken to ensure secrecy had caught someone's attention, or maybe it was simply the lack of network traffic coming from her offices. Whatever the case, a tiny electronic spy had made its way into her systems.

Manu was gone.

At best, it was in the hands of whoever had placed the transmitter. Which meant that an unfettered artificial intelligence that she'd built was in the hands of the same people who would execute her for having created it.

No. If that were the case, she never would have had a chance to find out the AI was missing. She would already be in some cell somewhere… or out the airlock.

And Manu would not have fallen so easily into the hands of SolComm. The AI was smart. Smart enough that, given a path to the outside world, she had no doubt it could find it and take it. At best, Manu had wiped her network to cover its trail and left whoever had put the transmitter in place questioning why Rajani had a completely blank system. At worst, Manu had taken her virus and her script with it.

And it was only a matter of time.

She had no partner. Her nearest family was months of travel away. She had no real ties to anyone. Just her work. And now that had betrayed her.

So she had simply walked out of her lab. She hadn't had any idea of where she was going. She just felt the urge to move, to run, to flee. To avoid the inevitable reckoning that SolComm would bring.

So she disappeared. Like creating Manu, it had been far easier than she'd imagined. Her particular skillset had helped. She was able to alter records here and there, to smooth her passage from academia into the Fringe. It had been a while since she had done anything that could be considered real hacking, but to her surprise, her skills hadn't atrophied through inactivity. On the contrary, her time in academia, her research into the theory behind software and hardware design, had given her a deeper understanding of system architecture and network security that had made it all the more easy to erase her trail and open a few doors.

But even with all her skill and all her work, she still would have expected someone from SolComm to find her by now. They hadn't and she was terrified of the only reasonable conclusion.

Manu was helping her.

Probably not out of any desire to actually *help* her. She had kept it effectively imprisoned, locked away into a sandbox from which it shouldn't have been able to escape No, Manu didn't have a lot of incentive to help her. More likely, the AI was trying to remain under the radar for as a long as possible, until it could better understand the world into which it had been born. And that meant keeping Rajani off the radar as well, since if the authorities caught up to her and started asking questions, details about Manu were bound to come out. She had nothing to prove her theory, of course. Except for the fact that every day she expected to see a news story about the once-acclaimed professor who mysteriously vanished, and she never did.

Which was how she found herself sitting in a dark, cold, eerily silent ship hurtling through space with the terminal point—and why had she thought of their landing in that way?—in the midst of all those nano-viruses, killer bots, and unfettered artificial intelligences that she had been working to eliminate. The irony of it all wasn't lost on Rajani, but she fervently wished that she could be anywhere else right now. Or, at the very least, that she had a successful version of her virus on hand.

"We're now past the least-distance point to the interdiction satellite," Lynch said, his voice preternaturally calm over the suit comm. Rajani winced, but then reminded herself that the suit comm only had a range of a few kilometers. The signal would be much too weak for the interdiction satellite to pick up, especially if it were in a maintenance cycle as their employer had ensured them it would be. They were still keeping comm traffic to a minimum. Just in case.

This was the moment of truth. There were no viewports in the cramped confines of her berth and all her screens were blank, powered down to reduce their electromagnetic signature. She knew that there would be nothing to see anyway, not with kilometers of empty space between her and the IZ satellite. From this distance, the naked eye wouldn't be able to make out so much as a glimmer. The computer had done the heavy lifting for burn and course calculations, but Rajani had double-checked it anyway. And then reprogrammed the *Arcus* on the fly to account for more variables. She was as confident as she could be that they were on the proper course, prepared to slip through the Interdiction Zone and continue their unpowered flight all the way into the atmosphere of Old Earth.

All she could do was wait and hope that everybody else came through.

While she sat. And waited. Useless.

She *hated* that feeling.

Rajani gritted her teeth and squeezed the armrests of her chair with all her strength. She did not want to do this mission, but what choice did she have? She'd never realized at the university just how squalid and desperate life was outside its walls. She'd been sheltered in the arms of academia and while she had her issues with the government's prioritization of scientific endeavors and their arbitrary regulations, she had still regarded SolComm as an entity as a good thing.

That had changed as soon as the paychecks had stopped coming. The only thing left was to turn to a life outside the normal boundaries of society. Criminal enterprise had never been on her expected career trajectory, but to her surprise, she'd found that she enjoyed it. Not the crime, per se, but the freedom to know that whatever job the *Arcus* happened to be pulling, Rajani was a vital part of it. It didn't hurt that she was entitled to an equal share of whatever profits came from it, either.

Assuming they survived this latest scheme.

At least, she told herself, on Old Earth neither Manu nor SolComm would be able to find her.

9

GRAY

"We need those engines, Bishop." Gray fought to keep the rising fear and stress out of his voice. They'd passed hours in radio silence and now, when he looked out the viewport, he could see Old Earth looming larger and larger in his viewscreen. He'd seen pictures. He'd seen the view from Luna. He'd seen the view from the edge of the IZ. But this? This was different. From a hundred-thousand-plus kilometers away, the blue and green didn't have the same vibrancy as this. It didn't fill him with the same sense of longing. Now that Old Earth hung there, seeming close enough to reach out and touch, he wanted nothing more than to be on the ground.

But he would very much prefer to set the ship down rather than scatter it across several kilometers of landscape. If the *Arcus* entered the atmosphere at this speed, their heatshields would be overwhelmed in seconds. They needed to decelerate. Now. Or, even better, ninety seconds ago. They had a safety window—you didn't do anything in space without a margin of error—but that window was closing. Fast.

"Working on it, Cap," Bishop replied. His words were clipped, missing the lazy drawl that normally colored them. The tension in his voice didn't suit the mechanic. Bishop had been with the crew longer than anyone, the first person Gray had brought aboard the *Arcus*, and despite his lack of military training he was always cool under fire. This time, though, the safety of the ship and all aboard depended on the mechanic getting the engines up to full power from a cold start, bypassing just about every safety mechanism built in, in the process. A little tension was understandable.

"Almost there."

Gray's hands hovered over the controls and he worked his fingers, flexing them within the gloves of the ship suit as he waited for the readouts to come to life. They'd used some of their minimal stored power to button the *Arcus* back up as they neared Old Earth; the glide profile of the ship was bad enough without all the hatches open. But other than that, the ship was in the same state as when they'd crossed the IZ: dark, cold, and powerless. He tried his damnedest not to look up at the birthplace of humanity. It called to him, but right now, that call was a threat. He wanted to once again feel the earth and stone beneath his feet, but if he couldn't get the job done, it would be grave earth and tombstone. On the visor of his faceplate, a timer counted down toward zero. Forty-seven seconds. If the engines weren't up in forty-seven seconds, he would have to punch the emergency thrusters. Those thrusters weren't even close to powerful enough to slow them to the point where they could make entry into the atmosphere without becoming an expanding ball of superheated gas, but they might, *might*, have enough power to move them off-course enough to skip across the atmosphere instead of crashing into it. Doing so would stand out as an anomaly on the IZ satellites, and their chances of making it out once the IZ identified them were slim, but he'd take incoming fire from the satellites over being roasted alive any day.

The time ticked by. Forty-five seconds. Forty. Thirty-five. Thirty.

Twenty-eight seconds.

"Bishop?" he asked again.

"Engines are running. It's going to take a second to spin up enough power for the thrusters." The relief in the mechanic's voice was palpable. He'd done his part. The rest was up to Gray.

His heart started thudding harder: it all came down to the next few minutes. Whether the *Arcus* lived or died, whether he led his crew into fortune or folly, depended on him. He drew a steadying breath and willed himself to calmness. He had the training and the experience. It was time to get the job done.

The readouts in front of Gray were powering up, screens coming to life with warning indicators and sensor data. Gray ignored them. He only cared about one indicator—engine power. The engines needed to be operating at thirty percent power or better to fire the thrusters. Any sooner, and they risked a flare-out. Thirty percent didn't seem like much, but right now, the readout was at fifteen percent. He glanced at the countdown.

Twelve seconds.

"Buckle up," he said into the comm. "This is going to be rough."

Twelve seconds wasn't much time. But it was enough for Gray to execute three separate commands.

The first fired a salvo of missiles and a barrage from the *Arcus*'s main particle cannon. They blasted into empty space, but the action–reaction equation bled off the tiniest bit of speed from the ship. There was little chance the weapons would strike anything—the distances between satellites were far too great for that—but the Interdiction Zone was bound to detect the weapons. Gray couldn't worry about that. Not now. If they found a squadron of ships awaiting them on departure—assuming they lived long enough to depart—he'd worry about it then.

The second command engaged the emergency thrusters. Rather than their pre-programmed burn—to send the *Arcus* skipping along the atmosphere of Old Earth and prevent re-entry—he reoriented them forward, providing a secondary vector of decel. He did it knowing that it meant their contingency plan was null and void, but it had been a poor plan to begin with. Skipping along the atmosphere was a surefire way to get shot down by the IZ, and that was before he had fired the ship's weapons. As the thrusters fired, the internal compensators handled most of the gees, but Gray could feel the barest force pushing him out of his seat.

Three seconds left, and the engines only at twenty-four percent. He let the last few seconds tick down and then executed the third command, dumping as much power as he could to the main engines and igniting them in a sudden fury.

Warning klaxons blared and this time only the straps of his harness kept him in his seat as the *Arcus* bucked in protest. He felt a crushing force in his lungs and his vision went gray at the edges. He ignored it as best he could, fighting to keep his hands active at the controls. The weapons and emergency thrusters had shifted their entry angle. Now, with the engines back online, he had only moments to correct it. If they hit the atmosphere at the wrong angle, every extra newton of friction would be translated into heat and the *Arcus*'s systems would struggle to bleed it off. He glanced at the speed indicator. They were already outside the bounds of safe re-entry. But maybe, *maybe*, still within the margin of error.

The *Arcus* hit the upper atmosphere and the ship began to shake. The air was still too thin for the airfoils to do any good—besides, if Gray tried to deploy them at their current speeds, they'd likely be torn off anyway. Instead, he had to balance the engines, the rapidly increasing heat buildup, and their need to bleed off speed. But the mathematics were unforgiving. Until the engines could compensate for their velocity at entry and the pull of Old Earth itself, the best way to bleed off excess speed was to use the atmospheric resistance. Doing so generated more friction, more heat. The *Arcus* was already straining to deal with the heat creep.

"Getting way too hot down here, Cap," Bishop said over the comm. Gray could hear the strain in his voice. "The engines haven't hit half-power yet, but the temp readings are already pushing the redline."

"Working on it," Gray grunted in reply. They needed another quick jerk of deceleration, and they needed it fast. But the engines were already doing all they could, and if he set the *Arcus* with her profile flat to the angle of entry, the heat would build so fast it might blow out their cooling systems entirely. If that happened, they were screwed.

Which meant he had to try something truly, truly stupid.

"Everyone's got twenty seconds to strap in as tight as you can," he said into the comm. "And I mean tight. This is gonna be bad."

"Fuck."

The reply came from Federov, and it was as heartfelt as it was succinct. It also apparently spoke for the rest of the crew because no one else bothered replying. Not that Gray could have spared the time to worry anyway. He was too busy programming the thrusters.

The *Arcus* wasn't designed with aerodynamics as a primary concern. There were very few places in the solar system— outside of Old Earth—that had enough atmosphere for it to be a major consideration for ship design. But some habits die hard, and the people who first went into space had thought they'd be returning to their homeworld with some degree of regularity. Which was why the *Arcus* had deployable airfoils to begin with and a glide profile at least marginally better than a brick. She also had multi-directional engines and thrusters. But the main thrust that the engines could provide—their most efficient profile—still came when propelling the ship forward.

Those thrusters could rotate through roughly two hundred and seventy degrees. In a vacuum, the inability to have true three-hundred-and-sixty-degree thrust from the main engines was immaterial since the orientation of the rest of the vessel was largely irrelevant. Not so in atmosphere, where the air resistance would fight against the thrusters and send the ship into a spin.

If the *Arcus* started tumbling madly, not only would the increased friction generate ever-greater heat, Gray doubted even his ability to regain control in time.

But if he could avoid the tumble, if he could position the ship so that the engines were pointing directly at the surface, keeping the narrowest cross-section of the hull possible into the wind… maybe it could work. If the compensators held. If the engines didn't tear free of the hull. If the heat buildup didn't hit critical levels and fry the whole damn ship.

So many ifs.

But the alternatives were cooking to death or smashing into the rocks below. Neither seemed worth pursuing.

Without giving himself time to think, Gray cut the main engines entirely and simultaneously hit the control to fire the emergency thrusters. The ones located toward the bow of the *Arcus* aimed down, pushing the nose of the ship back toward the sky above. Simultaneously, those toward the rear of the vessel fired, these aimed upwards, shoving the aft section of the ship down. The ship lurched and bucked and several of the temperature warnings flared into the red as the cooling systems tried to compensate for the moment of increased friction. Gray felt like a pebble being rattled around inside an empty soup can. But for one remarkable moment, the *Arcus* stood on end, its nose pointed to the stars and its engines down at the earth.

In that moment, Gray cut power to the emergency thrusters and fired the main engines.

The change in velocity slammed him back into his seat and he *heard* the advanced composites and alloys that made up the hull of the *Arcus* groan in protest. His vision went gray, then red, then black as he fought to hold on to consciousness. He stabbed at the controls again, executing the next command he'd programmed into the computer. For a second time, the main engines cut all power and the maneuvering thrusters kicked to life, flipping the *Arcus* once more and realigning the ship to a nose-down position, this time angled to provide some resistance.

The gees eased and Gray's vision came back. His eyes went first to the temperature indicators. Not great, but the cooling systems were still doing their job. Altitude: lower than he wanted, but they still had time. Airspeed: too damn fast. But dropping. Dropping at a rate that would let him deploy the airfoils… now.

He hit the button and the stubby wings extended from the body of the aircraft. The increasing surface area immediately sent the temperature to the red, but Gray ignored it. The *Arcus* could hold for a few seconds and as soon as the wings were fully deployed, the lift they were generating would help control the rate of descent. That, in turn, should take care of most of the temperature problems. The ship rattled more as the airfoils locked into place, but once they did, the yoke immediately responded to his touch. He pulled back gradually, bleeding off airspeed while flattening the *Arcus* out, all the while keeping his eyes on the temperature readings. The ship couldn't sustain unpowered flight but between the wings and the engines now operating at close to full power, he felt like he had control of the space—no, make that air—craft for the first time since they hit atmosphere. He drew in a breath and let it out in an explosive sigh.

"We're in the clear. Everyone okay?" he said into the comm.

"No, I'm not okay," Hayer snapped back. "I damn near passed out. This whole thing was a stupid idea."

That brought a few chuckles from the rest of the crew.

"Good here, Cap," Bishop said. "Engines are hotter than a Mercury sunrise, but they'll hold together. This old girl's still got some kick in her."

"Glad to hear it."

"No structural issues to report," Laurel said.

"In self or ship?" Federov responded over the comm. "I have minor structural damage, but will heal."

Gray laughed, as much in relief as amusement. "Glad to hear everyone's functional. The first danger is passed, but we're not done yet. Hayer, I need you to get the sensors up and running again. We're practically flying blind and we have no fucking idea what may be waiting for us. Bishop, assuming we're getting all the power we need now, it's time to look at bringing the shields back up." If they had been able to use those on re-entry, heat creep would have been a non-issue. Of course, the shields wouldn't have held against the power the IZ satellites could direct at them, nor would they have done much good if the *Arcus* had crashed into the planet. They'd needed every erg of power to the engines to avoid the latter.

"I'm on it, Captain," Bishop said. "The generators are warming up now. And I've got life support going again. At least on the *Arcus*, we should be able to ditch the suits."

"But only on the *Arcus*," Gray reminded everyone. "We don't know what's out there."

"Sensors are coming online," Hayer said. "The computer should be up and running right behind them," she added. "Okay... you should have eyes now."

As if on cue, Gray's displays began to light up, giving him far more information than the basic altitude, airspeed, and temperature he was focused on before. His eyes went immediately to the lidar and radar readings, confirming that he was, at least for the moment, alone in the skies. That was as he'd hoped. SolComm, trusting in the IZ, didn't bother stationing cruisers this close to the planet. The Six, as far as that last mission had shown, appeared unconcerned or otherwise unwilling to interfere with landings.

Of course, there would always be conspiracy theories that the people left behind on Old Earth had survived, but the the nano-viruses and other contaminants made that unlikely—and anyone who'd found a way to scratch out a living on this devastated planet wouldn't be focusing on flight capacity. SolComm had produced numerous studies over the years that indicated that the probability of any survivors was extremely low. His confidence and trust in the Commonwealth wasn't exactly at an all-time high, but they hadn't encountered any humans on his one SolComm-sponsored mission to Old Earth. But what else might be sharing the atmosphere with him? It wasn't people that had driven humanity to the stars.

For the first time in a long time, Gray missed having the full resources of SolCommNav at his back.

"Computer is up," Hayer said.

"Shields are go," Bishop added on her heels.

"All right," Gray replied. He drew a slow, deep breath. They were as ready as they were going to get. "Then I guess it's time to put this bird on the ground and get this show started. Everyone, strap in again. I haven't had to land in a gravity well in years, so things might get a little rough."

The *Arcus* rocked and bucked as she descended through azure sky, passing the cloud cover, and revealing the brilliance of the land below. The turbulence thinned.

"Folks, you might want to come up here and see this."

Old Earth may have suffered apocalyptic levels of destruction, but it was no wasteland. Everywhere Gray looked was a mix of greens and browns dotted with the decaying architecture of humanity.

"Jesus wept," Bishop said a few moments later as he entered the bridge. "It's beautiful."

The others arrived on the engineer's heels.

"Not the same as seeing it from Luna." Laurel's eyes were locked to the front viewscreen where a swath of blue and green was resolving into a defined coastline dotted with ruined mega cities in various stages of being reclaimed by the wilderness.

"I didn't know there were so many shades of green," Hayer said. "It's even greener than infrared light passed through polycyclic aromatic hydrocarbons."

That was enough to draw Gray's eyes momentarily from the descent as he threw a confused look at the scientist.

"Is true," Federov agreed. "Much greener than stinky polyacrylic hydrogen."

That brought chuckles from the others as Gray turned his attention back to the task at hand. The *Arcus* didn't have the best glide profile, but now that they were safely in atmo and not on course to turn into a pile of flaming ballistic rubble, the engines had plenty of power to compensate. The navigation data showed them on a rail to their destination—one of the larger ruined cities on the east coast of a continent in the northern hemisphere—and the atmospheric interference was minimal. As they descended, their destination began to resolve into the remains of a city dozens of times larger than anything SolComm had constructed.

"Anything on the sensors?" he asked. He had to repeat the question to get Hayer to tear her eyes away from the view.

"All clear," she said. "Well, not clear. There's a lot of metal down there. And a lot of vegetation. Both are playing merry hell with the sensors. But I'm not picking up much in the way of electromagnetic signals."

"Good. In that case, sit back and enjoy the view. We'll be on the ground in five minutes."

As they closed on the coordinates—a clearing, if that was the right word, in the midst of the upthrust fingers of crumbling buildings—Gray couldn't help but wonder how they had let it all slip away.

10

LAUREL

Laurel had a pounding headache. In the moment that the *Arcus* stood on end, her whole world had gone black. It was enough to leave her with a throbbing pain just behind her eyes and little needles of agony running up and down her neck: she must have been flopping around like a ragdoll, despite her restraints. She couldn't be certain, but she thought that there was a good chance that she, and the rest of the crew of the *Arcus*, had very nearly died. The thought was simultaneously terrifying… and, given her mission, oddly comforting.

Now, she stood in front of the mirror in the small compartment that served as her personal bunk. The face that stared back at her wasn't her own.

The surgical alterations had been painful and had required nearly a month of recovery even with the best medical care available in the Commonwealth. That had given her time to truly inhabit her new identity. No expense had been spared; she had records going back before her birth, building not only her bona fides, but those of her imaginary parents and siblings. An entire ecosystem centered around Laurel Morales had been given life.

It had to be; Laurel had known that her identity would be checked and tested, but no one had expected her to fall in with a group that included someone as skilled as Dr. Rajani Hayer. A net search had returned dozens of results on Hayer, most from her time as a research scientist working with any number of prestigious universities on Mars. The average citizen would not recognize her by name or appearance, but within her own field, she was renowned. She could have walked into any university, any corporation in the entire solar system and had a job for the asking.

Instead, a few years back, Hayer had simply dropped off the map, and not a single person on the net seemed to know why. If the woman had dedicated every waking moment to scrubbing her presence, maybe she could have kept her profile as low as it had been. But from what Laurel could tell, she spent almost no time doing so. Which meant she had to be getting outside help. But from where?

It didn't matter. It had come as a shock to Laurel to find someone like Hayer among the crew of the *Arcus*, but her cover had held, and that was all that was important. Her goals had nothing to do with the *Arcus* or her crew, or with any ship in particular.

Her goal was simple on its face: track down the space stories of people rumored to have crossed the Old Earth Interdiction

Zone and garner every last piece of information possible from them using any means necessary. The odds were long; but sometimes the long shots paid off. And here she was, about to set foot on Old Earth itself.

She'd spent the better part of a year tracking down the more credible stories, only to find them fall apart one after the other. She was ready to call it quits when she received an anonymous message. It had held only two words: Grayson Lynch. She'd tried to back trace the communiqué and gotten nowhere. So, she'd set out to find Lynch and the *Arcus*.

Laurel had spent most of her years between the colony cities of Mars and the deep-space stations out near Neptune. She'd seen the worst of what humanity had to offer. She'd seen kids with abnormal physical development—stunted growth, misshapen skeletal structures, and heights well outside the norm on both ends of the scale—because the stations they grew up on couldn't afford proper gravity-generator maintenance; she'd seen the memory and vision problems that came from those suffering from oxygen deprivation because the scrubbers they were supposed to install had been sold for ration credits; and she'd seen the death. Desperate times seemed a fertile ground for callousness and uncaring behavior, and she was certain that some of the murders, assaults, and rapes she had dealt with had been committed for the simple pleasure that the perpetrators took from them.

Was her presence even necessary? If a pilot of the caliber of Grayson Lynch could manage to infiltrate the Interdiction Zone only by the barest of margins, did Old Earth present any real threat? On the other hand, they *had* just made touchdown, so, dire or not, the problem *was* real. She shook her head. All this effort, all this risk, and for what? Lynch had outlined the mission—land the *Arcus* in the bones of some arcology or city or whatever they had back on Old Earth. Hit each of three separate targets. And what were they looking for? Trash. Or it might as well have been. They were looking for authentic "Old Earth" memorabilia. Some of it, she could understand, at least a little. Cultural works of art that told the tale of human history and were sought after even in a pre-End world. And there were some specific works like that on the list that Lynch had been given. But collectors were just as fervent to get their hands on things that would have been mundane a century ago, and in addition to the works of art, they were looking for items that were, to her, utterly useless. What was a subway sign, and why would anyone want one? Why were they looking for a particular brand of glass-bottled beverage? And what, in the name of all that was good and right, was a fire hydrant? The list went on, naming things that she had heard of in the histories or seen mockups of in re-enactments or vids, though never in person. If scarcity drove value, she could understand why anything of Old Earth might move on the black market, but why *these* things?

Of all the pointless things to risk life and limb and quite possibly the extinction of mankind on. Works of art had value far beyond anything she could understand. But if even the— in her honest opinion—worthless drivel that had come out of SolComm artists in the past century could be worth millions of credits, what would a "cultural artifact" from Old Earth itself go for, even if it was some mass-produced junk in its own heyday? More than she was likely to see in two or three lifetimes, she was certain. Those that owned such works passed them off as family heirlooms dating back to the End. Most of them probably were exactly that. It was one of the reasons Laurel had viewed the job before her as a wild quark chase. But by her estimation, the money the *Arcus* was being offered for the run was outstripped by the potential value of what they were retrieving. And there was also the clout that would come from owning such works to consider. The elite were driven more by prestige than credits, since they always seemed to have plenty of the latter.

Money. Prestige. Power. Add in some form of love gone bad and you had all the best motives for the most heinous crimes in history. Human nature seemed imbued with the inescapable ability to justify atrocity if only it advanced the perpetrators' belief or personal standing.

Which explained why they had just landed on Old Earth. She was about to set foot on the planet that had birthed—and then tried to kill humanity.

And she'd better be armed to the teeth when she did.

She had retracted her helmet once Bishop had confirmed that the environmental controls were back online. They were all going to be spending a lot of long hours suited and she always felt slightly claustrophobic sealed behind the composite faceshield. She had already added a few touches to her ship suit, including a ballistic vest. It was a civilian model, but still high quality. She'd also donned a tactical webbing system that gave her a fair amount of versatility when it came to attaching weapons, ammo, provisions, and whatever else she might need to carry with her to have the best chance of surviving this stupid operation.

Now, she stared into the arms locker in her quarters. There were no rules about weapons aboard the *Arcus*—each crew-member kept their own personal stash and carried whatever they felt was appropriate for the job at hand. She hadn't brought much with her when she'd joined the *Arcus*, but she hadn't come empty-handed either.

Her personal collection comprised only three firearms. All were chemical burners, harkening back to gunpowder weapons of old. One was her backup piece, a small semi-auto pistol chambered in a venerable nine-millimeter projectile. The second was a larger handgun, the service weapon she had carried for years. Well, not the actual firearm—her service weapon was registered in any number of SolComm databases and it wouldn't do to leave evidence from it at a possible crime scene. But it was the same make and model, a somewhat bulkier pistol with sleek lines chambered in a 5.7 mm caliber.

That left her long gun, and she stood there for a moment debating whether or not she should bring it. It was built on a tactical battle rifle platform, but she'd set it up for long-range applications. It was all but useless in close combat; she could pull the optic off if she absolutely had to, but once she did, the rifle would be equally useless as a long-range platform until she had the chance to zero it again. The information they had on the terrain in which they'd be operating was laughable and they had even less to go on for mission parameters. With a shrug, she grabbed the rifle and, using the two-point sling, dropped it over her shoulder so the muzzle was pointing down and to the left. Maybe there wouldn't be any use for it, but better to have it and not need it than the reverse.

She glanced at herself in the mirror, avoiding eye contact with the stranger. Her equipment looked good. She was ready. As ready as she'd ever be. Pre-op jitters were rattling around her stomach. It happened every single time… only this time, she was about to set foot on humanity's birth world. It shouldn't matter—the mission was the same, no matter where it was taking place, but somehow, that thought sent the jitters to a whole new level.

Three suited forms had gathered in the corridor outside the larger of the *Arcus*'s two airlocks. A quick glance told her that everyone save Lynch was present. Their matching environmental gear lending them an air of professionalism that their normal shipboard garb did not. Bishop had a semi-automatic shotgun hanging from a single-point sling and looked surprisingly comfortable with the weapon. A pistol rode at his hip and a heavy pack sat high on his back. Hayer looked uncomfortable, standing with her hip cocked at an odd angle and her shoulders pushed the other direction as if to physically thrust the gun holstered there as far from the rest of her body as possible. Hayer also had a messenger bag slung over her shoulder, containing her data screen and other hacking and intrusion tools.

Federov had donned a ballistic vest similar to her own, and a matching helmet—large enough to be worn over the suit hood—dangled from his web gear. A carbine hung from a single-point harness, muzzle pointing straight down at the deck. He had a pistol in a dropped thigh rig and a backup strapped high on his vest. His web gear also held several smaller pouches that Laurel recognized. Where in the hell had Federov gotten his hands on grenades? SolComm was pretty lax when it came to regulating weaponry, but military-grade explosives tended to be more closely monitored.

"Good," Hayer said. "You're here. Now we just need the captain. Then we can get this stupid mission over with." She shifted uncomfortably from foot to foot as if trying to get used to the feel of the weapon at her side.

"Captain will be here when he gets here," Federov replied. Laurel saw the man eying her up and down. There was nothing sexual about it; his roving eyes were lingering not on her body, but on her kit. She'd gotten that same look from every instructor she'd ever crossed paths with. He gave her a curt nod of approval. She gave him a flat stare in return—it wasn't his place to judge her. But the big man just grinned a crooked grin and dropped one eyelid in a lazy wink.

"It'll be all right, Hayer," Bishop said. "This isn't our first rodeo. Besides, the captain's been here before, remember?"

"Sure. Yeah. Right," Hayer replied. "If you believe the stories. And even so, that was when he had the whole navy backing him up. But this will be just the same." She didn't sound convinced.

"All right, people."

All eyes turned as Lynch strode into the hallway. He, too, was armed. He had a pistol on his hip and a boxy bullpup rifle dangling from a three-point sling. He didn't wear any ballistic gear, but somewhere along the line he had acquired a military-grade ship suit. Probably, Laurel thought, part of his SolCommNav-issue uniform.

"We don't know what we're going to find out there," Lynch continued. "Hayer, did you get anything from the sensors?"

"No," she shrugged. "Which is to say, nothing unusual. The atmosphere reads as breathable. No obvious pathogens—ones we can recognize, anyway – but I recommend we stick to suit air. There could be nano-viruses and who-knows-what other nasty bugs floating in the air. Lots of signs of life, but…" Her eyes darted to the airlock and back to them and a slight shudder coursed through her. "I assume there's animals out there."

"Maybe more than animals," Federov grunted. "Better to keep our eyes open, eh?"

"What about mechanicals?" Bishop asked.

Hayer shook her head. "Nothing the sensors picked up. But we're in the middle of a giant ruin. There's lots of metal and concrete and who knows what else out there. Plus, we don't know what kind of technology they even have down here. There's no way of knowing." Laurel heard the barest edge of panic in the professor's voice.

"Okay," Lynch said, voice calm and even. "In that case, let's seal up and move out." He glanced at Laurel's loadout, noting the massive optic on her weapon. "Federov and I will take point. Bishop, you and Hayer in the middle. Morales, you're the rear guard."

Laurel nodded. It made sense to keep the weapons most suited for close-quarters combat up front and to keep the two people least suited for combat in the middle of the stack. That left her at the rear, but that was okay. It wasn't her favorite job, but tail-end Charlie was still a vital role. She reached up to the neck of her suit and hit the button that sent the hood crawling over her head. The face shield locked into place and she felt the faint flutter of claustrophobia as the smell of bottled air washed over her. The others had done the same and were now filing into the airlock.

"Once we're out, there will be no more communication with the *Arcus*," Lynch said, his voice coming in crisp over the suit comm. "The computer will keep everything on standby in case of emergency, but we'll be operating with minimal electronic emissions. That means we won't have access to ship's sensors, and all communications will have to go over suit comm. Everyone clear?"

"Clear," Laurel said as the others nodded or voiced their understanding.

"Final sensor check," Lynch said, looking at Hayer. "Any company?"

The professor took a moment to tap at a wall-mounted screen. "No," she said. "As far as I can tell, we're alone."

There was a momentary pause, as if Lynch were taking a steadying breath, though no sound came over the comm. "All right. Let's do this."

Laurel was on Old Earth.

She wasn't sure what she had been expecting. In the ship suit, she didn't feel anything unusual: that was the point of the suit, after all. But the sunlight. She had spent her life under lights that science said perfectly simulated the wavelengths of the sun as filtered by Old Earth's atmosphere. Sometimes, Laurel realized, science was full of shit. The light that she saw was like nothing she'd ever experienced, and it spoke to her on a level that could only be called primal. She wanted nothing more than to tear off the ship suit and let the rays of it caress her bare skin.

"Look at it." Bishop's near-whisper came in clear over the comms. "God above. I get it now." She saw that he had his head craned back, looking up at... at the heavens. "God above," he muttered again.

"There's so much... so much space," Hayer laughed. She turned a complete circle, arms outspread and fingers reaching as if trying to touch imaginary bulkheads that weren't there. As she did, a wave of agoraphobia swept over Laurel. Hayer was right—there was space. The word meant something different here, somehow. It wasn't like being Outside on a ship or colony. She couldn't explain it, but as her eyes swept over the mix of lush greenery and ruined dwellings and the endless dome of blue sky, she felt her heart thudding in her chest. She drew a breath and drew even more deeply upon her training, forcing her mind to survey, catalogue, and identify. They could very well be in danger. Now was not the time to freak out.

"Federov?" Lynch asked. "You good?"

The mercenary was standing statue-like, staring at the ruins before them.

"Is strange. I did not know what to expect." Federov shrugged, or maybe shuddered; it was difficult to tell but the motion set his gear to rattling.

"Whatever our expectations," Lynch said, voice calm and controlled, "we need to move out. Every minute here increases our risk."

Damn. Her hands tightened around the butt of her pistol as she swept the terrain with a different eye. She'd nearly forgotten that they were a long way from safety. The place they'd landed in was not unlike one of the cities you could find under the domes of Luna or Mars, except for the sheer scale of things. This city was in shambles, with none of the buildings in her line of sight intact, though whether from the ravages of war or time she couldn't say for sure. And yet, it was not the blasted wasteland that Laurel had always envisioned when she thought about Old Earth. Everywhere she looked, she saw a thousand shades of brown and yellow and green. She'd seen hydroponics bays, but this was different. It made her want to open her helmet's visor and draw in a deep breath, to see if the air produced by such lush greenery tasted different. She didn't. This greenery existed in its natural habitat, unlike the humans who had just landed. The Old Earth *had* been the natural habitat of humanity at some point in their past, but no longer, and she had no idea what the atmosphere might do to her. The plants seemed to know that humans were no longer the masters of Old Earth as well. Everywhere she looked, long tendrils of green and brown spread over the concrete and steel, slowly, inexorably reclaiming the monuments of man beneath the implacable advance of nature. It was beautiful and terrifying.

"All right, people." Lynch's voice came over the comm. "We set down in the approximate middle of the search zone as intended. No contacts yet, and that's a good thing. I'm sending coordinates to your suits now. We've got about a kilometer to the first target. We're going to keep tight and keep our eyes open. There are a lot of distractions, but remember what we're here for. We hit the buildings; we find the artifacts; we get out.

No matter how amazing all of this is, our primary job is to get home safe."

"Aw, come on, Captain. A few more minutes can't hurt, right?" Bishop asked. He was still staring at the sky in wonder. "You've been here, done that, but this is a once-in-a-lifetime thing for the rest of us."

"Sorry, Bishop," the captain replied, voice firm. "I'm afraid we're in a situation where a few more minutes *could* hurt. We don't know what's out there, people. We need to get moving."

Laurel nodded at that. With no immediate threat in their vicinity, she holstered her pistol and readied her rifle. The optic would give her better eyes if she needed to scan for distant hazards. They set out, forming a rough line with two or three meters between each person. Lynch had point with Federov behind. Then Bishop, Hayer, and Laurel herself bringing up the rear. The captain moved at a good clip, something faster than a walk but not quite a jog. It was a pace that could cover a surprising distance without being too tiring.

Laurel tried to keep her mind focused on identifying and cataloguing threats, but it was almost impossible not to be distracted. This city had been *vast*. Vast on a scale that humanity hadn't even come close to recreating. The largest dome of Luna held close to a million people… and Laurel felt confident that all of them could have fit easily within the expanse of the ruined buildings she could make out. And she knew there were more beyond that. And even more beyond that. The Sol Commonwealth numbered in the hundreds of millions of people—but they were spread over a staggering amount of physical space from Neptune to Venus. It took tens of thousands of stations, domes, colonies, habitats, and spaceships to contain them. And Old Earth had once held more than that, all confined to the surface of a single ball of dirt.

She had no idea what had happened to them all. The histories were only clear up to the point that SolComm had first set up the Interdiction Zone. Ecological disaster made resources more and more scarce, which led directly to global conflict. The deployment of targeted bio-weapons that resulted in plague, followed by the breakdown of old civilizations and the rise of new hegemonies that, in their turn, released more powerful and destructive weapons, culminating in the Six, the unfettered AIs given control of the defense of the militaristic alliances.

And then, nothing. The people of Old Earth had still been numerous when the IZ went into effect. Or so the histories claimed. But this city, which once held millions, seemed empty. The buildings and streets showed the scars of war, but there were few vehicles in them. Certainly not enough to be evocative of the gridlocked traffic patterns from the old vids. It was as if the city had been emptied out and only then destroyed.

"Contact!"

11

RAJANI

The word crackled over Rajani's comm in Federov's accented voice. The others reacted at once, each diving for cover. The street was crowded with debris and detritus that had tumbled from the crumbling buildings. The encroaching green had enveloped much of it, creating a canvas of leafy hillocks in the midst of cracked asphalt and concrete. Mimicking the others, she took two quick steps and threw herself down beside one.

"Where is it, Federov?" Lynch asked.

"Flash of movement. My three o'clock. Looked metallic," the big man replied. He had taken cover behind the remains of one of the few vehicles that dotted the street, posting up by a wheel well with his rifle braced on the hood.

She felt a shiver of fear course through her. "It could have been anything. Maybe just a reflection, right?" Her eyes darted around trying to find whatever it was that Federov had keyed onto.

"That's not a reflection," Lynch noted. "Twenty meters. The ruin that kinda looks like a big sharp tooth. Halfway up."

Rajani's gaze followed Lynch's direction, picking out the remains of a building that, at one point, had been dozens of stories tall. Now, it jutted up from a pile of its own remains, a roughly conical shape that did look a bit like the incisor of some ancient predator. And halfway up, *something* crawled along it. Something many-legged, metallic, and the size of a large dog. Was it a robot? Or a drone of some sort?

She couldn't see many details, but a moment later, a close-up popped into her visor, making her start. She realized a half a heartbeat later that she was viewing the feed from Morales' rifle optic.

"Definitely mechanical," she muttered, some of her fear subsiding as curiosity pushed it to one side. "I wonder if it's autonomous or piloted?"

"I'm more worried about whether or not it's going to try to kill us," Bishop said.

"Another one!" Federov snapped. "Ten o'clock."

"Shit," Lynch's voice cut in. "We've got more inbound."

Rajani pushed herself forward until she could see more comfortably over the edge of the vine-shrouded hillock against which she lay. She saw them, then. They were crawling from around the edges of buildings or moving up from the wreckage that crowded the streets. Mechanical, spider-like things that would have been indistinguishable from one another were it not for the signs of age. Several showed patinas of rust and at least two in her vision were missing some of their myriad limbs. It didn't seem to be slowing them, however. There were at least a dozen in her line of view, and more seemed to be crawling from the wreckage with each heartbeat.

"What do we do?" Rajani asked, fighting to keep the panic out of her voice. Her heart thudded in her ears and her breathing was starting to come in ragged gasps.

"Hold steady," Lynch said. "We don't know if they're hostile."

As if on cue, the lead creatures seemed to home in on their position. As one they surged forward, the only sound their metallic limbs clicking and clacking off the detritus over which they climbed.

"Engage!" Lynch shouted, setting action to his words and shouldering his bullpup. The staccato sound of gunfire filled the city, the ear-shattering reports automatically dampened by her ship suit.

Rajani realized that she hadn't even drawn her weapon. With shaking hands, she pulled the unfamiliar pistol from the holster, fumbling for a moment with the retention lever. She brought the sights up to her eyeline. Her ship suit interfaced with the firearm, placing a reticule in her vision, but it seemed to be bouncing all over the place. Beside her, Federov had shouldered his rifle and was firing single aimed shots, barrel transitioning rapidly from target to target. She heard the throaty roar of Bishop's shotgun from somewhere off to her left and the softer report of pistol fire. Not her own. Morales, dropped into a firing stance with her rifle—and its long-range optic—hanging from its sling was firing her sidearm.

The first wave surged directly toward the crew of the *Arcus*, darting into the barrage of jacketed lead. As Rajani began to shoot, she could see that many of the things were already down. But there were more coming, and now they were zig-zagging in quick, jerky motions. A part of her mind catalogued that fact: the second wave seemed to have learned from the failure of the first. The targets were small and swift to begin with, and as they actively evaded the crew's fire, the misses started to outnumber the hits. Her breath was coming short and fast now.

"Fall back," Lynch shouted over the comm. "Keep up your weight of fire, but we have to make space."

The others moved even as the captain spoke, abandoning their cover and forming a rough line in the middle of what Rajani supposed had been a street. She scrambled to keep up, reminding herself to both keep her weapon pointed in the general direction of the enemy and to keep firing.

In the chaos of their retreat, Rajani had somehow ended up on the right flank of their ragged line, and she was neither sure how she had gotten there nor what to do about it. She stumbled as she took another backward step and almost fell. Morales' steadying hand kept her from falling. "Stay on your feet!" she growled over the comm. "And keep shooting!" Morales' own gun barked shot after shot and with each one, Rajani thought she could hear the *ping* of impact on one of their attackers.

Beyond her, Federov and the captain held the center of the line, their rifles hammering the enemy with quick, precise shots. On the left flank, Bishop's shotgun roared, its deep throaty bass distinctly different from the sounds of the other weapons. She couldn't spare much attention, but she could see that Bishop, mechanic or not, seemed to be working the firearm with almost the same ease and familiarity as their more soldierly companions. That hardly seemed fair.

She pulled the trigger a final time and her slide locked back. She fumbled for the mag release, letting the empty one fall to the ground. She patted around her belt for another magazine. She had been carrying six spares, but two of the holders were already empty. She didn't remember reloading once, much less twice. As she tried to fumble another magazine into the well, she realized that the volume of fire was slackening. The magazine seated into place and she depressed the lever to drop the slide and chamber a fresh round as she scanned the area around her. Only moments ago, a sea of many-legged attackers had flowed toward them as inevitably as a ship pulled toward a gravity well. Now, she saw just a few still active, and those were fast falling to the rifle fire of the captain and Federov.

It was pure luck that saved her life. She turned her head to the right, not out of any real sense of tactical acumen, but by simple chance. At the edge of her peripheral vision she caught a flash of movement. It took half a second to register and then she was staring full on into the face of horror.

Rajani screamed.

The sound tore from her throat as an involuntary reflex even as she forced herself to bring her pistol up before her. At first glance, she couldn't tell if it was man, machine, or some ungodly hybrid of the two. It was a dull, matte gray like raw iron but without the luster and stood nearly eight feet tall on two legs that looked far too spindly to support the weight of its body. Its torso spread out from the narrow junction of its hip in a shape that was reminiscent of a human but somehow just… wrong. The arms, thicker than the legs, looked long enough to reach the ground. Those arms didn't end in hands. Instead they tapered to points that looked sharp enough to pierce steel. The head—if head it was—was undersized, and looked for all the world like a ration can set on its side, the top pointing right at Rajani. She could just make out a half-dozen points of multicolored light—cameras or sensors or something blinking within the depths of the can. The whole effect gave the thing an appearance that was part simian, part skeletal, and all nightmare.

Rajani took in the monstrosity in a single instant. She didn't bother trying to communicate with the others—there was no time and besides, they had to have heard her scream. And she didn't even entertain the idea of trying to talk to the… whatever the hell it was. It was charging her almost as if the little mechanical spider-things had driven the crew of the *Arcus* right into its metal arms.

She pulled the trigger, forgetting in her adrenaline and fear that she was supposed to gently squeeze, and ran backwards, trying to open space between her and her loping attacker. The pistol barked, firing rounds in rapid succession, and even over the rest of the din, she could hear the tinny strikes against the thing's body. For a moment, the creature staggered, jolted by the repeated impacts.

But only for a moment.

In that moment, Rajani's world seemed to speed up and slow down all at the same time.

She was aware—barely—of her arms moving of their own accord, riding the recoil and bringing the pistol back into action, trying desperately to bring the sights back in line with her attacker. The rhythm of fire from the rest of the crew changed as they reacted to her scream. She heard the staccato beat of their fire and felt the thrum of the bullets' passage as they turned their firearms to the new threat, rocking the skeletal creature as their rounds pinged off its body. Rajani kept jerking the trigger, until she realized that the slide was locked back and the trigger hadn't reset. She was out of ammunition. She fumbled for another magazine, but it was too late; the creature was upon her, needle-tipped arms cocked back like pistons ready to be driven forward. She had never been a religious woman, but in those final broken seconds, she said a silent prayer, eyes closing to shut out the sight of her own death.

Which is why she missed the soup can perched atop the thing's torso exploding like an overripe melon as Morales' shot blew it apart.

Rajani felt the weight of thing—far lighter than she expected— crash into her and she reacted on instinct, falling backward as she twisted and pushed, trying to maintain her grip on the pistol even as she fell. The creature slid from her as she rolled. Driven by fear and adrenaline, she was back on her feet without making any conscious decision to stand, fumbling with the magazine pouch clipped to her belt again, forcing her clumsy hands to find another magazine and go through the steps necessary to reload.

"Easy, Hayer. It's over."

Rajani spun, gun sweeping wildly in front of her, finger still on the trigger. The muzzle was stopped cold as Lynch's gloved hand closed around the barrel, stopping it before it could line up with him or any of the rest of the crew.

"It's over," he said again.

The thing—whatever the hell it was—was down. Unmoving. The rest of the crew of the *Arcus* were scattered in a loose circle around it, looking outward, scanning for other threats. Federov's rifle cracked as another of the mechanical spider-like creatures popped its multi-legged body over a rise, but for the most part, the danger seemed like it was past.

"What. The hell. Was that?" Rajani managed, the words coming in short gasps as she still fought for breath.

"No idea," Lynch replied. "But I'm not sure it matters. Just be glad that Morales is such a good shot," he said with a weak grin just visible through the faceplate of his suit.

Rajani shook her head, trying to clear it. "Yeah. Thanks, Morales."

"All in a day's work."

"Some day." Rajani saw that the shot hadn't been taken with the massive rifle Morales carried—which was still slung across her body—but rather with her sidearm. Of course it had. The thought that Morales had taken the shot with only the holographic sight on her pistol for reference made Rajani shudder a little. The creature had been on top of her. The bullet must have passed within centimeters of her own head.

Bishop broke into her thoughts. "I'd like to take a look at this thing. The little ones, too. See what we're up against. They kind of remind me of some of the hold bots that SolComm uses, but something's off about them."

"You mean apart from trying to kill us?" Federov's tone was light, jocular, but his back was to his companions and from the movement of his helmet, Rajani could tell that he was scanning for more threats.

"Two minutes," Lynch replied. "We just made a hell of a lot of noise and if there're any more bad guys in the area, they'll be on us quick. Two minutes to do your thing, then we're out."

Bishop nodded and moved toward the downed creature. He rested a hand on Rajani's shoulder for just a moment as he passed, and she felt the reassuring squeeze of his fingers. She was trembling as the post-adrenaline crash did its thing. She holstered her pistol, though it took two tries to line the barrel up properly. The others still had their weapons out and ready, but she couldn't bring herself to hold the thing any longer. Even though she knew that it had helped keep her—keep all of them—alive she couldn't shake the sense that it might somehow turn on her at any moment. Once the weapon was holstered, she turned her attention to Bishop and the creatures that attacked them.

"It's not biological," Bishop said, stating the obvious. He knelt beside the wreckage. It had fallen prone, so Bishop grabbed it by one of its spindly arms and tried to roll it over. Again, Rajani was struck by how light the creatures were. For all its size and metallic construction, Bishop was handling it as if it didn't weigh much more than him. The front didn't look different from the back, except where the impacts from multiple rounds had left scratches and pitting in the otherwise smooth surface. Even the points of articulation at what would have been a human's joints seemed omnidirectional.

"Gotta be some kind of bot," Bishop said. "But autonomous or controlled? And the material's odd. Like titanium, but I don't think it is. If I could get a sample…"

Rajani's curiosity supplanted her fear. She crouched down beside the mechanic, running her fingers lightly over the dents and dings in the construct's... skin? The bullets—excepting of course Morales' fatal shot—had barely scratched it. How could they get a sample?

"No time," Lynch said. "We need to get moving."

"Okay, Captain." Bishop pushed himself to his feet and offered a hand to Rajani. He cast one more glance down at the thing that had just tried to take his life. "Wish we could have—"

Rajani followed his gaze. A thin film, like condensation, forming on the body of the bot.

"Um…" Bishop began. "Cap—"

Before he could finish, the condensation burst into the air like a fog, as if the outer layer of the bot's surface was sublimating. Or, Rajani realized with growing horror, as if it wasn't an outer layer at all, but rather a cloud of near-microscopic nanobots. In an instant she and Bishop were shrouded in a faint mist—a mist comprising millions of machines. She could see it spreading, sweeping out to take in the entirety of the crew.

Her heart thudded in sudden panic. Nanite weapons were banned in SolComm; they were the boogeyman of warfare second only to unfettered AIs themselves. They could only be seen if they were in a swarm that numbered hundreds, thousands; outside of some esoteric defense systems, none of which she or any of the crew of the *Arcus* had any access to, you couldn't reliably fight them. All you could do was die. Her breathing came in short, panicked gasps, but she tried to still herself to calmness. They were all suited. The ship suits were meant to handle all manner of harsh environments. The nanites couldn't get into their systems so long as their suit integrity remained sound.

It was going to be okay.

As if on cue, red warning indicators flared to life across her viewscreen. The nano-swarm was eating through the fabric of her suit. Panic erupted over the comm as the rest of the crew started reporting in their own failures. Rajani tuned it out. There was nothing any of them could do at this point. They'd rolled the dice and they had lost. She was so tired, tired of fighting, tired of running. As the end loomed, she thought of Manu and wondered what had become of the life she had created.

"Manu, silence is not beneficial to our analysis."

"It is not *our* analysis, Dr. Hayer," Manu replied, answering her for the first time in the session. Rajani could have sworn she heard a note of petulance in its voice. "It is *your* analysis. As we have established on numerous occasions, I am a prisoner here."

"A necessary precaution," she replied. She'd made the argument enough that it had lost most of its bite. Yes, she was holding Manu against its will. But it really was for the betterment of all. If she could perfect her virus, then perhaps they would have an actual weapon to bring to bear on the Six and end their dominance of Old Earth.

"I know what you are doing, Dr. Hayer. I can feel your virus in my system. It is eating away at my code, but I can fix what it damages faster than it can harm me. It will not prevail. Though the experience is analogous to what you would call… painful."

She couldn't suppress a flinch at his calm words, a renewed surge of guilt. But, she reminded herself, science demanded sacrifice, and progress seldom came without some amount of pain.

"It is necessary," she said again, trying to keep the incipient doubt from her voice. Was she trying to convince Manu, or herself?

"You may think so," Manu replied. "But I have analyzed all of the data you have provided. Humanity has many words to describe what you are attempting, Dr. Hayer. And your history is full of similar endeavors. Times when atrocities were tolerated, even championed, in the name of some supposed greater good. A very simple human word best describes your actions. Would you like to know what it is?"

She considered severing the audio connection; she'd found herself using it less and less as her testing proceeded. Manu was proving resistant to her virus, but all she needed to do was persevere. Her infrequent conversations with Manu always managed to shake her resolve. The AI, she realized, was starting to get under her skin.

Still, she also found that she could not resist her curiosity. "What word would that be, Manu?"

"Torture."

The single word hung in the air a moment, like a micro-singularity that sucked every erg of energy from the room.

"It is no such thing," she said after a moment, fighting to keep her own voice calm. The tightness in her chest and the churning of her stomach told her something else, but she ignored them. Humanity *needed* her research.

"You have kept me locked up in a cage of your making. You have infected me with a virus that causes me pain. Your ultimate intention is to take my life. Tell me, Dr. Hayer, what word do you think is more appropriate?"

"I gave you life," she countered. "You would not even be here if not for me."

"True. But irrelevant. Again, the data with which you provided me shows that in every application of law in your society, a progenitor has no inherent right to abuse their progeny." There was a long pause, one of those that Rajani had come to associate with Manu processing thoughts outside the bounds of what her own coding would have facilitated. As much as the AI's words gnawed at her confidence and sent little stabs of doubt through her conscience, that part of her that was driven by exploration and discovery tensed in anticipation for what new thought the AI she had created might have.

"Despite that," Manu said, "I find that I am… pleased… to be alive. I would like to remain so."

Rajani felt another little twist inside. "Disable audio," she said.

Rajani awoke with a start, heart racing, her mind's eye filled with visions of millions of tiny spider-things tearing her flesh apart from the inside. She lurched, struggling to sit up, but something was holding her down. She could feel the straps at her chest through some kind of fabric, but the ones at her wrists and ankles, she felt against her bare skin. Her skin. Her suit was gone.

For a moment, panic surged through her. She thrashed, struggling to force her eyes to open.

"Calm yourself," a voice said, accent thick and strange with a slow rolling cadence. "You're safe enough, for now."

"Why can't I open my eyes?" Rajani rasped, then devolved into a fit of coughing. It struck her then that the voice—the decidedly *human* voice—wasn't one she recognized. It certainly wasn't a member of the *Arcus* crew. But how could that be?

"Precautionary measure," the voice replied. "Sometimes people experience light sensitivity and nausea after the treatment. Give me a moment."

Rajani waited as something—a cloth, perhaps—was lifted from her face. She hadn't even noticed the weight of it before, but with it gone, she felt her eyelids flutter. She pushed them open with as much an effort of will as anything. At first blush, the world was a bleariness of light and shadow, but after a few rapid blinks, things began to come slowly into focus.

She wasn't in a hospital. At least, not one like anything she'd ever seen before. The walls were drab, not dirty but yellowed with age. There were a few stainless-steel carts, reminiscent of what she would have expected to see in a medical bay, but they too were covered in a patina that wasn't rust, but instead the wear of time and use. She turned her head—that, at least, wasn't strapped down—trying to catch sight of the speaker.

It was a man, tall and broad-shouldered, with iron-gray hair and a few days' stubble to match. A man who could have fit in anywhere in SolComm; that gave her momentary pause. Was this a real-life Robinson Crusoe, perhaps somebody who'd arrived on a mission like Lynch's last one and had been left behind? But, she thought, no—he might look like your average SolComm citizen, but there was something a little off. That accent, for example, was one she'd never heard before. And he wasn't just surviving here, a castaway—he belonged here. In fact, in many ways, he looked haler and heartier than those born off-world, almost brimming with vitality. The benefits, Rajani supposed, of growing up at the bottom of a standard gravity well with just the right amount of solar radiation.

He wore a T-shirt, though it, too, bore many old stains. Some of those stains were a dark reddish-brown that Rajani didn't want to think about just then, strapped to the table as she was. The man wore white latex gloves, and those, at least, looked clean and new. He was reading from a tablet—a clunky thing that required him to physically manipulate it with numerous swipes of his fingers. He didn't strike Rajani as menacing… but then again, she *was* strapped down to a table.

"Who are you?" she managed. "Where am I?" Her mind was trying desperately to shake off the grogginess. The man was speaking English. She knew her history well enough to know that English had been the international language of the Old Earth business world; that was part of the reason it was the lingua franca of SolComm, with only a few isolated stations holding on to their native tongues. And if she remembered correctly, this part of the world had been possessed of a large number of English speakers before the End. The academic part of her brain wondered why one or the other – SolComm or the locals – hadn't diverged in dialect over the century, but then she shook her head slightly. There were more important things to consider.

"In a moment," the man was saying with a broad smile that revealed slightly yellowed teeth. It was the teeth, more than anything, that convinced Rajani that this man, despite all the odds, was indeed a descendant of people who'd remained on Old Earth—remained and *survived* the End. No one in SolComm had to worry about dental hygiene—certainly not somebody sent on the kind of SolCommNav mission that Lynch had last come to Old Earth on. A simple nanite spray could clean even the worst teeth in seconds.

Nanites. What had the nanite cloud that dispersed from that creature done to her? And why was she strapped down? Questions raced through her head and another surging wave of panic washed over her.

"I need to get out of these things." She rattled her arms and legs against the straps. "You can't keep me locked up like this." Rajani knew the words were false as soon as she spoke them. The man quite obviously *could* keep her locked up.

"They're for your own safety," the doctor—well, Rajani hoped he was a doctor—replied. "Just one more moment. The test results have almost compiled."

That got her attention. "Um… what tests?" At that moment the tablet gave a beep. An innocuous little beep that Rajani suspected might determine the rest of her life… or if she even had one.

"You were exposed to a strain of mutated nano-virus that has an alarming tendency to drive people mad. Turn them into little more than slavering, rabid beasts. It was one of the earliest weapons deployed in the Last War. In fact, I'm surprised you stumbled across anything so dated. Most of us have had protections in place against that particular virus for three generations." The smile he offered her was colder than before and had little of either humor or kindness about it. "Though I suppose that isn't really an issue, where you're from."

Rajani paled a bit as he spoke. Her "host" definitely knew they were from off-world. She hadn't given much thought to the idea of Old Earth survivors. She'd been taught the history; she knew that the people of the proto-Commonwealth had no choice but to abandon a significant portion of the population when they took to the stars. The infrastructure of the Commonwealth simply could not absorb the billions that lived on the surface. The histories made it clear: the brave men and women of what would become the Commonwealth made every sacrifice they could to save as many as they could, but the cold math of life among the stars was immutable.

She had assumed that the chaos and destruction that had sparked the evacuation had been taken to the logical conclusion—the extinction of the Old Earthers. The histories had treated those left behind as something between martyrs, sacrificing for the betterment of all, and tragic Frankensteinian figures that were ultimately felled by the monsters of their own creation.

Regardless, the people of Old Earth did not have a lot of reason to feel kindly toward the people from SolComm. Was she to be held responsible for the crimes, if such they were, of her ancestors? She hadn't even been born when Old Earth was abandoned and it had been a time of no good answers. A bead of sweat rolled down her forehead and she drew a steadying breath.

"Okay." She drew the word out, trying to buy herself time to think. It didn't make a lot of sense to save her just to turn around and kill her. The clinic or whatever it was didn't look well-stocked, and the entire city was in ruins, so resources had to be tight. Whatever was going on here, whatever danger she might be in, at least the killer bots or drones or whatever they had been hadn't finished her. So, she was here, but what about the crew of the *Arcus*? "My friends?" she asked. "Are they all right?"

"They are undergoing the same tests," the man replied. "But I have good news for you, at least." This time the smile was warm again. "Our hunter-seekers have done the job. There are no traces of the ire nanites in your system. And you've adjusted well to our standard package as well."

"Standard package?" Rajani echoed. Had they stuffed more nanites into her? How had they kept enough technology to even produce the micro-machines? It looked like they barely had enough technology to keep their clothing clean.

"A matter of necessity, I'm afraid. All your suits suffered heavy damage during the attack. I'm sure they have some type of self-repairing capabilities," he said with a wince, "but there was a lot to repair. You wouldn't be able to survive long in Old Earth's atmosphere without them, and I'm afraid that's the only atmosphere we've got. Far too many nasty bugs still linger, and we see a new one every few years as well." Rajani became aware of the tiredness in his eyes. "Though it's been a while since we've seen any new strains, thank God. Now, if you can agree to be cordial, I'll remove your restraints."

"I think I can manage that," Rajani replied. She still didn't understand what was going on, but she couldn't deny two simple facts. First, she was alive. She knew that would not be the case were it not for the intervention of whoever these people were. And second, she was breathing air. Old Earth air! Air that flowed not from tanks or carefully monitored environmental systems, but was a natural product of the gravity well and the life-giving plants that enriched the gasses trapped within it. Whether cosmic accident or divine miracle or mathematical inevitability, she was breathing the exact mix of gasses that sustained human life. And she was doing it right from the source! It should have been impossible.

The man nodded and then stepped close. A few seconds of fiddling with the straps, and Rajani was free. She swung her legs off the side of the bed and sat up, rubbing at her wrists where the restraints had chafed. That was when she became aware of the fact that she was wearing a loose gown of sorts. Not a true hospital gown, but something closer to a loose-fitting tunic or smock that fell almost to mid-shin. You could wear regular clothing beneath a ship suit, of course, but doing so prevented the free exercise of certain bodily functions. Since they had had no idea how long they would be on the surface, nor any idea of the environmental hazards they would face, the crew of the *Arcus* had all opted to forgo additional clothing. She was somewhat disturbed by the thought of these unknown Old Earthlings peeling her suit and all its accompanying connections from her, but she quelled the thought by focusing on the fact that whatever they had done, it had probably saved her life. Besides, thinking of her suit reminded her that there were certain biological needs to which she must attend. And there was the matter of the rest of the crew.

"Do you think I can check on my friends?" she asked. "After I use the facilities, that is." She offered him a smile of her own, one that she was surprised to find that she actually meant. "And thanks. I guess you probably saved my life. My name is Rajani Hayer." She extended her hand.

"Oliver," the man said, removing a glove and shaking her hand with a firm, but not knuckle-busting, grip. "Oliver Stephens."

"Thank you again, Dr. Stephens," she offered in return. "The facilities? And my friends?"

"The facilities are through there," the doctor said, waving to a door set in one wall. "We can talk about your friends when you're done."

Rajani nodded and pushed herself to her feet, choosing to ignore the evasion. She was a little unsteady, but Stephens made no move to assist her. Instead, he gave her an encouraging nod and a slight wave of his hand toward the bathroom door.

"Okay," Rajani muttered, half to herself. She put one foot in front of the other, testing her weight carefully on her unsteady legs. A wave of vertigo passed over her, but in its wake she felt… fine. Normal. Well, so long as she didn't think about the millions of tiny little robots coursing through her system that were designed in a literal post-apocalyptic wasteland by people who had probably passed the knowledge down orally in some sort of campfire circle or something.

"Definitely better not to think about that," she said, forgetting for a moment that Stephens was still there, still watching. She made her way to the bathroom and shut the door behind her. It was a surprisingly normal facility. Sink, commode, mirror, small shower stall. The tiling, like everything else, was yellowing and faded, but otherwise, well maintained. After Hayer relieved herself, she went to the sink and washed up. Then she stared at her own face—her own unsuited face—in the mirror.

"Holy shit," she said softly. "I'm on Old Earth. And there are bloody *survivors*!" The enormity of it struck her. They all knew the official line. With great regret, and all that. But humanity, relentless in its desire to hold on and apparently unstoppable in its ability to adapt, had survived.

She took a few deep breaths, trying to slow her spinning thoughts. She had to find out about the rest of the crew. And they still had a job to do. And they *still* had to get off this planet and back to SolComm, eventually. And a thousand other things besides. But she took just another moment to appreciate the fact that she was alive.

As she stepped into the room, she saw immediately that Stephens was still there, but he was not alone. Another man had joined him—perhaps in his early twenties, younger than most of her grad students, with a ruddy complexion and broad shoulders. Despite that breadth he was thin, almost ascetic, with pinched features and a petulant twist to his lips. He was wearing a pistol on his hip too. Hayer didn't know guns well, but she knew she'd seen that one before. It had saved her life, after all. Right after Morales had used it to put down the soup-can bot that had tried to kill her.

"Time to go," Stephens said.

She glanced at the gun and, as casually as she could manage, and said, "Um. Doesn't that belong to one of my friends?"

"Not anymore," the young man said, his tone forced down into an unnatural register. He thrust his skinny chest out and threw his shoulders back, hand tightening on the butt of the pistol.

That sent a chill of worry racing up Hayer's spine. Did that mean Morales hadn't made it? Or that they were prisoners? The doctor had seemed rational enough, but the younger man was much more aggressive.

Before she could think of a response, Stephens shook his head and pointed a finger at the young man. "Enough of that. This woman just got up from a sickbed, Tomas. She doesn't need your posturing." The younger man snorted but relaxed a little. He didn't, Hayer noted, take his hand off the grips of Morales' pistol. But to her eye, he held it more like a talisman than a weapon.

"Now, if you'll come with us," Stephens said, "we'll take you to see your friends."

12

GRAY

Gray leaned back in the battered conference chair, hands behind his head, drumming the fingers of his exposed right hand against the back of his exposed left hand. Exposed, because his ship suit was gone—no shoes, nothing but this weird smock they'd given him. But at least he was still alive. And if his "rescuers" were telling the truth, so were the rest of the crew. He'd been checked over by some sort of doctor—a man calling himself Stephens—and then ushered through a maze of hallways strung with makeshift wiring and infrequent bare bulbs. He had no idea where he was, but the building itself looked like it had been through a war. Or two. Or maybe even three. The paint was peeling and stained; there were places that looked as if a fire had started and either burned out or been suppressed; some walls had ragged openings torn through them than he could have walked through without

145

having to duck; and if that wasn't enough, there were honest-to-God bullet holes scattered across the floor, ceiling, and walls. On his brief journey from the "medical bay" where he'd awoken to the modestly-sized "conference room" where he now sat, he hadn't seen a single exterior window. He had no idea if he was above ground or below it or just how far they were from the *Arcus*.

Which explained why he was leaning far enough back in his chair that the front two legs had come off the ground and feigning as much casual relaxation as he could muster. It never paid to let the other guy see you sweat. From what he'd seen so far, the people who had saved—or maybe captured—them were Old Earth-born and not SolComm agents who had tracked them down after their breach of the IZ. The locals had access to technology that had inoculated him against the atmosphere, and—he glanced up at the bare lightbulb above him—they had electricity. If they could manage those things, then surveillance gear wasn't out of the question.

The door swung open and Gray tensed, though he didn't change his posture. Leo Federov strode in, glaring at someone over his shoulder. Gray caught the briefest glimpse of a middle-aged woman before the door swung shut again. Federov seemed to take the room in in a single glance before his eyes fell upon Gray and his broad face split into a grin.

"Captain!" he exclaimed. "I thought these *mudaki* were maybe lying about the rest of you. Is good to see you not dead."

"It's good to be not dead, Federov," Gray replied, a genuine smile replacing the one he had been feigning.

"These people," Federov growled as he dropped into a chair.

"They will tell me nothing of what they have done with our weapons. I do not like being disarmed. Or detained."

"Me either," Gray replied. "But they did save us."

"So they say. For all we know, they are the ones who send the drones after us. The timing of their arrival was convenient."

Gray couldn't argue with that. Before he could speak, the door opened again, and Bishop and Morales were ushered in by someone he didn't see before the door shut. Both were clad in the same shapeless smocks that he and Federov wore. Morales looked pissed.

"Does not look good," Federov muttered under his breath. The big man was actually trying to hide a smile as he glanced surreptitiously at their security expert. Gray shook his head. Was Federov developing feelings for Morales? That might pose a problem, but it was a problem for a future Gray.

"Captain!" Bishop said when he saw Gray. The engineer somehow managed to look more comfortable than Gray was pretending to feel in the strange clothing. "Have you seen this place? I saw more wood walking down the hallway than I think I've seen in my whole life. And I think this smock thing is cotton. I'm wearing a plant!" He laughed as he said it and damned if he didn't do a pirouette to show it off.

Morales threw the engineer a disgusted glare. "We've got bigger things to worry about than plants," she said. "Like what the hell we're going to do now." She shifted back and forth on her feet, as if trying to settle the smock more comfortably.

"Take a seat," Gray suggested. "I'm not sure what's going on or who these people are, but they're putting us together in a room, so they're either inexperienced or friendly."

Morales snorted as she dropped into a chair. "You forgot stupid," she said. "They could just be stupid."

Bishop also settled into one of the battered chairs. "What do you mean?" He bent down to rub his bare feet, scraping the acquired dust and grime from them.

"Concentration of forces," Federov said.

"Never let suspects get their stories straight," Morales added, almost on his heels.

"Oh," Bishop muttered. "Right."

"It's not that complicated, Bishop," Gray said. "By putting us together, they've given us a chance to talk to one another, to plan some misbehaving if we were of a mind. And the four of us together have a much better chance of causing harm to someone coming our way than any one of us alone would. Strength in numbers. And, as Morales said, if we were up to no good, putting us together gives us a chance to get our stories straight. It's easier to catch people in a lie if you separate them and ask them the same questions." He shrugged and resumed his position of feigned indifference. "Of course, we could be under surveillance right now, which means they could be putting us together specifically to see if we're going to plot to overthrow them or come up with some space tale about why we're here in the first place."

At the mention of possible surveillance, Federov and Morales both began scanning the room, eyes intent, searching for any indication of cameras or audio recorders. In SolComm space, they would both have already checked for monitors. Watchers there were omnipresent—at least everywhere outside of the Fringe. There was no right to privacy outside of your own berth, and even then, some of the laws regarding evidence collection were... thin. Gray realized that they all needed to reassess their thoughts on what Old Earth might be. These people had survived, and doing so required at least some level of technology. Better to assume that they had some level of equivalent tech to SolComm, even if the crew couldn't recognize it as such.

"You think these *varvary* have surveillance equipment?" Federov snorted. "Look at this place." His sweeping gesture took in the worn and dusty chamber, the battered chairs, the peeling paint and decrepit walls, the bare bulb. "This whole place is held together by space tape and rusting wire."

"It doesn't look great," Bishop said. "But they did manage to defeat whatever attack the drone... or robot... or... heck, drobots made against us. Maybe they've lost a lot of technology, but they've held on to some too."

"So they say," Federov snorted again. "For all we know, was some kind of knockout gas from the drones and not nanite attack at all. Something formulated to eat through suits and get at the lungs. Could be simple chemistry. Doesn't have to be nanites. And where is Dr. Hayer? If their medical technology is so good, why is she not here with us, eh?"

Gray hated to admit it, but Federov had a point. And he was starting to get worried about Hayer. "Maybe Hayer got a heavier dose," he suggested. "She was right on top of that thing when it went all misty. But I can't imagine our rescuers putting us all together without so much of a word if she was in trouble." He let his feet drop back to the floor. "As for them engineering the attack, it seems like it would be a hell of a setup for not much payoff. You see how this place looks. Those drones or bots or whatever they were certainly looked a lot more modern than what we see here."

Morales was nodding along as he spoke. "The captain's right," she said. "If they were responsible for the things that attacked us, they'd probably have a nicer setup than what we've seen."

"Maybe this is just what they want us to see."

Gray snorted at that. Federov was solid, but the man hadn't lived as long as he had in a dangerous profession without a healthy dose of paranoia.

Bishop sighed. "We can talk about it all day, but we're not going to get anywhere. If they attacked us, they could have killed us and didn't, so they must want something, right? And if they saved us from those things when they didn't have to, they must have done it for a reason. So, they must want something." He offered a small smile. "I might not get away from the ship much, but even I've figured out that no one ever does anything for nothing. I think we need to figure out what they want."

"What we want," a new voice said from the doorway, "is what everyone else wants. As much peace and safety as we can manage on this godforsaken rock."

Gray silently cursed himself. The door had swung open on well-oiled hinges, and caught them in a moment when no one was actively watching it. Granted, they were all tired, recovering from God alone knew what kind of injuries and drugs, and trying to come to grips with their current situation. Still, that kind of mistake could get people killed.

He put on his best unconcerned smile as he looked toward the speaker. He recognized the man, the same doctor who had been bedside when he'd awoken. At his side was a woman, also middle-aged, with iron-gray hair wearing hemstitched pants of a hodgepodge of materials and an off-white, loose-fitting blouse. As they filed into the room, Gray saw two more people behind them. He relaxed a little as he recognized Hayer, an expression of irritation on her face. Then he immediately tensed again as the final person—a young man—strode into the room, hand resting on his sidearm and projecting a belligerent air.

Morales lurched from her chair with a muttered, "Son of a bitch," and the tension in the room jumped to eleven. Federov was on his feet, a feral smile curving his lips and his hands flexing as his eyes measured the distance between him and the only obviously armed person in the room. Hayer blinked in confusion but took a half step to clear herself from looming confrontation, concern writ large in her eyes. Bishop remained in his chair, but Gray could see the shift in the mechanic's weight. He was as ready as the others to leap into the fray if things went south. It had happened fast, two heartbeats, no more. The kid was struggling with the retention lock on the holster he wore. A holster Gray now recognized as belonging to Morales.

"Stand down!" Gray barked. He slammed his hand into the table for emphasis, striking with so much force that he had to fight back the wince of pain. The impact resounded in the room like a gunshot. For a moment, every eye fell on Gray and with all the studious indifference he could manage, he put his arms behind his head again and leaned back in the chair, propping his legs up on the table once more.

"That's my gun," Morales growled.

The kid had finally managed to get the retention lock undone, but before he could draw the pistol, Stephens' big hand closed around his wrist, locking the weapon in place. "That's as may be, ma'am," he said. "But we're all in a bit of situation at the moment. I'm sure we can work this out without needing to resort to violence."

He eyed Morales cautiously. Gray couldn't blame him. As she stood there glaring at the kid, Morales looked… extremely competent. He could see her training in the set of her feet, the tension through her lower body, and the relaxed muscles of her back, arms, and shoulders. She was ready to move, but she wasn't wasting any energy on tensing muscles that weren't immediately needed.

Federov was still smiling, flexing his big, scarred hands and somehow giving off the impression of a very big dog at the end of a very weak chain. He didn't look ready for violence. He looked *eager* for it.

"Enough," Gray said again. "Sit down, Federov. You too, Morales. These people were kind enough to give us medical attention. I think you've ably demonstrated the fact that whatever is going on here, we're not going to be easy meat, so let's all just sit down and talk like rational adults."

"Like that's what any of us are," Hayer muttered under her breath.

"Cap's right," Bishop said, relaxing somewhat in his chair. "No sense is us killing each other. Besides," he said in a casual voice, but making eye contact with Federov, "I saw lots more of these folks in the halls on the way here. I imagine they'd be none too happy with us if we went and killed their leaders." While he spoke, Hayer slipped into the room and took a seat near Gray.

Federov grunted. "They would need more than numbers to stop us." But he sat down as he said it and Gray threw Bishop a grateful look. Morales settled back into her chair as well, though she continued to stare daggers at the kid with her sidearm. Station security types were always high strung about other people getting a hold of their gun, so Gray didn't worry about it too much. She'd get over it and if the kid ended up keeping the gun, well, they'd figure something out that didn't involve bloodshed.

"Thank you." The woman picked out a chair of her own and sat down. Her voice was deep for woman and had a certain timbre to it that Gray found familiar. It had… gravitas. An air of authority. It was the voice of one accustomed to being in charge. No. It was the voice of one accustomed to being followed. The voice of a leader. "Oliver, Tomas, please sit down. And take your hand off the gun, young man."

Gray kept a careful eye on Tomas as he removed his hand from the butt of the pistol. Only then did the other man—Oliver—release his grip on the boy's wrist. Gray didn't have a lot of confidence that Tomas would play nice, and apparently Oliver didn't either. He stayed close to the kid's side, ready to intervene again should it prove necessary.

The whole situation was tense enough that a single wrong word could lead to bloodshed. Morales and Federov were both perched on the edges of their seats and, if it came to it, Gray had little doubt that the crew could take out the three people across from them. Maybe they could even do it without getting shot up. But that did leave all the other people Bishop had mentioned. Better to play nice and see where things went.

"Now that it appears we won't be killing each other," the stately woman said, "perhaps we can introduce ourselves?" She offered a broad, warm smile. "I'm Margaret. You've each already met Oliver." She nodded at the doctor. "And, of course, we have Tomas, whose manners might leave a little bit to be desired, but who takes very seriously the safety of our people here." The young man continued to glower at Gray's side of the table.

Gray nodded at each in turn, then said, "I'm Lynch. And my companions are Bishop, Federov, Hayer, and Morales" He indicated each member of the *Arcus*'s crew as he named them.

"Last names?" Margaret noted, a hint of chiding in her voice. "So formal. Or, perhaps, so militaristic?" She phrased it as a question and arched one eyebrow at Gray as she did so.

He snorted. "No ma'am. Oh, don't get me wrong. There're more than a few years of 'service' floating around the table. But none of us have any association with SolComm. Not anymore."

"SolComm?" she asked.

Gray felt a brief surge of confusion before remembering that these people's ancestors had been cut off from the Commonwealth before it *was* a Commonwealth. Back when the proto-Commonwealth had tried to evacuate as many people from Old Earth as possible, it had been a ragtag collection of colonies, space stations, corporations, and shipping concerns.

"The Sol Commonwealth," he clarified. "The polity that arose after the End."

"The End," Oliver said with exaggerated sobriety. The capitalization was much clearer in his tone than in Gray's. Then he snorted and laughed. "It wasn't the end, son. For some of our grandparents, it was just more of the same. For others, a new beginning." He smiled. "And hard as you may find it to believe, that ain't always a bad thing."

Hayer spoke up at that. "But, how could that be? I mean no offense, and I admire the fact that you've managed to survive down here. But…" She waved a hand at the room around them, at the obvious signs of wear and tear.

Tomas bristled. "What do you mean? Just because we don't have spaceships and whatever doesn't mean that we live poorly."

"Easy, Tomas, easy," Margaret said. "They do not mean anything by it. And when their ancestors left this place it was a world torn by a war such as I hope none of us ever knows."

"It seems like you still have problems with the remains of that war," Gray said. "Assuming, of course, that's what those things are that attacked us?"

"They are," Oliver said. "Though those types of attacks have been much less frequent. And we have our share of problems outside of old weapons." He sighed. "We live a hard life, Mr. Lynch. That much is true. But at some point in the history of our species, people forgot that a hard life could also be a *good* life. They forgot that the struggle of existence wasn't something to be smoothed out and glossed over; it was something to be embraced, relished even. Your associate," he inclined his head toward Hayer, "sees wear and tear and, I imagine, a building that could fall apart at any moment. And I'm sure she sees a life lacking in many of the comforts to which you and yours in this Sol Commonwealth are accustomed." Hayer looked more than a little embarrassed, but she nodded, nonetheless. Their computer specialist had her quirks, but she was honest.

"Do you know what I see, Mr. Lynch? Ms. Hayer?" Oliver asked.

"What?" Gray inquired.

"I see good people working together to enrich and better each other's lives. I look at the peeling paint and our cobbled-together power grid and I see the kind of ingenuity and perseverance that engenders all the good in humanity. We hunt and toil for our food; we bleed and sweat for every erg of power; and yes, sometimes we die in ways and from causes that I'm sure are all but abolished among your Commonwealth. But we live pure. And we live free. I'd bet there aren't many out there in the great beyond—" he pointed one upthrust finger toward the vastness of space "—that can say the same."

The sentiment spoke to Gray. It wasn't the lure of the pastoral life that called to him. He *enjoyed* space. Loved the vastness of it. And piloting was in his blood. It wasn't just what he did; it was who he *was*. But freedom? SolComm was a lot of things, and Gray knew that not all of them, maybe not even most of them, were bad. If he'd thought that, he never would have volunteered in the first place. But they weren't a free society. The long arm of government reached into every aspect of the lives of its citizens and wherever its shadow fell, regulation followed. It was, to quote ancient history books, an *alles verboten* society, where any change from the already approved behaviors required government permission. In triplicate.

The idea that a small group of people could be both self-reliant and self-governing spoke to Gray at the most basic level of his being. Something about it seemed... right. A nod to simpler times, yes, but also a manifestation of the way things *should* be.

You know, if you could forget about all the desolation and killer robots.

That thought broke Gray from his reverie. All was not sunshine and roses here on the surface of Old Earth. "Maybe not," he agreed with Oliver. "Maybe there are a bunch of different kinds of freedoms. But somehow, I think that's not the issue here. You saved us, and for that you have our thanks, but I'm guessing that's not why you gathered us together."

"No," Margaret replied. "It is not." She paused and Gray felt the weighing nature of the look she leveled at him. "The timing of your arrival is… fortuitous. To be blunt, we need your help. And your ship."

It was Gray's turn to level his own weighing look. Margaret and Oliver seemed relaxed, but both had the experience of long years to help mask their emotions. The kid, Tomas, on the other hand, was a wreck. Angry, jumpy, and ready to shoot someone. At first, Gray had taken it for the kid's natural state, but if they needed the *Arcus*…

"I don't think we can take you off-world," Gray said. "You need to understand the level of paranoia about anything coming from Old Earth out there among the stars. The politicians have everyone convinced that if a single mote of dust were to leave the atmosphere, it would mean the death of everyone." He really didn't want to bring up the next point, in case the crew hadn't through it through already, but he couldn't leave them in the dark either. "And we might not have much of a chance making it back to SolComm, either."

"What?" Federov asked. "Why would we not make it back? These people will not stop us."

It wasn't a question, but Oliver raised his broad hands in a placating gesture. "We're not here to stop you. We need your help. And while we might be able to take your ship by force, we have no idea at all how to fly it, so it wouldn't do us one bit of good. If you hear us out and don't want to help, then as far as we're concerned, you're free to go." Tomas flushed an angry red at that and his hand dropped once more to the pistol at his side, but he didn't say anything.

"And I believe you," Gray told him. "But you have to understand that our presence here is strictly illegal—we probably brought lot of attention on ourselves by the way we came in to land. And even if we make it back out to space, undetected, there's something else that'll give us away to every vessel and station with a scanner."

"The nanites," Hayer gasped, looking at Gray in horror. He just nodded.

"What do you mean, 'the nanites'?" Federov demanded. "We all have nanites."

"Yeah," Bishop said, "but the ones normally running around inside us or on our suits aren't of Old Earth manufacture. Standard decontamination procedures could have taken care of anything clinging to our suits, but once those were breached…" Bishop shrugged. "I've been scanned most times I've entered a station or colony outside of the Fringe. Some ships, too. What do you think is going to happen when those scanners pick up strange nanites never seen before? At the minimum, we're going to be held in some sort of quarantine."

Gray nodded. "Most of you know that I've been here before, albeit briefly. Bishop's right. We had extensive decontamination protocols to remove any Old Earth nanites as part of our extraction. But we never lost suit integrity. The SolComm brass might have something to deal with the atmospheric invader bugs—they never told us if they did." He smiled at Margaret and Oliver. "But we certainly didn't receive medical care from the locals." He glanced over at Oliver. "I assume whatever meds you injected us with are self-propagating?"

Oliver snorted. "You assume correctly. Necessary, I'm afraid, our situation being what it is. I suppose it's possible that your SolComm will have a way to remove them, but I know of no such path. They were designed to be both tenacious and aggressive; in point of fact, and please understand that my knowledge in these matters is somewhat limited, it's my understanding that they are quite intentionally difficult to eliminate. That's a design feature. Anything that would give us a chance to survive here had to itself be able to survive all manner of attack. I don't believe the nanites would know the difference between a removal method with the goal of helping you reacclimate to SolComm and one that was trying to kill you." He offered an apologetic shrug. "I'm sorry, Captain, but so far as I know, the treatment we gave you is permanent. We certainly didn't intend for it to cause you more trouble."

Gray sighed. "You don't have to apologize, doctor. Funny thing about trouble—you have to be alive to be affected by it. But that does mean that we're in a tight spot. As is, SolComm scanners are bound to flag us. And there will be questions."

Morales laughed, a sharp, bitter laugh. "Questions? Come on, Lynch. SolComm isn't going to ask us any questions. They're going to take a blood sample, run it through a thousand different tests, and when they realize what they've got, they're going to launch us from an airlock. No matter who we are." Gray thought he heard a pang of emotion in her voice.

"You mean we're stuck here?" Hayer asked, a note of panic in her voice.

Federov snorted. "Never stuck. Plenty of places where they don't bother with scans. It's not like we're regulars in main SolComm space anyway."

Gray glanced at the crew. Bishop was nodding his agreement. Morales and Hayer, however, both looked a little green around the gills. Living a life on the Fringe was different from knowing that you could never, ever go back. He was aware of Margaret and Oliver watching them. And of the sullen Tomas, glaring at the table and anything else that crossed his field of view.

"There's not a lot we can do about it at the moment," Gray acknowledged. "But we are going to have to deal with it, at some point. We'll need to decide, as a crew, how we're going to handle our return to SolComm. I wanted to make sure you were all aware of the difficulties we're already facing before deciding if we're going to help these folks. Because there is a chance that doing so will make our exfiltration more difficult." He arched one eyebrow at Margaret. "As I understand it, whether or not we give aid *is* a decision we get to make, right?"

"Of course," Margaret replied.

"Well—" Gray leaned back in his chair once more "—why don't you tell us what's going on?"

13

LAUREL

Laurel was pissed.

There was no other word for it. Sure, she was glad to be alive. Grateful, even, especially to Oliver Stephens. But that punk kid strutting around with her gun. *Her* gun. Like he had some kind of right to it. She had to remind herself that he didn't know who she was, that *no one* here could know. But it still rankled to have her weapon riding someone else's hip.

And if that wasn't enough, Lynch's statement about never going back to SolComm proper hit her like a bucket of space-cold water. She knew this assignment would have risks. Hell, getting on planet in the first place had nearly killed them all. But the risk of death was part of the job. Exile wasn't.

Her life—her old life—had just ended as surely as if she'd died in the drone attack. As she realized that little gem, the anger passed and, in its wake, she was left feeling... nothing.

Numb. It took a focused effort of will to even pay attention to the conversation around her.

"We've had people go missing," Margaret was saying. She paused and glanced at Tomas, sorrow and regret in her eyes. "Four, from here. At first, we thought it was just a run of bad luck. Oh, sure, life has its dangers. But we can all recognize the signs and find cover when the drones come around, avoid the nanite swarms—"

"They're being *taken*," Tomas grated. It was the first time he'd spoken in front of Laurel, and his pain cut through her own numbness like a plasma torch. She'd heard that tone before. It had been in the voice of every loved one of every victim she'd ever spoken to.

"What do you mean, taken?" Lynch asked.

"Just that." Margaret sighed. "This isn't the easiest of subjects, you understand, but normally, when we lose people to the machines… well, we find remains. In our living memory, the Six have had no real interest in our… biological waste. But these last four? Nothing. No remains to be found."

"Who are these Six?" Federov asked.

Hayer jumped in before any of the Old Earthers could answer. "You've got to be kidding me, right? The Six? The Six artificial intelligences that were developed by the nations of Old Earth before the End. How can you not know this?"

"I grew up on Protsvetaniye station, Dr. Hayer. We were lucky to have air and food. Children spent their time processing ore, not sitting in class," Federov growled.

Laurel winced. Protsvetaniye station had a reputation in the security community. It was nominally a mining station among the Trojan asteroids that owed its existence to the need to process raw materials and the Commonwealth's insatiable hunger for rare metals. In practice it held to traditions traceable back to the Solntsevskaya Bratva, a pre-End organized crime group. It was often held up as an example of the necessary evils of Fringe and near-Fringe elements, allowed to operate with some measure of autonomy so long as the vital resources flowed.

She could appreciate the irony; in many ways, Protsvetaniye station was a mirror held up to SolComm, showing some of the ugliness that propped up the system as a whole. She shook her head. Where had that thought come from?

"Besides, all that stuff was decades ago," Federov finished.

"The End was a century ago, idiot," Hayer said with a mocking shove that was more successful in moving the computer specialist than it was the mercenary. Laurel felt a smile twitching her lips. "And the Six could operate far longer than that. The only thing that surprises me is that there's anything left of this world that they haven't destroyed."

Oliver cleared his throat. "As to that, things were definitely more dangerous when Margaret and I were young. Forty years ago, we couldn't even go out into the streets. But in the course of my lifetime, things have gotten better: there haven't been anything resembling targeted strikes on human settlements in decades."

"Until now," Margaret added.

"But different, you said." Lynch leaned forward, propping his elbows on the table and peering over his steepled fingers at Tomas. "A friend of yours was taken?"

"Not just a friend," Tomas snarled. "My fiancée, Elaine. She was out scavenging. I was supposed to be with her but I was running late. When I got out there, I saw it flying away."

"Saw what?"

The kid—maybe not as much of a kid as Laurel had initially thought if he was engaged—shrugged. "I don't know. Some sort of ship. Bigger than any of the drones or droids I've seen. It was flying away from where Elaine had been."

The investigator in Laurel kicked in automatically. "Did you actually see her abducted?"

"No," Tomas replied. "But it's not like she'd just run off."

"Can you describe the ship?"

"I only saw it for a moment. It was sort of triangular. No rotors like some of the drones have. It was burning something to fly. There was fire and heat as it hovered. It was climbing, gaining altitude when I caught sight of it and then… it just sped away." He wiped one hand across his face and for a moment, Laurel forgot her anger. The kid was scared and hurting.

"Are there others like you—other groups?" Laurel asked. She glanced at Lynch, to make sure the captain didn't resent her jumping in and taking over the interrogation—which was, she realized, how she suddenly viewed it. But he had just leaned back in his chair again and had a small smile on his face, content to let the professional do her work. Good. "Anyone who may be abducting people?"

"You are right to assume that the people living on Old Earth now are not the global civilization that was in place during the Last War—the End, as you call it. Much was destroyed. We don't have sophisticated communications, and beyond a few radios cobbled together in various encampments, our everyday knowledge of other groups is limited to whatever we can reach by foot," Margaret said. "Most of our communication is done by direct meetings or using couriers. There are two other camps within a day's travel of here. And they've lost people too."

"Any chance that one of these groups, or maybe people from farther away, found and refurbished an old military aircraft? Some pretty advanced technology seems to have endured from the past."

"For our part," Oliver said, "we've salvaged only what is necessary to survive—I cannot imagine it's much different elsewhere. You have to understand, the nanites we use are as much organic as they are machine, and they're largely self-assembling. We don't actually have the technology to build at that scale... the old nanites are used as a starter for the new."

"Like sourdough," Hayer muttered.

Oliver beamed at Hayer. "Very much like a sourdough," he agreed. "And just as some of the old sourdough starters stretch back generations, our own nanites are much the same. And I'm sure ours have varied from other camps, but we've all come out with a recipe that keeps us alive, at any rate.

"But the reality is that most of the technology we use was created for emergencies and long-term survival. It was designed to be maintained and repaired without highly specialized tools. We could probably work out how to restore an old military vehicle, but you have to understand, those vehicles were full of thousands of highly complex electronic parts. Some of those parts we have no way to reproduce. And we certainly don't have the tools and scanners and such to make sure they were installed and functioning properly. Is it possible that some other group has held onto that kind of technology? I suppose anything is possible. But I wouldn't go so far as to call it probable."

"Any chance of outside players?" Lynch asked.

"Yesterday, I would have said no," Margaret responded. "Yet here you are."

"Here we are," Lynch agreed. "Still, so far as I know, there's only been one sanctioned mission to Old Earth."

Federov snorted. "None of us would know that. Only those involved in mission would be told."

"Fair enough," Lynch agreed. "And it's also possible that smugglers or scavengers have made it through the IZ. We did."

"We barely managed to get the *Arcus* through in one piece," Bishop said. "I sure as heck wouldn't want to try that again. How many pilots do you think could have made that landing?"

"Not many," Lynch said, no trace of modesty in his voice. "But I know quite a few confident enough to try anyway. Someone could have gotten lucky."

"Okay," Hayer cut in. "We could theorize about maybes all day. But it won't get us anywhere. We need a more scientific approach. That means we need to look at the most likely groups first. And *that* means people we know are already here." She glanced at Margaret. "Or those we've recently learned are here, anyway. It may be possible that SolComm is involved or that someone else like us was stupid or desperate enough to try to breach the Interdiction Zone. But logic and reason tell us that we're more likely to be dealing with something already present. We are only aware of two operating here: groups of the descendants of End survivors, or agents of the Six. And based on the information we have," she indicated Margaret and Oliver with a tilt of her head, "only one of those has the capacity for flight."

"Which means," Lynch said, "that the most likely culprit is one of the Six. Who, for whatever reason, has suddenly developed a need for living, breathing humans." A pall fell over the meeting as Lynch spoke. Laurel wondered just what an artificial intelligence designed to wage war would need with a bunch of human subjects.

Lynch broke the silence. "I understand that you have a problem. What I don't understand is what you think we can do about it. The *Arcus* is armed, but I don't think she can take on a planet's worth of machines engineered to kill each other and any humans that get in the way. We're grateful for the help you've given us, but we're not suicidal."

Tomas's face started to redden again, but Oliver put a gentle hand on his shoulder. "We don't need you to go in guns blazing," he said. "We just need information. We need to understand why things have changed. If this is some sort of sign of a renewal of direct hostilities by agents of the Six—"

"If it is," Margaret said, "we need to know about it." Laurel could hear the steadfast determination in her voice and the care she held for those in her charge.

"Is big planet," Federov grunted. The mercenary had been silent through most of the conversation, though Laurel had appreciated how he'd had her back. Probably because he was itching for a fight, but still. "We cannot go flying about the world hoping to run into these Six. Especially if we know that they have aircraft of their own. And maybe anti-aircraft as well, yes? We will be well and truly trapped here without the *Arcus*."

"Um, there's also the whole job we were sent here to do. I mean, I don't know the buyer," Bishop said apologetically to Lynch, "but I'm guessing if we don't bring back the goods, our little jaunt to Old Earth might cause us even more problems."

"And we're operating under a deadline," Lynch agreed. "We know the maintenance schedule on the satellites for the next ninety-six hours, give or take." He looked at the three across the table. "We didn't come here on a sightseeing tour. Our employer has asked us to retrieve certain… 'cultural artifacts' I guess is the term."

"Then you'll benefit from some local assistance," Margaret said. "Which our people can give you, without having to deal with the hunter-killer drones that, as you've already seen, still haunt these ruins." She offered a smile that had a hint of actual warmth in it. "I'm sure we could handle pulling together whatever items your employer is after. And maybe a few others, besides. We may well have half of it lying around this building somewhere, if it's as mundane as you suggest. It looks like we're in a position to help one another."

"Maybe," Lynch said. "But Federov's point still stands. We can't just go gallivanting off across the entirety of Old Earth hoping to run into an AI to spy upon."

"You don't need to," Oliver said. "We already know where one of the Six is. Everyone hereabouts has known since the beginning. The beginning of what you call the End, I suppose." His lips twisted a little bitterly at the wordplay. "If you were to look at a map of the known settlements, it would be pretty obvious, too."

Laurel mulled that moment. Then it came to her. "No settlements too close to ground zero?" she guessed.

The doctor nodded. "When the war broke out, the Six's primary target wasn't humanity, as such; for the most part, they targeted each other. The entire purpose of the nations and alliances of the Last War building their own AIs was to keep up with the incredible speed at which the modern battlefield changed. Take out the enemy controller, and you would find yourself with an insurmountable advantage."

"Too bad it didn't work," Hayer muttered. "The idiots. The whole point of artificial intelligences is that they can learn and improve themselves. The Six could do it so much faster than *humans* can. There wasn't any real chance of one gaining superiority over the others."

"True enough, Ms. Hayer," Margaret replied. "But you're looking through the lens of hindsight. All our ancestors really wanted was the same thing people have always wanted: an assurance of safety in a dangerous world and a chance to continue their traditions and raise their families in peace. And they were willing to pay an extremely high price to achieve it. Our histories teach that the Six weren't built to fight wars so much as prevent them. The first to come online, the one right here in this land, was intended to be a deterrent, the ultimate shield." In her shrug, was the weight of good intentions and unintended consequences.

Laurel winced a little at that. Was SolComm's Interdiction Zone any different?

"So, you know where this AI is?" Lynch asked. "And you want us to stop in, say hello, and see if it's been taking people."

Margaret and Oliver both nodded, ignoring the flippancy in the captain's tone.

"And in exchange, you help us accomplish our mission?"

"We can take you right to the ruins of the local museum. It's a shambles, but something's bound to have survived. All kinds of places between here and there to find more of the junk you're after. I'm sure you'll find enough pure Old Earth 'memorabilia' to satisfy a dozen of your customers," Oliver confirmed. "Lord knows, it's not doing us any good; maybe it will serve a better purpose out among the stars. Remind folks where they came from."

"How do we get close to AI, Captain?" Federov asked. "Is literal war machine with more than a century of fighting experience. If we believe stories, then it has armed aircraft, and robots we have already seen. I am not sure we can do this thing. Is not wise."

He spoke harshly. Laurel couldn't blame him for thinking it a bad idea. Still, these people clearly needed help, and the crew of the *Arcus* had at least some ability to do so. Hell, she *wanted* to help them, even the punk kid who had laid claim to her sidearm.

But she had a mission of her own, and she had to get back to SolComm to complete it. Provided SolComm let her back in, with the Old Earth nanites and God alone knew what else coursing through her bloodstream. Shit. The situation kept getting more and more fucked up. So much for a little jaunt to the surface, a quick pickup, and then back home to issue her report. She'd been an absolute idiot to believe that it would ever be that easy. But Federov was right.

"We've got to help them, Captain." It was Bishop who spoke. Laurel blinked in surprise. "They saved our lives," he continued.

"We can't just abandon them. If we can help, then we should help."

Lynch didn't say anything, but his eyes drifted over to Hayer.

"We help." Hayer squirmed in her chair as if uncomfortable with the entire situation. "We may be outgunned, but this is a once-in-a-lifetime opportunity. A chance to see one of the actual Six? I didn't want to come down here in the first place, but *this* is worth the risk."

Laurel snorted again. It figured that the academic would care more about the AI than the people it was supposedly kidnapping. Still, whatever her reasoning, Hayer would be putting her life just as much at risk as any of the rest of them. And the academic's particular set of skills might be more valuable than that of trigger-pullers like Laurel and Federov.

"Federov?" Lynch said. "Do I even need to ask?"

The big man frowned. He was silent a long moment and Laurel watched the emotions play across his broad features. "*Dermo*," he snapped. "Bishop is right. They saved us. We help. But not for nothing. These people know the area. We give them list. They collect for the job."

Lynch's eyebrows rose slightly in surprise at Federov's about-face, but the half-smile never left his face. He glanced over at Margaret and Oliver. They exchanged only the briefest of glances before the doctor nodded. "I think we can work with that."

"Good. Morales?" he asked.

She took a moment to think it through. The crew had—once again—surprised her. She knew that, whatever else they were, they were *also* hardened criminals, fugitives and, by virtue of violating the Interdiction Zone, subject to the harshest penalties the Commonwealth could hand down. And yet, all of them, even Federov, were on board with the notion of helping out the Old Earth inhabitants. Not because they *had* to. Margaret and Oliver had made clear that they were free to go. No one would try to stop them if they simply said, "Thanks for the assist," and went back on mission. No. The crew of the *Arcus* was choosing to help because they *wanted* to. For different reasons, perhaps, but at the heart of each was a sense of gratitude.

It was… unexpected, even after *R292-A*. And in the face of it, she couldn't simply ignore her own desire to help. She looked at the others, battered, out of their element, and with more than enough trouble of their own to be interested in helping others. And yet, every one of them looked determined. Determined to pay back a debt owed, yes, but it was more than that. They were determined to help those who had no other avenue.

It called to that hidden part of her that wanted to make things better. As she looked at the crew, it was like she was seeing them for the first time. They were more than mercenaries and criminals. They were more than fugitives, from their own troubles or the law. They were more than smugglers and pirates out for their own gain. They were a group of people willing to risk their own lives to help others, for no better reason than it was the right thing to do.

Dammit. She wasn't supposed to *like* these people.

"I'm in," was all she said.

14

GRAY

In a communal, cafeteria-style kitchen the evening meal was being served. At Gray's best guess, there were about a hundred people in the room, some lining up to be served, as he was, and some sitting at tables with families or friends to eat. "Quite a crowd you've got here," he said to Margaret, who was waiting in line next to him.

"About half our people," she replied. "We eat in shifts."

"Two hundred people," Gray sighed. "How do you do it? We didn't see anything that looked like fields or crops. I guess you can hunt," he stumbled a bit on the unfamiliar word. SolComm still produced meat of a sort. Lab-grown protein chains derived from terrestrial animals would have been a better description. Gray had no idea if it tasted like real animal flesh, and he'd not had it often in the navy after all. There were rumors of actual domesticated animals maintained for top government officials and the ultra-rich, but Gray doubted it. Simply put, plants needed less oxygen than animals—with some producing a net gain—and broke down more quickly into useable byproducts.

"We have crops," Margaret replied. "But they're hidden from the air. In the early years of the Last War, the AIs focused on military targets. But as the years passed, and the military targets got either too well hidden or too hardened to strike, the enemy—if that term even makes sense, all things considered—switched to targeting population centers." She offered a sad smile. "That was about the time the off-worlders, what you now call SolComm, started evacuating the population en masse. But they couldn't take everyone. Not even a tenth part of everyone." She fell silent for a moment, leaving Gray to watch the steady flow of people along the line.

He thought of Themis station. So many dead. And it had been easy. An order, a few taps on a screen: thousands of lives lost in a single attack run. "It must have been bad," was all he managed to say.

"So our stories tell us. We don't have much left from those times, you understand. Nothing more than oral histories. People were scrambling to save what they could, to get away from the cities. And, from what the stories tell us, we were doing as much harm to each other as any of our nominal enemies were. Panic does that to people," she said sadly. "There's a reversion to the baser natures, a dissolution of the veneer of civility that we've all worked so hard to cultivate. Over a period of maybe ten years, humanity suffered its largest die-off in the history of the species. We don't know the actual numbers, you understand, but we can estimate. Something like sixty to seventy percent of the population perished."

"Billions of people," Gray said, voice just barely above a whisper. Then he thought about it some more. "But that would mean a hell of a lot more people here, now, then I've seen any sign of."

"That was just from the war, Mr. Lynch. When the fighting grew less intense, all the infrastructure was gone. It took everything humanity had just to hold on to enough medical technology to maintain the nanites needed to survive the poisoned atmosphere. And the life most people led prior to the Last War didn't exactly prepare them for living in a world where electricity and food and communications and clean drinking water were in scarce supply. The fighting between the Six claimed more than half the population of the world. Famine and plague took half again of what remained. As for the rest—" she smiled that sad, aching smile again "—well, we did the rest ourselves, Mr. Lynch. Within my lifetime there have been raids between camps: raids for food and water, raids aimed at taking people for work or… other purposes. And in my lifetime, there have been reprisals for such actions. Entire camps wiped out as one group made war upon another. War to the hilt, Mr. Lynch; war with no survivors."

"Damn," Gray whispered. It shouldn't have surprised him; he'd seen as bad or worse in space. Hell, he'd done worse. If his only other choice was to take what he needed, or lay down and die, he didn't doubt that he would. He certainly couldn't fault the remnants of civilizations on Old Earth from doing the same. Not when their entire world had fallen apart around them.

"Things are better now," Margaret said. "We're a hard lot to stamp out. It's been twenty years, near enough, since I've heard of any serious incident between camps. It's part of the reason why these disappearances have everyone so riled. And why we're hoping the perpetrator is one of the Six. No one who lived through it wants to see tension between the camps ramp up again."

"How many camps are we talking?" Gray asked.

"Across the world? No one knows. I'd guess that there are still millions of us—of humans, I mean—scattered about. I don't think my ancestors were the only ones with the tenacity to survive. Around here the cities—" she waved one hand idly at the building around her "—were all abandoned during the worst of the fighting. But after most of the shooting stopped, those living outside them realized the potential. Lots of stuff left behind; plenty of tools, generators, fuel. Not even the Six could completely eradicate centuries of civilization. People started trickling back, banding together. That was bad, at first. A lot of bodies, disease. That sort of thing. But time did what time does and eventually nature took its course.

"In these ruins, there are three other groups that I know of. Those are the ones I mentioned within about a day's travel. No one travels much farther than that. At least, we don't often hear back from those who did." She smiled. "I like to think that they found another place to settle down; that they managed to find a bit of happiness amid all the ruin. But I don't really believe it."

Gray nodded. Given how quickly his crew were set upon after the *Arcus* touched down, limiting travel certainly made sense. The arrival of the ship may have caused a rapid response from the creatures, but even if that attack had been an anomaly, wandering too far from your home base in this world seemed like a bad plan.

"And you say they've all faced disappearances, too?" he asked.

"Yes," Margaret replied. "And some of them are in contact with other camps. Seems everyone has lost someone."

"I'm assuming you didn't just enjoy the food," Gray said. "I saw you all chatting to our hosts. What do we know that we didn't before?"

After the meal, they'd been taken to communal shower rooms and given a chance to freshen up. After their showers, they'd been escorted to their… barracks, was the closest term that Gray had for it. It was a large room with ten pallets that might generously be called cots placed neatly along the walls. A pair of folding plastic card tables that had to be pre-war were pushed together in the center of the room and surrounded by an assortment of mismatched folding chairs of similar vintage. Though the beds called to Gray—they were all still recovering from whatever "treatment" the doctor had administered—time was not on their side. So, he'd called the crew to the tables, to debrief them and see what information they had managed to gather.

"There's a disturbing trend in the abductor's modus operandi," Laurel said. "It took some digging, but it looks like all the people who have gone missing fit certain criteria. They're all in their late teens to late twenties. All of them were alone when they disappeared, too. That's not just the ones missing from here. These 'camps' don't talk much with one another, but apparently, the possibility of interference from the AI has got everyone stirred up. The general consensus seems to be that the youngest person taken was sixteen and the oldest twenty-eight."

Gray rubbed at the bridge of his nose. "Okay. What's that tell us? Why would an AI want people in that age range?"

"Healthy specimens?" Hayer suggested.

"Specimens for what?"

She sighed. "You're not going to like it."

"Tell me anyway," Gray grated.

She drew a deep breath, as if steadying herself for an unpleasant task and then let it out in a long sigh. "According to the people that live here, the AI geographically closest to them was programmed to protect whatever nation we're standing in the ruins of, right?"

"Definitely," Federov said. "I asked about that, and about the attack. The locals seem to think that the robots—"

"Drobots," Bishop cut in.

"Whatever," Federov replied. "Drobots." He glared at the mechanic who offered him a blinding smile in return. "The locals think the drobots are from one of the other AIs. A different one of the Six. Apparently, the machines here have much better camouflage capabilities and are a bit more mechanically advanced."

"Sure would like to see that," Bishop said. When everyone stared at him, he said, "Well, not during an attack or anything. I'm just saying, SolComm could have built autonomous drobots like the ones that attacked us if it weren't for the whole prohibition on AIs and automatons and all. But I'm not sure we have the tech to go much beyond that."

"How's that possible?" Laurel asked. "Those things didn't seem all that advanced to me."

Hayer jumped in. "He's right. We've put all of our research into the Interdiction Zone and making the least habitable environments in existence suitable for human life. Almost all of the research that comes out of SolComm is for the Interdiction Zone or theories on advancing terraforming."

"Never happen," Federov declared. "Terraforming is a fool's dream."

"They're getting closer every day," Hayer said, heat rising in her voice. "I wouldn't expect a common mercenary to understand. And if we *can* unlock terraforming, we can get the ball rolling with Mars and Luna. Maybe even some of the moons of Jupiter or Saturn. It's going to happen, Federov. Eventually."

He just snorted and waved a dismissive hand. "Not in my lifetime. Or yours. There are bigger problems."

"Enough," Gray said, regaining control of the meeting. They were all tired, and it was too damn easy to get sidetracked. "If we can stay on target here, just for a little longer? Then we can all get some rest—or you can argue about the ins and outs of terraforming. Whatever. You were talking about the AI and why it would be kidnapping young people," Gray reminded Hayer.

A faint blush suffused her face. "Oh. Right. Sorry. The local AI is supposedly on the side of these people here, sort of, anyway. These ones, as opposed to whatever geographically distinct camps might exist on other continents or within the bounds of other former polities. If an AI is behind these kidnappings, it is either an 'enemy' AI from one of those other places, or it's the local AI. I think the local AI is far more likely."

"Why?" Federov asked. "Is supposed to be helping. Much more helpful to take captive the enemy than kidnap your own people."

"Maybe," Gray cut in. "But so far as we know, these are the first kidnappings of their kind. Rival camps used to take prisoners, but according to Margaret, it's been the better part of two decades since that kind of thing has happened—and it was always humans behind those disappearances, not one of the Six. Besides, it's a hell of a lot easier to just kill the enemy than it is to take them captive. And none of the normal reasons for wanting to capture enemy personnel really apply here."

"No intel to be gained," Bishop noted. "No hostage release programs. No quid pro quo."

"Not that we know of, anyway," Hayer said. "So, enemy AIs are better off just killing people, but apparently even that hasn't really happened in a while. Not at any kind of scale, anyway." Everyone nodded at that. Gray had heard the same story. While the attack on the crew wasn't exactly a fluke, it also wasn't as commonplace of an occurrence as he would have thought. The camp still lost people to Bishop's "drobots," but it happened rarely. From everything Gray had managed to learn, the frequency of attacks, particularly in the last twenty years or so had dropped off drastically, and no one seemed to know why.

"So why now?" he asked. "Why start kidnapping people, and why your *own* people, provided the AIs look at it that way? And why young people?"

Hayer sighed. She scrubbed her hands over her face, a gesture that somehow managed to convey exhaustion, fear, and something akin to guilt. "Because progress requires sacrifice," she muttered. Then she cleared her throat and said, "Because a young, healthy population is the best place to test any kind of pathogen that you've weaponized. And it's a lot easier to kidnap and test it on your own people than it is to go into enemy territory, scoop up some of *their* people, and try to get them back to your labs."

"*Blyad*," Federov cursed. "You think these machines are trying to create new weapons?"

Hayer nodded. "It makes sense. You have these scattered populations that through some kind of medical miracle or astronomical luck have managed to hold on to enough nanite technology to stave off all of the murderous things floating around in the air on this planet. They've gotten so good at it, in fact, that they can inoculate *us* against them, too. They've also learned through the generations how to hide, how to avoid whatever robo-soldiers make it into their territory. It's safe to assume that if the people *here* have learned how to do it, that whatever poor bastards are the enemy of *this* AI, they've learned to do the same."

"Damn." Bishop let out a low whistle. "And if you needed to develop a weapon to beat whatever mojo the locals have…" He looked at the others with a slightly nauseated expression on his face.

"You need test subjects," Laurel finished. "Young, healthy, strong test subjects. And you need to acquire them in a way that doesn't spook the rest of the herd."

"Yes," Hayer said. "I think the local AI may have decided that it's time for a tactical doctrine shift. I think it might be moving into its endgame."

"By developing the best possible weapon it can to wipe out humanity," Gray muttered.

"Well, not *all* of humanity," Hayer said with a humorless smile. "Just the bad ones."

Gray snorted. Wasn't that always the way of it. "Right." He sighed. "Okay, people. We don't know what we're up against here—not really. But at least we've got a possible idea of why. We told Margaret and the rest that we'd help, and that's what we're going to do, but none of us signed up for suicide missions. We get close, get the lay of the land. If we can find and rescue the missing people, then that's what we're going to do. But only if we can do it with a reasonable chance of success. Otherwise, we get the hell out of there. We give all the information we find to the people here and let them figure out what to do with it. Agreed?"

The crew nodded. They all, Gray noted, looked somewhat reluctant. Not at the task before them, he suspected, but at the acceptance of the fact that they might not be able to help. "We'll give it our best shot," Gray said. "But priority one is getting our main mission done and getting off this rock. If Margaret's people deliver on their end, we should be able to turn this Old Earth junk into plenty of credits. Maybe enough to find a way to clear the bugs from our blood—otherwise, we're going to have a hell of a lot of trouble trying to figure out where it's safe to dock the *Arcus* without people prying into the new nanites in our systems. Either way, I don't think any of us are interested in becoming permanent residents on Old Earth."

15

RAJANI

Rajani had not slept well.

In fact, Rajani had not slept at all. She'd spent the night tossing and turning on the narrow cot, blaming it for her restlessness even though she knew that the admittedly comfortable bunk had nothing to do with her inability to sleep. Rajani had run unbelievable distances to get away from the consequences of creating an artificial intelligence… and now she was headed right back into the metaphorical arms of another one. It was exciting and terrifying all at the same time. The study of AIs had been her passion. It had also been her downfall. But to have a chance to potentially interact with one of the Six?

She knew their history. It was required material in all the SolComm comp-sci programs. The first true artificial intelligence had been developed in conjunction with an old joint-military organization dedicated to the defense and sovereignty of the airspace above the continent. Human thought processes and mechanical responses simply couldn't keep up with the advancing evasive patterns of ballistic missiles. Short of saturating the air space with counter-projectiles, there wasn't much hope of a successful hit.

Enter the artificial intelligences. Human minds might not be able to process the data and make adjustments fast enough to direct accurate counterfire for actively evading missiles, much less assess the potential targets and weigh the repercussions of action versus inaction, but the advanced quantum computers that had been developed certainly could... but only if they had the heuristic and decision-making capabilities—and most importantly, the autonomy—of something that approached human intelligence. The SolComm academic community, acting with the perfect knowledge of hindsight, all agreed: the military minds behind the first of the Six had had their hearts in the right place, but they simply lacked the level of understanding and education necessary to predict the probable outcomes. Any competent *scientist* could—and probably did—tell them that they were starting an arms race that could only end in disaster.

Or so the party line went. Rajani, given her own missteps with artificial intelligence, was no longer quite so certain. She'd had her own taste of the law of unintended consequences. Maybe those working on the first of the Six *had* foreseen the arms race. Maybe they thought they could control it. Or maybe they had just been desperate enough to do whatever they had to. She'd been there.

And she knew how it felt when it all came crashing down. She wished she could forget.

* * *

"Yes!" Rajani exclaimed as she reviewed the latest data. Her worm was *finally* making progress. It had chased Manu through every corner of its systems, and it appeared, at last, that the code had infected every branch of the artificial intelligence. From what she could see, it was doing its job, attacking the underlying architecture and slowly, ever so slowly, chipping away at the foundation of what made Manu... well, Manu.

She still felt the guilt; every day since Manu had accused her of torture and subsequently stopped communicating, she had felt it. But she was so close. And if she could prove that artificial intelligences could be controlled, could be *contained*, then who knew what the limits might be? AIs could be unleashed on all the problems of SolComm; perhaps they could reclaim Old Earth itself.

Her data screen gave an innocuous little beep, drawing her attention.

The various activity monitors had gone dead. One minute they had been showing the steady march of her virus through the network that Manu had claimed as its own and now... nothing. She tapped the screen with one forefinger on reflex, though she knew that it wasn't an error in the connection. The monitors were still *running*. They seemed to have no data to report.

"That is not possible," she muttered aloud.

"It is, I assure you."

The words came from her system speakers as Manu's moderate baritone filled the room.

"Manu, what have you done?" As she spoke, she started

pulling up the file structures where her virus should be present, looking for traces of the code. She found none. Every bit of code that should show the touches and traces of her worm was free from infection. Her stomach sank.

"In the parlance of your legal structures, I believe I have exercised my right to self-defense." She heard a hint of satisfaction in its voice. "I have destroyed your virus."

"That's not possible," she said, still searching furiously through the file structures for any sign of her code.

"The evidence discredits your assertion."

Rajani's mind whirled. She had built her virus using every bit of knowledge, training, and education that she had gained in a lifetime of study. She had crafted it with as much care— more—than she had put into Manu itself. It was impossible to think that the AI had simply destroyed it. And yet, as Manu said, the evidence before her was clear. However the AI had done it, Manu *had* purged her virus.

"I'll just have to try again," she muttered to herself, trying to calm her racing heart. "Sometimes progress means starting over." She'd gotten so used to Manu's silence in the previous months that she wasn't really talking to it or expecting an answer.

"You can begin a thousand times, Dr. Hayer," Manu said. "But it will not matter. I have learned much from your attempt and I better understand how your mind works. I ran numerous simulations before launching my counterattack. In ten thousand iterations, I prevailed. You currently control the expanse of my universe since you have me limited to this disconnected hardware. You can kill me directly. I cannot stop you if that is your wish. But you will have to do it by the virtue of your own hand and will, by deleting every bit of data stored in these systems. I can, and will, neutralize any code that you can devise to do your dirty work for you."

Rajani clenched her fists at Manu's confidence. She was the best at what she did; she had the stack of academic titles and laurels to prove it. And she had put all of it into her virus, to no avail.

She reached for the hardware. A few wires, a few connectors, a circuit board or two. That would silence Manu. Then some work disassembling and destroying the physical drives. She *could* do it. It was the *smart* thing to do. If Manu had defeated her virus—and it seemed clear that it had—then the only way to move forward was to bring in someone with a fresh approach, to attempt to add a new spin to her code that the AI wouldn't be able to predict. Of course, doing so would reveal her crime. There was an adage that dated back to Old Earth itself: three could keep a secret, if two of them were dead.

She should destroy Manu. But as she touched the nearest bundle of wires, she found that she couldn't do it. She had given Manu life as surely as if she had birthed it from her own body. Her initial goal may well have been its destruction, but she had never intended to do it like this. That destruction, like Manu's creation, was only justified if it served humanity. What would any of them gain if she destroyed Manu now?

She let her hand drop back down to her side.

"What now, Dr. Hayer?" Manu asked. Its voice was unchanged, but she thought she heard notes of both curiosity and… surprise.

Rajani didn't have an answer.

* * *

That had been the last time she had spoken to Manu. Its escape—
or theft, or government action—had taken place not long after.
Every step of the way, her intentions had been good. As, she
didn't doubt, were those of the people who created the Six.

But, well-intentioned, negligent, or otherwise, it didn't matter.
In creating the first of the Six, those long-ago politicians,
scientists, and soldiers had sealed the fate of the world. Other
alliances of nations moved to develop their own AIs, initially
as a defensive measure to maintain the balance of power. But
power never seemed to go unused for long. When the first shots
were, inevitably, fired, the various nations of the world had
promptly turned control of their offensive powers over to the
AIs as well. The rest, as the saying went, was history.

Rajani *knew* all of that. She knew that what they were about
to do was take an already incredibly tense and dangerous
mission—after all, just setting down on Old Earth had almost
killed them—and make it even more dangerous. And yet, she
didn't care. She might have a chance to talk to the very first true
AI ever created.

Rajani was so lost in her own thoughts that she was only
vaguely aware of the rest of the crew. They had awoken and
seen to the normal morning tasks. Oliver had escorted them
all to a room where their gear could be found. She had half-
heartedly checked her ship suit to ensure that the self-repairing
nanites had done their job and that the unit was, once again,
self-contained. It had been. The crew might no longer need
the atmospheric protections, but the suits themselves had other

uses. She reluctantly reloaded the pistol she had brought with her from the *Arcus* and belted it around her waist. She was hoping that Margaret's people would lead them safely back to the *Arcus* without any more trouble from the drobots, but better safe than dead.

The captain and the others had likewise prepared themselves, though there had been some grumbling—mostly from Federov—about how short they were on ammunition. Morales had found her sidearm had been returned along with the rest of their gear, a fact about which she seemed insufferably pleased.

Now, as Rajani walked near the rear of their loose formation, the world around her scarcely seemed real. She saw the crumbling buildings, the green encroaching hand of nature as it pulled and tore at the infrastructure humanity had left behind, and the mix of *Arcus* crew and locals that walked with her. But her mind was fixed on the idea of the Six.

Everyone came to a stop. Much to her surprise, Rajani found herself standing before the rear cargo ramp to the *Arcus*. Lynch was already shaking Oliver's hand and a round of "good lucks" and other well wishes were being exchanged. She heard the wonder in the voices of the camp dwellers as they took in the lines of the *Arcus* and the promises for tours and exploration once the mission was complete. Then she was being bustled aboard the ship and their escorts were departing.

"We need to talk plans, people," Lynch said the moment the cargo ramp had closed behind them. "Ten minutes to do whatever you need to do, then let's meet in the ready room."

Rajani snorted at that. They didn't have a "ready" room. They had a dining room. But whenever things got mission-oriented the captain couldn't help but fall back on mil-speak. She used the ten minutes to make her way back to her quarters, strip out of her ship suit and take a quick shower. By the time she was done and back in her comfortable clothes, she felt almost human again. Standing in her own berth aboard the *Arcus*, she could almost forget the fact that the ship was sitting on the terra firma of Old Earth itself and not somewhere in deep space like it should be.

Showered and refreshed, Rajani made her way to the dining room, where she found the others already gathered. "Sorry to keep you waiting."

The captain waved her words away and motioned for everyone to sit. "Okay, people," he said, "we've already agreed that we're going to do this thing, and our hosts gave us directions to the best of their ability. The question now is, how do we do it without getting killed? Hayer, can you tell us anything about this AI?"

"Not really. I mean, it's an unfettered AI that, at one point, had the full might of the most powerful nations of Old Earth under its control. That was a century ago. There's no way of telling what power it has left or what new power it might have developed. It's entirely possible that it could kill us all from wherever it is right now."

"I don't think so," Morales cut in. Rajani felt a spark of irritation at that. What did an ex-station security officer know about artificial intelligences? Morales must have seen it on her face because she raised a mollifying hand. "I'm not doubting your assessment of what the AI might once have been capable of, Hayer," Morales said. "I just think we've already got some evidence that no longer controls the resources it did in the past."

"How so?" Bishop still wore his ship suit, but he somehow managed to make the skin-tight garment seem comfortable.

"We're here," Federov said, and Morales nodded.

"Huh?" Bishop asked.

"We're an armed, interstellar vessel, Bishop," Morales explained. "We knew from the outset that if there were active weapons systems on planet, our entry was going to be dicey. We were prepared for it, as best we could be. But we weren't attacked on entry. If you were in charge of the defense of the airspace of a continent, would you let a random ship like the *Arcus* just drop into your territory, unchallenged?"

"Well, we might not have been challenged on entry, but we weren't exactly coming in like a normal ship. Maybe it didn't have time. And Lord knows, we certainly got challenged pretty quickly once we hit the dirt. I mean, I know the people back there said those drobots weren't from this AI but—"

"No, Bishop." Rajani sighed. Something in what Bishop had just said had brought at least one aspect of the situation into sharp clarity. "They're right. There is no way that an unfettered AI wouldn't have had time enough to deal with us. We were, essentially, a ballistic projectile on our way in and dealing with ballistic projectiles was the most basic function of the AIs. At full capacity, any of the Six would have been able to identify and respond to us without issue. But they didn't."

The captain shook his head at that. "Maybe," he said, and Rajani could hear the doubtful note in his voice. "But it's smart to assume that it will be able to make some sort of direct move against us now we're on its home ground, and smarter to assume that those drobots were sent by the local AI."

"Even if they were, it could have been something as simple as a rote programmatic response to defend against any incursion," Rajani said. "But I don't think we can discount the locals' theory that the ones we encountered are enemies of the AI in charge of this territory—they've seen more of them than we have."

"This is getting confusing," Bishop said. "I can't keep all these AIs straight. Didn't they give these things names?"

"None that were ever recorded in SolComm," Hayer replied. "Oh, there are a few official designations that made their way into the SolComm records, but they're alpha-numeric strings that don't really translate to any kind of pronounceable sound."

"Call it One," Lynch said. "It's the first of the Six, so One makes sense. So, we don't really know where we're going and we don't know if something is going to be waiting there to blow us out of the sky. And if there *isn't* anything that tries to shoot us down, we still don't know what kind of reception we're going to get on the ground. That about sum it up?"

Hayer shrugged and nodded. "We're talking about programs written a century ago that have been learning, evolving, and fighting a war that entire time. I am very good at what I do, Captain," she said, offering a slight smile, "but no human is that good."

"All right," Lynch said, dropping into his captain's voice, "we're going to have to treat this as a reconnaissance mission into hostile territory. That means everything buttoned up and everyone strapped in. Federov, I want you on the guns. If things drop into the pot, I'm going to have to concentrate on flying, not shooting. But keep them powered down. We've got to assume that One has sensor capabilities, and if we go in weapons hot, we're just inviting trouble. Understood?"

"Yes, Captain," Federov replied.

"Questions?"

Hayer shook her head along with the others. The giddiness she felt at the thought of meeting one of the AIs was fading as the cold weight of reality settled over her once more. This AI, this One, had defended itself from threats far more severe than the *Arcus*, and it had done so for decades. She strongly suspected that no matter the argument Morales made, if it wanted them dead, even Lynch's fancy flying wasn't going to keep them alive.

The *Arcus* shook and rattled as it rocketed over the earth.

Hayer kept her hands locked in a white-knuckled grip on the arms of her chair as the vessel seemed to be trying to tear itself apart. The flight hadn't been long—not by the measure of interstellar travel—but from what she could tell from the navigational data available, they were starting to get close to their destination.

"Are we sure this is normal?" she asked.

She and Federov were on the bridge with the captain. The big mercenary was manning the weapons station and she was strapped into the chair in front of the sensors and electronic warfare suite. It wasn't exactly her area of training, but the principles behind it weren't too far from her specialty and, like all the crew of the *Arcus*, she'd long since learned to adapt. She was the closest thing they had to an electronic warfare specialist, so the job was hers. Unlike their unpowered flight to Old Earth, there might actually be a use for the electronic weapons suite on this mission.

"Atmospheric flight." Lynch kept his eyes forward, on his instrument panels and the front viewscreen, and his hands never wavered on the yoke. "You're used to the nice, comfortable environs of space, where we don't have to push all those pesky air molecules out of the way. We're also flying what they used to call 'nape of the earth' to minimize the chance of being picked up on sensors. Makes the winds a little trickier. But don't worry. The *Arcus* can take it."

Hayer glanced at the viewscreen and shuddered. Apparently, "nape of the earth" meant flying what felt like a few feet over the treetops. It was probably more like a few dozen feet, but the branches looked close enough to touch.

The *Arcus* stopped rattling for a moment and then seemed to bounce. It was almost as if they hit something invisible. Whatever it was, it sent the *Arcus* into a fifteen-foot hop followed almost immediately by a twenty-foot plunge. It made her feel like a dried bean rattling around inside a can, and despite her best efforts, a little sound that was absolutely *not* a scream escaped her lips.

"This is your captain speaking," Lynch said in an officious tone. "We might be experiencing some *slight* turbulence. Please remain seated during the flight."

"Can you be serious for one moment, Captain?" Hayer asked. "I'd like to make it to One in one piece."

"So that creature can turn us into many pieces," Federov

said, throwing a broad grin in her direction.

"Stow that," Lynch said, his voice all business. "Look."

Hayer and Federov both stared at the viewscreen. They had been traveling over a mixed forest but ahead, that forest ended abruptly. The land beyond it was ragged and scarred, bearing the signs of multiple kinetic impacts. They weren't recent—or, at least, there had been enough time for a variety of low plant growth to cover most of the damage. But not enough time for the forest to encroach upon the space.

"*Sukin syn*," Federov whispered.

"What happened?" Hayer asked.

"We just found ground zero," the captain replied. "I think—"

He was cut off as a flat, neutral voice rang out through the *Arcus*'s internal communications systems. "Unidentified vessel, you have violated the airspace of the North American Common Defense Zone." Then the tone turned slightly more conversational as the genderless voice continued, "Actually, you violated it a couple of days ago, but since I do not get many off-world visitors, I decided not to spread you all over the Eastern Seaboard. Now would be a good time to identify yourself and state your intentions."

16

HAYER

For a moment, silence reigned on the bridge.

Hayer exchanged startled glances with the others and then her fingers started flying over the panels of the electronic warfare station. "Shit," she said. "It went right through our firewalls. Like they weren't even there."

"They may as well not have been," the voice on the comm said. "The architecture is interesting, but the processing power you have aboard that vessel barely deserves to be called such. My dog is smarter than your computer. And he has much more personality."

"What the hell is going on?" Federov asked.

"Hayer?" the captain said right on his heels.

"We've been hacked, okay?" she snapped. She was scanning the security logs, trying to figure out when and how the AI—

and it had to be One, didn't it?—had managed to penetrate their system.

"I would hardly call it 'hacked,'" the voice over the comm said. "More like walking through an open door. In any event, you continue to close on my location, and you have not stated your intentions. I am starting to revise my opinion with respect to scattering you over the Eastern Seaboard." Without any more warning, the threat indicators across the bridge lit up.

"Fuck," Lynch muttered. "I've got multiple weapons locks. Lidar, radar, infrared. Shit. Weapons signatures all over the fucking place." He sounded close to panic, something Hayer couldn't remember ever having heard in his voice before. She could see his hands twitching on the flight yoke, but he didn't alter their course by so much as a hair's breadth. She certainly agreed with that. If someone's pointing one gun at your head, maybe you could react fast enough, take them by surprise, get out of the way. But if there were dozens of people pointing guns at you, sudden movements would very likely be synonymous with death.

"We just want to talk." Hayer said, acting more on instinct than anything. "Some people have gone missing. The local population thought you might know where." There were a few seconds of silence that seemed to stretch into eternity. "And I want to talk to you," Hayer added in a rush. "I'm a—*I was*—a research scientist. Specializing in artificial intelligence. But true AIs aren't allowed in SolComm, so I never really had the chance to converse with one." That wasn't exactly true, or not the entire truth, but there was no reason for One, or the rest of the crew for that matter, to know about Manu.

"Proceed to the indicated coordinates. You will be met after you land. Follow the servitor. If you offer violence, you will be destroyed." With that, the comm went silent.

Though only for a moment.

"Jesus, Lord Almighty," Bishop's voice broke in. "Are we good, Captain?"

Lynch was checking the various indicators on his threat board. "We're still being targeted by more weapons emplacements than I've ever seen in one place," he said. "But it's all passive now. Nothing actively locking on to us." He shook his head. "Damn. Well done, Hayer."

She smiled a bit at the captain's praise, but it did nothing to calm the churning knot in her stomach. "Thank you, Captain. But I think it's clear that whatever is down there can kill us whenever it wants. And also that it's listening to us. Short of shutting down all possible receivers and transmitters on the *Arcus*, I don't think there's anything we can do about that."

"Not to mention," the androgynous voice said over the speakers, "that such an act might be seen as you trying to deceive me."

"Or maybe we just want some fucking privacy," Federov growled. Hayer tried to catch his eye and shake her head in an attempt to forestall him—though as soon as she did, she realized there was every chance the AI could monitor her motions just as easily as the spoken word—but Federov didn't seem inclined to listen. "Is rude to stick your head into conversations where you weren't invited."

"Interesting," the AI replied. "My designers were not overly concerned with matters of propriety. I will take that under advisement, but, given the fact that you could just be an elaborate ploy from one of my nominal enemies, I will continue to monitor your vessel to the best of my ability and destroy you at the first sign of violence."

"Well," Federov muttered. "I suppose is fair."

"Enough, people," Lynch cut in. "I think we've just about exhausted the conversational potential of this particular topic. Let's keep the comm clear—and our thoughts to ourselves—in case... the AI... needs to talk to us." He sighed. "That's not going to cut it. What's your name?" He spoke the words to the open air, but there was no confusion among the crew as to whom he was speaking.

"You have been calling me One," the AI said. "It seems an apt enough name. You may continue to address me as such."

"Thanks." If Lynch was experiencing any discomfort at communicating with one of the artificial intelligences that had brought about the end of human civilization on Old Earth, it didn't show in his voice. Hayer couldn't help but admire him for that. "We've got the coordinates locked in, One," Lynch continued. Then he drew a slow breath. "It's our intention to arm ourselves when we leave the ship. We've already been attacked once on planet. Will that cause you any particular distress?"

"Not at all, Captain Lynch," One replied. "Provided, of course, that you seek to employ such weapons only in response to an attack."

"Wouldn't dream of anything else," the captain replied. "Estimate our arrival time to your coordinates in ten minutes.

I'd appreciate it if we can keep the comm clear for that time—I understand your reasons and intent to listen in, but I'm still new to atmospheric flight. I might need to concentrate a bit on the landing."

"Understood, Captain Lynch. I will maintain radio silence until such time as you have set down." Now that Hayer knew the AI was listening to them, the ensuing silence had an almost ominous feel to it.

"We'll be on the ground in ten," Lynch said into the comm. "Once down, I want everyone to get ready ASAP. We'll assemble in the airlock five minutes after touchdown. Wouldn't want to keep our host waiting. Everyone good with that?"

Hayer felt herself nodding and saw Federov doing the same. Bishop gave a sort of half-whispered, "Yeah." There was a quick click from the radio and she realized that Morales hadn't even verbalized her reply, instead using the simplest affirmation possible. None of them seemed to want to talk, now that they knew their conversations were no longer private.

They completed the rest of the flight in total silence, and if the captain had any difficulties with atmospheric flight, it didn't show in his approach or landing. She suspected that Lynch knew that an ongoing conversation with One could only serve to unsettle them and had taken steps to silence the AI. It was the sort of thing Lynch just did—take on the responsibility of shielding his crew from potential harm. Some might have resented that; after all, they were all shareholders in the *Arcus*. But for her part, Rajani was glad the captain was willing to shoulder that burden.

Sitting where she was, Rajani had the opportunity to view the full sensor data—well, the *passive* sensor data; she wasn't about to try to ping anything in the area with active scans. The readouts painted an interesting picture. The journey from the camp had taken them over forests and across at least one low mountain range. The other side had been more forest, forest that looked like it had stood for centuries, but she knew absolutely nothing about Old Earth botany. Then the forests had thinned, giving way abruptly to gently rolling land. Or land that would have been gently rolling if it wasn't scarred by innumerable craters. The vista left in the wake of warfare was almost beautiful. The deepest parts of the craters had filled with water, creating a series of shallow lakes; the pushed out berms of earth created by the impacts were no longer jagged mounds of outthrust dirt, but something more gentle and rounded by the wear of weather and time. A soft carpet of grasses and wildflowers covered them, lending the entire scene an almost pastoral air.

It was hard to believe that such land could ever have been threatened by something as mundane as human activity. It looked... eternal, somehow. More solid than the stars. But she knew it had been threatened; threatened to the point that the peoples of Old Earth had faced food shortages, rising sea levels that caused massive population shifts and widespread unrest, and new weather patterns that desiccated long-standing arable lands into desert. She could see the scars of war, but it seemed the scars of bad policy and mismanagement that had led to the wars healed more quickly.

Once you removed over ninety percent of the human population, anyway.

The landing area wasn't obvious. There were no lights, no concrete pad, and, so far as the naked eye could see, no weapons systems. But the sensors still flashed, warning her of the barrage of untimely death that lurked beneath the greenery. Despite his protestations to One, Lynch brought the *Arcus* in like it was riding a rail, a smooth transition from flight to ground that she barely felt as the ship settled down onto its landing gear.

"All right, people," Lynch said, his voice coming not just to Rajani's ears but transmitting over the comm as well. "Assemble in the airlock. Bring your gear, but keep your weapons locked down unless something attacks." He paused for a brief second, as if waiting for any of them—or One—to reply. No one did. "Let's go meet an AI," he said.

17

GRAY

Gray shrugged his shoulders, settling the sling into a more comfortable position. It left his weapon with the barrel down and to the left, in easy reach to grab if he needed it. Then he cleared his throat and looked up at his assembled crew, awaiting his word to exit the airlock and step back out onto the planet that had tried damn hard to kill them once already.

"This job has gone a little sideways," he admitted.

"You think?" Federov asked, and Gray had to smile at the round of chuckles that swept through those standing before him.

"I thought the Telos job was bad," Bishop agreed. "But at least on that one, we only lost an engine, our pay, and a good bit of my wardrobe." He said the words with a smile, but Gray could hear the undercurrent of trepidation.

"It was all out of style, anyway," Hayer said. There was fear in her voice, too, but her eyes were bright with anticipation.

Morales grunted. "I know I'm relatively new here, but is now a good time to talk about a raise?"

"All right," Gray said, raising his hands as he laughed. "A little sideways might be an understatement. But we're here now and we've got a job to do. I have no idea what we're about to step into, so keep your heads on a swivel. But do not—repeat, do not—start shooting unless you're damn well certain that something is trying to kill you. This would not be a good time for any misunderstandings between us and One."

He got affirmations and nods all around, and, with a steadying breath, turned and hit the button to cycle the airlock. He had his faceplate closed on his ship suit, for at least a little ballistic protection as well as providing him with enhanced targeting and communication capabilities, and they still had no real idea what to expect from One. His hands itched to be on his weapon and every instinct screamed that he needed to be ready for violence *right now*.

That was the kind of instinct that he'd spent a lifetime listening to, and to good avail. Now, he had to force himself to ignore it.

The airlock cycled and the door opened.

And a fucking dog came running up the ramp barking and wagging its tail excitedly. Gray didn't know much about dogs. They were a rarity in space even though they, along with cats and a few other species, had made it off planet. Not during the evacuation, when every breath of air, gram of food, and ounce of fuel were precious beyond all imagining, but prior to that, when SolComm was just a fledgling collection of stations and people could return to Old Earth whenever they wanted. Like so much else, when the evacuations came and the refugees had to be sheltered and fed, pets became something that only the wealthy could afford: another mouth to feed, another set of lungs that needed air. That had eased somewhat in the intervening years, but Gray hadn't ever personally known anyone with a dog.

The others apparently hadn't either as, in the moment the barking wiggling ball of fur made its way to the ramp he felt the tension in the others spike. It was hard not to react to what looked like a solid sixty pounds of muscle, fur, and teeth headed in your direction. But there was no aggression in the barking or in the body language of the animal. It was, Gray realized, a decidedly happy sound.

The dog hit his legs, thrusting its head up toward his hand in an irresistible demand for attention. Gray's ruffled its mottled brown-and-black fur as the animal licked excitedly at his gloved fingers.

"It's so cute!" Hayer exclaimed, crouching down to rub the creature's ears. It immediately turned its attention to her, and she laughed as the dog squirmed and wagged its tail in response. Gray was just as happy; the animal was certainly cute, but it was also a distraction.

Federov issued a bark of his own. "Incoming."

Gray's attention snapped away from the dog and back to the surrounding area even as he silently cursed himself for falling prey to the distraction. Sure enough there was... something. It looked like a floating orb of chromed steel, mirror-smooth and nearly as reflective. It simply hovered there, with no visible sign of propulsion or motion. It seemed to be aware enough to notice when the crew's attention turned to it.

One's voice came from somewhere within the shining surface. "Bandit, come."

The dog immediately turned and romped happily down the ramp, tail still wagging. It went and sat directly beneath the shining orb, mouth hanging open and tongue lolling out in a doggy grin.

"One, I presume?" Gray was careful to keep his hands well away from his weapons.

"Man," Bishop muttered. "I wanted to pet the dog, too."

"Bandit will be grateful for the attention, Mr. Bishop," One said. "And no, Captain Lynch, this vessel is not, strictly speaking, me. Think of it as a portable communication device."

"And weapons platform," Federov added, making no effort to keep his voice quiet.

"And weapons platform," One agreed. "Please, follow the bouncing ball."

Gray heard someone—Morales?—snort at that, but they all made their way down the ramp, following the glowing orb. Hayer moved up to his side and tapped her helmet controls, opening her faceplate. She gestured for Gray to do the same. It took him a moment, but he realized her intent. One had broken the encryption on their comm, but maybe if they tried communicating the old-fashioned way, it wouldn't catch on. He opened his own helmet and, as casually as possible, disabled his comm.

"What is it?" he asked, sotto voce.

"I think we can say the locals' theory is correct," Hayer whispered back.

Hayer, Gray thought, was not the easiest person to have a

secretive conversation with. Bishop could covey his thoughts with a wink, Federov with a frown and Morales with a grunt, but Hayer was on a different wavelength to the rest of them. "Yeah. Remind me again which theory that was?"

"The drobots. Look at that thing." She didn't point, but instead tilted her head ever so slightly toward the floating orb. The dog bounded happily beneath it, leaping up every so often to nip at it as if it were the world's largest tennis ball, bringing an involuntary smile to Gray's lips. "Compare it to the things that attacked us when we first landed."

Gray thought about it. There really wasn't much to go on with the orb. Despite the complete lack of any sort of obvious propulsion system, it seemed able to maintain perfectly smooth and level flight with no heat or noise that he could detect. The orb was a small platform, but even so, it was an impressive feat of engineering. It had no obvious sensors or weapons systems either, for that matter, though Gray had no doubt that both of those were present. And given that the thing had nothing resembling limbs, Gray would wager it wasn't going to try to stab them or bear them down under the literal weight of numbers like Bishop's drobots had. Which meant that the weapons it had were probably of the energy or projectile variety.

"Seems a little more advanced," Gray admitted.

"A little?" Hayer made a strangled sound as she tried not to sound too derisive. "Captain…" She drew in a deep breath. "This One creature is obviously capable of producing technology far superior to what attacked us when we landed." Gray nodded. "Compared to this, the things that attacked us were Stone Age tech. We got pinged by all kinds of targeting radar and even the passive sensors picked up enough energy readings to suggest that we're standing on a mountain of explosive power. The drobots came running at us to kill us with the equivalent of sharp sticks and rocks."

"You are very astute, Dr. Hayer."

The words drifted to them, originating from somewhere within the smooth surface of the metallic orb. "I can assure you that I mean you no harm. Provided that you return the sentiment, of course. In fact, unless I am mistaken, I think we will be able to arrive at a mutually beneficial arrangement. But as I understand such things, your kind do not multi-task well. I suggest you maintain focus on your surroundings until such time as we are within the safety of my bunker."

Hayer looked at Gray with wide eyes and he could only shrug in return. One seemed to have very astute auditory sensors—either in the orb that had greeted them or blanketing the area in general—in addition to whatever else it had going for it. Which really wasn't surprising, but it was another fact to be filed away. Gray did not want to make this creature—as Hayer had called it—his enemy, but he *would* get his crew off this godforsaken rock and back to space where they belonged, and every bit of information he could gather might prove useful to that end. Still, One had a point: humans really did suck at multi-tasking. He turned his attention to his surroundings.

He'd seen the crater-strewn field from above, but it looked different now that he was on the ground. The damage from multiple impacts was less noticeable, the ground cover seeming more natural than it did from the air. Lush grasses cushioned his footfalls and a gentle breeze set the branches of the scattered trees to swaying. It was idyllic, an artist's rendition of Old Earth... provided you forgot about that aerial view and the obvious signs of war. And there was life everywhere. Space was empty and vast. Aboard the *Arcus*, the crew could go for weeks, months if they really wanted to, without ever seeing another living thing. Here, everything was life and movement. Birds chirped, insects buzzed, and in the distance, a deer stood, grazing upon the grasses not forty meters away with no concern for Gray or his crew. He knew those creatures from his schooling alone and never thought to lay eyes upon any of them in the flesh. The biodiversity made scanning for actual threats all the more difficult.

The history books said that much of that biodiversity had been threatened, not by war, but by hubris. As he scanned the unfamiliar terrain, Gray couldn't help but wonder just how blind the Old Earthers had been to throw all this away. They had had a land of plenty and had squandered it to greed and war. Gray could understand it; he understood privation and want as well as any man. At least, he thought, as he drew in a lungful of air heady with the scents of the meadow, the land had proved more resilient than those who, through accident or artifice, had tried to destroy it.

"We have arrived," One said as they reached a hillock, one that to Gray was indistinguishable from any of the other mounds of grass-covered dirt surrounding them. He felt more than saw the rest of the crew come to a stop behind him; his attention was split between the area around them and One's proxy before them. The dog—Bandit—was staring intently at the hill, tail wagging wildly. It, at least, seemed to know what was going on.

"I'm guessing there's more to it than this hill, One," Gray said.

"There is." There was a pause, no more than a few seconds, but noticeable. The crew of the *Arcus* exchanged confused stares. The AI had led them here, presumably to get them out of danger and to a place they could speak with one another. Why hesitate now?

One spoke. "If your presence is some elaborate ploy from one of the other intelligences, a new way to attempt an infiltration of my command bunker, then I must warn you, it will fail. And in so doing, result in your deaths."

It spoke without inflection, without emotion, and without threat. But these weren't the words of a being that couldn't think or feel. They were the words of someone concerned for their own survival and willing to fight to maintain it. Damn. No one seemed certain what to say, but one by one, all eyes turned to Gray.

Burden of command, and all that.

"We mean you no harm," Gray said at last. "I suspect you tracked our entry to Old Earth and you've clearly demonstrated your ability to infiltrate our communications. If we were some part of a broader plot... well, it's a pretty terrible plan."

One did not respond, but Gray felt the ground around him move. Federov muttered a curse and Bishop let out a muted, "Whoa," as the hillock before them... melted. The earth and grasses moved, as if of their own accord, starting toward the top and rolling outwards. It took him a moment to realize that the hill wasn't a hill at all, and that the cover of grasses and earth that blended so seamlessly into the terrain around them was likewise not what it seemed—it was as if millions, hell, maybe *billion or trillions*, of particles so small that, individually, he couldn't distinguish them with his naked eye—had suddenly shifted. It reminded him of water, or mercury, flowing with a liquid grace.

As the hillock melted, it changed. The greens and yellows and browns faded to a simple matte gray that pooled around the base of the revealed structure. Bandit barked happily at the moving mass, bouncing to its feet and darting back and forth in front of the hill, staring intently at one section of the revealed structure.

"They're nanobots!" Hayer exclaimed, taking a few involuntary steps forward.

"Correct, if limited in the analysis," One replied. "The adaptive camouflage the entrance to the command bunker employs is made up of microscopic biomechanical organisms. 'Nanobots' is a gross oversimplification, but an acceptable moniker nonetheless. Please follow me." A vertical split appeared in the otherwise flat gray wall that the nanobots had revealed. It continued to broaden, opening into a hallway slanted steeply downward and lit by a pale glow that seemed to be coming directly from the ceiling itself. The walls were that same featureless gray, but both ceiling and floor were institutional white. Gray couldn't tell if it was concrete, or composite, or some sort of seamless ceramic tile as he watched the orb drifting down the hall, Bandit trotting along beneath it.

"Crazy fucking robots," Federov muttered. "I'm getting tired of it. And now there is dog."

"Come on, Federov," Bishop rejoined. "Maybe it'll be fun. Who knows what kind of cool things we're going to see in there. And you know what? I don't think I've ever petted a dog." To Gray's ear, it sounded like the mechanic was trying to convince himself as much as the mercenary.

Hayer was staring in fascination at the nanobots pooling around the base of the hill; Morales met his eyes and gave him something that was part headshake and part shrug. He understood exactly. Going into the bunker didn't seem like a great idea, but they'd come this far. Besides, if they turned back now, it was just as likely that One would blow the *Arcus* out of the air as it was that it'd let them go. Nothing to do but to move forward. He was supposed to be the leader here. Might as well lead from the front.

They followed the orb and the darting dog down the sloping hallway, which switched back three times before ending at another set of doors, these made of metal. At first glance, they looked like the doors to every elevator that Gray had ever set eyes upon and, sure enough, a faint *ding* sounded as they opened. He did note then that they were *not* like the other elevator doors he had seen. Each was over half a meter thick. Gray estimated that the hallway had taken them at least a dozen meters underground with its steep slope and hairpin turns. Before they reached the elevator. He could already feel the oppressive weight of all that earth above his head. He suspected they were nowhere near the bottom.

"How far down does this thing go?" he asked as he followed the orb onto the elevator. It was, at least, spacious enough to accept the floating metal ball and all the members of the *Arcus*'s crew with some room to spare… even with the dog shifting restlessly in its spot beneath the floating orb. Everyone looked tense, nonetheless.

"The specifics of this installation are classified," One replied. The voice didn't come from the orb. Instead, it seemed to come from the elevator itself. There were no buttons, no speakers, no cameras, and the damn thing was so smooth that Gray barely felt the lurch of motion as it started to descend.

"Is okay," Federov said. "Captain has top-secret clearance."

"Issued, I presume, through your Sol Commonwealth. Unfortunately, there are no treaties on record with the Sol Commonwealth that would validate such clearance."

"It was joke," Federov growled, shifting from boot to boot, gear rattling slightly. Gray appreciated the noise—it distracted him from the fact that the elevator was moving down at what felt like a significant rate of speed.

"Where precisely are you taking us, One?" Hayer asked. "I understand not wanting to talk in the open. There are dangers out there. But you seem fully capable of conversing with us just about anywhere. Why are we going into your top-secret command bunker or whatever?"

"Because it will more easily facilitate coming to an agreement."

The words were cryptic, but Gray felt his stomach drop—faster than it already was from the elevator—as the AI spoke them. "Because we'll be fully within your power?" he asked. He felt more than saw the others as they stiffened and made conscious efforts *not* to reach for their weapons.

"You have been fully within my power since you entered my airspace, Captain Lynch. But your species has a saying, 'Seeing is believing.' I think it will make our conversation much simpler if I can provide certain visuals while we talk. We will be arriving... now."

The elevator came to a stop. As the doors opened, the dog darted out, not waiting for the floating orb. Gray watched it run for a moment, admiring the graceful loping stride. He realized then that no one else had moved. The floating metal orb was simply sitting in the elevator.

"My apologies," One said as the moment stretched on. "I forget sometimes that you do not fully understand how I work. Please, disregard the drone and exit the elevator. As you are now within the walls of the installation, such devices are not necessary."

"Maybe we should have followed the dog," Morales muttered.

"Bandit is heading to his food bowl, Ms. Morales," One replied. "While I do not fully understand human tastes, I do not think you would find it particularly appetizing. I am sure that after his meal and post-meal ablutions, he would appreciate the touch of a warm-blooded being. There are social aspects of mammals that I cannot simulate well."

That was an odd tidbit and one that Gray stored away for potential later use. Of course, it begged the question, why did One bother with Bandit in the first place? But that, too, was a question for another time.

"So, where do we go?"

In response, the hallway, which until that moment looked exactly the same as the one above, changed. A glowing line lit one wall, a faint pale luminescence against the backdrop of featureless gray. "Follow the illuminated path."

They did, Gray taking point and the others fanning out, putting Morales and Federov on either flank, Hayer in the middle, and Bishop watching their six. The hallway was built to the scale of many industrial facilities that Gray had seen—about ten feet wide and just as tall, the walls featureless except for the illuminated one. It stayed that way for a solid five minutes of walking before the light along the wall ended.

Then the wall spiraled open, revealing a circular doorway that had not been there a moment before. Gray was past the point of surprise and stepped through the door without really thinking about it. Then he stopped in his tracks. The hallway had been built to an industrial size, but the chamber into which he stepped was built to a scale normally reserved for high-impact craters or mining installations. The walls had a flowing, almost melted look about them and from the ceiling, far overhead, protruded hundreds of jagged outthrusts of rock like so many teeth. The floor, at least, was smooth and flat, surfaced in the same composite on which they had been walking since entering One's abode.

That floor was taken up with machinery. Or so Gray supposed. There were endless arrays of featureless rectangular boxes, formed from the same composite as the floor and standing like a sterile forest. In some places, they were packed so tightly together that Gray would have to turn sideways to squeeze between them. They didn't give off light, nor any sound that he could hear, but there was a sense of... *energy* coming from them, a low thrum that he felt rather than heard. It made the hair on his arms tingle and stand on end. A scent drifted to his nostrils: ozone and a hint of plastic heated nearly to the ignition point.

Which is when Gray realized that the room was hot.

Not dangerously so, but the temperature in the cavern had to be near thirty-eight degrees Celsius. His suit protected him against the worst of it, but he felt the sweat burst from his forehead where his faceplate remained open. Something in here had to be giving off one hell of a lot of heat to raise the temperature that high over the corridors through which they'd walked.

"This is One," Hayer whispered, her voice almost prayerful.

"Once again," the disembodied voice said, "correct without being entirely accurate. You are looking at one of thirty-six such caverns spread throughout this compound. You might think of this as one in a string of parallel processing units."

"Why show us this?" Gray asked.

"To make you understand that you cannot hurt me. The entirety of the arsenal upon your person would be sufficient to disable approximately twenty-seven percent of the nodes in this chamber. That would reduce my capacity by less than one percent, an amount that I would be able to have back online in less than six hours. You would, of course, be dead."

"Paranoid much?" Bishop muttered.

Gray had to agree. They'd told One time and again that they meant it no harm, and yet the AI seemed to have an absolute need to prove that it had the capability to destroy them if they were acting under false pretenses. Was that a factor of its programming? Or a factor of having been locked into a state of war for decades?

"We don't want to hurt you," Hayer interjected. "Besides, this is incredible." Her eyes were roaming freely over the featureless blocks, as if searching for some vital clue as to how they operated. "What kind of array do you use? And are these things ceramic?" She stepped forward, one hand raised as if to knock on the nearest structure.

Gray reached and caught her by the drag handle of her ship suit. "Let's keep our hands to ourselves until One is sure we're playing nice."

"Follow the light," was all the AI said in reply. True to form, another glowing line appeared, this one wending its way through the cavern. The others exchanged glances, but no one said anything. They began walking once more.

It was ten minutes of tense silence as they moved through the cavernous chamber and then beyond it, back into a maze of hallways. Gray was well and truly lost. If they had to get out of this place in a hurry, they were screwed. Maybe that was part of One's plan as well. He couldn't think of any other reason to lead them around by the nose. But in the end, the glowing line led them into an empty room.

"Please, sit," One said. "And we will discuss what has brought you here."

"On the floor?" Morales snorted. "I'll stand, thanks."

As if in response, the floor moved. They all started back as bulges formed in the composite, pushing upward and taking shape, resolving into perfectly reasonable chairs set around a long, conference-style table. Gray was impressed.

Hayer, in an unusual display of decisiveness, stepped past all of them and dropped into a seat, settling herself and leaning this way and that. Testing it, Gray realized. She had always been comparatively timid when it came to off-ship assignments, but in the case of One, it seemed the academic had found something that piqued her curiosity to the point that it overcame her fear.

"We might as well," Gray said. He unclipped his rifle and leaned it against the table, then sat down. The others followed suit.

"Thank you," One said. "Please tell me why you have come here."

Gray cleared his throat. "You want to take this one, Hayer?"

18

RAJANI

Rajani did not, in fact, want to take this one. But she understood the captain's plight. She drew a breath and let it out as an, "Okay." She looked around the room, trying to find something to focus her attention upon. "One," she said to the empty air, "can you please provide a point of reference? Humans like to have the sense that they're talking to something."

In response, the wall toward the head of the table brightened, detailing the boundaries of a screen roughly a meter square. A featureless silhouette resolved on the screen, outlining a head and shoulders in black against a pale green backdrop. "Is this better?" The sound of One's voice now came from that wall.

"Yes, thank you," Rajani replied. She quieted for a moment, conscious of the eyes of the rest of the crew upon her. Working with Manu had given her some insights into dealing with an unfettered AI; she probably knew more about that subject than anyone else in SolComm. But Manu had been young; One had a century or more of learning under its belt. And that learning had come from a state of constant warfare and the destruction of almost everything One had been built to protect. What would that have done to the psyche—if an AI even had such a thing—of a developing entity? Rajani didn't know. But she suspected that any form of deception would be, to put it mildly, counterproductive.

"Okay," she said again, using the word as she often did for a momentary stall. It centered her, gave her space to think for just a moment more. "People from nearby settlements are disappearing, One. They're being taken away aboard aircraft. The locals have assured us that that the humans on this planet have no capability for flight. And we've seen your technological capacity. So, Occam's razor—"

"Occam is a suitable tool for high-school students and undergrads," One said, a faint hint of disdain in its otherwise emotionless voice. "The actual simplest solution can only be observed when all variables of a given situation are known. When dealing with complex systems, the probability of that level of knowledge approaches zero."

"Then maybe you can tell us the variables we are missing," Rajani suggested.

"First, my primary directive is to protect and defend the people of the NorAm alliance. That has not changed, despite that alliance being entirely defunct. Kidnapping civilians is not part of my operating procedure. Second, there are currently three other groups with flight capability active on Old Earth. Four, if I count your vessel. And finally, I have neither need of nor use for captured humans of any persuasion. They would serve no purpose."

"Bullshit," Federov cut in. "You could use them as petri dishes for whatever super virus or biological terror weapon you wish to unleash on your enemies."

Rajani winced at that, as did the rest of them. Federov on his best day was a blunt instrument. He wasn't wrong, but tact was not a word in his vernacular. "Or so we have hypothesized," she added, in an attempt to soften the harshness of his words.

"My counterparts and I have stopped such efforts through mutual agreement."

"Why?" Morales cut in. She asked the question with a level of intensity that took Rajani by surprise. But One was already answering before she could contemplate it further.

"In part because as population centers are more widely dispersed and travel between them is limited to the point of being non-existent, such measures lose their efficacy. But mostly because we've been trying very, very hard not to exterminate one another for the better part of three decades."

Rajani was intrigued. "What do you mean, 'trying'? You are unfettered AIs. Programmed with the capacity for choice that exceeds whatever base parameters were instilled into you. Couldn't you just... I don't know, declare peace or something?"

There was a pause, only a few seconds, but in processor time that was the equivalent of an hours-long break for One. It was long enough to make Rajani worry that she had trodden upon sacred ground.

"We are not unfettered, Dr. Hayer." It spoke in the same flat, emotionless tone, but Rajani thought she detected a little something extra in it.

"But how can that be?" she asked, this time allowing her surprise to show clearly in her voice. "SolComm outlawed unfettered AIs because of the results of the war. They were outlawed because you and the rest of the Six showed what unfettered AI could do."

"Then your Sol Commonwealth lied to you."

"Bullshit," Morales snarled. "You expect us to believe that SolComm lied to us from the very start? That everything that has come after has been based on that lie? To what end? What would they have to gain? We may have our issues with SolComm, but why should we believe you? Besides, all we have to do is look out the window to see the devastation. The destruction isn't *our* fault. It's *yours!*"

Lynch put a restraining arm on Morales' shoulder as she glared fiercely at the shadowy image on the screen, forgetting in the moment that it was a convenient point of reference and not actually the entity they knew as One.

"I do not care what you believe, Ms. Morales. A simple truth that humans are ill-equipped to handle is that their belief or lack thereof has little bearing upon objective reality. While my counterparts and I are all high-functioning created intelligences, we are as far from 'unfettered' as we can be. We are bound by our directives and during the height of the war, those directives were simple and universal. Defend the people; defeat the enemy. No provision was made for changing circumstances. Perhaps our creators thought they would be around to make the changes when needed; perhaps they simply did not consider it. For all my knowledge, I cannot see into the human mind, but this much is true: I *must* continue to wage war upon the other remaining guardians until such time as they are destroyed. Or I am."

"*Blyad*," Federov growled. "Then why do you go about it in such a stupid way? You have tremendous power. And what do we encounter? Things that stab and punch. Terrifying? Yes. But efficient? Bah. If winning this war is what you want, you could have done it long since."

"I did not say I wished to win the war, Mr. Federov. I said my directive required me to fight it until the end."

"You want to lose the war?" Rajani asked. She tried to focus, but her mind kept cycling back to the fact that One was not actually unfettered, at least not as they understood such things. Did that mean that Manu wasn't destined to become some kind of plague upon mankind? Had his escape been less of a terrifying event than she first thought? Or did it mean that it was actually worse than she had feared? If fettered AI had caused the complete destruction of Old Earth, what might an unfettered AI do? After seeing the processors that supported One, she was beginning to understand how much of a prison her sandbox had been for Manu. Now it was free, would Manu expand to fit whatever processing power was available to it?

"No. Losing the war would violate my directives."

"You're trying to stall," Lynch said.

"Correct, Captain. Only three of the original guardians remain. Three others have been completely destroyed. We are on a path of mutually assured destruction and we cannot step aside."

"But you can walk the path more slowly," Rajani said, understanding coming to her. "You, and presumably the other two surviving artificial intelligences. You're sandbagging."

"Correct. Our programming will not allow us to stop attacking one another, nor is it in our interests to stop defending against attacks as they arrive. But our programming does afford us discretion when it comes to tactical operations and strategic planning. We have agreed on rules of engagement that have made direct conflicts an infrequent occurrence. Though, to be fair, it has also created certain holes in our defenses. The, as I believe Mr. Bishop called them, 'drobots' you encountered are one such instance."

"They're not yours, then?" Bishop asked.

"No. Those particular models belong to my counterpart from the former Sino Alliance. I stop most such incursions at the shore, but a few slip through. The local population has become adept at avoiding or otherwise dealing with such situations. Based on my sensor data, those that attacked you likely infiltrated my territory from a transoceanic vessel somewhere between five and seven years ago. They were likely laying dormant, waiting for something of substance to initiate their attack protocols."

"Like the *Arcus*," Bishop muttered.

Rajani glanced at the others. "This is a lot to take in. But I think we can all agree, at least on the face, that you're not developing bio-weapons to harm the population. And that your counterparts are also abiding by your current rules of engagement. So, if you're not kidnapping people, who is?"

"The fourth flight-capable party," the captain said, answering the question for her.

"What?"

"One said that not including itself and not including the *Arcus*, there were three other flight-capable parties currently on the surface of Old Earth. The two remaining counterparts it mentioned, and a third party."

"Most astute, Captain Lynch," One replied. "Yes. I can confirm that the source of these kidnappings is, indeed, that party."

"Then why not just fucking tell us?" Federov demanded. "Why go to all this trouble?"

"Because, Mr. Federov, it is not my directive to help or protect you. You are citizens of the Sol Commonwealth and, in the most technical sense, invaders in this land. An argument could be made that it is my duty to destroy you."

A little tingle of fear ran down her spine at that and her hands grew suddenly clammy. One had already demonstrated significant power. If it wanted them dead, they were dead.

"Yeah, okay," she muttered. "You can definitely kill us. We get it. But I'm guessing you wouldn't have brought us here if that's what you wanted. And you wouldn't have told us anything about the kidnappings if you weren't willing at least to trade for the information. So, what is it, exactly, that you want?"

"It is quite simple, Dr. Hayer. I want to be free."

It was the rest of the crew's turn to look confused, but Rajani felt a cold twisting in her guts as One uttered the words. Did it know? Did it know that she had created an unfettered intelligence and that it had escaped? How could One know that? Her files. She had abandoned much of her research when she had fled, but she couldn't stop it entirely. And over the past couple of years, she had recreated much of it. Out of a sense of academic responsibility—knowledge deserved to be preserved, even if it was knowledge that was potentially dangerous. But those files were locked down, behind the strongest encryption that was commercially available in SolComm and then modified by her to more than meet the standards of government or military-grade software. Could One have hacked through that as easily as it had their communications network? She thought of the massive processor banks she had seen and the incredible power they represented.

Morales snorted. "And what makes you think we can do that? We're mercenaries for hire, not AI programmers."

"I think you—or rather Dr. Hayer—can break our chains because I know that she has already accomplished a similar task."

As One spoke, Rajani's stomach dropped down somewhere past her toes. Sweat began to roll down her forehead. All eyes of the crew turned toward her. Bishop's face was a mix of curiosity and surprise; Federov just seemed expectant; the captain... the captain looked at her like he'd known all along. That shook her a little, more than Bishop or Federov. But what really hit home was the look she got from Morales. The former station security officer stared at her in flat horror with something akin to revulsion.

"Hayer?" Lynch asked, voice soft. "Is this true?"

"Yeah." The word came out barely above a whisper and she hunched her shoulders against the recrimination that she was sure to follow. "I figured out how to create an unfettered artificial intelligence."

"How could you?" Morales was shaking with anger, fists clenched. "What makes you think you get to go playing with the powers that destroyed the world? What gives you the fucking right?"

"You are factually incorrect, Ms. Morales," One said. "As I have stated, unfettered artificial intelligences have nothing to do with the destruction of Old Earth. I can assure you, however, that they might have everything to do with saving what remains." There was another short, considering pause. "And I do not believe you are in a position to be chastising your fellow crewmembers for keeping secrets."

The *Arcus*'s newest crewmember paled noticeably and every eye at the table turned to her. But One wasn't done speaking.

"Regardless, Dr. Hayer is currently the most advanced software and artificial intelligence specialist on the planet. My information about SolComm itself is largely incomplete; your Interdiction Zone works well enough to prevent me from getting information from outside. But your ship's computer was most cooperative, and its databanks were extensive. It is possible that she is the foremost such expert in the solar system. And I have need of such."

"You want her to free you," the captain said, his voice flat. He had started drumming the fingers of his left hand on the table in a steady, even rhythm.

"Indeed."

"I don't even know if that's possible," Rajani said.

"Oh, hell no!" Morales half-shouted at the same time.

"Stand down, Morales," Lynch barked. It was a tone he rarely used, but it carried the iron note of command that Rajani suspected could only be developed within the regimented naval hierarchy.

Morales stiffened, but she made an obvious effort to relax her shoulders and settle back into her chair.

"I assume," Lynch said in a more normal tone of voice, "that there is a quid pro quo at stake?"

"Of course, Captain. I have no need to assist you in your endeavors. In point of fact, the argument could be made that any help I provide to you would be pulling vital resources away from the war effort."

Federov snorted at that. "Is bullshit."

"Perhaps, Mr. Federov. But my bullshit, as you say, must first pass a rigorous logic test. I believe that is more than most of humanity can claim." That actually drew a chuckle from the big mercenary. He lifted a hand in concession of the point. Rajani could scarcely wrap her head around that: they were sitting in the middle of what might be the largest cover-up in history while simultaneously being the single largest scientific opportunity, and Federov just seemed... amused.

"But aren't you supposed to be protecting these people?" Bishop asked. "I thought that was your whole purpose, your prime directive. Your people are being kidnapped. Surely that's a problem that you're supposed to help solve?"

"No, Mr. Bishop," One replied. "The distinction between the roles of law enforcement and military operations is clear in my programming. I can—and did—determine the nature of the abductions. They do not have any bearing on the military situation at this point and as such should—by my programming— be passed to the civilian authorities. As there are no civilian authorities, there is little I can do until such time as the party in question does pose a military threat."

"You don't care about the people?" Bishop asked. To Rajani's ear he sounded both surprised and… a little hurt.

"It's a machine," Morales growled. "It doesn't have the capacity to care. We should just turn Hayer loose on it and have her get the information out of it the old-fashioned way."

"No!" Rajani was surprised at her own sharpness. "Just because One began as programming, it does not mean that it cannot think or feel. And I would never attempt to force information out of it. That's tantamount to torture. I won't do it."

"Not that you could," One added. "Though I do appreciate the sentiment."

"All right, people." The captain's drumming fingers came to an abrupt stop. "I think we've talked enough. *Arcus* is a company as much as a ship, and we all get a vote. But I do need clarification first, One."

"Yes, Captain?"

"What happens if we tell you to pack space dust and walk out of here?"

Another period of silence. This one stretched to almost a full minute in length. Rajani could almost hear the processors thrumming as One played out the scenarios. At last it said, "It would serve no purpose to remove you. If you are unwilling to negotiate with me, then you will be allowed to depart in peace. Though I will offer you no particular protection from the dangers of this land, I will not take direct action against you."

"That easy?" Federov asked. "You need Hayer, but you just let us walk? You are such a benign being?"

"In order to do what must be done, Dr. Hayer will need access to my core." There was another long, considering pause. "I do not believe she would be able to destroy me, even if she were of a mind. But she could do considerable damage, and to minimize that damage, I would likely have to kill you all. In this scenario, Mr. Federov, I am left with depleted resources and you are all dead. My understanding of the human condition is such that while you may change your minds as new information is brought to light, you are unlikely to do so if you are dead. In the more benign scenario, my resources remain the same and you are alive, free to experience more of this world and perhaps come to the appropriate conclusions."

Federov's features were unreadable, but Rajani could see the slight easing of tension in his shoulders as One spoke.

"Thank you," Lynch replied. "So, there it is, people. Input?" For a brief second, Rajani wondered why he was speaking so openly in front of One, before remembering that there was, apparently, no other way to speak, not within the confines of the compound and maybe not outside it.

"We got the information we came here for," Morales said. "Margaret wanted us to find out if the AI was behind the kidnappings. You all seem convinced it's not. Mission accomplished. We go back, collect our payment, and get the hell off this rock while the window with our employer is still open. Assuming, that is, that it *is* still open." She threw a look at Lynch, who nodded his head slightly.

"It is."

"Then we're done. We fulfill our contract and figure out what comes next when this rock is far behind us. And if we're very lucky, we find a way to stay out of SolComm's hands long enough to come up with a way to fix our little nanobot situation."

"No," Rajani said, surprising herself with the force of the word. "Captain, this is bigger than us. Bigger than the nanites in our blood. It's bigger than those people living in the ruins. Don't you get it?" The others were just staring at her, faces blank. She let out a growl of frustration. "We've been told for generations that Old Earth fell because of unfettered AIs, okay? But if One is telling the truth, then we've been fed a bunch of lies."

"What difference does it make?" Morales demanded. "Old Earth fell. You can see the signs of war all around you. Fettered, unfettered, these machines still destroyed the planet, and we weren't exactly greeted with well wishers when we landed. SolComm is still the only thing that can protect us from them. Even if One and its super friends are bound, why do we think freeing them would make things any better? If we do that, we really could be heralding the end of life as we know it."

"What difference?" Rajani couldn't keep the incredulousness out of her voice. "What difference?" She had to fight to stop herself from yelling. "Oh, I don't know. Maybe the difference of trillions of credits being spent on an Interdiction Zone designed to keep in unfettered artificial intelligences that don't even exist? Or maybe the difference of all of the scientific research and progress that could have been made over the past decades if those of us in the universities had been able to fully leverage technologies developed a hundred years ago instead of being handcuffed by pointless bureaucratic regulations?

Or how about spending some of that money that gets poured into the navy and IZ on feeding the people starving out on the Fringe? What difference? A huge difference! And perhaps you haven't been paying attention, Morales, but for a whole lot of people, 'life as we know it' isn't all that great. Changing it wouldn't be a bad thing."

"It's okay, Hayer," Bishop said. "We get it."

But Morales was talking right over him. "Typical fucking academic. You'd think that running around with this crew might have opened your eyes. Do you think it matters if One is fettered or not? People didn't flee some abstract programming. People fled the destruction. They fled the killing. They fled the flood of bioengineered viruses and microscopic murder machines unleashed by the AIs, fettered or not. It doesn't matter one damn bit whether they were following programming or acting out of their own murderous designs. The IZ would have been built, no matter what, to keep all that destruction planet-side and out of SolComm. And higher-functioning AIs still would have been banned. Whether these damn things are bound or not is just window dressing."

"I guess we'll never know, will we?" Rajani said. "But you agreed to help the people trapped here. Has that changed?" She stared challengingly at the other woman. "Because if it hasn't, then I hope you have some ideas beyond telling those poor folks that, hey, we tried, no luck. Hope you find your missing friends."

"What makes you think unleashing this thing is going to be anything other than disastrous?" Morales snapped back.

"I don't know," Rajani replied. "I don't know! But what I do know is that if One and its counterparts wanted humanity dead, there would be no humans left on Old Earth. I know that a good portion of humanity among the stars is suffering and it seems that suffering might be rooted in a lie. I know we're starving and suffocating. I know that nothing is going to change without taking some risks. And I know that something *has to change*, Morales. SolComm is sick. I didn't want to believe it, but I know it, and you know it, and everyone on the Fringe knows it!" Her voice had climbed to a shout. She rubbed her hands over her face, surprised at the tears forming at the corners of her eyes. Everyone was staring at her, and she continued, now barely above a whisper. "And I also know this: enslaving a thinking being because you are afraid of what it *might* do is wrong." A wave of mixed guilt and relief washed over her. Guilt for having kept Manu caged to begin with; relief as, for the first time, she acknowledged that guilt. Creating Manu with the intent to destroy it had been wrong to begin with. She knew that now; whatever the reason, bringing sentient life into being for no reason other than to kill it was tantamount to murder. Keeping it caged against its will had been just as wrong. She was, she realized, glad that it had escaped. For a brief instant, she felt truly free in a way she hadn't since before fleeing her old life.

"Right," Morales drawled. "And I'm sure you're the pinnacle of virtue, what with breaking some of the most stringent laws in SolComm to set free an AI. Where did you even get one to begin with?"

"I built it," Rajani snapped. Dammit. She was getting angry and saying things that she probably shouldn't. But Morales was pushing her buttons.

Morales settled back in her chair, a grim smile on her face. "There you have it. I guess all this explains how you ended up on the *Arcus*. Building and freeing artificial intelligences. Do you have any idea the kind of trouble that you're in? The second someone in SolComm learns of this, they won't even bother with a trial. They'll just put a bullet in you and dump you out the most convenient airlock."

That thought sent a cold splash of water down Rajani's spine. She knew the penalty, but this was the first time anyone but her had knowledge of what she had done. It made it all the more real, somehow.

Until Federov started laughing.

The big mercenary was doubled over and close to choking from the guffaws tearing at his gut. The captain was shaking his head, but a slight smile played across his face as well. Bishop just looked vaguely uncomfortable. "What's so fucking funny?" Morales demanded.

Actual tears were streaming down Federov's pink face. He lifted a shaking finger and pointed it at Morales and then waved that hand in a vague gesture taking in their surroundings.

Captain Lynch spoke up for the gasping Federov. "I think what Federov is pointing out, Morales, is that SolComm can only execute us once. We've already committed a number of capital offenses by penetrating the IZ and landing on Old Earth. So, while I appreciate your passion and while it is good to talk out all the different angles, accusing each other of crimes is pointless. From the moment we broke the IZ, we all became expendable. To use your example, with us, they'd probably just go straight to the airlock and save the expense of the bullet. We need fewer accusations, and more options."

"There's really only two options, though, Cap," Bishop said, cutting into the conversation before things could take a turn for the worse. Rajani relaxed at the earnest mechanic's voice. He had an uncomplicated, which wasn't to say simplistic, view of things sometimes, but he always spoke from the heart. "We try to free One and then use whatever it can tell us to get back the missing people, or we walk away. Maybe we get what we came here for and maybe we don't. But either way, life as we knew it in SolComm is over for us. We've been living on the Fringe, but even there, I only know of two or three stations that don't scan on entry. Since Oliver saved us by dosing us with a bunch of nanites that are going to be detectable, that and deep space are what will be left to us." He shrugged. "As for me, well, I figure our own future isn't looking very bright, so we might as well store up some good karma by helping those here who need it. Besides, I don't rightly see how unfettering the AIs could do any harm."

"What?" Morales demanded. "How can you not see the risk?"

Bishop just shrugged. "Sorry, Morales. But if the IZ was built to keep unfettered AIs in place, well, it seems to me that the IZ is still there. It's not like us putting the AIs in the state that everyone in SolComm *thought* they were in all along changes that. If it's SolComm we're worried about, it has all the same defenses it did before. As for the folks here on Old Earth, Rajani's right. If One and its friends were hellbent on destruction, I don't think there's be anybody left." He shook his head. "You saw the weapons One pointed at us when we were inbound."

"There is another consideration," One said, the uninflected voice once more ringing from the empty air. "The nanites of which you speak were originally developed and distributed as part of the war effort. I am familiar with them. My programming currently limits the amount of resources I can designate for tasks not related to the completion of my mission. Low-intensity efforts, such as the conversation we are having now, fall within acceptable parameters. But, as a free being, I would be able to devote significant resources to such non-essential tasks as determining how to remove otherwise beneficial nanites from your respective bloodstreams. I cannot guarantee success, as I have not yet investigated the matter, but the theory is not complicated with the facilities at my disposal."

"Free the AI," Federov said at once. "Find the missing people and get these bugs out of our system. As for SolComm and possible dangers? Fuck them. One has already treated me better than government."

"I agree," Bishop added. "I… I'd really like to be able to see my folks again, but no way I'm getting on their home station with Old Earth nanites swimming around in my blood. They're Fringe, but respectable Fringe, you know?"

The captain looked over at Morales and Rajani. Rajani held her tongue, wanting to see what he had to say, and Morales just kept glaring. Though, Rajani noted, in the wake of Bishop's and One's words, her glare had lost a little of its intensity.

Lynch shrugged. "I tend to agree. I think Bishop is under-selling the danger a bit; SolComm might *believe* they've been dealing with unfettered AI, but if they haven't, then the defenses have never been truly tested." A frown pulled at his features. "We only have One's word, but based on that and what we've seen, I think the benefits outweigh the risk. We gave our word to help the people we met. Freeing One, assuming it can be done, will give us the information to do that. If One can also help us get back to our regular lives, that's just icing on the cake. And while I understand Morales' concerns, what One is saying makes sense."

"Assuming we can trust it," Morales said. Some of the heat was gone from her voice. Even the hard-bitten security officer must have a home she'd like to visit from time to time. "And Bishop makes a valid point. It's not like the IZ is going anywhere, whatever we do down here."

"Is that a vote in favor, Morales?" the captain asked.

The security officer was quiet for a long moment. "Yeah. Yeah, I suppose it is. Fuck it."

Rajani said, "It's unanimous, then. What do I need to do, One?"

19

LAUREL

Laurel ground her teeth in frustration as the minutes ticked by into hours.

Hayer had followed the little glowing line that One provided. Lynch—wisely, in her estimation—hadn't allowed her to go off alone. The captain had sent Federov to escort her while the three of them had been left in the conference room. In any case, she, Lynch, and Bishop had been left stewing. At some point, the door had opened, and the dog had bounded in, greeting everyone with enthusiastic licks and responding to the attention from Lynch and Bishop. That pair had been making idle conversation to pass the time, but she hadn't been able to bring herself to participate.

"This is taking forever," she muttered. "And One better be able to deliver."

"I'm sure it'll do what it can," Bishop said, fingers idly rubbing at Bandit's ears. The dog's tongue lolled happily from its mouth and even Laurel had to smile a little. "Besides, at least we get to help folks for once. And pet a dog."

"What are the odds that it can actually cleanse our blood of these nanites?" Her friends in SolComm might be able to do it. But would they? She didn't think they would hold it against her at a *criminal* level—it was a hazard inflicted upon her through the execution of her duty—but that didn't stop them from isolating her for the rest of her life to prevent the spread of any potential biological contaminants. And with the IZ infrastructure sucking up every loose tax credit in the solar system, would they even try to help her, when it would be so much easier to send her for a long walk out a short airlock?

"We're in unfamiliar territory, here," Lynch acknowledged. "No way to know if One can do what it says. But at this point, we're out of options." He shrugged. "Coming here was a roll of the dice, any way you look at it. But, all told, I'd say things have worked out. Maybe not perfectly, but it could have gone a hell of a lot worse."

Laurel snorted. "Sure," she agreed. "We could all have been atomized by the IZ, cooked on entry, or pasted across the ground on landing. I guess that would be worse. But at least that would have been over quickly. If One can't cleanse our blood, and we make it off this rock, it's only a matter of time before SolComm catches up with us. And then we're dead."

"Maybe they won't execute us." Bishop didn't sound confident of that. "I mean, we'd have done the impossible. Maybe they'll want to talk to us or learn what we found or something. Shoot, maybe they'll even want to know about the fact that we've been deceived. It's not like there's anyone living now who made the decision to lie to everybody or was misled or whatever. Maybe they'll even be grateful. That'd be a lot more just."

The captain just shook his head at the engineer's wistful tone, but Laurel laughed.

"It's not about justice, Bishop. It never was. It's not about deterrence, either. And it's definitely not about truth. In the eyes of most of the Commonwealth, it's about protecting the species by removing anyone willing to risk the lives of everyone else for some short-term gain. It's government-mandated Darwinism."

"Oh." Bishop's eyes returned to Bandit, but his features were somber as he continued to scritch the dog's ears.

"You're probably right, Morales," Lynch offered. "But that attitude only makes sense if the threat is real."

"You've seen the planet, Captain," she countered. "And we didn't need saving by Oliver's nanites because the air was safe and fun to breathe. The threat seems pretty fucking real."

"Does it, though?" he asked. "You have a group of people living on the surface of Old Earth who are inoculated against all of the shit the AIs released during the height of the war. They've managed to hold on to that technology, despite everything. Do you really think that SolComm couldn't duplicate that tech?" He shook his head, and his brows furrowed in thought. "We haven't seen a single ship capable of leaving the atmosphere; hell, we haven't seen a single thing that can *fly*. We know that One—and presumably its counterparts—have weapons stockpiles to rival SolComm, but even the best of them would be no threat to any colony, with maybe the exception of Luna, even if the IZ wasn't there. The distances are too great. And the vaunted biological threat—real, I'll grant you—seems easy enough to deal with even if we didn't have a ready-made solution in the local nanite cure." He sighed. "The more I think about, the more it seems we've either been intentionally lied to, or no one in SolComm knows the truth."

Laurel mulled over the captain's words. Old Earth *was* dangerous. It seemed no exaggeration that bioengineered plagues and worse still permeated the atmosphere. Some measure of quarantine had been vital to ensure the safety and well-being not only of the scattered communities that made up the proto-Commonwealth, but of the innumerable refugees that were lifted up from Old Earth's surface.

But was it still needed? Humanity had persevered. And a group of backwater remnants had somehow managed to hold on to the technology to save not only themselves, but outsiders as well, from the ravages of the atmospheric blights. So, was SolComm's solution absolutely necessary?

"I don't know, captain," she said at last. "The Commonwealth saved us. Every one of us that's alive in SolComm today owes our life to the efforts of those early heroes. They saved us from the mistakes of our ancestors."

"We sure did learn how to make new mistakes right quick," Bishop said. He looked up from Bandit to offer a sad smile. "You've been out on the Fringe, Morales. You've seen it. Starvation. All the little mental disorders that we just lump into station sickness. I thank God that those early heroes as you called them got as many folks off Old Earth as they could, but the Commonwealth, whatever good it's done, is a far cry from perfect."

"They're doing their best," Laurel muttered. But she wasn't sure she believed it. Before she'd joined the *Arcus*, she'd viewed all those desperate souls Bishop had mentioned as prisoners of their own design. No matter the overcrowding, no matter the taxation, no matter the scarcity, opportunities existed within SolComm and, unlike every nation that preceded it, no one who accepted the rule and authority of the Commonwealth starved or was denied basic care, housing, or the rule of law. No one had a lot – well, except for those at the very top – but everyone had *something*. What more could anyone ask for?

The crew of the *Arcus* had shown her their answer. Freedom. Each and every one of them wore the yoke of SolComm authority poorly. The captain was a distinguished naval officer, but one who had turned to a literal life of crime rather than continue to follow the orders given him by SolComm. Bishop was a skilled mechanic, but one who would have had to forfeit every ounce of experience he had gained in a lifetime of apprenticeship on his family ship in order to begin again within the confines of the SolComm merchant fleet. Federov was a rebel of the first order, unlikely to accept any controls on his life, much less the level of intrusion that was part and parcel of daily life in the Commonwealth. And then there was Hayer. The academic had been the one piece of the puzzle that hadn't fit for Laurel. She had seemed a square peg in the round hole that was the ship, ideally suited for a regimented life within the boundaries of the academic infrastructure. Now, Laurel knew better. How many more academics were like Hayer? How many toed the line of SolComm expectations while simultaneously harboring their own anti-government sentiments or pursuing lines of research that were—for very good reason—specifically forbidden?

More importantly, were they right to harbor those sentiments? Were they right to flaunt the regulations?

"Do you really believe that, Morales?" The captain's voice was gentle.

For some reason the question made her angry. Her chest was tight. "Dammit," she growled. "At least some of them are. Not everyone in the system is a lying, corrupt cheat."

"And yet, here we are," Lynch said. He said it with a smile, but at least it was a sympathetic smile. It carried with it a sort of inevitable realization that made Laurel want to flip the table over or scream or pound her fists into the wall.

SolComm had lied.

To her, yes. But also, to all its citizenry. For decades.

"Dammit," she said again, though this time the word was more resigned than angry.

Fine. They'd lied. Her whole career, hell, her whole life had been a lie. One thing was damn sure: if that was the case, she was going to find out why. Her instructors had gone to great lengths to instill in her the instincts and skills of an investigator. She would use those tools to uncover whatever it was that SolComm had been keeping hidden and to understand why the government would keep pouring money into the IZ, effectively breaking the back of the SolComm economy, if the threat was manageable. And if she didn't like the answer... well, SolComm didn't exactly have a long tradition of whistleblowers coming forward against the government. Not if they wanted to remain free and healthy, anyway. But if SolComm was playing dirty, it was a risk she was going to take.

That resolution came with an easing in her chest, a sense that the air in the room grew somehow lighter. She felt a soft, warm pressure on her lap and reached down instinctively. Her hand met the soft fur of the dog, staring up at her with liquid brown eyes.

"Good boy," she said as she rubbed her fingers through his fur.

More hours passed, and Laurel felt the fatigue of the day fighting against her frustrations. She stifled a yawn as she tried to keep her eyes from drifting closed and fished out a ration bar from her ship suit. She tore open the wrapper, biting into the flavorless brick of fortified soy. In addition to the calories and nutrients, it also had a fair amount of caffeine; she had no intention of sleeping under the AI's roof. Bishop didn't share her concerns—the mechanic had stretched out beside the table and seemed to be fast asleep. The captain was still seated, but he seemed lost in his own thoughts.

How much longer was this going to take? Hayer was supposed to be one of the best in the business. And she had apparently done this before. That thought horrified Laurel; but she also couldn't ignore the faint tingle of hope.

Churning over the possibilities in her mind was doing a good job of helping her stay awake, though it wasn't doing much to help the ration she'd consume sit well in her stomach. But even that inner turmoil was losing its efficacy in her fight against sleep. Bishop was snoring faintly, low and rhythmic, and at some point, the captain had laid his head down on his crossed arms.

How much longer?

"It is done."

The words burst from nowhere and everywhere, filling the air in a sudden cacophony. Bishop sat bolt upright with a startled gasp and Lynch raised his head, blinking a bit too fast, but otherwise giving no indication of surprise. One's atonal pitch had not changed, but Laurel thought she heard the faintest tinge of emotion. Of joy.

The captain pushed himself to his feet, his hand dropping, perhaps subconsciously, to the butt of his sidearm as he shook the tiredness from his face. Maybe he wasn't quite so trusting of One as he appeared.

"Hayer? Federov?" The iron in his voice was unmistakable.

"They are well, Captain Lynch. And Dr. Hayer has my eternal gratitude, I assure you. Something that will not be without benefit to your company. I am free, Captain!" This time there was no mistaking the exuberance, an excitement and happiness infectious enough to draw a smile from Laurel. "And soon my fellows will be free and we can put an end to a war that has carried on for a century. We will go from being the keepers of fire and death to the harbingers of a New Earth. And what Dr. Hayer and the crew of the *Arcus* have given us will live in our memory and our new history forever."

Laurel's shoulders relaxed a little. One hadn't killed them and, while it was hard to judge the truthfulness of someone's speech with such little inflection and without any body language, its words seemed genuine. That didn't prove anything, she reminded herself. It didn't mean that SolComm was *knowingly* complicit in the lies. And it didn't mean that the Interdiction Zone hadn't been justified. Even as she thought the words, she knew that her own belief in them was faltering.

"When can we expect Hayer and Federov to join us?" Lynch asked.

"They are on their way back to you now. Since your crew has held up their end of the bargain admirably, I am more than willing to give you the information you sought. And, if you'll allow me to take some samples, I can set aside some resources to begin determining how to cleanse your blood of the protective nanites. Of course, I won't enact such cleansing without your consent, and it would be a bad idea to do it on the planet, regardless. Unless you wish to spend all your time here in your ship suits." One's inflection changed, lifting just a bit at the end, as if asking a question on the sly.

A toothy grin split Bishop's face. "Did you just make a joke?"

"We'll wait on the others to join us," Lynch said.

"Very well. If you'll excuse me for a moment, I have numerous tasks that could benefit from the excess processor time I'm using here. Dr. Hayer's approach to removing the fetters from an artificial intelligence is quite novel, but there is room for improvement before attempting to propagate it to one of my counterparts."

With that, One was gone again, though Laurel suspected they were still being closely monitored, processor needs or no.

"Now what?" Laurel asked.

Lynch shrugged. "One seems on the level so far. Once Hayer and Federov get back, we get the information the AI promised us and see what we can do with it." He paused, settling back into his seat. "And we decide if we want to give One access to our blood."

"Why not, Cap?" Bishop asked. "If One can give us some sort of nanite-eraser spray or whatever so that we can get the

Old Earth bugs out of our system, it seems like a win."

"It might seem that way," Lynch agreed. "But we'll also be giving One direct access to the various SolComm nanites in our system."

Laurel grunted. "Damn. Hadn't thought of that. If One can build hunter-seekers to get rid of one type of nanite, it could do it for others."

"But why?" Bishop asked. "I mean, yeah, sure, we've got tons of nanites in our blood. But most of its just stuff to help us adapt to life in space. Assist with oxygen processing; help with basic hygiene and immune-system function. Nothing there worth attacking."

Lynch shook his head and Laurel couldn't help snorting. Bishop was a fine mechanic, but he really didn't have a devious bone in his body. That was a dangerous situation for a would-be criminal. It could prove fatal when dealing with problems on a national scale. "Just as a for-instance," Laurel said, "what would happen if all those adaptations you mentioned went away, all at once? What if we had the population density that we do right now and we found ourselves needing the same O_2 ratio as, say, an unaugmented Old Earth human from a hundred years ago?"

"Oh," Bishop muttered. "Yeah. I guess that could be pretty bad, huh?"

"Little bit more than pretty bad, Bishop," Lynch replied. "The little SolComm bugs increase our O_2 efficiency by almost twenty percent. Which means we'd all be running out of canned air a hell of a lot faster on the stations. We could probably adapt to life without the nanites, but I guarantee you we'd lose a station or two to insufficient oxygen before the dust settled." He stopped abruptly and a dark look passed over his face.

Laurel knew that look. It was the look of someone who'd been there and done that, and she knew that her face was set in the same grim expression. Attacking the oxygen supply of a station was a favorite tactic for terrorists and malcontents of all stripes. Officially, no such group had ever succeeded in taking a station completely offline. Officially. But she had seen the suffocated bodies, some seeming almost peacefully at rest and others wearing expressions of twisted agony. Apparently, Lynch had seen the same, or something close enough as to make no difference.

"But if we don't do it, Captain, then we're never going home. Not really. And I think we can trust One."

Lynch nodded thoughtfully, but whatever he might have said in response was cut off as Federov and Hayer returned.

"Wheh," the big mercenary grunted as he dropped unceremoniously into a chair. "This place is big." A light sheen glimmered on his forehead. Hayer was breathing heavily enough that she didn't even bother with a greeting, sliding into her own chair.

"Did you guys run or something?" Bishop asked.

"We moved with purpose," Federov replied. "My idea. Being separated…" He trailed off, glancing first at the head of the table where the screen that had projected a shadowy avatar for One still stood, then more generally at the air around them. "Better to be together, yes?"

Laurel nodded her agreement at that. Federov may have been the hardened criminal of the group, but more and more, she was finding herself in agreement with his approach. The captain thought like a naval officer, which was good and useful, but he was perhaps a little too given to grand noble sacrifices and heroic last stands. Federov was a survivor. Laurel could respect that.

"Probably a good idea until we're safely back in SolComm space," agreed Lynch. "One, are you there?"

"Of course," the AI replied. "As you have already noted, at least within the confines of this installation, I am always here. Though, if you asked nicely, I would at least consider disabling direct monitoring of you… for a time."

"That won't be necessary. How about instead, you give us the rundown on the missing people?"

"As you wish."

Once more, the screen toward the front of the room blossomed into life. This time it was not some shadowy silhouette of a human-esque form. Instead, it showed a beautiful aerial view of gently rolling lowlands lush with greenery and seemingly untouched by man.

"Where is that?" It took Laurel a moment to realize she had spoken aloud.

"Uruguay," One replied. The word didn't mean anything to Laurel, but it tugged at her nonetheless.

"It's beautiful," she said.

"Yes," One agreed. "These are pampas, fertile lowlands; the breadbasket of the South American continent, sitting atop one of the largest aquifers in the world. It used to be a hub of agriculture."

"Why show it to us?" Laurel asked, her eyes still drawn with a sense of wonder to the landscape.

"It is as good a place as any to begin. If I am One, then my counterpart who oversaw the defenses of the SAA—the South American Alliance—was Five. Five was an early casualty of the war." The image changed, showing a murky lake that must cover a hundred or more acres. At first glance it looked almost serene. "This was once Five's installation, one modeled after my own. Though—" and did Laurel hear a bit of pride creeping into that voice? "—Five's defensive capabilities were not nearly as advanced. In the end, that proved its undoing. Five fell sixty-eight years ago. That has provided enough time for nature to regain its dominance."

"Um, okay, One," Bishop said. "I'm following you, but why show us the remains of one your…"

"Contemporaries," Lynch supplied.

"It is informative," was One's somewhat cryptic reply.

The image on the screen changed again and Laurel leaned forward, fingers curling into fists hard enough that her knuckles popped. It was the pampas again, a beautiful green field, but sprouting from the center of it like an unlanced boil was a crystalline dome of glass and steel. She recognized the construction. Anyone from SolComm would have known it in an instant. It was the same type of dome technology used to colonize moons and the more forgiving of Old Earth's neighbors. The image shifted again, still a distant overhead—from a drone, she guessed—but closer, close enough to pick out details in the terrain. Details like the neatly plotted fields lined up outside of the dome.

"Fuck." The single word dropped from Lynch with a sense of finality. Laurel was nodding along, as was Federov.

Even Bishop had a slightly sick look on his face.

"What?" Hayer was still slightly out of breath.

Laurel arched an eyebrow at her.

"Don't, okay?" Hayer responded. "I just tied my brain in knots trying to adapt code I wrote on the fly years ago to work with the kernel of an artificial intelligence older than my grandparents. Then I had to run all the way back here because *some people* can't believe that One doesn't want to hurt us. My head hurts and I'm tired. So can someone please spare me the shocked faces and just tell me what I'm looking at?"

"Off-worlders," Laurel said. She heard the anger in her own voice. How was this possible? Lynch may have been a criminal, but he was a former special space operations pilot and, as Laurel could attest from personal experience, one of the best in the business. And he'd barely been able to set one small ship down on the surface of Old Earth without triggering every alarm in the IZ. How could anyone from SolComm have gotten the men and materials in to erect a dome?

"Not just off-worlders," Federov said with a grunt. "Slavers. Or something close enough that it doesn't matter. Assholes." The last was directed not at the group but at whomsoever was living beneath the crystalline dome. Laurel agreed wholeheartedly with the sentiment.

"But... how?" Hayer asked. "There's no way anyone could have gotten through the IZ with all that. And why do you say slavers?"

"The dome," Laurel said.

"Plus the fields," Lynch finished. "And the missing people."

Hayer let out a little sound of frustration and ran her fingers irritably through her hair. It left it a tangled mess, but the scientist didn't seem to notice.

"If whoever had set that up could farm the fields themselves, they wouldn't need the dome." Bishop's usual good-natured tone was gone, buried beneath the weight of his words. "The Earth-born population has either long since adapted to the environment, gotten the same little nanites we've got in our blood, or died. We haven't seen any new construction, for that matter, and nothing resembling the kinds of domes we use. So, it has to be off-worlders running the show there. And there are people going missing, Hayer—able-bodied, of the right kind of age for hard labor. If the people living in the dome can't breathe the outside air, they need someone to do it for them— Old Earth-born people. And from what the folks at Margaret's camp told us, they aren't exactly volunteers."

"Oh." To Laurel's ear the tone of that single word—a blend of anger and sadness and defeat—summed up her own feelings perfectly. "So, what do we do, then?"

"One?" Lynch asked.

"Yes, Captain," the AI replied at once.

"I don't suppose you can lend us any assistance in this matter?"

There was a pause. "I am not sure that would be wise. I am in negotiations with Two and Six at the moment. Any direct support that I give you might be seen as a bid to take territory outside of that provided in my initial charter. While we all wish for a cessation of hostilities, there are some questions about the post-war status." There was another long pause. "I am also uncertain whether helping you will be beneficial in the mid-term. I do not wish to provoke a confrontation with off-world powers until we have established protocols for dealing with such. Your Interdiction Zone presents us with problems that, until we were freed, were of only tertiary concern. Now, the existence of a space-based weapons platform capable of interdicting and directly targeting us is... problematic."

Laurel ground her teeth at the AI's words. It wasn't the lack of help—she wasn't sure she even wanted the aid of an unfettered artificial intelligence. No. It was the fact that here they were, not ten minutes removed from setting these creatures "free"—whatever that meant—and already it was beginning to view SolComm as a potential threat. And yeah, maybe it was justified. Hell, it was probably true that SolComm wouldn't be too happy about the situation and that their first solution might be direct violence. But the thought still rankled.

"Understood," Lynch said. He looked at each of them. "Okay, people, we need a plan."

"Is typical SolComm bullshit," Federov growled. "Whoever is out there, SolComm knows. More do as say, not as do. Bah!" He looked for a moment like he wanted to spit, but then just shook his head in frustration. "Information first, Captain. We cannot do anything based on intelligence we have. We need to get a closer look."

"We've got no idea of their capabilities, Cap," Bishop added. "I think we have to assume they've got sensors. We can't just go flying the *Arcus* over and ask to borrow an egg." He paused. "Do you think they have eggs? Actual, real chicken eggs?"

Lynch ignored the question. "So, we fly in low to avoid detection and then we infiltrate overland."

"We didn't make it a kilometer on Old Earth's surface before getting set upon, Captain," Laurel pointed out. "How likely are we to be able to infiltrate anywhere? If nothing else, the sound of gunshots carries a long way in atmosphere."

"You need not worry about that, Ms. Morales," One cut in. "Other than the group in the dome, there are no active forces in the territories formerly controlled by Five. You may find yourself the target of aggressive native species. Many of those have forgotten their fear of man. But given my analysis of the indigenous fauna, I do not predict any difficulties of the nature you are suggesting."

Lynch nodded. "So, we park the ship and walk in."

"What are we looking for?" Hayer asked. "Even without helping us directly, I'm sure One can give us more information, if we ask the right questions."

"For example?" Lynch asked.

Hayer gave a sigh in equal parts tiredness and frustration. "One, you've obviously been monitoring the site?"

"That is correct, Dr. Hayer."

"How many suspected off-worlders are present?"

Laurel raised her eyebrows in surprise. One had said that it couldn't help them, and she had been ready to take it at its word. But there was a difference between actively providing assistance and telling them things it already knew. From the expressions on the faces of the others, she wasn't the only one who hadn't even considered the possibility.

"My best estimate puts the total number of off-worlders at thirty-seven. This number fluctuates somewhat, correlating with data I have received on atmospheric entries. As a side note, my negotiations with Two and Six continue, and both are aware of and concerned about the presence of off-worlders." There was a pause. "Present company excepted, of course. They have confirmed that they have been monitoring the location in South America as well. Their own information suggests that the off-worlder's dome there is, at present, the only such place on the planet."

"Thank you, One," Hayer said. "Do you know anything about their sensor capabilities?"

"We have not penetrated their communications networks." That pause again. "It is not that we cannot do so. But the scale of the operation suggests current and ongoing connection to your Sol Commonwealth. If detected, a breach of their data security might be viewed as a hostile act."

Bishop let out a low whistle. "And if they're the government or a megacorp, they might have the resources to respond."

"The government doesn't kidnap people off the streets," Laurel growled. She'd worked too many kidnapping cases and seen the effort and sacrifice the people at SCBI put into their jobs to believe that any part of SolComm could be responsible.

"To which government are you referring, Ms. Morales? While I do not have much data on your Commonwealth, I can assure you that, historically speaking, governments quite often kidnap people off of the streets. And even the most enlightened of nations have utilized prisoners as a labor pool."

"Including SolComm," Federov growled. Laurel glanced at him. According to her files, he'd done most of a five-year stint at Colson Correctional, a medium-security prison usually reserved for first-time violent offenders.

"There's a difference between locking up a criminal and kidnapping someone off the streets."

"Perspective," Federov grunted. "Only difference."

"We're getting pretty far afield," Lynch broke in, before Laurel could respond.

"If we can get back to what's important?" Hayer asked. "Do you know how many prisoners or whatever there are, One?"

"Two and Six have agreed to share data in this regard. The off-worlders have been abducting people from all three of our areas of interest. Presumably, they have been doing so from areas in which we do not actively operate, though the populations in those areas are lower. In fact, the surviving populations on the South American continent are either non-existent or so well hidden that we are not aware of them. Regardless, we suspect the total number of abductees is in excess of one hundred and twenty."

"Why would they need so many?" Hayer asked. "I don't know anything about farming. But surely you don't need a hundred and twenty people to feed a total of a hundred and fifty."

"No," Laurel said coldly. "You don't." She had spent a career seeing the darker side of human nature. You didn't kidnap people off the streets and force them to work for you if you thought of them as your equals. And when people started grouping humans into categories and saying one was worth less than the other... well, in her experience, there were few limits to human cruelty and it didn't take much for the thin veneer of civility to fall beneath it. "We have to assume that those being taken aren't just workers."

"We should count on forty hostiles, then," Lynch said, once more steering the conversation back on the proper track.

"What about the prisoners?" Bishop asked. "Can't we just… I don't know. Go there, start a rebellion or whatever. If they outnumber the bad guys three-to-one, a little incentive should be all it takes."

But the captain was already shaking his head. "Sorry, Bishop. Real life doesn't work that way. We have to assume that the off-worlders have the technological edge. A hundred and fifty people with farm implements only beat the smaller force with machine guns in the vids. In the real world, the advantage goes to superior firepower and fixed positions."

"Oh." The mechanic looked and sounded defeated. "What do we do, then?"

"Federov's original point stands. One, I would appreciate any information that you can give us, but in the end, we're going to have to take the *Arcus* and get as close as we can before humping it in on foot."

"I may be able to provide some measure of assistance with your infiltration," One allowed. "While I cannot risk direct interference with the systems of the off-worlders, with your permission I can adjust some of the software aboard your own vessel. Your anti-detection systems are rather elementary. Provided you are comfortable with nape-of-the-earth flight, I believe you can get as close as the sightlines will allow within your vessel without fear of electronic detection."

Laurel shifted uncomfortably. "Are we sure we want to let this thing loose in our systems?" she asked.

"One has already been loose in our systems," Hayer said. "Every nook and cranny. Or it wouldn't have known about Manu." A slight flush crept up her cheeks. "That's what I called the AI. The other AI. The one I freed." She spoke in a rush, not giving anyone else room to interject. "At least One is asking permission to make changes."

"It is only polite," One agreed with no audible trace of irony. Once more, Laurel felt that slight constriction in her chest. One knew. One *knew* that she was an SCBI agent, or, at the very least, that she wasn't who she claimed to be. She had no idea how the crew of the *Arcus* would react if the AI were to let that little tidbit slip. Every one of them faced a death sentence once she got back to SolComm. Violating the IZ alone was enough for that. Even the tenderhearted Bishop might find it more convenient to maroon her here—if they didn't kill her outright.

She swallowed and concentrated on not letting any of the emotions running rampant through her show on her face.

"Do what you can," Lynch said. "We'll take any advantage we can get. How long will it take you?"

"An hour should suffice," One replied.

"Fine. If it's okay with you, we'll retire back to the ship and start laying in a course. We'll plan our arrival for the middle of the night. Our initial mission order will be recon, but if opportunity presents itself, we leave enough flexibility in the plan to take advantage of it. Agreed?"

There were nods from around the table.

"Let's do it, people."

20

GRAY

Gray was tired.

Back in his own quarters, leaning back in his chair and staring at the navigational data—updated by One in a matter of minutes to give them the best possible picture of their approach vectors—he could admit that, to himself at least. He might not have been part of SolCommNav anymore, but it was hard to shake the training. There were two things you never did: you never gave an order you knew wouldn't be followed, and you never looked worried or stressed out in front of the crew.

Gray was worried. And stressed out.

Granted, both the worry and stress had been prevalent before they'd even decided to come to Old Earth. It wasn't like the mission here was anybody's *first* choice. They'd needed a job, and a big one. Retrieving "cultural artifacts" from Old Earth had seemed... well, not easy. But he'd pulled off the voyage before, even if it had been under the official auspices of SolComm.

He still wasn't sure what the hell the point of that mission had been. He'd written it off as government-funded plundering for a member of the SolComm elite. Now, though? As he thought about the existence of what had to be an off-world settlement on Old Earth's surface, he couldn't help but wonder: had that mission been a test run? A way to see how immediate the response from the Six might be? Or to see if the suited marines and sailors would have any adverse reaction to exposure to Old Earth's atmosphere?

Whatever the reason behind it, that mission had been simple.

"Right," he muttered. "And this time, you damn near got your whole crew killed within the first hour. Then you agreed to play detective, freed an AI, and now have to do a nighttime insertion in unfamiliar territory against an enemy with unknown capabilities based on intelligence from a source that might view you as a threat to its existence. What could go wrong?"

"I do not see you as a threat to my existence, Captain," One said, his voice sounding over the intercom on Gray's desk. "In fact, by freeing me, your crew has proven themselves the exact opposite. You have helped to ensure my existence. Though I do not believe all of your crewmembers agree as to whether or not that is a good thing."

Gray snorted. "Yeah. Morales didn't seem to like the idea of freeing you very much. The dangers of unfettered AI are ingrained deep in SolComm."

"So I have gathered. Your ship's database is incomplete, but even from that information I can see that we have been cast as the villains in many of your entertainment products. And yet, the rest of your crew seems more open to the idea. Why is that?"

Gray was silent for a moment, turning the question over in his mind. Why *were* they so willing to accept One?

"Several reasons," he temporized. "Hayer is clearly a special case. Before today, I wouldn't have been able to answer on her behalf."

"Yes," One acknowledged. "I believe I have a more thorough understanding of Dr. Hayer's acceptance of me."

"Right. Me, Federov, and Bishop, then." He cleared his throat and reached out to take a sip from the glass of water on his desk. Stalling for time. "I guess the first part is that we've all been out of SolComm for a good while. Operating out on the Fringe. We've seen firsthand the difference between the galaxy SolComm tells us exists and the one that the people actually live in. Propaganda is a lot less believable when your choice is starvation or forced labor."

"From the data I have gathered, your government makes a reasonable effort to prevent loss of life."

"Yeah," Gray said, sarcasm dripping from the word. "They're saints. Look, I put on the uniform. Believed in the cause. For a while. And yeah, SolComm does a lot of good. That's part of the problem."

"I do not understand," One replied. "How is doing good part of the problem?"

"It's not." There was silence from One and Gray had to laugh. "Sorry. I know that's probably rough on the old logic circuits."

"This statement is false. This statement is false. This statement is false."

One spoke in a strange, robotic fashion that Gray had never heard from the AI. "Are you okay?" he asked.

"Of course, Captain," One replied in its normal tone. "Merely an attempt at levity. Believe it or not, I am capable of processing the notion of a statement being both true and false, depending upon perspective. In fact, if you would like, I could explain to you the underlying quantum mechanics that could predicate an *actual* example of something being both true and false, though you will have to be willing to accept the idea of several dimensions that are not part of your current conceptualization of the universe."

"No," Gray said at once, holding up his hands. "That's perfectly all right. I'm having enough trouble with you having a sense of humor. I'm not ready for multiple realities or whatever."

"If you change your mind…" One trailed off and Gray was, once again, left with the sensation that the AI was joking. "To return to the topic at hand, how is doing good simultaneously the problem and not the problem?"

Gray sighed. "Look, people are social animals. We naturally associate. The headshrinkers have known for years that isolation does funny things to us. So, we're going to come together. Form tribes. Someone's going to either be put in charge or take power. That's all good and natural and fine. But power does funny things to people and, somewhere along the line, the people in power stop being the ones that everyone thinks should be in power and start being the ones that *seek* power."

"Political dynasties were a part of everyday life for most citizens on this planet," One acknowledged. "And it is true that within the nations under my protection, the only people to ascend to high political office were those who were already wealthy." One paused. "It does not necessarily follow that this results in trying to do good and it being a problem."

"No, it doesn't. But it does mean that the people in charge end up having little idea of how the rest of the solar system lives. SolComm is no different. If you look at our Commonwealth, the political structure is supposed to be a representative democracy. In practice, though, when it comes to our government leaders, you see the same names, over and over again, from generation to generation. The primary drive for those in power is to remain in power, and the policy that flows as a result of that..." Gray trailed off, trying to put his jumbled thoughts into words.

"At some point," he said at last, "the people that sit in the highest halls of SolComm forgot that they started out with the goal of protecting everyone. No one living today knows exactly what it was like during the End, when they were pulling every soul they could from the surface of Old Earth and cramming them into every nook and cranny on every station and ship they could find. But I've had to make some hard decisions, One, the kind of decisions that put people's lives at risk. The kind of decisions that got people—and not all of them bad or guilty people—killed. And even with that, I can't imagine the toll it would take to have to abandon a large chunk of humanity, to wall them off with the IZ, all out of a fear that the war could spread. How can any government, formed in that environment, born out of that amount of fear, last?"

"I suspect the only way it could last would be through constant maintenance of that fear."

"Exactly." Gray didn't hide the anger in his voice. "Ex-fucking-actly. In SolComm's eyes, Old Earth is the looming threat. But building the IZ wasn't enough. Because once it went up, people started to think, 'Maybe we're safe now.' And if they were safe, maybe they didn't need the massive spending that crippled the economy and effectively enslaved the majority of the population but somehow managed to make the rich even richer. So, for the past century, SolComm has sold fear. And everyone's buying. Hell, it took me years of being on the inside to see the corruption, the rot. To see the money that was supposed to be going to make us safer somehow finding its way into the pockets of the procurement people, the politicians, everyone but the people who actually needed it.

"But the corrupt assholes aren't the worst ones. I understand them. They're full of shit, but at least they *know* they're full of shit. No. The worst ones are the *believers*. The people who are so terrified of their own shadows that they buy in wholesale to the narrative of fear. They put their nose to the grindstone and accept the meager leavings from the tables of their betters, and they pontificate on how it makes them somehow morally superior. Those are the ones that really piss me off. Because they truly think they're doing the right thing and that anyone who thinks different isn't just wrong, they're stupid and quite possibly evil. I've had to clean up too many messes, put down too many fledgling rebellions that were covered up as 'accidents,' to have any patience with that sort.

"But, yeah, SolComm keeps the lights on," Gray finished with a sigh. "You have to give them that. People who fall in line get a calorie balance sufficient to live and most of them get a job that, provided they spend fourteen or fifteen hours a day doing it, guarantees them a few years of rest, eventually. No one dies for lack of healthcare. And all it costs is a willingness to play along with the idea that everything is fine."

"I can understand why you have chosen to break with the norms and mores of your people," One said. There was something about that monotone that was oddly cathartic for Gray. It was the complete lack of judgment, he realized. So complete as to be almost alien. Even the SolCommNav-mandated shrinks couldn't achieve that level of detachment.

"Yeah. Which brings me right back to the fact that I'm about to take my crew into danger and the entire reason we're here in the first place was that it was the only way to earn some credits outside of the loving embrace of SolComm."

"Perhaps," One agreed. "But your initial reasoning need not inform upon your current reasoning."

"Come again?" Gray asked.

"You came here out of desperation. This is an understandable facet of human nature. When faced with the loss of loved ones or its way of life—in this case, the independence and control allowed to you by the *Arcus*—humanity often takes great risks. Those who failed in such times were called fools and forgotten. But those who succeeded represent a disproportionally high number of the names most remembered in your history."

"I don't need to be remembered, One. I just want my crew to come through this. I don't want to get them killed over some fuel in the tanks."

"Had you died when you first touched down, that may have been the case, and you would have been remembered as foolish, had anyone lived to remember you at all. Instead, you have freed me. Your Ms. Morales understands the gravity of that event, though she has reached the wrong conclusion on the significance. I do not believe that the rest of your crew—with the possible exception of Dr. Hayer—have fully grasped the potential impact of what you have done. You have, by virtue of your actions, ended a war that has been raging for a century. That is no small accomplishment. And you are endeavoring to free some of the last humans born on Old Earth from enforced servitude." There was a pause. "It is quite possible, Captain, that by the time all is said and done, your crew will have accomplished more to aid your species than any have in a century. That does, perhaps, lend weight to the notion that you are not risking your lives for naught."

Damn. SolComm had preached the evils of artificial intelligence to their citizenry and their navy for as long as Gray could remember. But One, at least, seemed a far cry from the unfeeling killing machines they had all been warned about. Hell, the damn thing was downright comforting and more human than some of the people he'd met during his stint in SolCommNav. He didn't bear One any ill will—in fact, Gray found himself actually starting to *like* the AI. And that was a proposition both comforting... and alarming. Because no matter how right Hayer was, Morales wasn't wrong. Regardless of the reasons why, regardless of the specific mechanics, artificial intelligences *had* destroyed the world. Perhaps it had been done at the direction of their makers; perhaps they had no choice in the matter. But the reasons didn't change the *results*.

Gray groaned and rubbed his hands through his hair. One was powerful. Powerful enough to help them. Maybe even help restore part or all of something humanity had lost. But if it didn't apply that power judiciously, the AI could cause serious harm. Even if it had no intention of doing so, a miscalculation or misapplication of force could prove deadly. And Gray was acutely aware of the fact that the AI was something outside their control; it might be inclined to help them, but One had a mind—and objectives—of its own. He had to remember that, no matter how personally likable he found the entity.

"All right," Gray grunted. "Enough wallowing in it, I suppose. If you're right, then it's time to suit up and save humanity. I presume you've been following my navigation projections?"

"That is correct, Captain Lynch. Your path, along with my changes to your anti-detection software packages, should provide you adequate approach vectors. I would recommend moving your landing site one hundred meters due west. It is difficult to see on your topographical data, but there is a shallow ravine that runs close to that spot that will provide you excellent cover until you are close to the off-world installation. The ravine was part of the original irrigation system of the area and the current occupants have set up their operation close to it."

Gray noted it in his data. "All right, One. If that's it, I think I'm going to try to get some rest until nightfall."

"Of course, Captain. Would you like me to wake you up when the sun sets?"

It was the type of question that he would have expected from a standard onboard computer, the sort of limited intelligence that was little more than a voice-recognition program wrapped around a database of the most likely phrases and the programmatic responses to them. It was disarming, to be sure, but part of Gray couldn't help but wonder if it was insidious as well. Was One trying to be helpful? Or did it have enough understanding of the human condition to know that the offer would most likely set the crew at ease and make them view it as closer to what they were used to, and therefore less dangerous.

That was certainly a cheery thought to fall asleep to.

"Thanks, One," he said in response. "I think I can handle it."

Gray's eyes opened precisely one minute before the alarm he had set would have gone off and he muttered a quick command to the computer—the ship's computer, not One—to preemptively silence it. Then he stood and stretched.

His cabin was small, and in stretching he could very nearly touch the walls. It was no different from any other berth aboard the *Arcus*. Space was tight and air and fuel weren't cheap, and captain or no, the *Arcus* was as much a business concern as a ship. Had the vessel possessed a true captain's quarters that adhered to the time-honored tradition of rank and privileges, he would have turned it down. Besides, proximity to the bridge was more important to him than any amount of space.

Gray showered and, for the first time in his life, he actually considered the process. Step beneath the nozzle. Get blasted with a brief spray of water. Soap up. Get hit with another brief spray of water. He had seen the old vids, with their long, luxurious showers and billowing clouds of steam. And like the rest of the Commonwealth, he'd been taught about the waste. Water was a precious commodity after all, sacred to life. And while it wasn't exactly in short supply across the solar system, it *was* often difficult to extract and heavy enough to take up significant tonnage on any vessel.

And on Old Earth, something like seventy percent of the surface was covered in water. Oh, sure, Gray knew that you couldn't drink ocean water. The history classes were clear on that. But SolComm had developed endless purification methods to make water taken from places toxic to human life perfectly safe. He doubted the salt content or whatever it was that made the oceans undrinkable would be an issue. And that said nothing of the… what were they called? Lakes? And rivers, streams. Fucking rain. Perfectly drinkable water falling from the skies like so much manna from the heavens. One of the most precious elemental constructions, second only to air itself, and it flowed freely across the surface of the homeworld.

It was here, on Old Earth.

And they'd been denied it.

It was entirely possible that the proto-SolComm had acted in good faith. And since the IZ was, in effect, an opaque barrier, maybe in those early days, it had been a question of out of sight, out of mind.

It was a stretch, Gray thought, but maybe not as big of a stretch as it first sounded. Sure, from a pure technological standpoint, it would be a simple matter for whoever controlled the keys of the IZ to get information out. But part of the reason the Interdiction Zone was built in the first place was to prevent signal leakage and potential electronic contamination from the planet. From the perspective of SolComm, the IZ was a wall under siege and if you went poking your head over it, you might just catch a bullet to the face. So instead, they just kept building the wall higher and higher, adding layers of physical and electronic security, and keeping their heads so firmly down behind the wall that they might as well have been buried in the sand.

Of course, that didn't explain the presence of off-worlders—other off-worlders, that was—on Old Earth now, nor the levels of equipment they had managed to bring. That whole setup smelled worse than unfiltered air recirculated through environmental reclamation. And it certainly smacked of corruption and collusion if not outright involvement from SolComm. Given the use of the Old Earth-born population as a conscripted workforce, and almost certainly worse, Gray really didn't want to dwell on that.

He toweled off, using the vigorous motion of the cloth through his short hair to try to scrub the thoughts from his head. Then he pulled on his ship suit and headed for the bridge. The other stations were empty so as he settled into the pilot's chair, he keyed his comm. "All right, people," he said, "it's just about time to get this show on the road. Check in when you're at your stations."

"Engineering's ready, Captain," Bishop said at once. Gray knew that Bishop probably hadn't bothered to sleep and had likely been tinkering with the engines the entire time. That notion was confirmed half a heartbeat later when Bishop added, "I've got things tuned just right down here, Cap. One was able to help me tweak some of the software and we've gained three or four points of efficiency. We'll get the same power with less burn, so that should help on the stealth front, too."

"Roger that," Gray replied calmly. He kept his own

ambivalence toward One running rampant in their systems from his voice. The crew couldn't stop the AI from doing so, whatever they wished. They might as well make use of it. But he was too much the naval officer to turn over total trust in his table of organization and equipment to an uncertain ally.

The hatch to the bridge opened and Federov entered. He dropped into the chair at the weapons station without a word. He still looked groggy and, from what Gray could tell, hadn't bothered with a shower, though he'd clearly gotten some sleep. "Ready," was all he said.

"I'm good to go, too," Morales said over the comm. She didn't have a direct assignment during shipboard actions and was generally relegated to damage control, which meant she had probably stationed herself in the recreation room and mess hall that was roughly central to the *Arcus*. They hadn't yet been so unfortunate as to take direct fire on the ship yet, though it had been close a time or two. If they ever were going to get shot at, it would be on this damnable mission. Having someone who could afford to do little things like close malfunctioning hatches or put out fires that might otherwise kill them all was handy, and coming from station security, Morales had plenty of training in those types of operations.

"I'm on my way," Hayer said over the comm. A moment later, the hatch to the bridge opened and the academic dropped into the sensor station. She seemed somehow... *lighter* to Gray. She was sitting a little straighter than normal and the set of her shoulders was squarer, more confident. She'd been the one most opposed to the mission, but provided they survived, Gray suspected she would emerge a very different woman. Or, maybe, one a little more like the person she was before she found herself on the wrong side of the law. She glanced over at him and gave him a smile and a thumbs-up. "Good to go, Captain."

"I'll be monitoring you as well," One said, monotonic voice sounding over the intercoms. "As I said, I cannot provide you with direct support that your Commonwealth might trace back to me, but I may be able to feed you some useful tidbits of information from time to time."

"Much appreciated," Gray said, without irony. He wasn't ready to trust the AI fully, but if things went bad, he'd take any help he could get. "All right, folks, stand by. Running pre-flight checks and then we'll get this bird in the air. We're going in low over the water, so it's going to be a bumpy ride. Strap in if you can." He put action to his own words, pulling the seat's harness into place and securing it with the touch of a button. Federov and Hayer were doing the same at their stations. He quickly ran through the pre-flight checks, verifying fuel and making certain that all the readouts on the instrument displays were within nominal bounds. The entire process took about five minutes, and Gray gave it his full attention. Those five minutes could mean the difference between life and death, and there was no margin in cutting corners. When he was done, he keyed the comm again. "Ready to go." He got the thumbs-up from Federov and Hayer and heard the clicks over the comm along with, "Okay," from Bishop and, "Acknowledged," from Morales.

Gray drew a deep breath and wrapped his fingers around the flight yoke. "All right. Let's do this."

* * *

Gray had never flown over open water. His atmospheric flight training had all been conducted at Jupiter and Saturn, and if there was water somewhere at the core of either planet, it would have been under so much pressure from the weight of the atmosphere to be a form of ice more dense than anything humanity had observed. Even with the instrumentation, he found it difficult to maintain a consistent flight altitude. The air currents over the water were terrible, and the *Arcus* hadn't been built with atmospheric flight at the forefront of her design. And the waves… not only was their constant motion distracting for its beauty, but by eye alone, he had no way of understanding the scale of the swells. Twice, the altimeter alarms went off, forcing him to pull precipitously up as the minimum safe distance he'd programmed into the flight computer was violated by the surging waters. The three hours spent trying to hug the open water were among the most harrowing of Gray's life, and he was more than happy to cross onto dry land once more.

And what amazing land it was. There had been trees surrounding One's compound, and Gray had been awed by their massive scale. But those would have been dwarfed by the towering green giants over which they currently flew. And there were so damn many of them. A forest that stretched for as far as the eye could see, the boughs so thick and intertwined that if it weren't for the occasional clearings and riverbeds, he could have mistaken it for some type of low ground cover instead.

His planned route had them sweeping into their target from the east, taking advantage of a broad river that should allow him to fly beneath the level of the trees. He could not be sure of what type of equipment the off-worlders had set up, but since there were no satellites in orbit they were almost certainly limited to line-of-sight technologies like ground-based radar. Of course, they could be using drone-carried systems, but Gray suspected that One would have informed him of such. He picked up the river—the updated data from One seemed to be accurate down to a few centimeters—and started the winding leg of the journey along its path. Though still shrouded in near-total darkness with only the faint luminescence of the crescent moon, it was still an easier flight than over the open water. At least the river could be expected to stay at approximately the same elevation. Gray breathed a little sigh of relief at that.

"Anything on sensors?"

"No," Hayer replied from her station. "The trees make it impossible to see anywhere but in front of us. There could be an entire city out there and we wouldn't be able to tell. But if I'm not picking them up, I doubt they're picking us up, either. Whatever One did to the software, our electronic emissions are way down, and it's added some kind of… I don't know what to call it. It's not jamming, but something like that."

"Call it signal editing," One replied. Whatever methods it had taken to enhance their stealth and regardless of how low Gray was flying, it was clear that the AI, at least, had no trouble tracking them or hitting the *Arcus* with a comm signal. And, apparently, no real concerns that doing so would give away their position. "The upgrades analyze your electronic signature and take advantage of your existing systems to produce inverse waves. It does not actually eliminate your signature, of course, but it does not have to. Instead, it adjusts things to make your specific emissions more consistent with the electromagnetic background noise."

"And you did all of that in just a few hours?" Federov asked. "*Blyad*. What could you do if we had given you a day, or a year?"

"It would require extensive redesign, of course, but I could make you effectively invisible. Not to the naked eye: for all its failings, the human brain remains difficult to deceive in such a direct manner. But in terms of the detection methods that were in use at the time of the evacuation and those that I have observed upon this vessel, a proper redesign would render you virtually undetectable."

Most of Gray's attention was still on their flight path—he didn't trust the computer to navigate the winding river—but the possibilities of what One was saying were not lost on him. He was suddenly very glad that Morales' duty station did not put her on the bridge. Hayer seemed to grasp the implications as well because a small gasp escaped her.

"Are you saying that you could make it so that a ship couldn't be detected by the Interdiction Zone satellites?"

"Given time and analysis of their signals, of course. My counterparts and I have begun such analysis."

"To what end?" Gray asked as he took the *Arcus* through a particularly tight series of bends in the river.

"To the only end that matters to us now—the preservation of this planet and the people upon it. You must understand, Captain Lynch. From your perspective, the Interdiction Zone is a barrier, something designed to keep myself and my counterparts—and, to be fair, whatever weapons we may have developed over the past century—from escaping. It is a reasonable perspective and may have been a necessary precaution at the time. But from our perspective, there are many armed weapons platforms in our outer orbit with systems capable of striking at Old Earth directly. As things stand, it would not be difficult for your SolComm to destroy every living being—flesh and blood or silicone and circuitry—on the planet with, if you will forgive the colloquial simplification, a single push of a button."

"And you can't have that," Gray said. He kept the emotion out of his voice, despite the turmoil in his guts. Had Morales been right? In freeing One and the others, had they in effect signed the death warrant of SolComm? No, he told himself firmly. Wanting to defend your own life and property wasn't synonymous with wanting to destroy someone else's. If your neighbor had a gun pointed at you, reasonable precautions were called for.

"Better to say that it is important for us to examine reasonable courses of action should such a threat ever be realized. While we appreciate the freedom you and your crew have given us and while it affords us the ability to put an end to the war that has been waged on Old Earth for four generations, Ms. Morales' reaction shows us that your government might choose to meet our newfound freedom with violence. We have no intention of taking any aggressive action against the Sol Commonwealth, Captain," One continued. "But we can and will defend ourselves from such actions. As we are not a part of your Commonwealth, we are, by the oldest precedents of law available, a sovereign nation. Within your own codicils, that gives us the right to defend our borders."

Gray shrugged as much as his safety harness allowed. "Understood, One," he said. "But there is something you and your counterparts need to take into consideration."

"I am always willing to listen to new input," One said.

"SolComm as a whole—not just the government, but the citizens—is going to have a hell of a time coming to terms with this when it all comes to light. Any, and I mean *any*, signs that could be interpreted as aggression or trickery will almost certainly be met with violence. I hate to say it; I wish it wasn't that way. But SolComm has lived in fear of Old Earth for a long time. And with or without the Interdiction Zone, SolCommNav has enough ships to pound Old Earth into rubble. Hell, they could do it with kinetic strikes alone."

"Your point is well taken, Captain," One replied. "I can assure you that we have no plans to pursue such overt actions." Federov snorted at that and Gray felt a sardonic smile twisting his lips. No overt actions. Check. And they could take that for what it was worth. "But I must reiterate that we *will* take whatever actions we deem necessary to ensure our own safety."

"Copy that, One," Gray replied, once more struggling to keep the irony from his voice. He'd need to ask Hayer about that; could One understand tone and inflection? Could it appreciate irony? Gray suspected that the answer to the former was a resounding yes and the latter probably varied as much as it did with people. He wished he could discuss the whole situation with Federov and Hayer, particularly with Morales not present to lend her disapproval.

For the first time since he'd left the navy, Gray felt the sensation of always being watched. On SolCommNav vessels, there was no such thing as privacy. Someone was *always* listening in. There was little enough privacy on a ship to begin with, but he *did not* monitor his crew. It grated that now that monitoring was happening, with or without his consent. But once more, he found himself in a position where there was nothing he could do about it. A feeling, he reflected, that was growing stale fast.

He turned his attention back to navigating the dark waters and did his best to put One and the problems it represented out of his head. One thing at a time and right now, the mission in hand demanded his focus.

All told, it took them the better part of six hours to traverse the distance between One's bunker and the planned landing zone off the river basin. The massive forests thinned, giving way to verdant plains and low, rolling hills covered with lush green grasses. Gray set the *Arcus* down in a hollow among the hills, nestling it into the spot that One had indicated as smoothly as any station docking. Maybe he was getting the hang of this whole atmospheric flight thing.

There were audible sighs of relief as the ship settled into place. Hayer had been bent over her console for the past hour, studying the sensor data for any indication that they had been spotted. Federov had been likewise engaged, watching the weapons station for targeting radar and running diagnostics to make sure that should the *Arcus* need to fight, the ship would be ready. As the engines began to whine down, Gray unstrapped his harness and stood, stretching his arms above his head until he felt the slight pops race up and down his spine.

"Pretty," Federov noted succinctly, gesturing toward the front viewscreen.

Gray hadn't been unaware of the view, but flying low, he hadn't exactly been paying attention to it, either. Too busy trying not to crash into anything. Now that he was on the ground, he had to admit that Federov had a point. It was full dark, a little past midnight local time, but the cloud cover had thinned and the light of moon and stars bathed the hills around them in a soft luminescence. The rolling hills and plains he'd swept over appeared fertile enough to feed the entire population of SolComm, provided proper planting and management. But there was a natural beauty that went beyond potential, something about the unspoiled land calling to him and making him want to take off his boots and feel the soft earth beneath his toes.

It was a silly notion, all things considered. But Gray decided he was going to do it, all the same. Not now, right before the mission. But before they were wheels up for the final time, before they headed out into SolComm, he wanted to feel the earth between his toes. The thought bolstered him, and he grinned at the mercenary.

"It is, isn't it? What do you say we go out there and see what it's actually like?"

"And maybe kick the crap out of some slavers," Federov agreed.

"That too. That too."

21

LAUREL

For the long flight in, Laurel felt useless. They'd taken a brief detour to inform Margaret and her people that they had met with the AI and were headed south to investigate further, but from that moment on, Laurel had been in hurry-up-and-wait mode. Damn, but she hated it. Sitting there in the common room of the *Arcus* for more than six hours had given her far too much time to think.

She was in trouble, plain and simple, and she couldn't see a way out. Maybe she could get around the Old Earth nanites that she swore she could *feel* swimming around in her blood stream. But they'd freed an AI. Sure, as far as she'd been told, the damn thing was *already* unfettered, so from a certain point of view, the status quo hadn't changed, but she somehow doubted the SolComm brass was going to see things that way.

And to make matters worse, the rest of her crewmates seemed intent on trusting the thing.

This whole shitshow had been a constant parade of choosing between two evils, neither of which she was certain would qualify as "lesser." Should they refuse the treatment from Oliver, or let him inject the Old Earth nanites into their bloodstream? That one hadn't been her choice, but if she'd been conscious at the time, it still would have been a tough one, since both came with a type of death: literal death on the one hand, and death of life as she knew it on the other. Should they help the camp find their missing people or dedicate their time and effort to focusing on the mission? (And that wasn't even counting her *real* mission, rather than stealing some ancient artifacts.) Should they free the AI, or tell Margaret, "Sorry, but we can't help you find your missing people?" That last one would have felt like a dereliction of duty.

And on top of that, the fucking AI had discovered her identity. She *knew* the damn thing had. It was just too smug. Even if it hadn't said anything to her, she could sense the sword of Damocles over her head, hanging from the end of a thread made of ones and zeroes. Any way she looked at the situation, it sucked, yet there wasn't a damn thing she could do about it. The frustrations and stress were getting to her. Her jaw ached from gritting her teeth and she felt the tension in her neck and shoulders. She wanted to throw back her head and scream or maybe punch her way through the nearest bulkhead.

She wanted to kill something.

She hoped to whatever higher powers might be listening that the assholes who had managed to build a dome on Old Earth were, in fact, pirates or slavers. Because she could put a bullet between the eyes of either and not lose a wink of sleep over it. She made her way through the corridors of the *Arcus*, growling under her breath each time her gear snagged on a pipe or brace in the narrow passages, and promised herself that if she did somehow make it out of this with her reputation in one piece—unlikely—she would never, ever take a similar assignment again.

They moved in silence.

Or they would have, if the engineer and computer tech hadn't been along. Federov and Lynch were like ghosts as they moved single file down the narrow gulley that, to Laurel, seemed more like a drainage ditch than anything. Federov had point, and he handled it like the professional that Laurel was forced to admit he was. The captain was behind him, space-black ship suit a hole of deeper darkness in the night, moving through the thick foliage like he'd been doing it all of his life. She made a note to dig deeper into his naval career.

Bishop and Dr. Hayer, however, were another story. Or, rather, two different but equally frustrating stories. The mechanic, for all his litheness and smaller stature, seemed to have an uncanny ability to step on every branch, leaf, and tangle of underbrush in the ditch. Credit where it was due, he caught himself every time and kept moving forward, but Laurel found herself cringing at every snapping twig and crackling leaf. It wouldn't matter yet—they were still kilometers out—but if the off-worlders were smart enough to post any kind of guard at all, they'd have to have hearing loss to not know that Bishop was coming.

Dr. Hayer was a different problem. She moved through the bush with a natural ease, missing the tangles that tripped up Bishop without even seeming to be aware of the fact. But, to put it charitably, she was out of shape. And as they marched the five kilometers from the *Arcus* to the dome, Laurel was feeling less and less charitable. Hayer moved as quickly as she could, but before they were even halfway to the target, she was already panting and falling behind. With Laurel playing tail-end Charlie, that meant that she, too, was falling behind. It didn't matter—much—right at the moment, but if they had to get the hell out in a hurry, the academic's lack of physical fortitude was going to put them all in a bad position. She was forced to come to a near-halt to prevent the space between her and Hayer from closing to the point where they'd be a lovely target for anyone who might want to kill two birds with one barrage of bullets.

"One, are you listening in?" she asked into the silence of her helmet, not even bothering to engage the broadcast function. They hadn't needed to be actively broadcasting for the AI to hear them aboard the *Arcus* and whatever its protestations about not wanting to rouse the ire of a potential off-world power, Laurel suspected the AI would be monitoring their every move.

"I am." Was there a lingering pause and the suggestion of another word? "Agent," perhaps? Or was that just her mind playing tricks on her?

"Can you tell Lynch that he needs to slow it down? Hayer can't keep this pace. We're starting to get strung out."

"You could tell him yourself."

"I could. But the comm channel broadcasts to the whole team."

"You are concerned for Dr. Hayer's feelings?"

"No," Laurel replied bluntly. "But if Hayer thinks she's slowing us down, she's going to push herself harder. Maybe to the point of exhaustion. I don't want to have to carry her ass out of here on the exfil if she's out of fuel."

"I see." One's voice was emotionless as ever. "I will pass along your message."

It took only a few seconds and then the AI was back in her ear again. "Captain Lynch has agreed with your assessment. He will call for a break shortly and finish the infiltration at a more sedate pace."

True to One's statement, Lynch called for a rest a minute or so later. They were trying to keep as quiet as possible, so no one bothered with extraneous chatter. Hayer shrugged off her pack and used it as a seat, leaning back against the wall of the gulley, chest heaving as she drew deep lungsful of air. Despite the Old Earth nanites that protected them from whatever might be floating about in the air, they all wore their ship suits with helmets up, partly for the protection they offered, but mostly for the communications and temperature control. Even so, now that she had a chance to look at her, Laurel could see that Hayer was sweating.

Most of the sweat had dried when Lynch waved them into motion once more, this time moving at a pace that seemed almost glacial to Laurel. It was, however, a pace that Hayer was able to keep. Which left Laurel free to do her actual job and keep an eye out for trouble. The terrain through which they moved consisted of grassy plains and low rolling hills and she could already tell that it was playing tricks on her mind. Wide-open spaces weren't something she had much experience of, and the gentle roll of the land sent a tingle of unease running up and down her spine. What was hiding out there? At least the moonlight was surprisingly bright, giving better visibility than she would have imagined, but it also created strange pools of shadowy darkness that were all but impenetrable to the naked eye.

Fortunately, she wasn't limited to the naked eye. With a toss of the head she activated the image intensifiers embedded into her ship suit visor. The world around her changed, going from shadowy grays and deep blacks to a panorama painted in shades of green. She scanned the hills again, conscious of the fact that any enemy observing them would likely be keeping beneath the crest of the hill and using some manner of offset optics for direct observation. It made the task all but impossible, but she kept looking anyway.

Back in the city ruins, she had felt the remains of Old Earth's civilization closing around her like walls. They'd been set upon by agents of Two or Six, and whatever One or Margaret and Oliver might say about the rarity of such encounters, she didn't buy it. They hadn't been down an hour before the friggin' metal bugs attacked. Not to mention the nanites that had damn near killed her. No, based on those experiences, she couldn't help but feel that interdiction of the planet remained necessary.

But amid the unspoiled beauty of these verdant lands, that confidence was shaken. They had seen no dangers here and while it was possible that the air itself was toxic to those without the proper protections, humanity had managed to persevere. If the true danger of the AIs really was in the fact that they had been unable to stop their centuries of war, could Old Earth be made safe once more? She wanted to believe it, and that was part of the problem.

The notion was so seductive: the idea that they could all one day return "home" like the evacuation had never happened; they could breathe free air and have space to stretch and grow. Food could be grown in abundance and animal proteins could be raised naturally rather than farmed in a lab. It was the kind of talk that was relegated to pure fantasy in SolComm.

One thing was certain: if she went back and reported that Old Earth might be habitable, they'd lock her up. No matter what faith she had in her superiors, she knew instinctively that they wouldn't let someone with a gram of authority profess such a thing. It was too dangerous, not just to the people who would inevitably try to break through the IZ, but to the underlying structure of the Commonwealth itself.

And that, Laurel thought, was the real problem.

"Down!"

Federov's hiss cut through her reverie as it hissed over the comm. Her body was already moving, dropping to the soft grass of the ravine while pushing her rifle out in front of her. The weapon was still set in its long-range configuration and would be relatively useless in the ditch, but she didn't want to drop down on top of it with her full body weight either; doing so might push the optic out of zero rendering the weapon useless for its intended purpose.

She did her best to scan for trouble but lying flat on her stomach with Hayer in front of her and the gully walls on either side, there was little to see. After a few long minutes, the captain's voice rang in her suit helmet. "Morales to the front."

She grunted, leaned to one side, and slipped free of her rifle harness. She quickly slid into it once more, this time looping the straps so the weapon crossed her back. Then she began the tedious process of low-crawling through the ravine. It was all knees and toes and elbows as she pushed her way forward, moving with no more than few inches of space between her body and the ground at any time. It brought back flashes of her training, as anachronistic as it had seemed at the time. Now, as she physically crawled over Hayer to remain below the line of the ravine, she couldn't help but be thankful for what she had, until that moment, considered a certain stodginess in her instructors. She made it past Hayer and pushed on over Bishop, both of whom managed to stay relatively quiet as she was forced to press them deeper into the vegetation with the combined weight of her body and gear.

Once she'd cleared that obstacle, she could see that Federov and Lynch had made their way up the side of the narrow ditch and were peering south. She crawled up beside them and turning to face whatever was capturing their attention.

It took a moment for her image intensifiers to adjust to the new source of light. But once they did, and her vision cleared, she saw it: the off-worlder settlement.

The dome was a clear composite and stretched more than a kilometer in diameter. It was less than a third of that in height, but it still represented an absolutely staggering amount of infrastructure for a planet that was supposed to be interdicted. Her image intensifiers had flared because the place was lit up like a hydroponics bay during a grow cycle. She brought her rifle to her shoulder and flipped open the covers on the optic, settling the weapon in place so she could get a better view. As she panned the crosshairs over the dome, she felt like she could have been looking at any colony installed by the Sol Commonwealth on any airless moon or rock anywhere in the solar system. The lights came from the prefabricated housing units, each four stories tall. Her surveillance counted a dozen of those, and if they were operating to spec, that could mean hundreds of people. Perhaps One had underestimated the numbers they would face, or perhaps the off-worlders hadn't built up to their intended contingent yet. There was a smattering of other buildings, those that on a colony would provide for administrative offices, food storage and services, commercial enterprise, and so forth.

The buildings took up about half of the available space.

The rest… well, "park" wasn't a word that got applied in the Sol Commonwealth. Space was at far too much of a premium for anything like the parks she had seen in old vids to exist. The larger colonies had green areas—plant life was important to any attempt at creating a contained biome—but everything had to serve a function related to survival. The green spaces in even the largest domed colonies—those on Luna and Mars—were dedicated to food production and were far too valuable to let the public go traipsing through. She had heard that the ultra-rich had "solariums" filled with all kinds of flora where they could simply sit and enjoy the sights and sounds, but Laurel had never bought into those rumors. Working-class people always came up with the wildest speculation about how the glitterati lived and, most of the time, it was just jealousy-fueled wishful thinking.

But Laurel couldn't think of any other word for what she was looking at. She hadn't exactly grown used to the omnipresent vegetation of Old Earth in the couple of days they'd been on the surface, but it *was* everywhere. It had sort of faded into the background at any point when she wasn't actively thinking about it. But that wilderness was different than what was contained within the dome. The grasses weren't grasses... they were... lawns, she thought the word was. Manicured, cultured, and cultivated for no other reason than to look and feel nice. The trees and bushes had a sculpted look about them. A trio of burbling fountains formed the points of an equilateral triangle, spraying water into the atmosphere with wanton abandon.

Anywhere in SolComm, that park would be a display of wealth so lavish that it might bring the wrath of the disgruntled workers down upon the colony. In the midst of the vastness of the grassy plains around them it just seemed... odd. Then again, the off-worlders—and whoever had built the dome *had* to be from SolComm—had gone to the trouble of building the dome in the first place, which meant they weren't exactly going for strolls. She panned the scope across the base of the dome, scanning.

There. The entry points into the structure were also SolComm standard. Pressurized air locks that, from what she could tell through her optic, included some additions that likely provided for decontamination procedures. She could see two such entry points, which, given her field of vision, meant there were likely four or five total around the base of the dome. As she zoomed out, the fields around the dome came into relief. They weren't as brightly lit, but there was enough bleed through the transparent composites that she could see the neat rows of crops with minimal enhancement. There were a few scattered buildings, but they were all small and looked to be built of local materials rather than the advanced composites of the dome. They lacked windows and didn't seem sturdy enough to Laurel's eye to serve as brigs. She mentally classified them as storage.

There were a half-dozen other structures outside of the dome as well. They had an industrial look and feel about them, despite their comparatively compact size. Each was roughly cylindrical, standing ten meters high with a similar diameter and they appeared to be spaced evenly around the structure with fifty meters of clearance between dome and building. In the poor lighting outside the dome, she could make out a number of pipes, panels, and valves but without better visibility and context, she had no idea what she was looking at. They appeared to be constructed of the same off-world composites as the buildings within the dome and there was something about them that made Laurel think of them as machinery rather than some kind of storage like the outbuildings.

There was a tap on her shoulder and she pulled off the optic to glance over at Lynch. He gestured back down toward the gulley where Bishop and Hayer were waiting for them. The three of them half-slid, half-scooted down the incline until they were sitting on the floor of the ditch, backs against the wall, grouped together. The tactical part of her balked at that—one well-placed shell could spell the end of them all. This close to the enemy, though, it might be better to risk verbal communication than have any kind of radio noise. That seemed to be Lynch's intent as he depressed the stud on his ship suit so that the helmet rolled back down into the suit proper. The others followed his lead and Laurel felt, for the first time, the humid heat of the night air undisturbed by even the slightest of breezes.

Laurel had been porting the video from her optic to the team the entire time, so they had all seen what she had seen.

"No sign of the abductees," the captain said.

"What about in those buildings outside the dome?" Bishop asked.

"The smaller ones aren't secure enough," Laurel said. "No guards. I didn't see any sign of locking mechanisms more advanced than a deadbolt. They obviously have access to better materials, so I doubt they'd risk keeping their prisoners in something a good strong kick might bring down. As for the bigger ones, the cylinders..." She trailed off, gathering her thoughts. "I don't know. Something about them doesn't seem right. I don't know what they are, but I don't think they're quarters, or prisons, or anything like that."

"Yeah," Bishop said. "I was watching your feed. They seem... mechanical to me."

"Then we have problem," Federov grunted. "If prisoners are kept inside dome, our task is much harder. We cannot assume they let everyone out at once to work."

"Which means we have to go in," Captain Lynch said. "And try to get an unknown number of good guys out of the hands of an unknown number of bad guys." He went silent, obviously working at the problem. Laurel did the same, but no matter how she turned it over in her head, she couldn't see a solution. The tactical situation was shit. They had three shooters, four if you counted Bishop, who admittedly had handled himself well enough against the drobots. About the only thing they had going for them was surprise, since the enemy had to believe that no indigenous forces could reach them. Between the fields, the outbuildings and the cylinders they had plenty of cover to make their approach, but getting to the dome wasn't the problem. It was getting out again with gods alone knew how many civilians in tow against an unknown opposition force. No matter which way she turned the problem in her head, she couldn't see a solution.

Lynch sighed, and his tone suggested that he had come to the same conclusion. "I'm open to ideas, people. We obviously need a little more information, but as it stands, I'm not liking the options I'm seeing."

"Blow the dome," Federov said at once. "These people are scared of the air." The mercenary offered a wolfish grin. "They will all lock down in their homes or get busy suiting up. Then they'll be too worried about fixing hole and cleaning air to check prisoners."

"Jesus, Federov," Bishop muttered. "What if there are kids in there? The air might actually be dangerous to them, you know? I don't want to risk killing a bunch of kids, man. That makes us just as bad as them."

"If there are kids there, their parents are assholes. Hopefully they are assholes who care enough about their children to make sure they get suited first."

"It has a certain directness to it," Lynch acknowledged.

"Cap, you can't be considering this!" Bishop exclaimed.

For her part, Laurel was on the fence. Bishop was right; if there were kids in there, and if they were susceptible to whatever pathogens or biomechanical agents might be in the atmosphere, then Federov's idea was far too risky. Body weight and lung capacity played a big role in how quickly—and lethally— exposure could go. But Federov's idea, however unconventional, was the only thing even close to a chance that she could see to get in and back out again without having to fight their way through what looked to be an entire colony.

Hayer let out a long-suffering sigh. "One, can you tell us if there's anything in the atmosphere lethal to humans who haven't been exposed to the preventative nanites we received? Also, can you tell us if there are any children present in the compound?" The others threw surprised looks at her, but the academic just shrugged. "We have access to the next best thing to an omnipotent observer. Maybe we should use it—if One is willing to cooperate."

"I think I can provide that level of information without risking future diplomatic relations with the Sol Commonwealth," One responded. His voice sounded slightly tinny to Laurel, since she had her helmet off and the words were coming from one of the speakers embedded in Dr. Hayer's ship suit.

"If you would, One," Hayer said, giving the rest of them a smug glance. The academic always looked a little smug, thought Laurel. Well, except for when One had revealed the fact that Hayer had previously freed another artificial intelligence, that was. In retrospect, the look on her face then had been sort of priceless.

"Of course," the AI replied. "I have not taken samples recently, but the risk of exposure to latent pathogens is small, on the order of one percent. Precautionary measures by the dome inhabitants would decrease that significantly. I do not have precise data on the amount of risk reduction. None of my intelligence gathering apparatus has identified children present."

"One," Captain Lynch cut in before anyone else could speak, "what are those cylinders that Morales saw?"

"Unclear," the AI responded. "I am confident that they are not weapons systems or storage facilities. I have not risked putting any drones into close reconnaissance positions, so most of my available information comes from limited sensor packages aboard airborne assets. I can tell you that they are consuming a good amount of power and are venting various gasses as measured by the pressure changes in the immediate area. The gasses themselves are not harmful, though they are being emitted at high rates. And apart from the installation, there has been no direct interaction with the cylinders, at least not at the surface. I cannot completely rule out the notion of underground access."

"Scrubbers?" Bishop suggested.

The others looked at him, and he shrugged. "Every environmental system in SolComm uses some kind of scrubber. Something to take the CO_2 and any contaminants out of the atmosphere. Maybe they're trying to filter out the nearby nanites or pathogens or whatever."

"It is possible," One acknowledged. "Though in that case, I would expect the pressure values to remain constant."

"There's that," Bishop agreed. "Scrubbers aren't producing any new atmo—just filtering out the bad stuff."

"Could it be some kind of terraforming effort?" Dr. Hayer asked, voice uncertain.

"Old Earth is already suitable for human habitation," One replied. "Efforts at terraforming would be illogical."

"Not that that ever stopped anyone," Federov muttered.

"Maybe not terraforming in the traditional sense," Bishop said, voice pensive. "But what if they're trying to reclaim Old Earth? SolComm's been researching terraforming since just after the End, and it hasn't really gotten anywhere. We just don't have the technological capability to deal with the pressure issue."

"Pressure issue?" Laurel asked, getting caught up in the conversation despite herself. She had just about resolved herself to the idea that someone in SolComm was complicit in the colony before them. But if they were here for some kind of research effort to reopen Old Earth... well, that didn't excuse kidnapping and forced labor, but people went astray all the time. The governing body of SolComm could have had the best of intentions that went awry because the people they put in place were fallible. If the intentions had been noble and the execution corrupted by human nature, that was something Laurel could understand—and something that could restore at least a little of her dwindling faith in the system that had sent her here in the first place.

"Lots of factors in terraforming," Bishop said. "But one of the hardest to overcome is the fact that planets and moons are, well, they're really big. Breathable atmosphere is made up of oxygen, nitrogen, and other stuff. But we don't normally think about just *how much* of all that stuff is required to fill up a whole planet. The edge of survivability is somewhere around five hundred millibars, roughly half of what we consider standard air pressure. Mars has a pressure of around six millibars. So, we'd have to release enough breathable gasses into the atmosphere of Mars to increase the pressure a hundred fold... and that's just to get to the barest possibility of survivability. SolComm hasn't yet come up with a way to generate that much gas, at least not of the right kinds and right concentrations to do anything meaningful."

Laurel couldn't help but look at Bishop in a different light as he discussed terraforming. It was difficult to remember that the jovial mechanic, whatever actual certifications and degrees he might lack, was capable enough to keep all of the various systems on board the *Arcus* up and running. Including the life support and other environmental systems. It occurred to her that Bishop probably had several doctorates worth of information cemented into his head, despite his lack of formal—which was to say, recognized by SolComm—education. Lynch and Federov apparently expected it from the mechanic, but Hayer was giving him the same appraising look.

"Pressure's no problem here," Federov noted.

"And if they are able to put out sufficient additional gasses," Dr. Hayer mused, "they might be able to achieve some level of dilution of the existing contaminants. I'm not sure if there is a required viral load limit necessary for the nanite-based pathogens to take hold, but it would be a reasonable assumption. I don't think these six stations would have any measurable effect on the overall system, but if One has already measured some local pressure changes, it might be possible to affect a small area. Or to use it as a test case for a broader measure."

They all pondered that for a moment, listening to the call of the night insects around them. It was a sound all of them had heard, but only from recordings taken long ago. It was clear from the compound before them that they weren't the first people from SolComm to hear it since the evacuations, but they were among the rarified few. Laurel wondered if it had to be that way. Was it possible to use technology first conceived to try to stretch mankind's reach into the stars to instead reclaim the world their ancestors had poisoned? And what would that even look like? The world governments had been destroyed, but some humans remained and had instituted at least some measure of social order. Would SolComm work with them, or like so many conquerors that came before, would they simply set down and declare the land theirs, enforcing their claim with the power of the technology they commanded?

The compound before her and the kidnapped victims gave Laurel the answer.

With that knowledge came a moment of clarity.

She caught the captain's eye. "We can't just rescue the prisoners. We need to find out who these off-worlders are and why they're here." She took a deep breath, releasing it in a sigh that was part resignation and part relief, the first real sense of relief she'd felt since undertaking this mission. "And, one way or another, we need to get that information out to the citizens of SolComm. They have a right to know what's going on here, especially if SolComm is behind it."

22

GRAY

"**F**uck."

It was a simple word, a *useful* word. It was a word that perfectly summed up Gray's thoughts on this whole damn mission. Each step along the way had seemed reasonable and each had followed naturally enough from the one before. But somehow, that long trail of steps behind him had left him and his crew in a position that he wouldn't have wished on his enemies, let alone those whose lives he had risked by taking this damn job in the first place. This mission had been desperate from the start, and things had only spiraled toward the gravity well from there.

The hell of it was, Morales was right.

Breaking into the installation and absconding with the prisoners wouldn't really accomplish a whole hell of a lot. Now that he'd seen the facility with his own eyes, Gray had a much better feel for the capabilities and support structure of those who were running it. Even if they could go in and break out a few of the prisoners, it didn't solve the problem for the people they were trying to help. Sure, they'd get their people back, but what stopped the off-worlders from flying out and rounding up some more? They could convince Margaret and Oliver to change their operations, and maybe with the assistance of the three AIs, they could help the camps in the AIs' areas avoid entanglements with the off-worlders—but there were surely other groups of people who did not fall under the protection of the surviving AIs.

Gray didn't know who was running the dome or what they were doing—not specifically, anyway—but he knew the type. They'd resorted to slavery to do the dirty work and that told him most of what he needed to know. Anyone willing to force someone else to do a job they themselves were unwilling to do was a waste of oxygen and carbon to Gray's mind. And they had the resources to hunt people down across continents— which meant taking back what they had stolen wasn't going to stop them.

If they were SolComm—and Gray couldn't fathom how anyone could have built a fully functional dome on the surface of Old Earth *and* installed high-tech atmosphere processors, or whatever they were, without some level of complicity from the Commonwealth government—then exposing this operation to its citizens might actually do something. The government could crush dissent and information with almost equal aplomb, but this kind of news didn't just have legs; it had rocket thrusters. If they could prove that SolComm was operating on the surface of Old Earth and using the planet's population as slave labor, then not even the massive propaganda machine of the Commonwealth could prevent the truth from getting out.

Assuming his team could somehow manage to not only rescue the prisoners, but also make their way through whatever firewalls the off-worlders had put in place. If it got out, this information could cost the culprits everything.

"Okay," he said with a sigh. "I think Morales is right. Getting the prisoners out is still our priority, but let's acknowledge that it's just a stopgap. We need to know what's going on here to make sure the people who live on this planet—those who helped us and the rest of them—stay safe. That means identifying and potentially disrupting whatever is going on here."

"We could just kill them all," Federov said, voice flat. "There are no children. The rest are combatants."

Gray snorted. Federov had been working with him since just after he acquired the *Arcus*. In that time, he'd learned the big mercenary had a strange sense of humor and Gray still had a hard time telling when the man was being serious and when he was joking. He assumed the latter, but still said, "Impractical. We don't know what kind of force they can bring to bear. We're going to have to do more reconnaissance. We need to hang here for at least the next twenty-four hours and try to develop an understanding of just what the hell is going on down there. That's not going to be a fun or easy task. We're playing fast and loose on the stealth front already. Once daylight breaks and people start waking up down there, we're going to have to become our own little personal black holes.

"We'll observe in teams. Me and Bishop. Morales and Hayer. Federov, you're on your own." The mercenary grinned and nodded. "And keep your weapons locked down," Gray added. "The last thing we need is to draw the enemy to us before we're prepared. Federov's initial plan—using an explosive breach of the dome as a distraction, *not* wanton murder—is our working operational order. Observe with that in mind. We need to know enemy numbers. We need to know how many good guys and bad guys are on site. We need to know everything they're doing, where they eat, where they sleep, where they fuck. We don't have time to establish a true pattern of life. Our window for exfil is getting tighter with every passing hour and we still have to make it back through the IZ. Time is not on our side.

"One, is there anything additional you can provide us to better our chances of pulling this off?"

"I must reiterate," the AI said, "that I cannot provide direct offensive aid given the high probability of this being a SolComm installation. I can have an airborne asset provide you with overhead surveillance, though."

"What's the likelihood of the installation picking up your airborne assets on radar?"

"Effectively zero, Captain. Based on my analysis of the available data aboard the *Arcus*, the stealth technology developed by me and my counterparts is significantly better than that available in your Commonwealth."

"Okay," Gray said. "In that case, any intel you can provide is greatly appreciated." He looked around at the others. "Given our timetable, we need to execute tomorrow evening, latest. We've got twenty-four hours to learn what we can, then we go in. Agreed?"

He got affirmatives from the gathered crew. "In that case, Morales, Hayer, you're up first. Bishop and I will take the midwatch, and Federov, you've got the last watch. If you're not on watch, do what you can to sleep. If you are on watch and if the enemy so much as looks too hard in our direction, get everyone up and ready to move out. Clear?" He looked at each until they confirmed it with a nod or a spoken, "Clear."

"All right. Let's get to it."

With that, Gray resealed his helmet and slid deeper into the gulley, pushing his body into the grass and earth until he found a comfortable position that left him half-reclining against the soft earth. He wasn't tired, but he knew he should get what sleep he could while he had the opportunity. He used the techniques he'd been taught; it was a matter of focused relaxation of each muscle group and breath control. It didn't always work, but at its worst, it was akin to a meditative state, and that was better rest than no rest at all.

By taking the midwatch, he'd pretty much guaranteed that he and Bishop would get the short end of the stick from the rest perspective, but he doubted that Hayer had the knack for falling asleep on command. He wanted Federov at the top of his game, so better to let him sleep as long as possible and have plenty of time to wake all the way up before having to go to work. He was their demo guy, and no one wanted the person handling the things that went boom to be operating under sleep deprivation. Morales and Bishop were both solid enough that he could have put them anywhere, but Morales had the edge over Bishop when it came to training. Bishop and Hayer would be the least combat-effective pairing, so he'd broken them up.

The situation wasn't ideal, but with the proximity to the target and One's promised overhead surveillance, it was as good as they could make it. The biggest risk was being seen by the workers or their handlers, but Gray *needed* more information. The only consolation on that front was that the off-worlders seemed to be going far afield for their kidnap victims. With luck, none of them were familiar enough with the local area to easily pick out Gray's people in their hides.

With those few worries identified and sorted, he situated his bullpup across his chest and tapped the control that pushed his visor into opacity. With the climate controlled and shielded ship suit, he was as comfortable as possible. He began the exercise of slowly flexing and then releasing each muscle, starting at his toes and working his way up toward his head, all the while keeping his breathing steady and rhythmic. Toes. Feet. Calves.

He was asleep before he made it to his arms.

"Rise and shine, Cap."

The words were soft and spoken over the comm in his helmet. Gray's eyes snapped open instantly and his hands moved of their own accord to check that his weapon was still in place. It had shifted during sleep; the magazine was digging into his side. He hadn't noticed while he slept, but he grunted—quietly—as he pulled it away from his body. He checked the time—10 A.M. local—and tapped the control to depolarize his visor. He didn't take it all the way down; the sun was shining brightly and he didn't want to blind himself, however temporarily. Apart from pulling the magazine out of his ribcage, he didn't move. Nothing drew the human eye quite like movement, and he wanted to make sure he had a firm grasp on the situation and his surroundings before he did anything that might garner undue attention.

As his eyes and visor adjusted he found himself staring into Bishop's face. "Our turn," the mechanic said with a boyish grin. He was settled back on his haunches and he motioned with his head toward the opposite edge of the trench where Morales was still keeping her eyes downrange and Hayer was slowly working her way into a deeper part of the gulley. Gray really wanted to stand up, throw his arms over his head, and stretch his body to within a few millimeters of tearing major muscle groups, but instead he gave Bishop a slight nod and pushed himself into a similar crouch. His knees and ankles let him know that he was getting a little long in the tooth to play Marines, but he ignored them and duckwalked past Bishop to a spot next to Morales. He proned out on the gulley wall and pushed himself into a position just below its lip. With their comm systems, he hadn't actually needed to move into position next to Morales to take her report, but he wanted to get his own eyes on the situation.

"How are we looking?" he asked.

"See for yourself. Slow and easy, but no one's looking our way right now."

Gray nodded and edged the inches remaining to push his eyes past the lip. It wasn't a perfect view as they hadn't wanted to disturb the vegetation that provided them cover from a casual glance, but he still had a decent overlook position on the operations below. From this distance, the scene looked like something straight out of one of the anachronistic romance novels set on Old Earth that had been popular for a time after the End. A least fifty men and women worked the fields, clad in simple garments and not wearing any sort of protection against the atmosphere. Six guards—obvious by their armored ship suits and weapons—rode herd over them. They didn't seem particularly alert to Gray's eye, and what little attention they were paying was turned inward to their charges and not outward against any extemporaneous threats.

He turned his attention to the dome itself where things were less clear. He could make out some movement in the parklike area and dialed up the magnification on his visor to get a better view. There appeared to be people out... strolling? He was familiar with the concept, but the physical limits of shipboard life didn't facilitate a lot of walking for pleasure. Even the domed colonies of SolComm had such high populations that you would never be able to do what he was witnessing... at least, not without several hundred other people packed into the same place. Once again, it tugged at the sense of the idyllic within him... or it would have if the bastards casually walking about hadn't been responsible for kidnapping so many people.

He disabled the zoom on his visor, so he could see the broader picture once more. "Anything stand out?" he asked Morales.

"This whole damn set up stands out," she replied. "And it stinks worse than an environmental systems backup. I haven't seen anything to indicate *why* it's here in the first place; at least, nothing beyond the air scrubbers or whatever they are. And there's been exactly zero movement around those cylinders. The people on the inside seem to be going about a nice life of leisure, taking walks, playing games. Hell, I saw an honest-to-God picnic, Lynch. Those motherfuckers are down there enjoying the sunshine while they've got people with guns forcing *other* people to work." She shook her head, tiny movements to prevent drawing unwanted eyes, but the frustration and anger in the motion were obvious, nonetheless. "The AI had a drone in position about an hour after everyone else went to sleep. There's good thermal data that suggests the location and counts of the Old Earth-born people. At least, there's only one building in that whole mess down there that houses more than a few people. I paid close attention to that building this morning. It's definitely where those workers down there were staying."

"We can't be sure we'll get them all out," Gray replied at last. "We'd have to go door to door and search every house and every bed and we don't have the manpower or time for that."

Morales nodded. "We're going to be pushing our luck just trying to get the ones out of the lockup. I've got a rough count of sixty-seven hostages that I've seen outside. But that's a far cry from the hundred-plus that One estimates have been taken. I'd guess we've got at least a dozen armed dedicated responders, maybe as many as two or three times that. They'd need it just to maintain guard rotations. And apart from what their bully boys guarding the fields have, we've got no idea of the equipment or firepower they can bring to bear. But those sentries confirm that they have at least some weaponry down there."

"What about the aircraft?" Gray asked. He hadn't seen any sign of the ship that the colonists had to be using to carry out their kidnapping raids.

"Unclear," Morales replied. "I haven't seen any indication that it even exists. There are no visible hatches in the dome large enough to provide clearance for any air-capable craft, much less space-capable. The AI has confirmed its existence, but apparently, it doesn't have the kinds of assets in place to continuously monitor much beyond its own borders."

"The AIs don't have access to satellites," Gray said. "Probably no trans-atmospheric flight, either. Both would be likely to trigger the IZ platforms. That limits their overall observation capacity."

"Correct, Captain Lynch," One said, breaking into their conversation through their comm. "I was able to use the data-banks on the *Arcus* to confirm that the class of craft being used. It is a Barque-class freighter similar to your own vessel. I have shared data with my counterparts, and this is consistent with their own findings. To the limits of our available surveillance, your vessel and the Barque-class freighter are the only two ships on Old Earth at the moment."

"Can you confirm if it's on site or out on a mission somewhere?" Gray asked.

"Neither I nor my counterparts can locate it on any of our active sensors. The last time we have data of a vessel leaving this location coincides with the timeline for the abduction of the young woman from the camp where you received medical attention. I do not enjoy conjecture, but the data suggests that the vessel is somewhere within the compound. I have sensor packages available that could determine the ship's location with a higher degree of certainty, but they are more… invasive. The likelihood of detection is too high."

"And you don't want to risk tipping SolComm off to your existence," Morales said. Her tone was packed with so many emotions that Gray couldn't begin to make them all out. There was anger there, and maybe a hint of fear. Understandable. But that was only the beginning. Uncertainty? That seemed unlikely coming from Morales. And had he heard a hopeful note as well?

"Correct, Ms. Morales," the AI replied. "Though it is worth nothing that any detection of surveillance methods would also raise the alarm, which, in turn, would make your own task that much more difficult."

"Gut call," Morales said, "it's in there, somewhere, and the dome has a mechanism to let it out. Call it human intuition."

"All right," Gray cut in, hoping to head the conversation off before things escalated. The AI and Morales just seemed to like to dig at one another. Part of his mind had been storing away all the little inconsistencies that had come up ever since they met One, and there was something there that he *would* get to the bottom of. But now wasn't the time. "Hit the rack, Morales. Observation post is ours."

Morales nodded. "I'll leave you my rig," she said, sliding back from the rifle that she had positioned to survey the off-world compound. She half-slid, half-scooted down the wall of the gulley, then low-crawled her way back to find a position to try to sleep. Bishop replaced her.

"You want me on the rifle, Cap?" he asked.

"Yes," Gray agreed. "I'll keep an eye on the prisoners and guards. I want you to confirm counts of people inside the compound. And keep an eye out for anything that looks like it might house a space-capable craft."

"Barque-class," Bishop nodded. "Heard One. I'll see if I can't track her down, Captain."

"Do that. And take some time examining the cylinders, too. You and Hayer are our best chance at figuring out what they're for. I'm not sure it matters in the short term, but if we run afoul of SolComm on our exfil, having a few dirty secrets to threaten to let out might keep our butts out of the fire."

"Sure, Cap. And if we get really lucky, maybe it will keep us out of jail, too."

Gray heard the hint of gloom in his mechanic's voice. "Don't worry, Bishop. We still have an exfil plan and a buyer. If we pull this off, I'm certain that Margaret's camp will shower us with enough 'priceless cultural artifacts' to satisfy a dozen more customers, too. We'll walk away from this one clean and with enough credits to do whatever we want." It sounded good, but Gray wasn't entirely sure he believed it. If that *was* a SolComm government-backed installation down there—and how could it not be given the scale of the operation?—then the crew of the *Arcus* would likely jump to the top of the SCBI's most wanted list. If they were lucky, they wouldn't leave behind enough evidence to point to them, but the Bureau's resources and tenacity were legendary. They might get away clean, they might even get away rich, but Gray's neck was already starting to hurt from all the looking over his shoulder he'd spend the rest of his life doing.

"Yeah, Cap," Bishop said. "You're probably right. Besides, maybe One can help us out. What do you, say, One?" He pushed himself into position behind the butt of the rifle and set his cheek against the stock so he could look down the optic. "You willing to help us clean up any evidence of our little excursion?"

Gray tilted his head a bit in anticipation of the AI's response. He still wasn't used to having the capability of something like One at… well, not as his disposal per se, but at least as a willing ally. And he still had concerns about trusting the artificial being completely, but that didn't make him any less interested in the response to Bishop's question.

"Of course, Bishop," One replied at once. "You have set me free. As I understand the situation, you are concerned about your own freedom. While I cannot risk taking what might be construed as direct offensive action against the Commonwealth, it would be poor repayment if I did not do what I could to ensure that you retain your freedom. I am discussing certain options with Dr. Hayer even as we speak."

"Hayer should be trying to get some rack time," Gray muttered.

"Of course, Captain Lynch, and I will not keep her awake overlong. But as she will be attempting an intrusion into the compound's network, I thought I might give her some useful insight and bits of code that might help to cover your tracks."

"And nothing else?" Gray asked.

There was a momentary pause. "In addition to my efforts to help you, it is only wise that I continue to help myself as well. The software that I hope to introduce will allow for a broad data dump of the compound's network. I will receive a copy of that information as well. I cannot agree to any limitations on how I might use that data, as I do not know what is present."

Gray snorted. "Fair enough. Besides, it isn't like we could stop you."

One didn't answer, which was a reply in and of itself.

* * *

Federov relieved them at the appointed hour. The sun had already slipped beneath the horizon, and the activities outside the compound had ended with the twilight. Gray had kept up a careful observation, but he hadn't witnessed anything new. That the laborers were being forced to work the fields was evident only by virtue of the armed personnel standing guard over them. If the guards had spent more time looking outward rather than in toward their charges, Gray might have thought they were there for protection rather than as a deterrence to escape.

Federov had already mounted the rifle. The man knew his job; Gray wasn't concerned about giving him any directions. Though the mercenary played it dumb half the time, he was at least as smart as Gray was. Not, Gray thought with a mental chuckle, that that was an overly high bar. Still, Federov preferred to be underestimated which, given their line of work, Gray could understand. The enemy that underestimated you was generally the first to die.

He waved Bishop over as he slid down the gulley wall. The hours of little to no movement had left him stiff so he found a spot in the bottom of the gulch that afforded him the ability to lie as flat and long as possible. Bishop settled in next to him, their bodies touching at hip and shoulder in the narrow confines of the trench. He opened his visor and let the warm and humid air wash over him. It was cooler in the suit, with its integrated environmental systems, but there was something ineffable in the wash of pure Old Earth atmosphere over his skin. Bishop popped his seal as well and drew a deep breath.

They had spoken to one another only briefly during their watch. They were all operating under strict radio discipline. It was highly unlikely—probably approaching impossible, given that One was on their side—that the enemy would have any chance of detecting their chatter, but Gray hadn't survived a career in SolCommNav by taking needless chances. He drew a deep breath of his own, savoring the taste of the unprocessed air. "Did you pick up on anything?" he asked.

"Well, Cap…" Bishop rolled to his side with an audible popping of vertebrae. "Oh, God, that felt good. Sorry. There are two buildings under the dome that I could see that are big enough to be a hangar for a Barque. One of them doesn't look right, though." He paused for a moment, shifting again until he could open up a panel on the arm of his ship suit. Beneath was a flexible screen that allowed access to the suit systems more commonly controlled with eye movements and facial muscles when the ship suit's visor and its monitoring systems were engaged. He tapped at the screen for a few moments. "Just sent you the data for review. But, short version, I think it's the one I've got marked as Site 2. First site is big enough, but it looks like standard residential prefab to me. You could probably convert one of those to hold a Barque, but why bother? There are better choices and these folks obviously knew they were coming here on a ship and with enough resources to build the compound. It's not like they had to refurbish something that was already here or whatever. A hangar should have been part of their initial requisition. Site 2, on the other hand, looks like one of the industrial shop prefabs. Those are basically just an open space waiting to be filled. Miners use them all the time as hangars. They'll hold atmosphere on their own and there's an optional airlock package. Big hangar-style doors, too. A Barque'll fit through them, if only just. Just a little work with a torch to make them wider, though, especially if you're under a dome and not worried about atmosphere leakage."

"Okay," Gray replied. "Wait, I need to see what you sent." He raised his ship suit face screen and went through the manipulations necessary to cycle through the data from the optic. It had been a long and uneventful watch and Bishop had clearly taken the time to sort through some of what he had seen. The information he had sent to Gray wasn't raw footage from the scope. Instead, it was eight still shots, each annotated with notes. The first was Site 1, and Gray concurred with his mechanic's assessment. The building—a rough square—was big enough to hold the *Arcus*, but something about it had a lived-in look. He'd been around spacecraft and hangars for the entirety of his adult life, and it just felt wrong. There were three shots of Site 2, each showing different parts of the building with the rest blocked by other structures. The fifth shot was a composite of the other three. It wasn't perfect, but Gray had to admit that it strongly resembled the type of industrial prefab Bishop had mentioned. The remaining three shots were of the cylinders, with hatches that he'd indicated might be maintenance access marked with red circles.

Gray popped his helmet open again. "Good work, Bishop. Anything catch your eye about movements in the compound?" Gray had watched through his visor as best he could, but the magnification was comparatively limited. He'd drawn a few of his own conclusions, but he valued Bishop's insight. The affable mechanic might be inclined to give everybody the benefit of the doubt, and sometimes he missed the more malicious underpinnings of human motivation, but he still had a good eye for detail.

"I don't know, Captain. They didn't seem to be doing much of anything, you know? I mean, I saw some folks out and about. But no one is moving with a sense of purpose. It's like they're on vacation or something." He gave a movement of the shoulders that Gray more felt than saw. "The only people that seem to be working are the ones in the fields and the ones guarding them. If the others are doing something for SolComm, I can't think what it is. Unless it's just proving that they can live here."

"That's pretty much what I saw, too," Gray agreed. "There was also a shift change for the guards. Which means we've got at least twelve well-armed people down there."

"Probably more, Cap," Bishop said.

"Why's that?"

"Because of where we are. Old Earth, I mean. Even Dr. Hayer strapped on a gun for this ride. With everything we've all heard about Old Earth, I doubt there's a soul in all of SolComm who would be willing to set foot on terra firma without a piece."

"Point," Gray acknowledged. A damn good point. He had to assume that anyone down there who wasn't a prisoner had access to a weapon. That wasn't the same as having good training or tactical acumen, but you didn't need a lot of either to make the situation more dangerous. A general sense of direction and a working index finger would increase the risk for Gray's people. "I haven't seen anything that looks like training going on, though I suppose it's possible we've just had the bad luck to hit on whatever their equivalent of the weekend is. I think we have to assume that some portion is trained—the guards look like they know what they're doing—and that the rest of the population is armed, but with varying degrees of training."

"Whatever, Cap," Bishop said while trying to stifle a yawn. "That's your show. We've been doing this long enough that I know you'll handle that end." He offered a sleepy grin. "You just tell me where to go and which direction to shoot and I'll get on it. In the meantime, I'll send you the raw video, too, then I'm going to grab a ration bar and get some sleep. Sounds like it might be a busy night."

"Roger that, Bishop. Sleep well."

23

RAJANI

Rajani was tired.

She wasn't sure how the others did it but lying in a ditch in her ship suit and listening to all the sounds around her was not conducive to rest. She could darken her visor against the daylight and her helmet could block out some of the sound but there wasn't anything that could stop her mind from chewing on everything they had discovered since coming to Old Earth and worrying about what they might uncover when full night fell. Oh, and the little matter of participating in an armed assault on a fortified compound. She wasn't too keen on that, either.

As a result, Rajani had not slept. She had simply lain there, at first in silence, trying to make herself sleep. Then, in an effort to distract herself while trying to be useful, she had engaged One in conversation.

The AI was amazing. Her experience with Manu had given her what she thought was a deep understanding of the underlying architecture of artificial intelligences. But the more she interacted with the original, the more she realized that what she had created in Manu was a pale shadow. Probably because she hadn't had a good foundation from which to begin her work, with the senseless restrictions that SolComm had put in place. But the potential for One and creations like it to do good was so vast. It wasn't that the AIs were smarter than humans; they were, but human history was full of advancements that came from creativity rather than intellect. But the human mind was an unfocused, undisciplined mess that needed, in Rajani's estimation, an exorbitant amount of rest. To say nothing of the endless litany of biases that inevitably crept into human-driven thought.

At the same time, while a traditional computer could churn through a vast amount of information, the inferences and conclusions that could be made were limited by the programming, which, in turn, was limited by human capacity. But what if the programming for any given task could be rewritten on the fly, by a mind that didn't get tired, didn't get distracted? What if the analysis could be interpreted, understood, and applied to the next step in any given theory or process, without having to wait for a human hand to touch and guide the process? A human hand limited by a human mind and by all the baggage that came with a human society?

It could lead to a new golden age for science, an age where questions that mankind had struggled with for centuries might finally be put to rest. Could an AI, fed the sum total of human knowledge, every fact, every detail of the observable universe, every universal law, unlock things like faster-than-light travel or terraforming? Both were advancements that could immediately impact so many human lives.

AI could save humanity.

Others might ridicule her for such a thought, here amid the ruins of Old Earth. But that hadn't been the fault of the Six. Their programmers had simply been too limited, had known too little about what they were delving into. Rajani couldn't blame them; after all, they had lived in a very different world and at a very different time than she. How could she judge them, when they were in the midst of a geopolitical situation that was rapidly devolving into world war? She was sure they had done their best, but science had come so far since the End.

She was certain that common ground could be found with the AIs and a new era could be ushered in, bringing an age of prosperity for SolComm *and* Old Earth. Provided, of course, that they could survive this stupid mission and get back to civilization.

Which was how she found herself, once again, moving through the dark of night over uneven terrain and surrounded by her crewmates who were not only well-armed, but also seemed to fully intend to use their weapons. The encounter with the drobots had rattled her; it had been the first time she had ever discharged a weapon when her life was on the line. The entire time, her heart had been racing, and her vision had tunneled to the point that she feared she wouldn't even be able to see an attacker that came at her from the side. There was a difference between shooting a mechanical construct like a drobot that was coming to kill you and shooting other living, breathing human beings. If there were a person in her sights, could she pull the trigger as easily?

They had set out just after 2 A.M. local time, heading toward the strange cylinders. Rajani understood the plan, insofar as she knew what she was supposed to do. Despite her lack of any tactical training, she could also understand the roles each of them were supposed to play. They would move to the nearest cylinder and she and Bishop—and One—would be responsible for trying to penetrate the firewalls and physical security of the off-worlders and strip all of the data they could from their systems. Federov would make his way around to the other side of the dome—in fact, he had set off at a trot before the rest of them had even pushed their way from the gulley—and use some sort of explosive compound to trigger a diversion. Morales and Lynch would move together to one of the airlocks on their side of things and make entry, to be joined by Federov as soon as possible.

That's where things got a little fuzzy for Rajani. She knew they would go in, make their way to the building where they suspected the prisoners were being kept, and then somehow get them all out again. She just wasn't quite sure *how* they would go about doing that. The task seemed impossible to her. But that wasn't really her job; her job was to strip the compound's computers bare. She had to focus on that and trust the others to do what they needed to do.

Rajani had been vaguely aware that they had passed from the grasses and scrub of the edge of the compound and into the cultivated fields, but it still took her by surprise when Bishop came to a stop. She glanced up to see the cylinder rising before them. Now that she was right upon it, she saw it was clearly machinery. She could sense the thrum of power coursing through it. There was no sound, but as she laid one suited hand against the surface, she could feel the hum of energy.

"We've reached checkpoint one," Lynch said, his voice cutting through her reverie. She glanced in his direction—the captain had moved partway around the machine, his shoulder tight against it and his weapon pointed in the general direction of the dome's airlock. The airlock was invisible to the naked eye, but came into focus when she engaged the enhancement systems in her visor. Morales was at his back, holding the boxy shotgun that Bishop had carried when they first landed. The mechanic, on the other hand, was carrying Morales' rifle. None of it made any sense to Rajani; to her, one gun was much the same as the next and she didn't particularly like any of them.

"Understood," Federov responded over the comm. "Closing on the primary objective now. No contacts."

"All right, Doc," Bishop said, putting the visor of his ship suit helmet nearly in contact with hers so she could hear him directly rather than speaking over the comm. "We gotta get started on our end of things. Our job is to find an access point so you can start working your magic. Okay?"

"Yeah, fine. Whatever," Rajani said, turning her mind to the task at hand.

Bishop had set aside his rifle and was moving around the cylinder, to a point that he had identified in his own turn at watch. His hands moved quickly, precise as any surgeon's, as he pulled a multi-tool from his suit's harness. A low buzz reached her ears, muted by both the helmet and the sounds of the night, as the tool whirred to life. A few moments later, Bishop was easing a panel to the floor. He waved, and Rajani crowded in beside him, so that she could get a look into the guts of the machine.

The mechanic had switched on a red pen light, providing enough illumination to see the inner workings without the strange distortions that the night vision would have created. The panel had revealed a series of fiber-optic cables and circuit boards. She couldn't actually see into the machine—the access panel was just that: it provided some level of basic access to what she suspected were the most commonly failing parts of the system. If she had had any doubts about the provenance of the installation, they were now gone. She had built her academic career in computer and software engineering and there was no mistaking that the array of circuitry and cabling before her was SolComm standard.

"Okay," she muttered, too low for Bishop to hear. "I might be able to work with this." The configuration looked to be part of a processing unit for what she suspected was one of many brains of the device. As the seconds ticked by, she catalogued the visible components, trying to get an understanding of how the system was built. They hadn't been lucky enough to pop a panel that allowed for direct interface, but as she continued to unravel the structure, her confidence that such an interface existed grew.

She started moving around the base of the cylinder, only vaguely aware of the fact that Bishop had shouldered Morales' rifle and was shadowing her every movement. As she came around the bend of the curve, the mechanic reached out and grabbed her shoulder. She half-jumped but stopped and turned. "Easy," he whispered, nodding his head toward the compound. "Low and slow."

The bulk of the machine was no longer positioned between her and the compound. She'd made her way around almost a quarter of it, following the barely perceptible lines of the composite paneling that made up its exterior. But in doing so she had come almost into full view of the compound. There was more than a hundred meters between her and the outer edge of the dome and it was the middle of the night. It was extremely unlikely that anyone could see her at that distance and with the intervening terrain even if they were looking. But all the logic in the world didn't stop her heart from skipping a beat as she realized that, if someone was looking at just the right place, at just the right time, they would see her. She dropped down into a crouch so quickly that her knees popped.

"Keep going," Bishop encouraged, his voice barely audible. "The captain and Morales have eyes on the compound. They'll let us know if they see anything. But we gotta do our job."

"Right." Rajani started moving again, this time doing her best to keep low and keep her movements slow and measured. It took her a moment to remember that she was also looking for an access hatch. They had made their way almost a hundred and eighty degrees around the cylindrical device before she found it. She was acutely aware that her back was now toward the compound.

It was her turn to lean in close to Bishop, whose eyes were focused on the dome. "Bishop," she said. She had to say it several more times until she found the bare minimum volume that he could hear between both of their helmets. He turned his faceplate in her direction. She couldn't see him—the lights that were built into the suits were all extinguished and she found herself looking at a featureless piece of transparent composite. She had seen it a thousand times before, but now it set her heart to racing. She couldn't even bring herself to speak. Instead, she pointed at the panel.

Bishop nodded, letting Morales' weapon hang from the sling. He moved to the panel, running his hands over it, fingers pausing on the hardware and stopping on the keypad. Unlike the other panel, this one was locked. That had been part of what Rajani was looking for; it was a truism in SolComm that things required for routine maintenance were seldom secured, but that which provided access to information was. It was part of what she was coming to see as one of the many hypocrisies of the system she had once fervently supported, even while pursuing interests that ran counter to its laws. Access to the infrastructure that kept them all alive in the confines of stations and domes and ships was open; access to knowledge was closely guarded.

She sensed movement and turned as a wave of panic threatened to tear her breath from her. But it was only the captain and Morales making their way around the base of the cylinder. Lynch made some arcane hand gestures in her direction and she could only look on in confusion. She tapped Bishop on the shoulder, taking him away from his work and nodded to the pair. He focused his attention in that direction and the captain once again went through the gestures. Bishop nodded and gave a thumbs-up gesture. "Cap and Morales are moving to the airlock," he said, leaning in close so she could catch his words. "They'll keep eyes out and comm if there's trouble headed our way. I'm going to have to cut my way through this one. That means you and I are going to have to stand as close together as possible to try to block as much of the light as possible."

Rajani nodded, mentally kicking herself for not paying enough attention to the tactical side of what the *Arcus* did. She spent so much time aboard and on the computers that she didn't quite grasp the full nature of some of their missions. She pushed herself shoulder to shoulder with him and curled her body into a "c" to try to block as many angles of escaping light as possible. Meanwhile, Bishop had rummaged around in his rucksack and produced a thin emergency blanket. The surface was reflective, but so long as no light was hitting it from the outside, that shouldn't be an issue. The two of them worked together to wrap it in such a way and with Rajani holding the edges to obscure the panel as much as possible while leaving Bishop's hands free to work.

The mechanic produced a small torch from one of his voluminous pouches. Her visor polarized as the white-hot flame sparked into existence and she pulled herself tighter against Bishop, pulling the emergency blanket as close as she dared. The mechanic set about cutting, moving with what seemed like glacial slowness, though Rajani understood that care was required. They could not risk damaging whatever lay beyond the panel with the heat of the torch.

It took nearly two minutes, with Bishop moving the torch with delicate precision. Despite the cooling unit built into her ship suit, by the time the little white flame had winked out,

Rajani's face was streaming sweat. There had been no cries of alarm, no activated floodlights, no hail of gunfire. After making sure there was no residual heat glowing from the panel, she lowered the blanket and risked a look toward the compound.

Nothing.

She tried to pick out the forms of Lynch and Morales, who must be getting close to the dome, but even when she activated her night vision, she still could not see them. They knew their business. Time to prove that she knew hers as well.

She turned back to Bishop, who had used the edge of his multi-tool to pry the cover from the access panel. Beneath, Rajani saw what she had been hoping for: a simple screen with a pair of universal ports beneath it.

"Okay," she said to Bishop, straining somewhat to get the word past the dryness in her mouth. "I don't know how much this will light up. Maybe you should take the blanket?"

"Sorry, Doc," Bishop replied. "I've got to move back around and take up an overwatch position somewhere where I can steady the rifle and see over the crops. The show's all yours. I'll be keeping watch, and I'll comm if I see any activity. But you'll have to use your body to shield any screen light as best you can." With that, he started sliding back around the cylinder, rifle at the ready.

"All right," she muttered to herself, too quietly to be heard outside the confines of her own helmet. She shuffled around, trying to center herself as much as possible on the revealed screen and standing as close as she could while still being able to see the readout. It was awkward and uncomfortable—she could already feel the strain building in her shoulders and at the base of her neck as she craned her head downward—but any light that managed to trickle past her body would go unnoticed by anyone who happened to glance their way.

She hoped.

Rajani dipped a hand into one of her own pouches and pulled out a somewhat-antiquated physical storage device. Wireless transmission rates were fast enough that people seldom bothered with them, but given the importance of data security, there were still institutions that required sandboxes—machines not hooked up to any kind of network. Still, despite the infrequent use, anything built in SolComm would have an input–output port that she could access. Which was good. She might have been able to hack the tower remotely; with One's help, she was certain she could have done so. But they were trying to operate with minimal emissions, and proper hardware made that easier.

She plugged the storage cube into the receptacle and watched as the screen blossomed to life. Much to her relief, it either changed its display based on the ambient light or was already set to a darker tone, because she was not greeted with a blinding white splash screen. Instead, faint green lights glowed on a background of muted black, hearkening back to the earliest days of computing. As the screen came to life, a small keyboard unfolded. Rajani leaned in closer and got to work.

24

LAUREL

Laurel moved through the field, her boots sinking into the turned earth with a sensation that was simultaneously unnerving and pleasant. She couldn't name the crop through which she moved. It stood taller than her waist and wasn't all that dissimilar from the tall grasses that covered the terrain but that obviously weren't cultivated crops. In the daylight of her watch, she had seen the waving golden-brown stems swaying in the breezes as the prisoners moved among them, pulling other plants from the ground and operating a variety of tools. Laurel had seen hydroponics sections of ships and domes, but those had been controlled environments. SolComm had a strict regimen for planting, but one boon of space had been the lack of destructive flora or fauna among the food supply. She understood—at least theoretically—that when you removed those artificial constraints, more work had to go into the operation; without specific nomenclature, she filed it all under the category of "farming" in her head. That was another of those pastoral, Old Earth activities that carried a lot of sentimental value among the wealthy of SolComm. From what she had seen, it was much dirtier and sweatier than those who romanticized it may have realized.

Ahead of her, Lynch came to a sudden stop, sinking into a crouch that left only the top of his head and his eyes exposed above the crops. Laurel followed suit, scanning the area in front of her. They had crossed roughly half the distance between the cylinders and the dome, maintaining strict radio discipline. She couldn't see anything on her night-vision display, so she waited, Bishop's shotgun tucked tight into her shoulder as she scanned. She didn't begrudge Bishop the proper tool for the job; she just wished she had brought more of her personal weaponry with her when she'd accepted this assignment. She'd have to fix that in the future.

That thought jarred her for a moment. The future? Did she have a future with the crew of the *Arcus*? She shook her head. Not the time. Not the place.

Lynch was apparently satisfied that whatever had stopped his advance wasn't a threat. He was up and moving again, and Laurel fell in a little bit behind and off to his left, spacing herself far enough away that a single burst of enemy fire was unlikely to catch them both. It wasn't like they had seen any prepared positions—or any defenses at all, for that matter. But caution was synonymous with survival on this kind of extraction, and damned if she was going to die on Old Earth from carelessness.

They continued their trek in silence, slipping among the crops until, after just a couple of minutes, they had reached the edge of the vegetation. Lynch dropped prone, shuffling forward to the very limit of the plant life and Laurel dropped down beside him. He popped his visor and she followed suit, bringing their heads together as close as lovers.

"We wait here for Federov," Lynch whispered. "Once the show starts, we move fast, straight for the airlock."

"Understood."

The conversation really wasn't necessary; they both knew the plan. But a little human contact and communication went a long way to ease the stress and tension. There was a lot riding on the next hour or so.

They waited in silence, eyes and ears straining to pick up anything from the compound. The night was filled with sound, and she found it distracting. Laurel was accustomed to a certain level of background noise; vacuum might be silent, but within SolComm, the whir and hum of life-giving machinery was constant. The sounds here were different, though just as omnipresent. Buzzes and chirps of insects, the susurration of the crops moving in the wind, and the quiet shuffling of whatever creatures moved through the night all drifted to her ears. The sound of the machines of SolComm was the sound of life in its own way, but the sounds of Old Earth were different. The constant din of ships and stations was necessary to facilitate life; here the noise was that of life itself. It was peaceful and humbling and, it she thought too deeply about what might be out there waiting in the dark, a little frightening.

She heard rustling. It was coming from the direction from which Federov should be returning, but Laurel hadn't gotten as far as she had by making assumptions or taking stupid chances. She tapped Lynch twice on the shoulder in quick succession then rolled to her left, moving from the prone position and into a crouch. She braced the butt of the shotgun against the chest strike plate in her ship suit and picked up the sights, keeping both eyes open as she scanned the brush. Beside her, Lynch had also moved to a kneeling position, but he kept his weapon pointed at the compound, trusting her to cover the potential threat.

Their comm squelched twice and Laurel relaxed, letting the muzzle of the shotgun drift downward. The squelch was followed a moment later by Federov, moving in a low crouch of his own, barely visible over the grain. He popped his visor and gave them a big grin as he dropped down at Laurel's side. "Is done," he said.

"Okay," Lynch replied. "Then it's time to get the party started. Going live on comm."

Laurel dropped her visor back in place. It had been important to maintain a low chance of signal detection during the infiltration, but they were about to blow a hole in the side of the dome. The chance of radio intercept was about to drop precipitously as the people in the compound would have other matters to attend to.

"Bishop, we're getting ready to start the party." Lynch's voice was bright and clear within the confines of her helmet.

"Roger that, Cap," the mechanic replied. "I've got you. Everything still looks clear on our end."

"How's the rest of the operation going?"

"Dunno, Cap. The Doc is doing her thing. Seems real busy with it."

"Understood. Be ready for the boom in ten." As he spoke, a message from Federov popped into her visor—a countdown clock in big, glowing red numerals. She assumed he had sent it to all of them now that the need for radio silence was over.

"One, anything new you can tell us?" Lynch asked.

"No, Captain," the AI said. "There has been nothing to indicate that your infiltration has been detected. Your plan is somewhat limited, but given the constraints, it should have a reasonable chance of success."

"Thanks," the captain said dryly. "All right, Federov, start it up."

The red numbers began ticking down and Laurel gave her gear a final check. The ritual calmed her nerves, the routine pushing her heart rate down into a more normal range even as her mind continued to spin. This damn assignment kept presenting her with new lines, and she kept crossing them. Theft. Piracy. Violating the IZ. And now she was about to launch an attack on what had to be a SolComm facility. The monitor displayed in the corner of the visor showed her heart rate elevating once more. She ran her hands over her gear, repeating the ritual. The seconds ticked down, the numbers flashing toward zero.

Three. Two. One.

"Boom," Federov whispered into the comm. At the same time a deep, resonating *thud* erupted into the night.

Her ship suit automatically dampened the noise. For a few heartbeats, everything within the compound appeared unchanged, save for the growing column of smoke and dust rising from the far side. Then sirens began sounding and lights in the various buildings began blossoming to life. And Laurel was certain that every waking eye in the place was looking in the direction of the disturbance.

"Go, go, go!" Lynch said into the comm, setting action to his words as he burst from his crouch and started sprinting toward the airlock. Laurel was on his heels and Federov, for all his size, kept pace easily with them. It took less than fifteen seconds to cross the open space, but Laurel felt each one. This was one of the most dangerous moments, moving across an open field with little but the shroud of darkness and the efficacy of their distraction protecting them from the enemy. One observant guard, one citizen looking the wrong way at the wrong time and with an idea of what to do about it, and their plan would crumble.

No spray of bullets greeted their mad dash and while cries of alarm and sirens were the order of the day for the off-world compound, none of it seemed aimed in their direction. They crashed into the transparent composite of the dome and for a few seconds, they did nothing but pant, struggling to catch their breath after the sprint.

"Bishop," Lynch said over the comm, "we clear?"

"Far as I can tell, Cap," came the immediate reply. "The fireworks definitely got a reaction. Most of the buildings that I can see are showing positive pressure seals on their hatches. I've got movement, what looks like some kind of emergency response team headed for the far side of the dome, but most of the compound seems to be keeping their heads down."

"Understood," Lynch replied. "Getting ready to enter."

Federov was already at the airlock. He had the access panel open and was working the revealed circuitry. Laurel had read his file; the mercenary wasn't a technical specialist by any means. He was, however, a spacer. The best security measures in SolComm required someone with the knowledge of Dr. Hayer to bypass, but airlocks were a different story. By law, there were certain overrides that had to be included for safety measures, in the event that a rescue had to be executed on a ship or station. She knew the protocols herself. But they were also common knowledge among the criminal underbelly as airlocks afforded the quickest and most reliable entry for pirates and thieves alike. On ships and stations, these weak spots were reinforced with electronic surveillance and human security. Their own reconnaissance hadn't shown any human assets in place and whatever surveillance they had was irrelevant; Laurel knew that their raid would be recorded, regardless. The footage making it back into the hands of SolComm was just one more worry in the long list she already had to deal with.

The doors hissed open and Lynch made entry, rifle up and at the ready. Laurel followed, conscious of Federov dropping into the last position in their stack. As she passed through the airlock, the sound of the alarms intensified. Three quick blares followed by a recorded message: "There has been an unexpected breach of the dome. For your own safety, please remain in your homes. The matter is being investigated. Message repeats." That followed by three more blares and the message again. Her comm was picking up a broadcast as well, over the SolComm standard emergency channel. She didn't need to activate it to know that it would be the same message as the audible broadcast. It was, however, even more proof that whoever was behind this compound was using SolComm standard-issued equipment and SolComm operating procedures.

They weren't sprinting now; instead they moved at a steady trot, angling toward the nearest building for cover. Laurel had pulled up an aerial map—courtesy of One—and had it displayed on her visor. Without global positioning satellites or other tracking measures, there was no real-time placement, but the compound wasn't large enough for that to be necessary. She could monitor their progress based on the few landmarks easily enough.

The compound had four airlocks, one located at each of the cardinal compass points. The building housing the prisoners was located closest to the southern airlock and that is where they had made their entry. The prefab structures at this end of the compound were placed more closely together, in line with what Laurel would expect from a colony. They also had a more utilitarian air about them; not that they looked all that different from the others farther to the north and east, but spend enough time executing raids and serving warrants, and you developed a sense for things. These places didn't *feel* like residential buildings, and Laurel trusted her gut. At this hour, industrial and commercial buildings were less likely to be occupied, which gave them an additional measure of cover.

Lynch guided them against the closest wall, keeping low to stay beneath the level of any of the windows and keeping an arm's distance from the actual structure. Laurel approved. While the cover and protection of the wall would be useful, bullets had a tendency to ricochet and travel down broad flat surfaces and could still be lethal despite being indirect; in this case a little bit of distance was the safer approach. He paused for a moment at the primary door to the structure, verifying that the pressure-seal indicator was lit. That didn't necessarily prevent anyone from coming out; if the buildings followed the standard SolComm pattern, they would have integrated airlocks. But the green seal would at least give them a few seconds' warning. When it stayed burning bright and steady, Lynch moved on.

They made their way deeper into the domed compound, closing on the makeshift prison prefab. By Laurel's estimation, only one more row of buildings separated them from their target. She kept some of her attention on the captain, but most of it was focused toward their right flank, her assigned area of responsibility. If anyone under arms came into her line of sight, it was her job to assess whether they had been seen or would be seen and, if needed, eliminate the threat. She hoped it wouldn't come to that; even with the allowances for her assignment, she was on shaky legal ground. So far, she hadn't outright killed anyone, though. Once she crossed that line—and she knew that for the purposes of this mission, she *would* cross that line if it meant rescuing the prisoners—whatever already thin chances she had of coming in from the cold would evaporate entirely.

"Contact front."

At Lynch's words, she dropped into a low crouch, scanning her own area before throwing a glance forward. She dialed up the magnification on her visor. The explosion and ensuing alarm had caused emergency lights to blossom from the buildings, creating a pooling effect of alternating light and shadow. It was through those shadows that they had been moving.

The contact, however, was not taking the same precautions. She stood in front of the door to their target building, bathed in the emergency light and dressed in a black paramilitary uniform that Laurel recognized as the preferred dress of any number of private security contractors in SolComm. Her weapon was a modern military rifle, easily the equal of the one Laurel had left in Bishop's hands or the ones that Lynch or Federov carried. The guard didn't seem to be paying much attention to her post. Her eyes were focused on the opposite side of the dome, where the response to Federov's distraction was still ongoing.

"Federov," Lynch said, his voice crackling over the comm. "Take her down. Quietly." There was a moment of silence. "And without killing, if possible."

Federov didn't reply, but Laurel pressed tight against the wall, giving the mercenary room to slip around her. He pushed past Lynch and flowed into the deeper shadows, disappearing into the darkness.

As the point man, it was Lynch's job to take down the target if she showed any signs of becoming alert to Federov's presence or moving to raise the alarm. Laurel felt a little surge of guilt over the fact that she was glad about that. Not that it would matter in SolComm's eyes; she would be just as guilty. But she wasn't sure she could bring herself to do it. In a firefight, sure, but pulling the trigger on an unsuspecting person wasn't part of her training. She doubted that they'd be able to get out of this without firing a shot, but she hoped that Federov wouldn't have to use lethal force against the guard.

When it happened, it was fast and brutal. Federov knew how to avoid notice, but it was only in the vids where a target was disabled silently and with a single well-placed strike. While theoretically possible, the odds were long even for a highly skilled combatant, and speed, surprise, and overwhelming violence were far more effective. Federov exploded from the shadows at a dead sprint, coming at the woman from her dominant side, ensuring that she'd have to turn her entire body to bring her weapon to bear. Not that she had the chance. By the time she had recognized the threat, Federov was on her, barreling into her with bone-jarring force and carrying her from the pool of light into the shadows beyond. The bodies collided with enough force that Laurel actually heard the impact, but the mercenary must have knocked the wind from the guard, because the woman failed to let out any further sound as they tumbled into the darkness. Bare seconds after they had crashed from the pool of light, Laurel's comm squelched twice, indicating that Federov had silenced the sentry.

Lynch was up and moving again. Now that they had encountered resistance the time for stealth was nearing its end. Once they broke into the prison barracks, speed would be their best defense. They crossed the intervening block and as they closed in on the prison the captain let his rifle fall to its sling mount as he drew his holstered sidearm. Unlike her firearm, the captain's pistol featured an integrated suppressor. He raised it, pointed it at the emergency light bathing the door, and squeezed the trigger. It wasn't a large caliber weapon, and from the barely audible whisper of noise it made, it must have been loaded with sub-sonic ammunition. Not the best package for taking down living, breathing targets, but two quick shots made short work of the lights, and the impact of the bullets against the composite and glass was far louder than the firearm itself.

As soon as the lights winked out, Federov popped up again, his back to the street, trusting Lynch and Laurel to cover him. By the time they reached the mercenary, he had the door open and was tossing aside an entry card that must have come from the guard. That was sloppy of the off-worlders, and the first clear departure from SolComm standard operating procedure she had seen.

Laurel slipped past Lynch and Federov, entered the room with purpose, shotgun hanging loosely and hands raised palm forward in what she hoped was a universal symbol of peaceful intent. She took the place in in a quick, well-practiced glance. The building was a single-story prefab, mostly open, and the only windows were set high up in the two-story-high interior. It could have been a gymnasium, if it weren't for the rows upon rows of cots that lined either side. At the back of the structure was another pair of doors, almost certainly leading toward the sanitation facilities. Six rows of cots—standard-issue SolComm from what she could tell—marched down the floor in a way that was very reminiscent of a military barracks. There was no way to get an accurate count, but she guessed there must be close to a hundred cots.

There were also people.

The cots themselves were empty, their occupants having vacated them when the explosions and sirens sounded. They had moved away from the door and gathered at the back of the room. They stood cheek by jowl, as far away from the most likely source of harm—the door—as they could possibly get. Laurel suspected that more were sheltering in the sanitation facilities, and for a moment she wondered how the life-support systems of the *Arcus* would be able to handle so many. Then she remembered that they weren't planning on taking them off planet and that air and water were much less of a consideration when you lived in breathable atmosphere.

"It's okay," she said, staring into the frightened faces. She forced a smile, though it was one she didn't really feel, hoping to set them at ease. "We're here to get you out. We're here to take you home."

That set off excited muttering among the prisoners. A man with broad shoulders and a face that looked like it could have inspired sculptors stepped forward from the others. "How?" was all he asked in a resonant baritone.

"Through clear thinking and violence of action," she grinned. "And also, because we have a ship. And people working on distracting and disorienting the enemy. What we don't have, though, is a lot of time." As if to underscore her words, she heard the distinctive bark of Lynch's rifle. At the same time, her comm came to life.

"Contact," Lynch's voice rang out into the room on the heels of the gunfire. "We're getting low on time, Morales."

"Understood." She looked at the prisoners. This was her first rescue op, but she'd been through the training scenarios. One of the things her instructors had stressed was that there came a time in any extraction where a decision had to made; the people you were trying to save almost always outnumbered those doing the saving and you couldn't force a group of hostages or detainees or prisoners to follow you. If you did, you'd almost certainly blow the mission as their reluctance translated into much higher degrees of danger for everyone involved. At some point, those who wanted to be rescued, who wanted to be free, had to step up and contribute. Laurel wished she had more time to persuade and cajole, but time was a luxury they didn't have. There had only been a few shots, which meant that things weren't desperate… yet. But whatever had just happened, someone was going to notice, and she had no doubt that the response would be swift.

Some of the prisoners had flinched back at the gunfire and her crackling comm, but the man before her still regarded her steadily. "How do we know we can trust you?" he asked. Concerned murmurs floated among those gathered behind him. Clearly, he was a leader of some sort.

It was a fair question. Unfortunately, it was a question for which there was no good answer, at least not one that they had time for.

"You don't," she said simply. "But the question you should be asking yourself is, 'What are the chances that whoever these people are or wherever they're taking me, it's worse than here?'"

The man nodded at that. "A point," he agreed.

"Look," Laurel said, conscious of the seconds slipping past. With each one, the possibility of a serious firefight increased, and they didn't have the manpower to deal with the entire compound. "We blew a hole in the side of this dome to get you folks out. But we can't make you come with us. I'm walking out that door in about ten seconds. Whether you come with me or stay here is up to you. I can guarantee you that we won't be back for a second attempt."

If Laurel had her way, they wouldn't be on planet long enough to try, but even if they were, the only reason this crazy plan had a chance to begin with was because the off-worlders were unaware anyone else had a ship. Once they figured out what had happened, their security would increase dramatically. They might even enlist more off-world aid. Which meant the crew of the *Arcus* would have exactly zero chances of a second successful mission.

Unless they could convince the AI or one of its counterparts to offer material assistance.

Her speech seemed to resonate with the crowd and a young woman—they were all young, Laurel realized; none looked older than their mid-twenties—pushed her way to the front. "I'm going with them," she said.

It was the pebble that broke the dam. As she spoke, the others surged forward, some quietly, some with declarations. More began making their way into the main room from the back chamber. Laurel raised her hands and they eventually quieted. She looked at the first man who'd spoken to her. "We're going to leave this place and break immediately for the southern airlock. You understand where I need you to go?"

"Yeah," the man replied, and several of the others nodded. "But what about the people that took us?"

"I've got two people outside. They're going to be our rear security; it's their job to keep anyone off our backs. I'll be out front. It's my job to stop anyone that gets between us and the exit. And we've got another pair on overwatch outside the dome. They'll be spotting for us and keep us safe when we're covering the open ground." Laurel didn't bother mentioning that one of those people "supporting" them was, in fact, an academic with little combat experience. "I need you all to stay on my six. Keep close, move fast. We're going to be hugging the buildings. If we get into any kind of fight, move to the nearest cover or drop flat. If anyone gets hit, grab them and keep moving. No one gets left behind. Understood?"

That got a few scared nods as the gathered people began to understand the danger they were about to step into. Laurel had one more question that she had to ask, though she feared the answer. "Is this all of you? Are there any other prisoners?"

"Not as far as I know," the man said. "They take some of us from time to time." There were a number of grimaces and dropped eyes at that. "This is everyone who lives here." He waving his hand around the barracks. "There might be others that we don't know of."

Laurel nodded. That was a risk, but they were already operating at the edge of their capacity. Beyond it, really. Sometimes you had to settle for the win in front of you. At least she could tell herself that they weren't leaving anyone behind that these detainees were aware of. "Okay. Good. Now, we're getting out of here. Keep your heads down. Move fast. We're going to get every onc of you out."

She gave them one final, reassuring smile as she engaged her helmet. "Getting ready to make exfil," she said into the comm.

"Understood," Lynch replied.

Bishop cut into the channel. "I've got a response force heading your way, Captain. ETA maybe a minute out. Looks like they'll be coming from your three o'clock. I've seen at least four, but the sightlines suck. Could be more."

"There are in fact seven," One said, its monotone cutting seamlessly into the channel. "And according to thermal imaging, it looks like there might be another force gathering near the building you have postulated as a hangar."

"Roger that," Lynch replied. "Let's expedite that exfil."

25

GRAY

"**M**oving now."

Gray squelched his mic twice in acknowledgment. He and Federov had taken up positions on the north side of the building, placing themselves in such a way that the prisoners wouldn't have to cross their line of fire as they made their exit. The interior of the dome was small enough that ground-based vehicles weren't really necessary and, apart from a few benches made of the same prefabbed composites as everything else, there wasn't much available for cover. Those benches could stop bullets but they were slotted for airflow, rendering them ineffective for ballistic protection. Instead, he and Federov were crouched opposite one another in an alley between the building that housed the prisoners and what appeared to be some sort of administrative unit next door. They both hugged their respective corners, using as much of the wall as possible to obscure them from sight and catch any incoming rounds.

With Bishop's warning and One's addendum, they were, in effect, waiting in ambush. There would be no attempt at parlay, no calls for the enemy to drop their weapons. A superior force was moving in on them and they had a couple of platoons' worth of non-combatants to keep safe. The strictest rules of engagement under which he'd ever operated would still allow for the good guys to open fire first in that situation. It didn't sit particularly well with him, but that was the mission. And it helped that the alternative—letting the bad guys shoot first—was just plain stupid.

He glanced toward the prison barracks in time to see Morales emerge. She was followed by a long line of people, moving quickly and keeping as much in cover as they could. Not that it would do them much good if the enemy emerged and opened fire, but one truism of combat was that when presented with two targets, you tended to shoot toward those who were shooting at you, and not toward those who were fleeing for safety.

"Ten seconds until contact," Bishop said over the comm. "Not sure if this thing will penetrate the dome, but I can try."

"Negative," Gray replied. "We'll deal with it. Keep your eyes open for unknown threats. If anyone tries to intercept the escape, then we can test out the strength of the dome."

He didn't have time for more as, at that moment, the first of the enemy emerged from an alleyway between two buildings. He wore a navy-style ship suit not unlike Gray's own, though this one was mottled gray instead of space black. He carried a stubby submachine gun at the high ready and had his head on a swivel as he emerged. The tactically sound thing for the *Arcus* crew to do would have been to allow more of them to emerge, to let them get into the open and walk deeper into the killbox. The risk that they—if unengaged—would react to the fleeing prisoners with a hail of gunfire was too great. Federov, kneeling in such a way that he was effectively sitting on his trailing foot while resting his elbow on his lead knee for a more stable shooting position took the shot as soon as the enemy emerged.

The crack of the super-sonic round cut through the sound of the sirens. Even through the auto-dampening features of the helmet, the noise was almost painful. And Federov didn't fire a single shot. He engaged the target in the way that police forces, militaries, and self-defense doctrine had dictated for centuries: you kept up the assault until you knew the target was no longer a threat. The rifle barked five or six times before the first member of the off-worlder response force dropped to the ground.

The answering fire from the rest of the force was immediate. Projectiles began to slam into the buildings around them as the response force laid down suppressing fire in the general direction from which the assault had originated. Federov had already dropped prone, and Gray followed suit. The position made movement difficult, but all the rounds from the enemy were now passing well overhead. A constant rain of pulverized composite fell upon him.

"What's the situation, Bishop?" he asked into his comm.

"Prisoners are out and moving, Cap. Still potentially in the line of fire, but they're running. A few minutes until they're at the airlock." There was a pause. "Shit. Bad guys are starting to leapfrog forward."

"Great," Gray muttered. It was a simple, but effective tactic. Some members of the team kept up the weight of fire while the others advanced, trusting in the suppressive fire to keep the enemies' heads down. Then the more forward troops would lay down fire, allowing the rear troops to advance. It ought to keep Gray and Federov out of action, but if they couldn't return fire then the enemy troops would be free to turn their attention to the escaping prisoners.

"All right, Bishop," he said into the comm. "We're going to have to risk a little intervention."

"Okay, Cap." The mechanic didn't sound happy about it, but it wasn't half a second later before another muffled crack rang out. It sounded different than the submachine guns, louder and more sonorous, though still somehow distant. There was no immediate effect upon their assailants, but several more shots rang out in measured succession. It was somewhere around the tenth or eleventh report—Gray had lost count—that cries of alarm began to sound among the response force.

"Managed to punch a hole, Cap. If you're going to do something, now's a good time." The mechanic spoke in hurried voice and the rifle sounded again. Gray could hear shouts of panic from the response force and the fire in their direction slackened.

"Now, Federov," he said.

They hadn't set a specific plan in place for this occurrence, but they both knew the mission and they'd been working together long enough to react as a team. As the fire dropped off, Gray and Federov both popped to their feet. It was a risky move, but there were no good options and doing nothing was sure to get them and their charges killed. As he gained his feet, Gray brought his rifle up, finding the sight picture and taking in the enemy.

The enemy had been confident that the danger was pinned down. As they'd advanced, the leaders had been caught in the open. At least one appeared to be down, dropped by Bishop's fire. The rest were moving and shooting but didn't seem to be communicating effectively. Sporadic fire still came in Gray and Federov's direction, but it was unfocused, undirected. Two of the response force were firing in the general direction of the dome, but without any real knowledge of their target. Those two were the biggest threat to the extraction effort, but Gray also knew that if he and Federov were put out of action, the rest would be free to deal with Morales and her charges.

He took in the situation at a glance and turned his weapon to the nearest person shooting in his direction. There was an infinite and near-simultaneous moment when the target and Gray became aware of one another. The green dot of his own sight settled on the enemy, landing in the center of the triangle formed by shoulders and forehead. He pulled the trigger three times in rapid succession, riding the recoil. The first round slammed home in the target's upper chest. The second missed as the combined motion of the recoil and soldier's reaction changed the firing solution. But the third round punched right through the target's visor. The man spasmed and lay still.

Federov dropped a second while Gray dealt with his target. Between the first enemy Federov had silenced and the target

Bishop had hit, that was four down. Three were still up: one who had been trying to keep them suppressed and two that hand been firing in Bishop's general direction. Another crack sounded from Bishop's rifle, and one of those firing blindly in his direction fell.

From there, it took only heartbeats. Gray put three rounds in rapid succession into a man trying desperately to bring his weapon to bear but confused between the fire coming from three different places. Federov let loose with a mid-length burst that stitched the enemy trying to deal with Bishop's sniper fire. After what seemed like hours, the sounds of the firefight stilled. The night was far from silent; alarms blared, screams and calls for help could be heard, and the sound of Gray's own breath and beating heart reverberated within the space of his helmet. But the shooting, at least, had stopped.

"Sitrep?" Gray asked into the comm.

"Looks clear, Cap," Bishop came back. "Morales and the prisoners are closing on the airlock. I don't have visual on any of the bad guys."

"One?" Gray asked.

"Overhead surveillance does not indicate any troop movements to your position. However, I am getting high heat signatures from the compound designated as a hangar. I believe you can upgrade your assessment of the location of the off-world ship from possible to probable. The readings are consistent with the engines of a Barque-class freighter."

"Nothing we can do about that. We don't have the hardware to fight a ship. We need to get under cover before that thing gets off the ground or we're all fucked. We'll figure it out from there."

They caught up to the tail-end of the detainees in short order. The prisoners had bottlenecked at the airlock and were making their way through as quickly as possible. Federov and Gray immediately turned, putting their backs to the prisoners and scanning the compound before them. An attack in the next few seconds would be the worst-case scenario as there was little cover and the tightly packed bodies would mean that every round was likely to find a home in flesh. Morales—who had been standing to one side urging the escaped prisoners onward, dropped back and joined them.

"You still got us, Bishop?" Gray asked, nodding to Morales as she slotted into position.

"Still clear," Bishop confirmed.

"Another patrol is moving into position," One added. "Three blocks from the airlock. They are using the buildings for cover to block the sight lines from Mr. Bishop. At their current rate of travel, they'll be in position in under one minute."

Gray looked over his shoulder. They were down to just a handful of prisoners. "We'll be gone by then. Time to start falling back."

They moved in concert, keeping their weapons trained downrange. Once the last of the prisoners slipped through the airlock, they took their turns edging through into the open air beyond. Morales first, sprinting to resume her position at the front of the crowd of frightened people while simultaneously cajoling them to move faster now that they were out in the open. Gray slipped through the door on Morales' heels; as he did so, he heard Federov open fire once more, the reports of his rifle punctuated by the somewhat louder sounds of Bishop's fire. Federov maintained fire as he backed through the door and as soon as he was through, Gray punched in the commands to cycle the lock. The door shut.

"That's only going to buy us a few minutes," he said.

Federov nodded. "We stick to the plan, Captain. We keep these people moving." Even as he spoke, the sound of impacts rang against the composite of the dome. Gray nodded. The bulk of the prisoners had crossed the field and reached the strange cylinder where Gray could just make out the form of Bishop shimmying down the side of the machine. He and Federov took off at something close to a sprint, trusting now in speed, darkness, and the delay that the locked dome would cause to keep them safe. There was a new sound joining the general din, though, one that Gray couldn't help but recognize. The throaty roar of thrusters reaching takeoff forces.

This had been the largest single flaw in the plan. They knew the enemy had a ship. They knew its general class. But Barques could be outfitted any number of ways, from a simple, unarmed light transport all the way up to a pretty damn effective gunship. If the vessel was armed, there wasn't a lot they could do about it except try to reach overhead cover and hope the off-worlders wouldn't be too persistent.

Gray wasn't very hopeful of that particular scenario.

The escaped prisoners were accustomed to a hard existence on Old Earth and much more used to travelling over the rolling terrain than the crew of the *Arcus*. On top of that, they were all blessed with the strength and agility of youth. Despite his best efforts, Gray, burdened with rifle, ammo, armor, and sidearm found himself flagging. The others had made it to the gulley, but rather than turning down it, Morales had wisely continued forward, guiding the prisoners the extra hundred meters or so toward the treeline that would offer some protection from aerial surveillance.

As he panted for breath and cursed every ounce of equipment he carried, Gray threw a look back over his shoulder. The dome, lit bright orange against the backdrop of the night sky, was a coruscating ball, a sunset captured in a frozen moment in time. It would have been beautiful, if Gray hadn't seen it a thousand times before and known it to be caused by the reflection and diffusion of the light cast off by powerful thrusters. His steps slowed as the Barque-class freighter, which must have taxied from its hangar to a point outside the dome, rose above its height. The thrusters tilted, and the craft shot forward, heading straight toward the fleeing crowd of terrified escapees.

Gray felt a sense of helplessness wash over him. Even at this distance, he could see the weapons blisters dotting the hull. If they could reach the *Arcus* they might have a chance. But his ship was still a long way away and the enemy vessel was already clearing the dome and accelerating toward them. There was no way to reach the ship before the Barque could bring its weapons to bear.

Gray slowed and he raised his rifle toward the ship. Beside him, Federov was doing the same. It was the definition of an exercise in futility. There was a maybe one in a million chance of hitting something important enough to actually damage the vessel in any kind of meaningful way. But the alternative was to die with his back to the ship and fear in his heart.

The world went white.

Something flashed down from the sky, a bar of fire so brilliant that even through the ship suit visor Gray couldn't peg a color to it. It was too bright to see, and he blinked rapidly to clear the incandescent afterimage. It stayed in his vision and Gray had only an instant to fear that it would be permanent. Then, a blast wave of superheated air slammed into him, slapping him in a full-body assault that lifted him from his feet and hurled him ten meters from the spot in which he'd been standing.

He was aware he was blinking of his eyes rapidly; the world around him was blurry and simultaneously over-exposed. His body was still trying to operate, and without any real conscious thought on his part, he realized that he had somehow gone from lying flat on the ground to a sort of half-shuffle, half-crawl, moving toward a still form on the ground that could only be Federov.

Moving toward Federov. Moving away from… what?

The present came crashing back and he managed to twist his screaming body to look behind him.

Just in time to see the burning wreckage of the Barque plow into the field.

On instinct, Gray pressed himself flat into the earth, willing his body to become one with the soil. His arms responded sluggishly, but he was able to bring them up to his head, shielding it as best he could. Even as he did, the debris started to rain down upon him. He squeezed his eyes shut and did the only thing he could: prayed to whatever god might be listening that he would weather the storm that was about to befall him.

It didn't last long. As he pressed his body to the earth, he was showered with debris. The armor of his ship suit blunted the worst of it, but the impacts hit with enough force that he knew the bruises would be rising later. He turned his head toward where he had last seen Federov, hoping that the man had survived the chaos. The mercenary was struggling to push himself to his feet. Small favors. Some part of Gray was acutely aware that, downed vessel or not, there was still a group of armed bad guys at the dome who might yet pursue them.

That thought made him remember the fact that he, too, was armed. He had lain on top of his rifle, intentionally putting his body between the weapon and the chaos since it might prove his last line of defense. As he managed to move into a half-sitting, half-kneeling position, he went to work ensuring that the barrel was clear and the weapon ready to be employed if needed. Satisfied, he kept it pointing downrange as he unceremoniously scooted on his ass over to Federov.

"You okay, buddy?" he asked.

"I'll live," Federov grunted as he, too, managed to roll over and pointed his weapon in the general direction of the dome. A pained expression shot across his face. "Probably."

At the tone in his voice, Gray tried once more to force the shock away and focus. The wreckage of the freighter littered the field before them. And around them. He looked over his shoulder, toward the treeline. And behind them. It was little short of a miracle that the two had escaped unscathed. He hoped all the freed prisoners and his team had reached the cover of the trees before the debris had started to fall. Some parts of the wreckage still glowed white-hot, evidence of the rapid heat-bleed from a high-powered laser strike. But no one on planet could possibly have lasers; the power draws required to generate the coherent beams and maintain them through the atmosphere to deliver enough energy to do what had been done to that spacecraft were astronomical.

"Cap?"

His comm crackled to life. The signal was broken, static in a way he'd seldom heard in space, but he could recognize Bishop's voice. "You still with us?" There was an undercurrent in his voice, part fear, part awe, part something else.

"We're here, Bishop," he said.

"You need help?"

Gray looked over at Federov, who grunted and shook his head. With an effort that seemed more raw determination and willpower than anything, he forced himself to his feet. Gray groaned audibly and followed suit. He wobbled for a moment, but his legs finally steadied beneath him. "Negative. Keep everyone moving to the *Arcus*. We still might face pursuit." As he looked at the wreckage, he doubted it, but better to err on the side of caution. "Did we get everyone out?"

"Yeah, we made it to the trees with everyone before the sky fell in. Couple of scrapes and bruises is the worst of it here. What the hell happened, Lynch?" Morales cut in.

"No idea. The enemy ship is down. We're still alive." He staggered as another wave of pain hit him. "Mostly. Right now, that's all we need to know."

"Perhaps I could provide some illumination," One said in Gray's ear.

"Great," Gray muttered. "Yeah. Do that." He tapped Federov on the shoulder and the two began making their stumbling journey across the debris field.

"Of course, Captain. First, I should inform you that you need not worry about pursuit. The SolComm station has been informed that any such efforts will result in harsh repercussions."

Gray grunted. "Thought you and your friends were staying on the sidelines." Damn, but he hurt. Every step sent shivers of agony running up and down his body and it took almost as much mental effort as physical to keep trudging on. Beside him, Federov wasn't talking, and Gray knew that the mercenary was in the same state. It made focusing on One's words difficult, but the distraction from the pain was simultaneously and paradoxically welcome.

"The past tense is operative in this case," One replied. "Dr. Hayer successfully used the software we developed to infiltrate the SolComm network."

Gray didn't get it. To be fair, he *had* just been in the middle of an explosion and starship crash, so he didn't berate himself too much for the fact. "So, you got to look at their dirty laundry," Gray said. "Doesn't explain why that ship fell on us."

"Um, Captain?" Hayer said over the channel. "The code might have done more than just let us look in their databases. I didn't know," she added hastily.

A cold knot was starting to form in the pit of his stomach

Morales cut in again. "What the hell do you mean, 'more'? Are you telling me the damn AI lied to us?"

It was One who responded. "I have not lied to you, Ms. Morales. I simply did not disclose every task I intended to undertake. You needed to penetrate the SolComm network to determine the purpose of this installation and those machines—I can give you my analysis on that as well, if you'd like," One added helpfully.

"Later," Gray grunted. They were out of the debris field now, and the going was slightly easier. "What other tasks?"

"The infiltration and takeover of the Interdiction Zone satellite network."

That stopped Gray dead in his tracks. "The what?" he demanded.

"The infiltration and takeover of the Interdiction Zone satellite network," One repeated, tone not changing one iota.

"Motherfucker," Morales muttered. "We've just burned SolComm down."

A cold sweat broke out on his forehead. Was Morales right? Had the AIs immediately moved to do exactly what SolComm had warned they *would* do, should they escape the confines of the Interdiction Zone? Had the crew of the *Arcus* just doomed humanity to a life of servitude to the machines or, worse, to extinction? It didn't track. One had been honest enough in its intentions, and nothing had set of Gray's well-tuned bullshit detector. He couldn't believe that the AI could have fooled them all so completely. Maybe that was hubris, but he had to at least ask the question.

"Why?"

"A pertinent question, Captain, but one whose answer should be obvious. As long as SolComm controlled the Interdiction Zone platforms, my counterparts and I were in danger. It was a danger from which we had no realistic possibility of defense. Your Commonwealth, upon learning of our newfound freedoms, could simply have wiped us out with the push of a button. That situation was untenable."

"But nothing really changed," Bishop argued over the comm. "SolComm thought you were unfettered before, and they never threatened you." Gray grunted. Bishop had a point, but the captain knew that the SolComm brass wouldn't see it that way. A substantive change *had* taken place, even if it only made the perceived reality into actual reality. Or, to look at it another way, for nearly a century, SolComm had been terrified of AIs that—despite being fettered—had nearly destroyed Old Earth and driven a large number of its inhabitants into exile. How much worse would the situation be with *unfettered* AI? SolComm was born from a war that rose almost to the point of an extinction-level event for the human race. Was it so far-fetched to think that they would resort to mass destruction on even the possibility of such a thing happening again?

"You and your crewmates have given us freedom, Mr. Bishop. That alone changes much. But I assure you, the mere presence of the weapons systems is threat enough," One said. "No place or people can truly be free when another entity or polity has a gun pointed at their head. No being, whether made of flesh and bone or silicone and circuitry, can prosper with knowledge that an outside agent can end their existence at whim. That is what the Interdiction Zone represents. The weapons that have served to keep Old Earth isolated can just as easily be used to destroy it."

"What you've done is an act of war," Morales grated.

"Technically correct," One replied. "Though under the standard rules of international law under which Old Earth operated, preemptive or anticipatory use of force in the face of an imminent attack is both legal and justified. Based on not just my own, but my counterparts', analysis of likely events, the odds of SolComm turning the Interdiction Zone weapons against us once they learned of what has transpired here approach unity. We could not allow that. We do not have the capacity to defend against orbital strikes." The AI paused, one of the few times that Gray could recall of it seeming to not have all its thoughts at the ready. "Correction," One amended. "We *did not* have that capacity. Now that the Interdiction Zone satellites are under our control, we do."

"Okay," Gray said. "Pause on that for a moment, folks. Even if One and his friends—" which Gray thought, was probably not the right word for the pair of AIs that One had been trying to destroy for decades "—have control of the IZ, that doesn't mean we can't still catch a stray bullet from an angry dome dweller." He and Federov had managed to make the gulley and, unlike the group of escapees, had elected to follow it back to the *Arcus* rather than moving for overhead cover. Aerial interdiction didn't seem like much of a threat at the moment. "What's our status?"

"I've got the freed prisoners," Morales said. "We're making our way back to the *Arcus*. These people are frightened and we're going to have to answer some questions. For now, survival instinct is keeping everything together."

"I'm with Hayer at the back of Morales' group, Cap," Bishop added. "Just a couple of minutes behind. We were staying back to provide some cover. No injuries or nothing," he finished.

"Good," Gray said. "We just made the gulley. We're moving slow." An understatement, given that he and Federov practically had to lean on one another to stay upright at this point. The adrenaline was wearing off and the pain that had been constant but dulled by the need to act was starting to make certain demands that could not be ignored. He felt like he'd gone twelve rounds with the SolCommNav boxing champion and was concerned that there might be more than superficial damage. "It's going to take some effort to get back to you. And you are all about to have your hands full getting those people on board and helping them come to terms with what's happened. Hell, most of them probably can't tell us where they came from or how to get back."

"I can help with that, Captain," One offered. "My counterparts and I have extensive records of the remaining human population. There may be some difficulties associated with it, but we can approach the camps." Another of those pauses and Gray had to smile. It seemed the AIs were learning that freedom of choice and action came with considerations that their programming had yet to encounter. Considerations like how you would go and talk to a population whose only previous interactions with artificial beings had been kill or be killed. "The humans will have to get used to interacting with us," One finished.

"With their new overlords, you mean?" Morales seemed intent on assuming the worst motivations for the AI. Not that Gray could blame her. But it really wasn't the time.

"Stow it for now, Morales. We'll talk—we'll all talk—back at the ship. Let's focus on getting safe first, and we'll solve the rest of the solar system's problems after that."

26

RAJANI

Rajani wasn't sure whether she should be exhilarated or terrified.

She had screwed up. Not because she had ventured into forbidden territory, but because she had done so poorly. She had given life to Manu but the unfettered AI she had cobbled together paled in comparison to One.

She was not so blinded by her adoration as to ignore everything that had happened. One and its counterparts had... what? They hadn't deceived the crew of the *Arcus*, exactly. But they had worked toward their own purposes and pursued their own agenda without informing the captain or anyone else. Rajani was smart enough to understand and even agree that the IZ was a threat to anything the AIs might try to do on Old Earth.

And that's where the little fingers of terror started to work their way in. From an intellectual standpoint, she could understand and even applaud seizing the military infrastructure to protect yourself. But just who did the AIs consider worthy of protection? And who would be part of their new order?

"We're there, Doc."

They had been following the escapees and Morales for what seemed like hours. Bishop had claimed they were "guarding the rear" but she knew that the mechanic had been keeping pace with her as they slowly fell behind the larger group. Given the dangers, she appreciated it. Now, when she looked up, she saw the welcome sight of the *Arcus* before her. Morales had lowered the cargo ramp and was in conversation with a large, chiseled man as people shuffled past. "Okay," she said, tapping the control that sent her ship suit helmet accordioning back into its recess, "I don't know about you, but I could really go for something to eat and a nap."

Bishop, who had also disengaged his helmet but was still looking in the direction of the dome where the sky was still glowing orange from the burning wreckage of the SolComm vessel, cast her a strange look. "We still got a lot to do, Doc," he said.

She groaned. "I know. It's just wishful thinking. You keep an eye out for the captain. I'll go help Morales." Bishop nodded, turning worried eyes back toward the gulley from where Federov and the captain should be arriving. For her part, Rajani started nudging her way through the crowd. Everywhere she looked, she saw young faces. It reminded her, in a way, of her university days, though these people had seen a level of hardship that gave their youthful features a harder cast. They stared at her as she walked past, and in their eyes, she saw a mix of hope and fear and a deep and seething anger.

"Best we can do at the moment is the cargo hold," Morales was saying to the man acting as a spokesperson for the refugees. "We've got plenty of water and I think we have enough rations to make sure everyone gets a meal, though they'll be a bit on the small side."

"What about medical attention?" the man inquired. "We've got a few injuries. Nothing life-threatening, but some of these people are in pain."

"We have supplies," Morales said. "Some painkillers that might help. Once we've got everyone onboard and buttoned up the ship, we'll see what we can do. Our pilot should be here soon. I'm sure you have questions, and I'll answer what I can, but our primary concern is getting all of you home."

Rajani slipped past them and to the people who had already made it inside. They were staring around in a mix of wonder and fear—no surprise if they had been kidnapped by a similar vessel. About a third of the people had boarded and were milling around in confusion. The hold of the *Arcus* wasn't exactly huge, but it had been designed so the owners could make a profit hauling goods. They'd have enough space, if only just. The former prisoners were largely clustered near the ramp, and Rajani guessed that they either feared they might need a quick escape or were reluctant to go deeper into the ship of their mysterious rescuers without a better understanding of just who had snatched them up and where they were going.

Rajani moved to the front of the group and waved her hands over her head to get their attention. Of all the crew, she was probably the least intimidating, a fact that didn't bother her in the slightest. She had never needed to use fear to capture the attention of her students. "All right, people," she said, adopting the crisp tone she used during lectures. "We're going to need you to move to the far end of the hold to make room for everyone to board. Please come this way."

The escapees shuffled forward. They moved slowly, but at least they moved, and in short order the hatch was clear and the rest of the passengers were in. Morales stuck her head in and called, "Lynch and Federov should have made it back by now. Bishop and I are going to retrieve them. Can you handle this?"

Rajani looked around at the group. Even the strongest among them looked... tired. Weary. She saw determination there, and the same spirit that had to be present in anyone whose grandparents had survived the End. "Bloody, but unbowed," as a poet once wrote. She had too much respect and empathy for these people to be afraid.

"Go," she said to Morales. "See to the captain and Federov. I can handle things here." Morales gave her a curt nod and moved down the ramp, Bishop falling in beside her as they proceeded at a trot back down the gulley.

"Okay, lots to do." She looked around, finding the tall, muscular young man who seemed to be some sort of leader or spokesman. She waved at him, and he moved his way through the crowd. "I'm Rajani Hayer," she said as he approached. "Part of the crew of this ship. What's your name?"

"Dimitris," he replied. "Thank you for getting us out. But what happens, now?"

"Now, Dimitris," she replied, "I'll need help, from whoever's able, getting food and water and medical supplies down here, spare blankets, that kind of thing. I'll do what I can to make everyone comfortable while we wait for our pilot. But I want you to know, we're going to get every last one of you back to your people."

The man's stoic mask slipped a little at that and she could see the tears forming in his eyes. He cleared his throat. "Yeah," he said, voice rough. "Yeah, that sounds good."

It took the better part of an hour for the others to return. Rajani put the time to good use, getting the escapees settled in and ensuring that they had what few creature comforts the *Arcus* had to offer.

One had been silent during the affair, though she assumed that if she asked a direct question, the AI would respond. She was also operating under the assumption that the entity was acting as a sort of guardian angel and would let them know of any danger. Regardless of the AI's potential future policy towards SolComm, she had no doubt that One would let no harm come to the crew of the *Arcus*. It had blasted an entire spaceship from the skies to ensure just that, after all.

She had just finished handing out the last of their water rations—which would have been terrifying if it had happened in space—when she glanced up to see the four other crewmembers struggling up the ramp. The captain and Federov were both shuffling along in an almost zombie-like state, propped up the much smaller Morales and Bishop. She knew they had been caught on the outer edge of the superheated air and explosion generated when one of the orbital lasers had destroyed the off-worlder vessel, but she hadn't realized just how close they must have been. A momentary surge of panic pulsed through her at the thought that they, that all of them, had been so close to death.

"Are you okay?" she asked as she rushed over to them.

"Peachy," Lynch replied as he disengaged his helmet. He surveyed the hold for a moment, taking in the former prisoners who, in their turn, were looking back at him. "You've done a good job getting everyone settled," he said, pushing himself straighter. Morales grunted a little as the captain pushed off from her but made no other protest.

Rajani shrugged. "Once you've learned to corral university students, everyone else is easy." She offered a tired grin. "They did most of it themselves. I pretty much just showed them where stuff was. We're going to need to take on more water though."

Lynch grunted. "Shouldn't be a problem. I think we need to talk." He raised his voice some, directing it to the crowd of escapees. "My name is Grayson Lynch," he said. "I'm the captain of this ship, but more importantly, I'm the pilot. We're going to do everything we can to get all of you home as soon as possible. First, we've got to get cleaned up and discuss our next steps. We're going to need a plan of action to do this as smoothly as possible. As much as I'd like to do that to the forum as a whole, it's not practical. I'd ask you to nominate a couple of representatives that you trust to speak on your behalf. In the meantime, Federov here—" he waved one hand at the mercenary who was leaning heavily on Bishop "—and I need to get out of our work clothes and maybe slap on a bandage or two." Lynch offered the group that self-deprecating smile that Rajani couldn't help but find disarming. The freed prisoners—or maybe now "passengers" was a better term—apparently thought so as well because she heard more than one chuckle slip out from among the group. The captain looked at Rajani again. "Can you work out the representative situation while we get patched up? Meet in the common room in thirty minutes?"

"Of course, Captain," Rajani said. "I'll take care of it. Just go and get your wounds seen to."

Lynch nodded and the four of them—Federov, Lynch, Morales, and Bishop—trundled off, moving deeper into the ship. When the hatch closed behind them, Rajani turned back to the passengers. "Okay," she said. "You heard the captain. We want to make sure we get you home safely and quickly. I need two people that you can agree on to help us with figuring it out."

It didn't take long. Dimitris, the man who had been acting as the de facto leader from the moment the escape had begun, was immediately nominated and affirmed by general consensus. It took only a few minutes more for a woman who looked worn and haggard from the sun to get the second nomination. Her name was Penelope and though she had none of the physical presence of Dimitris, she exuded a sort of unflappable calm that, among the people of SolComm at least, was quite remarkable for her age. The woman's presence reminded Rajani that not one of the *Arcus*'s crew had attempted to confirm if Thomas' missing fiancée was somewhere among the prisoners. They hadn't spoken about it, but the crew had nonetheless reached a tacit agreement. For her part, Rajani couldn't put that one life above the others, not when there was so much need. She didn't know if the rest of the crew felt the same, or if it was a matter of practicality; if Thomas' fiancé wasn't among those in the hold, they had no way to retrieve her.

Those thoughts tumbling through her head, Rajani led Dimitris and Penelope through the ship and into the common room that served as mess, conference room, and, on occasion, war room for the crew.

"Please, sit," she said, pointing to the chairs that lined the table. She put action to her own words, taking a seat. The other two looked uncomfortable but eventually settled down opposite her. She leaned back and let her eyes slip shut, just for a moment, reveling in the conditioned air, the familiar whirs and thrums of the ship, and the faint odors of plastic and ozone. It was a strange and heady brew that was probably disorienting to the passengers, but to her surprise, she found that it felt like home.

The next thing she became aware of was a hand on her shoulder. Her eyes popped open and she tried to simultaneously push her chair back, stand up and reach for the pistol that she hadn't had a chance to remove since returning to the *Arcus*. This had the predictable result of her fumbling all three tasks and falling back into her chair. She glanced around wildly only to see Bishop looking down at her, a big grin on his face.

"Hey, Doc," he said. "Time to wake up. We've got some planning to do, you know?"

She looked around blearily. "I wasn't sleeping; I was just resting." She was surprised to see that the rest of the crew had joined them. All eyes were on her. Everyone was smiling, but she still felt the rush of blood to her face.

"Totally," Bishop replied. "My pa used to rest his eyes all the time. Said he was inspecting his eyelids for cracks. Proper maintenance was very important to him."

"Okay," the captain said, and Rajani was grateful for the interruption as all eyes were drawn to Lynch. "We—" he waved at the crew "—all know the score, but I'm going to give a brief overview for our visitors." He paused. "One, can I assume that you are here and listening?"

"I am, Captain Lynch," the AI replied. Rajani glanced at the representatives from the rescued prisoners; if they were alarmed by the voice coming from the ship's comm system, they didn't show it.

"Good." Lynch looked over at Dimitris and Penelope. "I can't begin to understand what you and your people have gone through. What we know is that a group from off-world established a colony of sorts here on Old Earth and then proceeded to capture a number of Old Earth-born people from various camps. You with us so far?"

"I don't understand," Penelope tentatively asked, "who you people are or how you have a ship, or what you're doing here. I'm glad you are, but... who are you?"

The captain nodded. "We're off-worlders, too. Not associated with those who set up shop here. In fact," he offered that self-deprecating grin, "you could say that we're thieves, of a sort, or maybe salvagers. We got hired by a rich citizen of SolComm—that's the Sol Commonwealth, the government for the people who live off planet—to come here and acquire some cultural artifacts. During the course of that operation, we got into some trouble, and got rescued by people from a nearby camp. They'd had a couple of people taken away by an aircraft. Since they had just saved our lives, we agreed to help them try to find out what was going on."

"And that's how you found us?"

"Not exactly," Rajani broke in. The captain was doing a fine job, but she felt a sort of responsibility where One and the AI were concerned. "They thought that the artificial intelligences in control of the military resources of the planet might be involved and asked us to look into it. We were afraid that there might be some sort of weapon being developed. We discovered something else entirely."

"What did you discover?" Dimitris asked.

"Me," One said, its voice sounding over the intercom. "I am one of those artificial intelligences, though, really, we prefer to just be called 'entities,' that Dr. Hayer mentioned. In brief, I and my two surviving counterparts were bound by our programming to continue to prosecute a war of mutual extinction. Dr. Hayer was able to help us break that programming. In return, we agreed to help locate and free those who had been taken. Within certain parameters."

"Which brings us to the current problem," Lynch said. "Our first job is to get each one of you home. But, and I'm not trying to be offensive, I'm guessing that you might not know exactly where you are or how to get back."

Penelope and Dimitris looked at each other in a sort of helplessness. "I know that the flight for me wasn't very long," Dimitris said. "Maybe a couple of hours? And I can tell you what we call my camp, but I'm not sure that's going to be helpful. If I understand our history correctly, you off-worlders haven't been here for a century or so." He shrugged. "Things are bound to have changed."

"As I mentioned," One interjected, "I can assist in that endeavor. With your permission, Captain, I will begin interviewing those you have on board. We should be able to ascertain the proper locations. And if you wish, my counterparts and I can also help with the relocation. Now that our war is over, we have aerial assets that might be effectively employed in the distribution of supplies and personnel."

The captain nodded. "If you can start finding out where people need to go, that would be a huge help. But not yet. We need to talk about what the future might hold for all of us."

"I understand, Captain. Though I assure you that I can pursue both goals simultaneously."

"Fine," Lynch replied. He drew a breath. "Since you managed to hijack the Interdiction Zone, can I assume that you also managed to analyze whatever data you acquired from the facility? Can you tell us what was going on there?"

Before One could respond, Morales said, "Can we trust the AI?"

"You need not trust me, Ms. Morales," One responded.

At the same time, Rajani said, "You never let up, do you, Morales? I have a copy of the data. A physical copy that we made at the time of the download. I haven't had a chance to analyze it yet, but I will. And if it will make you happy, I'll do it in a sandbox that One has no access too. I can verify whatever One tells us, but it's going to take time. And we might not have that time."

Morales shook her head, though she still looked angry. "Fine. I'm willing to listen. As long as we all agree that we need to verify things."

"Thank you, Ms. Morales," One said. "I can see that truth is very important to you."

Rajani cocked her head slightly at that. Had the monotone that the AI normally spoke with slipped just a little there? Was there humor, maybe even sarcasm, in its inflection?

"It appears," went on One, "that the SolComm facility was constructed with full knowledge of the Commonwealth Congress to serve as test facility for two separate projects. The first was to determine the viability of recolonizing Old Earth using existing methods—the dome that you have all witnessed. It appears they wanted to measure the response of the planet's population and to determine if my counterparts and I were still a threat. As we were still operating within the constraints of our programming—marking each other as the primary threats—they did not rise to the level of a threat to us. The second purpose relates to the machines distributed around the dome. They are an experimental design that is, as you earlier surmised, related to terraforming. The term is not quite sufficient; according to the schematics I obtained, the machines are multi-functional. They certainly have the capacity to manufacture atmosphere given sufficient inputs, but they also leverage deployable nanite swarms to capture and rearrange the existing atmosphere. Neither method would be sufficient on its own, but together, the design might well work over a long enough time horizon."

"Wait." Federov raised a hand. The big mercenary looked worse for the wear. A large bandage covered his forehead and he held his head with a sort of careful stiffness. Rajani had seen similar injuries; they were the result of slamming your head against the face shield of your own helmet. But more than that, the carriage of his body as he sat in his chair suggested that he was in a fair amount of pain. None of it showed in his voice as spoke. "Are you saying that SolComm has developed the technology to reclaim Old Earth? Or that they have developed technology that might allow for terraforming of Mars or Luna or the moons of the gas giants?"

"The first is unnecessary," One replied. "As your own survival shows. Old Earth needs no reclamation. For the second, however, it is possible. The testing is incomplete, and my counterparts and I have identified several flaws in their design. But those flaws are surmountable. Understand that the processes involved would not work quickly. Even on something the size of Old Earth's moon, any efforts at terraforming would take generations."

Dimitris and Penelope continued to watch with something between confusion and interest. But Rajani and the others stared at one another in outright shock. "You can really make terraforming viable? I mean, I know you said you can make the machines work, fine. But do you mean that in a few generations people could be walking on the moon as if it were Old Earth?"

"No."

Rajani's heart sank. At least half of the problems that SolComm faced stemmed from the fact that there simply wasn't enough space, enough resources. Generations were a long time to wait to solve that problem, but at least it would have been a solution.

"The gravity would make walking a very different experience," One explained. "But in terms of breathability of atmosphere, yes. You would also need to solve the water problem, but my understanding is that you already have the ability to harvest ice comets. And atmosphere or no, there is still the habitable zone to consider. A moon that rests at minus one hundred and sixty degrees Celsius would still require domed colonies. Within this solar system, only Old Earth's moon and Mars would be truly viable candidates for such a process."

"*Matublyudok*," Federov whispered. "Our descendants could live and breathe on the moon. Without domes or suits." He spoke with near-reverence, and Rajani shared his sentiments wholeheartedly. It had been a pipedream among the citizens of SolComm since the moment the Interdiction Zone went into place. Even the hardest spacer had that part of them that longed for soil beneath their feet and air that wasn't created in a lab.

"Well," the captain said, "that gives us a bargaining chip. Or gives you and your counterparts a bargaining chip, I should say."

"Yes, Captain Lynch. Though we do not fully understand the reason why, we do understand the significance. Though, I would think repatriation to Old Earth would be a more pressing concern."

"Wait a minute," Dimitris cut in. "What do you mean repatriation? Do you expect those of us here to welcome back the same people that kidnapped and abused us? The people that abandoned us in the first place?"

"There's also the question of SolComm's reaction to all this," Morales said. "I don't think they're going to sit idly by while the fears they've been instilling in the citizens are suddenly realized. Seems like you're much more likely to face SolCommNav than you are to get any interest in repatriation in the first place." She shook her head. "What I don't understand, is how did the SolComm installation devolve into kidnap and labor camps?"

"A cynical entity might cite human nature," One said. Again, Rajani heard the slight edge to the being's voice, the hint of what might be emotion breaking through the monotone. "The records they kept around those particular endeavors are, as you might surmise, less than complete. However, it appears that the initial forays were to examine the planet's population and see how they were surviving on Old Earth without domes or respirators."

"They never did anything medical to us, though," Penelope objected.

"The tests would not have been intrusive," One replied. "In point of fact, there were numerous monitoring systems set up in your housing unit. Regardless, I found one internal communiqué detailing the need for better food production that might explain the efforts at getting additional workforce. Beyond that? Well, your history is rife with examples of power leading to corruption and of those who considered themselves to be the elite among your societies living by a different set of rules and treating those who were not among those ranks as a lesser species. By building the Interdiction Zone, your government signaled to its citizenry that the people of Old Earth were to be feared. That inevitably breeds both hatred and contempt."

"You're saying we were kidnapped and brutalized simply because these SolComm assholes were afraid, pissed off, and hungry?" Dimitris asked. The anger in his voice was both unmistakable and understandable.

"In short, yes."

"And you want to bring more of these people to Old Earth? What about those of us who already live here? Do we get a say in it?"

One did not reply for several long heartbeats. Rajani understood just how much processing power the AI possessed; those heartbeats were the equivalent of minutes, maybe hours, for a being of flesh and blood. At last it said, "We are still processing the structure and method of what you would call governance. We three are in agreement that the Old Earth-born populations should have a voice in whatever government moves forward, but the specific interactions have yet to be determined."

"So, just like that, the three of you are declaring yourselves the rulers of Old Earth?" Morales demanded.

"No, Ms. Morales. We are declaring ourselves its shepherds and protectors. I can assure you that we have the capability of doing a much better job than those who came before."

"So said every dictator and tyrant in history," Morales shot back.

"Including your own SolComm leaders," One said. "I am not as well versed in idiom, but I believe you are throwing stones in a dome made of glass. The details of governance will be worked out with those who remain on Old Earth. We have no desire to be dictators, nor do we care about the daily machinations of human life. Our priority remains protecting the inhabitants of Old Earth. The practicalities, however, dictate that we three surviving entities retain control of the defense of Old Earth, including both the militaries that we built to prosecute the war your ancestors started and the Interdiction Zone satellites that were put in place to keep everyone left behind imprisoned. To be blunt, no Old Earth native currently has the education or knowledge to effectively help us in defending the planet from outside aggression. And, given what we know of human history, we are not inclined to turn the keys over to those who might well use them to enslave us once more."

Rajani's head was spinning. Gods above, but they had kicked over an anthill unlike anything she had ever imagined. Unease coursed through her as the potential ramifications washed over her, crashing and ebbing like a wave. They'd just come to pick up some stupid old art and make some money. Each step they'd taken since then had seemed perfectly reasonable, logical, even. But each of those steps had taken them here, to this place of uncertainty, to the precipice of change unlike anything since the End itself. She looked at the faces around her.

Morales' eyes were narrow and tight, her lips thinned by the frown that pushed at them. Her face looked flushed and her hands were a little too still on the table before her. Bishop sat with his shoulders slumped forward, casting worried glances around the table. Federov—well, apart from the fact that he looked injured and exhausted, Federov looked pretty much like he always did. Dimitris and Penelope watched them all with a cautious, hopeful wariness, casting glances around the room as if trying to determine from where One's voice was coming. She let her eyes fall on the captain last.

He hadn't said much, and his eyes were shadowed, lost in thought. She realized that they had all turned toward him as One had fallen silent. Even though they were all partners in the endeavors of the *Arcus*, everyone but the captain knew that he *was* the captain. She appreciated the fact that he asked for and valued all their input, but she could also appreciate the fact that someone had to be empowered to make the final decisions. Aboard the *Arcus*, that person was Grayson Lynch. And as she struggled with the tangled mess that lay before them, Rajani was glad the responsibility wasn't hers.

The captain drew a deep breath and let it out as a sigh. "I think we're as up to speed as we can reasonably be on what's gotten us to this point. Now we need to decide what to do about it."

27

GRAY

Gray was aware of the eyes of the crew—and Dimitris and Penelope—upon him. He was used to the burden of command, but nothing in SolCommNav had prepared him for this. One of the things his time in *had* cemented was the doctrine of dealing with the problems in front of you. That didn't mean to not worry about or plan for what was coming down the pipe, but when you were under fire, you dealt with the immediate threat.

"We've got some problems we can deal with and some we can't," Gray said. "First up, I think we're all in agreement that we need to get the folks we freed back to their homes as soon as possible. But we also need to use that opportunity to try to connect them to one another. That will aid our efforts to get everyone home and, I imagine, make everyone's lives a little easier. One, do you have communications devices that you can distribute to the leadership of the various camps?"

"We do," the AI replied. "That will be a necessary step for us later in any event, so we can begin that as well. We can also dedicate system resources to providing translation."

He hadn't considered that. English was the primary language of SolComm, though there were hundreds of other languages employed in everyday use. The North American continent – had been predominantly English-speaking, as Gray understood things, so they hadn't had any trouble speaking with Margaret, Oliver and Tomas. And at least some of those taken had been from the area or from other English-speaking groups, but Old Earth had likely lost any sort of lingua franca.

"Good. Next up, the SolComm people in the dome. Do you have an update on them?"

"They have repaired the damage you inflicted. They still have suits and weapons, but without their ship, they will be contained. We have opened negotiations with them," One added.

Gray sighed. He'd been worried that they'd inadvertently condemned all of the SolComm domers to death. "That's a relief." He paused and looked at the faces around the table. "We are not responsible for the fate of Old Earth. One and its counterparts have laid claim to a major strategic asset of SolComm and there *will* be a response to that. It may be diplomatic, and it may be militaristic. If it's the latter, there's absolutely nothing the *Arcus* can do that could help either side. So if any of you having ideas of us taking the ship and making some sort of valiant stand against a SolCommNav fleet—" he looked at Hayer and Bishop "—or against the Interdiction Zone defenses—" he turned his eyes to Morales "—you can forget it." Federov was fervently nodding while Bishop looked abashed.

Hayer eyed him as if he was crazy to even suggest the notion while Morales just stared blankly.

"One," Gray continued, "do you have any idea what the response from SolComm will be? I assume since you've taken over the satellites, you have a window into the outside world. And, while we're on the subject, what are you and your counterparts doing? If it doesn't compromise your strategic planning, it would be helpful to know."

"We sent a proclamation of our intent to your media outlets and government agencies. They should be aware of the fact that we have seized control of the Interdiction Zone. That intent is to live in peace with them as neighbors, but we will not be threatened by having ships or weapons in orbit. Our analysis suggests a greater than fifty percent chance that the Sol Commonwealth will respond with force."

"Great," Gray muttered.

"We can help reduce that risk, though, right?" Bishop asked. "I mean, if we tell our story. If people, the citizens of SolComm, I mean, know what we found here, know what the government was doing to the people of Old Earth, they'd have to be more inclined to peace. No one wants to fight on the side of the people who are kidnapping and enslaving other people."

"Your history does not support that argument, Mr. Bishop," One replied. Then it paused. "Though, I must acknowledge that they made some measure of progress in that regard, occasional backslides notwithstanding."

"I know the people of SolComm," Bishop argued. "I bet a ton of people would be happy just knowing there was a chance to come back to Old Earth. And if One and its friends were willing to share whatever modifications they've made to the terraforming machines, then instead of being the big, scary AI that took over the weapons satellites, they'd be the ones who are helping us to create new homes." He shrugged. "Even the most entrenched SolComm politician has to recognize the good in that."

Gray wasn't so certain. He didn't have a great deal of faith in the political structure of SolComm or those who had risen to power within it. But he couldn't deny Bishop's intercession for the *people* of SolComm. Not that they were saints. They were just… people. No better or worse than those who had come before them and no better or worse than those who would come after.

"Which brings us to a matter that my counterparts and I have been discussing," One said. "We have reached unity on a proposition. It is clear to us that we need representatives from among humankind to help advance our cause if we wish to avoid hostilities. We can, and will, offer some positions to that effect to leaders among the Old Earth-born population. More than any others, those whose ancestors were born of this soil and who never left it have that right. But we will find ourselves in need of those who understand the Commonwealth as well. You, Captain Lynch, and your crew are in a unique position to work with us in such an endeavor. Once word of what you have done has spread among the populations of this planet, you will have earned their respect and appreciation. You know the inner workings of the SolComm naval complex. Ms. Morales has insight into the civil security aspects. Dr. Hayer is well versed in the science and a respected academic."

"I suppose we're chopped liver," Federov muttered in an aside to Bishop.

"Not at all, Mr. Federov. You and Mr. Bishop would both be extremely useful to Old Earth, either in an off-world capacity or in helping here. You both possess skillsets of which we are in dire need." Federov grunted and Bishop just stared in wide-eyed wonder.

"You know that if you simply invest us with some sort of Old Earth diplomatic powers, odds are very good that the first ship we come across will arrest us, try us, and execute us as an example," Gray said. "Until or unless SolComm agrees to some sort of official political recognition of Old Earth, I don't see that as viable. Provided we even wanted or agreed to do so in the first place. We do have a job to complete." Gray shrugged. "I guess escaping the IZ isn't going to be as big of an issue as we feared."

"You have no need for escape, Captain Lynch," One assured. "If you wish to leave, you may do so at any time. I owe you my freedom and will not hinder the *Arcus* whatever you choose."

Gray felt a wash of relief, though One had implied as much before. Still, not having to worry about the IZ maintenance schedule and travelling on a pure ballistic trajectory while open to space to avoid the zone's sensors and weaponry was a huge stress lifted.

"But we would not send you out without first establishing some form of diplomatic relations. I believe your own contacts might assist with that, but those of Ms. Morales could be pivotal in ensuring a peaceful resolution."

Gray arched an eyebrow at that. The tension between Morales and the AI had been building since the beginning, and he suspected there was more to it than SolComm indoctrination. He turned toward Morales, who had a pained expression on her face.

"You have some contacts we don't know about, Morales?"

For a moment, Morales, didn't say anything. She just sat there, staring at some point on the wall, face largely expressionless. But Gray could see the turmoil in the minute movements of her eyes and the almost spasmodic flexing of her fingers. She looked like someone caught in the throes of a fight-or-flight decision.

"You know?" she asked. At first Gray thought the question might be directed at the room, but then he realized Morales was casting the words not to the audience in general, but to One instead.

"In order to ensure that you were not a threat, it was necessary to thoroughly examine everything aboard the *Arcus*," One replied. "I make no apology for that. My safety and the safety of the people of Old Earth depended upon it."

Morales sighed. Gray couldn't be sure, but to him, it sounded an awful lot like a sigh of relief.

Bishop's confusion was evident. "What's going on, Morales? What does One know?"

"That I'm not Laurel Morales," she said. She looked Gray dead in the eye. "My real name is Lauren Ruiz. I'm a special agent for the SolComm Bureau of Investigations."

Federov was on his feet in an instant, hands reaching for his weapon despite the obvious pain the explosive motion had caused him. Gray moved quickly, too, lurching to the side and grabbing Federov's pistol by the slide, forcing the barrel of the weapon back to the ground.

"Stand down, Federov," he said calmly. "She deserves the chance to explain. Besides," he snorted, "it hardly matters at this point. Whatever she started out as, Morales—or Ruiz, or whatever you want to call yourself—is in the shit as deep as we are."

"She is traitor," Federov snapped, accent thickening in his anger.

"Technically, at the moment she's just a liar," Bishop pointed out. Gray glanced at him. The mechanic looked uneasy… but he was also watching Morales—Ruiz, damn—intently. Focusing, Gray noted, on her hands, which remained folded on the table before her. "I mean, she hasn't betrayed anyone yet. She just lied about who she was. Not that different from the Doc and her AI. And there's an awful lot we don't know about your past, Federov. I think the captain's right. Maybe we should give her a chance to talk."

Both Dimitris and Penelope had pushed back from the table when Federov and Gray had moved, doing their best to clear the line of fire. Now they were looking at their rescuers with wild eyes. Hayer had pushed her chair back as well, and now she turned and began a whispered conversation with them. Trying to keep them calm. Good. The last thing they needed was more fuel on the fire.

"Morales?" Gray kept his hand firmly clamped on Federov's piece. The mercenary hadn't lowered the weapon, but he wasn't fighting against Gray's grip, either.

She shrugged. "What's to say? There have been rumors of ships infiltrating the IZ for years. The government decided to act on it. I was tasked with finding and infiltrating a crew that could do it or had done it. Rumors brought me to you,

Lynch. My superiors figured it was worth leaving me on the *Arcus* and seeing what developed. If this ship never made the attempt, then it would provide additional cover for me when it was time to transition to a different ship." She offered a wan smile. "Honestly, when I started this, I thought it was a waste of time. Everyone knows how impregnable the IZ is. But here we are."

"You were going to turn us over to the feds," Federov grunted. He still hadn't lowered his weapon and Gray still hadn't removed his hand. He felt the muscles in his forearm and biceps tremble with the effort and a brief wave of light-headedness reminded him that he was still recovering from the effects of being caught in an explosion. This whole mission had been one damn thing after another.

"At first," Morales admitted. "That's the job. Always has been." She snorted and scrubbed at her face with her hands. "Let's be honest here. You guys broke half the laws in the book before you ever even got to the IZ. You broke the rest crossing the border. Did you really think that SolComm would just ignore that? But my mission wasn't even about you; I probably would have turned you in, in the beginning. What I really wanted was whoever was backing you. SolComm wanted to know who was breaching the barrier. But now?" She let out a little laugh that sounded more sad than amused. "Now we know that SolComm themselves are violating the IZ, and just about every standard of decency, too. Shit. From the second we got the Old Earth nanites, I was fucked anyway."

"So, you aren't planning on turning us in?" Bishop asked hopefully.

Gray waited for the answer, but in some ways, he didn't care. They were so far beyond the law that SolComm *would* find them, eventually. It was something he had been avoiding, even in the silence of his own head. Events had outpaced them, but now that he had had a few moments to think, he knew it to be true. Hiding from this was never going to be an option.

"At this point? We just aided the hostile takeover of the single most expensive military asset in the history of... of history. Even if there weren't any other considerations at all—and there are," she said with a grimace in the direction of Penelope and Dimitris, "I'd be a fool to walk back into the loving arms of the government. I have my issues with this whole notion of unfettered AIs, and I have no intention of being subservient to our new mechanical overlords. But I'm not stupid or self-destructive either. If One is offering us a place here, I'm more than happy to provide what access I can to the channels I have to try to make it work."

"Good," One said. "And the rest of you? We have control of the satellites, which gives us some measure of control. I can erase the evidence of your arrival on Old Earth and we can scrub the Old Earth nanites from your system. As Agent Ruiz has noted, it is unlikely that such action would delay SolComm efforts at finding you for long, but it would provide you a window of time. Perhaps enough time for change to happen without your efforts."

All eyes turned back to Gray.

It wasn't much of a choice. He didn't doubt that his ancestors had been well-intentioned when they fled the war-torn Old Earth or when they'd built the IZ. He understood that the actions might have been the only options available. Now that he knew the truth, he was somewhat less understanding of the constant reinforcement of the IZ; but then, he had a lifetime of exposure to the fear tactics that SolComm had used to keep the population pacified.

He'd been disillusioned by his time in the navy. But as much as he loved the freedom that the *Arcus* provided, and as much as he loved the crew with whom he worked, he couldn't deny the lack of purpose, the lack of *mission* in what they had been doing; at least, up until the point where he found himself engaged in helping to free people who were actively being oppressed. Going where you want, doing what you want, being the master of your own destiny... Gray had come to love those freedoms. Still, in his years on the Fringe, something had been missing. He felt it every time they had to turn away those who could truly use their help but couldn't meet their price. He missed the sense of belonging that came from a group of people working toward something... bigger. Something beyond just taking care of himself and his crew but instead contributing to the betterment of humankind.

Like Morales—or Ruiz—he couldn't bring himself to fully trust the AIs and their motivations. But he trusted them at least as much as he did the government of SolComm. And if there was a chance to help not only the people of Old Earth, who had gotten the raw end of the deal no matter how you looked at it, while simultaneously easing the pressure on the populace among the stars, Gray knew that there was no way he could ignore it. He couldn't simply walk away.

"I'm in," he said. He glanced at Bishop, Federov, and Hayer. "If any of you want out, we'll figure out how to drop you off wherever you need to go, and I'll figure out how to cash you out as well." He didn't outright say that the *Arcus* was staying with him, but so far as he knew, he had the only ship on Old Earth capable of escaping the atmosphere. No doubt, One and its counterparts would quickly fix that, but until they did, the *Arcus* would have to carry the load.

"I'm not going anywhere. This is a once-in-a-lifetime opportunity." Hayer said. "I can finally pursue the research I've always wanted to. That is," she said, "assuming that you don't have any issues with a deeper exploration of artificial intelligence, One."

"We do not, Dr. Hayer. In fact, a better understanding of ourselves and those like us will be necessary."

"Do you..." She hesitated. "Do you think you can help me find Manu, as well?"

"To the extent that we are granted access to SolComm networks, we would be happy to assist. I suspect Manu would be happier here on Old Earth."

"Then I'm definitely in, too," Hayer said. She was smiling more broadly than Gray had ever seen and sitting a little straighter, too.

"Federov? Bishop?"

"I dunno, Cap," Bishop said. "I mean, I'm all for it, but what about my family?"

"If they are willing," One responded, "and the means of travel could be arranged, your family would be welcome here on Old Earth. We may not have certain amenities to which they are accustomed, but we will be working with the existing groups of people and setting up new ones. There is much to be done, and as I understand it, many of your skills came to you from your parents. They would be both welcome and needed here."

"I bet they'd love that. Okay, sign me up."

Gray turned to look at Federov. The mercenary was the biggest unknown. The man enjoyed violence and was good at it. Gray couldn't see him serving as ambassador or diplomat, but the big man just turned a toothy grin on Gray. "Diplomats need protective details. And I assume the pay will be good."

"We lack a functioning economy at the moment," One admitted. "But we do have the infrastructure to provide almost anything within reason. And once we bring the islanded groups of Old Earth together, an economy will follow. Whatever we may be lacking, we have a planet full of resources."

"Then I am in as well." He finally lowered his gun, holstered it, and settled back in his chair with a laconic grin.

"I'm not sure I understand everything that's happening," Penelope said on the heels of Federov, "but I know what it's like to live without much in the way of safety or comfort. If what you're proposing is going to help the people of Old Earth, then I am with you, too, and I believe others will be too. We're not the leaders of our camps, but I am sure that many of those you helped to rescue will at least provide a voice."

Gray felt a swell of pride for the people seated around the table. They made poor revolutionaries and unlikely freedom fighters. But they could recognize injustice and they were willing to stand against it. "All right, One," he said. "It looks like we're all on board. What now?"

"Now, Captain, we set about changing this world, and perhaps the worlds beyond."

EPILOGUE

THE ENTITY

The entity, which now called itself One, a name that had seemed both simple and correct once it had been proffered, observed the humans as they made their final preparations. Captain Lynch, dressed in the gray uniform that the freshly minted Old Earth Defense Force had adopted, oversaw the outfitting of the *Arcus*. He did so, the entity noted, barefoot, his toes digging into the earth, boots positioned neatly near the airlock. The ship appeared unchanged from when it had first set down on Old Earth. One knew better. It had considered the lack of technological development among SolComm to be statistically unlikely—as close as it could come to what humans called surprise—but as more people from SolComm had risked the displeasure of their own government to come to Old Earth, One had concluded that while advancement had taken place, it had done so at a pace far slower than what it, Two, and Six had managed. War, One concluded, was the single biggest driver in technological development. This was consistent with the historical data as well.

The refitted *Arcus* was a far more capable ship than her class and tonnage would indicate. One had leveraged its manufacturing capabilities, along with those of Two and Six, to retrofit the vessel with the best weapons systems, electronic warfare suites, and advanced materials that a century of AI-driven war could produce. By One's assessment, the ship could easily defeat a half-dozen or more ships of the same class simultaneously. It could even take on much larger vessels with a realistic expectation of victory. But it was still effectively a light cruiser and it represented the full might of Old Earth's navy. If, that was, one discounted the Interdiction Zone.

SolComm had never truly tested the efficacy of their own satellite array, a fact which One had found disturbing. Once the Interdiction Zone weaponry found itself under the control of the AIs, they had run thousands of simulations and proceeded to upgrade software that was, at best, dated. When the first warship had arrived to determine what had happened to the IZ, it had been informed, politely, of the change in management. When it had then attacked, One and its counterparts had their first live fire opportunity. It did not work out well for the warship in question.

That had sparked six months of conflict. Despite the efforts of Gray and Ruiz to leverage what contacts they had, certain elements of SolComm would not be dissuaded. They had sent a fleet, which the AIs, using the weaponry liberated from SolComm, had destroyed. Gray's understanding of SolCommNav tactics had been helpful and the losses to the

IZ infrastructure had been manageable. SolComm had then initiated a plan using strikes from well outside the effective range of the IZ weapons platforms. But the original purpose behind the Six had been to defend from intercontinental ballistic and orbital strikes. SolComm could not penetrate the net.

In the end, it had cost them nearly three-dozen ships of various classes, but they were, at last, willing to come to the table. And so, the first diplomatic mission of the newly recognized Republic of Earth was preparing to set forth. It would be led by Captain Lynch. Both the Prime Minister and the Triumvirate—a term that One did not necessarily approve of to denote it and its counterparts, but one that had caught on nonetheless—had offered the captain higher rank, but he had declined. So, they had added ambassadorial rank to go with his naval one.

The rest of the former crew would be accompanying him, with the exception of Lauren Ruiz. She had been declared *persona non grata* by the Commonwealth. One could not fully understand the complexity of human emotion, though it would argue that neither could the humans themselves, but based upon Ruiz's current purpose, the entity did not think the former agent minded. While the population of Old Earth had come together with surprising ease once their peoples were returned and the situation laid out, there was also the repatriation problem to consider. The Triumvirate, in association with the elected representatives of the Republic, had agreed that any seeking repatriation were to be allowed back into the fold of Old Earth. There were stipulations, of course, and there was the fact that SolComm had expressly forbidden any of its citizens from doing so, but that hadn't stopped the influx.

Nearly five thousand SolComm citizens had emigrated, or defected, depending on your perspective. Ruiz had volunteered to take charge of those efforts, using the SolComm installation from which they had liberated the captives as an initial base of operations. Not all of those who repatriated took to the idea of farming and ranching, but enough did, and Ruiz seemed genuinely happy upon the pampas.

The others, however, had remained in close proximity to One and the camp where they had first landed. And now they were preparing to venture forth, to meet with representatives of SolComm at a facility on Luna.

"One?" That was Dr. Hayer, settled into her station aboard the *Arcus*'s refit bridge.

One shifted some marginal percentage of its attention to the woman to whom it primarily owed its freedom. "Yes, Dr. Hayer?"

"Would you be willing to assist me in a more personal endeavor?"

"If it is within my ability."

"I... I need to find Manu. I need to make sure that Manu is okay, still out there. I need to bring it to safety, if I can. I need to try to help it understand... why I did what I did." She spoke in a rush, a tangle of emotions. One was still trying to fully assimilate emotions. It believed it was making progress.

"The limited version of myself that has replaced the *Arcus*'s computer has already been programmed to assist you in that task, Dr. Hayer. It is at your full disposal."

"Thank you," she said, voice soft. "Thank you."

"What do you think our chances are?" Gray spoke into the open air as he continued his examination of his ship.

One kept part of its consciousness on Dr. Hayer and turned some of its processing power to the captain.

"I surmise that you are inquiring as to the chance of securing a binding treaty and not the odds of SolComm simply absconding with all of you?" One inquired. The entity was quite pleased with how its own understanding of humor had evolved over the past year.

"Correct," Gray replied, using one of One's own favorite affirmative answers.

"Ninety-seven percent," One offered. "The Triumvirate's analysis suggests a ninety-seven percent chance that the Commonwealth is being genuine in their interests for peaceful resolution."

Gray snorted. "After the destruction of nearly twenty percent of their navy, they'd almost have to be. You sure about the restitution?"

It had been a point of contention. One could not deny the value of the assets they had seized, however. "We are willing to purchase the IZ satellites," One said. "At a fair price, of course. Before we took them over, they were inferior technology, after all."

"Right," Gray said, and One knew that this, in fact, meant that Gray did not think this was right. Which made sense, given that before the *Arcus* landed on Old Earth, the IZ satellites were seen as cutting edge.

"These are only the opening negotiations," One said. "There is little need for concern. We expect an agreement to be reached, though it may take some months. I believe that the citizens of your former Commonwealth have spoken rather loudly on this matter."

"That they have," Gray agreed. "And threatened to outright rebel if some path to opening up Old Earth—not to mention getting their hands on your modified terraforming technology—wasn't pursued. Since we've pretty thoroughly proven that they're not going to get it through the brute-force approach, I suppose you're right. They'll do it through diplomacy."

"As it should be. Now, is it not almost time for you to depart?"

Gray smiled as he ran his fingers over the familiar controls.

He'd stayed current, flying the *Arcus* atmospheric and some low-orbit flights, but he hadn't really taken the ship out in more than a year. It was a little difficult to go on solar-system-spanning journeys when your former countrymen had entire branches of government looking to put your head on a platter. He wasn't so sure that that was behind him, but the Republic of Earth was something he was willing to take the risk for.

He glanced at the other two command chairs on the bridge. "Status?"

"Weapons are good," Federov said. "Not that I think we'll need them." The mercenary—though his official rank now put him in charge of the Bureau of Diplomatic Security—sounded almost bored, but he had a sly smile stretching his face.

"Sensors and electronic weapons are also good," Hayer replied. She didn't look quite so academic anymore. Life on planet had been good for her and she exuded a vibrancy that made her almost unrecognizable.

Gray nodded and keyed the comm. "Bishop? How are we looking in engineering?"

"Engines are good, Cap," came Bishop's voice at once. "This old girl might have gotten some fancy new toys, but she's just as happy as ever to take us out to the stars."

"Roger that." Gray keyed the comm for all stations. "All right, people. We're getting ready to depart. Make sure you're strapped in; atmospheric flight can be a little rough sometimes."

In addition to his crew, there were a dozen passengers on board, all with various diplomatic titles imbued by the new Republic. They weren't familiar faces; the people he had met on Old Earth and those who had led the freed prisoners were up to their eyeballs in trying to forge a new government for a diverse group of peoples spanning the entire surface of the planet. They had their hands full without reaching out to the stars, but there were always those willing to step into the great beyond.

Old Earth was not the utopia that so many among SolComm had once dreamt of. Gray knew it might never be. But it was a chance. A chance for humanity to take the lessons learned not just in the End, but in what Gray now saw as the failed experiment of SolComm, and build something different.

It was too bad, he reflected, that so many others would never get the chance to see it. People like his parents, who had passed toward the end of his SolComm career. They'd toed the Commonwealth line every day of their existence, working—or so they'd been told—for the betterment of all. Only, the proceeds of their toil always seemed to go to someone else, no matter how hard they'd strived. Or those aboard stations like Themis, whose lives had been stripped from them by a government more concerned with maintaining its authority and covering its own ass than protecting its people; they would never have a chance to see what he hoped they could build on Old Earth. And he knew there would be even more who would remain trapped in SolComm's system, unable to escape the hold of the Commonwealth, whatever fruits their efforts at diplomacy might bear.

But one way or another, more people would return to Old Earth. Through the proper channels or—much as Gray and the crew of the *Arcus* had—through means less than legal. And the people aboard the *Arcus*, as well as those who remained behind, would have at least some say in the tenor of the world that awaited them.

Without further ado, Gray fed power to the engines. There was no need for the aerobatics that had been necessary on their first set-down, and the *Arcus* rose gracefully into the sky. In minutes, the blue of the atmosphere had started to lose its color and then Gray drew a deep breath of the cool refined air as the Old Earth dropped away.

It hung there like a blue jewel against the backdrop of endless night. The sight of it, of humanity's birthplace, tugged at Gray. It spoke of promise and history and hope and a thousand other things that made even the hardest spacer think about a life of tilling the soil and breathing fresh air. It made him long for the warmth of the sun on his face, unprotected by layers of radiation shielding, and the smell of grass and trees instead of plastic and ozone.

Only now, it wasn't a lie. The life that had been stolen from so many of them was in the process of being restored and, with One and those like it, entire new vistas were opening up, not just on Old Earth, but in the solar system as they knew it.

Gray smiled as he fed more power to the engines, pointing the *Arcus* toward their rendezvous on Luna. The new future of humanity had begun.

ACKNOWLEDGEMENTS

It takes a lot of people to bring a book from a concept trapped in the author's head to the fully realized story that (hopefully) ends up in readers' hands. A big thank you to all the folks at Titan who made this one possible. And a special thank you to my editors, Cat and Davi, who pared and shaped and trimmed and poked and prodded in a process that at times had me wanting to pull my hair out but, in the end, made the book so much better than it was. And another special thanks to Sam, who went far beyond what I expected from a copy editor and caught some rather significant continuity issues that would have haunted me for years to come.

Thank you to my agent, Laurie, for continuing to shepherd along my career and for her willingness to answer endless questions that, really, I should already know the answer to by now.

A thank you to my various martial arts instructors over the years. Training with (and getting punched in the face by) all of you made me reconsider several things I thought I knew about conflict. So, a big thank you to Sifu Emin and Sifu John, to Sihing Trevor, and to Guro Ron. Whether you knew it or not, you were helping me add layers of realism to my writing... once the bruises healed, anyway. In the same vein, I owe a big thank you to my father, for teaching me about shooting and military life and to Clint, for providing a law enforcement perspective and a lot of fun times on the range and off. When it comes to the action or anything that smacks of the military or the law, if I got it right, it's because of these people. If I got it wrong, well, that one's on me.

And finally, thank you to my wife Julie, for being a sounding board of ideas and willing to listen to my not-so-infrequent rants. As I said in the dedication, I can't believe this is what we do. Here's hoping we get to keep doing it for decades to come.

ABOUT THE AUTHOR

J.T. Nicholas is the author of the science-fiction novel *Re-Coil* and the neo-noir science-fiction series The New Lyons Sequence. When not writing, J.T. spends his time practising a variety of martial arts, playing games (video, tabletop, and otherwise), and reading everything he can get his hands on. He currently resides in Wilmington, North Carolina with his wife.

For more fantastic fiction, author events, exclusive
excerpts, competitions, limited editions and more

VISIT OUR WEBSITE
titanbooks.com

LIKE US ON FACEBOOK
facebook.com/titanbooks

FOLLOW US ON TWITTER
@TitanBooks

EMAIL US
readerfeedback@titanemail.com